The Crafter's Dilemma

A Dungeon Core Novel

Dungeon Crafting – Book 3

Jonathan Brooks

Cover Design: Yvonne Less, Art 4 Artists

Edited by: Celestian Rince

Acknowledgements

I would like to thank all my friends and family who have supported me on my writer's journey, as well as providing much-needed encouragement. You're the best!

In addition, this book wouldn't as great as it is without the help of my Patrons on Patreon and my beta-readers!

Aaron Wiley
Alex Canavan
Brian O'Neil
Brian Oles
Drew Welcher
Emma Baker
Glen Shepard
Grant Harrell
John Debnam
Joshua Chausse
Kevin Caffrey
Kilsharion Deborah Land
Nate Martin
Paul S.
Rei S
Rickie Brown
Ricky Kukowski
Sean Hall
Steven Genskay
Tania Bay
Tom Davidson
Tyller James
Zack Devney

Table of Contents

Recap

Sandra was born a merchant and died a merchant – but that wasn't the end of her existence. She was born with crippled hands that prevented her from crafting all but the most basic materials; because of this – and the ability to *see* but not *manipulate* all of the elements – she spent most of her life learning as much as she could about anything associated with crafting. After indulging in her hobby a little too much, she over-reached and ended up being sacrificed to fuel an enchantment from the very person she was hoping to learn it from.

Reborn as a Dungeon Core – centuries in the future – in a place uninhabited by Humans, Sandra was thrust into a small, hollowed-out underground space without a clue of what she was and why she was there. With the help of a Dungeon Fairy named Winxa, however, she was able to learn how to create Monster Seeds, Dungeon Monsters, rooms, tunnels, and even traps.

After building her dungeon and practicing as much crafting as she could manage, a Half-Orc/Half-Dwarf appeared at her entrance chased by huge Bearlings. Sandra managed to save Kelerim with her dungeon, and through a unique application of her Core abilities she was able to designate Kelerim as a "Visitor". Over time, she taught him the correct way to blacksmith, fixing and improving his meager skills so that he could go back and help the land of Orcrim against the pervasive attacks of the nearby "normal" dungeons.

Fate had other plans as Kelerim's previously unknown half-brother Razochek Bloodskull – an Orcish Warband Leader – stumbled upon Sandra's dungeon while hunting Bearlings near the Orc village of Grongbak. Sandra – with Kelerim's help – fought against Razochek, and the Half-Orc/Half-Dwarf killed him with some help from her unusual Dungeon Monster constructs.

Affected by the slaying of his own flesh and blood, Kelerim set off to find his father and to start his own smithy, bringing much-needed quality to the progressively poor work done by the existing Orcish blacksmiths. As soon as he left, Sandra was able to finally concentrate on crafting – or so she thought.

In an effort to acquire additional crafting material – wood, specifically – her dungeon was inadvertently discovered by the nearby Elven village. When Echo – a relatively young Elf Ranger in Elven society – discovered that Sandra had multiple elements at her disposal, the Elven village of Avensglen called in an Elite dungeon-destroying team from the Elven capital. With limited time until they arrived, Sandra used her resources to upgrade her Core Size, opening up additional avenues of defense – and accidentally causing problems at the same time elsewhere.

Because of her expanded Area of Influence, one of the local Dungeon Cores was able to exploit a loophole; by possessing an identical element and having a smaller Core Size, the reptile-based Core was able to use Sandra's Area of Influence as if it was its own. As a result, an army of reptiles assaulted the nearby Gnome village of Glimmerton, killing most of its residents in the process. Sandra sent her constructs to save the Gnomes and destroy the reptiles, but unfortunately only managed to save a handful of them.

In order to heal one of the wounded Gnomes, Felbar Warmaster, Sandra needed to bond with him – which placed him in a temporary coma. In the meantime, she also bonded with the others, before sending most of them back to Gnomeria – the land of the Gnomes – with a wagon full of raw materials; Violet – an Apprentice Enchanter – helped to enchant a Hauler with her specialized knowledge, as well as helping Sandra set up a Repository that helped preserve how enchantments were created.

Meanwhile, Echo – the Elf who first found Sandra's dungeon and who was tasked to watch her – nearly died because of a snakebite and was only saved by a last-minute bond with Sandra and her Repair Drones. While Echo recovered in a bond-induced coma, Sandra upgraded her Core Size to 20, unlocking the Advancement System; using the Advancement Points she had accumulated, the crafty Dungeon Core upgraded her Classification and acquired an Unstable Shapeshifter in an attempt to find something that could craft better than her Constructs – as well as being able to communicate with the Elves. While the Shapeshifter could finally manipulate elemental energy for use in enchantments, she still wasn't able to verbally communicate.

Unfortunately, the Reptile-based Dungeon Core that had destroyed Glimmerton had its sights set on the Elven village Avensglen. With no way to communicate with the elves, she couldn't warn them of the approaching Reptile army, so Sandra decided to destroy the attacking Core herself. She ended up sending just under half of her Constructs to assault the foreign dungeon and managed to keep enough of them alive to make it all the way through it, destroying the Core in charge – but that didn't end the threat. The reptile army was following its last directive, which was to kill everyone in the Elven village; there might've been a group strong enough to repel them, but the Elite Elves had arrived and were in the process of assaulting Sandra's own dungeon.

Using a special technique to negate the traps inside her defensive dungeon rooms, making them practically useless, the Elite Elves tore through her Constructs with ease. It was only towards the last of her rooms that they started to run out of elemental energy; before they could be killed by one of Sandra's Iron-plated Behemoths in the last room, Violet stopped them. Offering them a compromise, as well as a newly crafted Energy Orb that gradually restored their elemental energy, the Elite Elves had their lives spared and were sent away to defend the village – on the condition that they would help in a future endeavor regarding cooperation with the other races.

With her dungeon and the people inside of it – as well as the Elven village – now safe, Felbar and Echo woke up to find that their world had changed drastically while they were out...

Chapter 1

"...and this place is...what? A garden of some sort?" Echo asked, still confused at her current situation – but starting to understand that the dungeon she found herself in was quite a bit different from any she had heard of before. While it had been obvious that it was unusual from her previous observations, the voice in her head was trying to explain just *how* unusual it was.

** Sort of...it's my Growing Room, where I can rapidly produce different types of plants and trees at a rapidly accelerated rate. Those Apple, Pear, Peach, and Orange trees, for instance, were grown and matured in a matter of hours instead of the years it would normally take. I was also able to grow Flax, Cotton, and even an Oak Tree inside here – all so that I could obtain the proper materials I needed to craft what I wanted. **

That's definitely...strange. The dungeon – whose name was "Sandra", apparently – had explained what happened in the outside world while she was in some sort of healing coma; she really didn't remember anything after being bit by that blasted snake, so an update of what was going on was much appreciated. That was, of course, if she could trust the voice in her head; the dungeon's believability was still in question – at least concerning the circumstances. Waking up alone and surrounded by stone walls had been a shock to say the least, but what was even more shocking was the "Visitor's Bond" she had apparently been subjected to without her permission. *Though, if it keeps me alive and allows me to communicate with the voice in my head...unless the poison from that snake is making me lose my mind. That's definitely still a possibility.*

A little of the information "Sandra" had told her she had already known – like the devastation of the nearby Gnome village – but most of it was new. The arrival of the Elite team from the capital in Avensglen, their assault on the dungeon where she now found herself, and how they were almost killed – which was honestly unbelievable in and of itself. She had heard stories of Porthel and Alanthia before, and the fact that such a new dungeon could defeat them seemed impossible; again, if the dungeon could be believed, that impossibility had actually occurred.

Then there was the fact that they were *spared*; not only that, but they were sent back to Avensglen to protect it from being destroyed by a force of the same reptilian monsters she had seen wipe out the Gnome town. The dungeon had been a little sketchy on the details regarding the deal it made with the Elites, only briefly mentioning that something was provided to them as an incentive. What that could possibly be, though – Echo had no clue what a dungeon could give them to make them turn away from their sworn duty of destroying Dungeon Hearts.

Or, rather, Dungeon "Cores", which was what the dungeon evidently called them. That was only mentioned when Sandra purportedly destroyed the Heart—*Core*—of the reptilian dungeon that attacked the Gnomes and her village. *One dungeon destroying another is the hardest to believe, I think.*

"So, you like to...craft?" As crazy as the other things that she was told sounded, a dungeon using its own dungeon loot to craft things was relatively...normal.

** I definitely do! In my previous life, crafting was my passion and with the ability to craft anything I want – as long as I have the materials and proper tools – it has been an interesting experience. Of course, it would be even better if people weren't trying to destroy me every few weeks, but I'll take what I can. **

From an outsider's perspective, Sandra seemed to be just a dungeon that wanted to be left alone so she could craft to her Dungeon Heart's content; in that context, Echo felt *a little* bad about being the source of the Elites attacking the dungeon. However, whether or not there was an ulterior motive behind all of the "crafting" still had to be determined. Just because those stronger than her were convinced of the dungeon's benevolence, that didn't mean there wasn't something sinister going on.

For the moment, though, Echo was inclined to believe most – if not all – of the information she had been given; not only was she *alive* when she should probably be dead, but she was also told that she wasn't a prisoner and could leave at any time. At least, that was what this "Sandra" had told her, though how the young Elf was supposed to find her way out of the strange place she found herself in was something else entirely.

The "tour" she took around the dungeon inadvertently helped to expand her knowledge of her whereabouts; after eating what she could of fruit from the trees inside the Growing Room, she was shown different workshops that seemed capable of making hundreds or thousands of different items. Not only that, but she was shown a storage room of sorts that held a myriad of different finished products; the sheer amount of knowledge needed to make the different types of weapons and few pieces of armor she saw was impressive enough, but she was also told that Sandra had produced many other items from their most basic, raw forms – like thread, cloth, and wood.

The workstations themselves were unique in the fact that they could apparently function and operate with the use of an elemental power that the dungeon called Mana; she was shown a forge that could heat up without having to use any type of visible energy source, the finishing station had grinding wheels that spun automatically, and even a crude saw connected to a table would rotate without any obvious means so that it could be used to cut and shape wood. There were other things in the rooms she was shown that she had no idea their importance even after having them explained to her, but they obviously did what they were intended for.

The only thing that was missing – which she thought odd – was any sight of the unique dungeon monsters that Sandra possessed. There was currently no one – or no *thing* – working at the crafting workstations, despite the dungeon...*Core's*...obvious enthusiasm over every part of her production rooms. Echo had to admit that what was built underground in the wastelands was impressive, but she was starting to have serious doubts about the truthfulness of the dungeon...because there didn't seem to be any crafting going on.

At least, not until she arrived at a room that made her stomach growl before she even entered. Echo inhaled the delicious smell of cooking meat that had a unique scent accompanying it; fortunately, "unique" didn't mean bad, just different. When she finally arrived in what appeared to be some sort of cooking area, she got her first glimpse of a dungeon monster – and it was unlike anything she had seen before.

It was approximately three feet tall and looked vaguely like a person; it had a head, two arms, two legs, and a torso – but that was where the similarities ended. Just like the others she had seen outside of the dungeon, it appeared to be made completely out of metal and moved smoothly without any apparent source of energy – though its range of motion was more limited than a living person's. Despite that, it was easily moving a few copper pans – and well-made copper pans at that – around on top of an obviously heated cooking surface. In one, she could see – and smell – a fairly good-sized hunk of meat that appeared almost done cooking; in the other were two, smaller chunks of meat that smelled just as delicious.

** Go ahead and take a seat; the food will be done soon. **

Tearing her gaze away from the dungeon monster that was *cooking* – which was something that she never thought she would see – she saw that there was a rather short table on the other side of the room made completely out of stone. Accompanying the table were three chairs, two of which were small – as if made for children; the other seemed more normal-sized, though still on the small side. *Probably so it can fit under the table, which also seems a bit small for my liking.* Echo didn't mind, though, because her stomach growled loudly again; apparently it didn't care where she sat, as long as it was getting food.

Immediately after she took her seat, Echo started to stare at the strange dungeon monster cooking food; however, before more than a half a minute passed, she heard voices over the sizzling meat sounds coming from a tunnel she hadn't been down yet. She tensed up when she didn't recognize the language they were speaking, though for some reason it *almost* sounded familiar – but she couldn't place it.

** Calm down, relax, and don't worry – it's just Violet and Felbar coming to eat with you...I did tell you about them, didn't I? **

Sandra sounded genuinely confused, as if she was sure she mentioned them. "No, you certainly did not. Who are they?" As soon as she spoke aloud, the voices coming down from the tunnel stopped, though her keen hearing could pinpoint whoever owned them still walking closer. Echo went to grab the dagger at her side, but she belatedly realized she was completely unarmed; instead, she snatched one of the sharp steel knives that were on the table, which she assumed were there to help cut the meat the dungeon monster was cooking.

** Oh, they're two of the— **

"Gnomes," she finished for the dungeon, as two small figures walked into the room suspiciously. One was a young-looking woman that seemed harmless, while the other was a grizzled older man that appeared to have seen his share of battle. She vaguely recognized them from the battle inside the Gnome village and their subsequent retreat towards the dungeon in the wastelands.

** They're my friends and visitors here in my dungeon just as much as you are. Actually, Violet here played a big part in convincing the Elites to leave the other day, so you also have her to thank for keeping you alive; if I had been destroyed, it's likely you would've died without ever waking up from your coma. **

Echo briefly wondered what the relatively innocent-looking Gnome had done to turn the Elites away, but then the part about "relaxing" that Sandra had mentioned finally penetrated her mind; looking down, she realized her knuckles were white as they held onto the steel knife as if her life depended upon it. With deliberate care, she relaxed her hand and placed the stone implement back on the table; out of the corner of her eye, she saw the grizzled Gnome slip his own small knife – that she hadn't even seen him holding – back into a sheath placed at his side.

The two Gnomes took their places at the table, and it was only when they were seated that she realized that the table was originally made to accommodate those of their small stature; looking around at the area, she realized that *she* was the odd one of the bunch, as it seemed like everything was originally made to accommodate Gnomes – not Elves. Echo had been thinking how strange they appeared up close with their small size, but she was starting to feel like she didn't belong there; *at least the rest of the rooms seem like they're suited towards larger people.*

Most of the distrust Echo was feeling towards both the dungeon and the two Gnomes was lost as she saw the dungeon monster approaching by her side; before she could react, a stone plate filled with the larger hunk of meat she had seen cooking earlier was laid before her, looking and smelling perfectly cooked. She could see tiny granules of what appeared to be salt on top of the seared steak – of some unknown animal...*at least I hope it's an animal* – though she couldn't see any other seasoning.

Next to the steak was the source of the unique smell she noticed earlier, though it had been lost under the overwhelmingly delicious smell of cooking meat. What appeared to be apples and pears were sliced up and practically falling apart inside of some sort of sauce that smelled of citrus.

** My repertoire of cooking ingredients is sorely lacking, but I've been experimenting. The Bearling Meat is seasoned with Salt, after marinating for a couple of hours in a thin orange juice to tenderize it a little more – I've heard it can be a little chewy otherwise. I also baked some apples and pears in an orange reduction, though I wish I had access to some grains so I can bake some sort of pastries or bread. And some sort of sweetener like sugar, or a myriad of different seasonings...anyway, enjoy! **

Echo didn't have to be told twice; while the fruits she had consumed down in the growing room had filled the gnawing hole in her stomach and reduced some of the weakness in her body, she felt like she was still starving. She tore into both the steak – which was remarkably tender – and the fruit concoction, which was also delicious; however, it only took a few bites of each before she started to fill up...and uncomfortably at that. She saw that the others were finishing up at nearly the same time, though the young Gnome woman ate quite a bit more than the older man.

** Felbar just woke up from a coma as well – or at least he did shortly before you regained consciousness. You'll both have to wait until your bodies can handle food again after your periods of forced* *sleep, but this should help alleviate most of your hunger issues at the moment. **

There was also a stone cup of fresh, cool water that was brought over to the table, and Echo wanted to gulp it down as extreme thirst hit her; however, just like the steak and fruit, she could only consume a little bit before her stomach started to cramp up and hurt. *I think I'm going to throw up...*

Fortunately, the feeling subsided after a few minutes and she felt fine; during that time, she could see what she figured was a similar look to her own on the older Gnome's—*Felbar, I believe his name was*—face. The shared discomfort made her feel strangely more comfortable with the Gnomes, and for the first time since she woke up she felt herself relax a little.

** Now that you're all fed, it's about time we discuss what the plan is from here on out. Now, Echo, like I told you before, you're free to go anytime you want to. However, I would like to offer you an opportunity that I hope you'll accept, as it will make negotiations and cooperation between myself, the Gnomes, and your people much smoother. Especially when you see and experience for yourself what I have to offer. **

Echo could see that the young Gnome woman...*Violet, I think*...was smiling and idly fondling two strange-looking glowing orbs fashioned around her neck in some sort of necklace.

Obviously, the dungeon is talking to everyone here at the same time – good to know. "And what is that, exactly?"

** Let's head up to the workshop up near the surface and I'll show you. **

Now that she had eaten and most of the discomfort in her stomach had passed, Echo was eager to get moving again. If they were indeed heading towards the surface, that was all for the better; despite being saved from death by a snake bite, kept alive during her convalescence through some unusual means, treated like a guest in someone's home, and fed a delicious meal (even if she could only eat a few bites)...she still wasn't entirely sure she could trust the dungeon. Being near the surface in case she needed to escape would be beneficial; listening to what Sandra had to say would likely be worthwhile, because now her curiosity was piqued.

As they got up from the table, the stone plates, cups, eating utensils, and even the uneaten food disappeared as if it had never been there. She jumped when she saw that, partly startled, and smiled at the grizzled old Gnome when she saw that he did the same. *Maybe we can escape together if this dungeon turns out to be deceiving us – I'd hate to leave anyone in this place if I have the means to help them.*

With that thought buried in the back of her mind for the future, because she wasn't exactly sure if being "bonded" to the dungeon meant that it—*she*—could read her mind, Echo followed

Violet out of the room as she seemed to know where she was going. As she watched the young Gnome enter another room and walk to a delineated spot on the floor, she stepped back in surprise as a massive gust of air shot her small form upwards through a hole in the ceiling.

Echo shared an incredulous look with the old battle-hardened Gnome, who shrugged and walked without hesitation to the same spot. As he too shot upwards, the astonished Elf couldn't help but shake her head in wonder.

This could be more interesting than I thought...

Chapter 2

Sandra was glad that her guests – despite being different races – were getting along. *Well, **getting along** might be too strong of a phrase; **tolerating each other** might be better.* Regardless, they didn't appear to want to kill each other, though it could be because Felbar and Echo were both still a bit wary of Sandra and the dungeon, so they were grasping at anything living nearby that seemed normal. At least the older Gnome had Violet to help ease him into the situation, but the Elf only had Sandra's voice in her head to explain things.

Not for the first time she wished that they could speak a common language, but even when the Elites (who were quite a bit older than many of the other Elves) were being addressed by Violet, only one of them was actually able to understand the Gnomish language; having the ability to speak foreign languages was obviously a bit of a rarity. It was too much to hope that Echo – who was reportedly much younger – would have that kind of knowledge, especially considering that there really hadn't been much contact between most of the races for a lengthy period of time.

Regardless of the language barrier, *Sandra* could at least mentally communicate with everyone and translate where it was needed; there hadn't been much need yet, but she was sure it would eventually be vital towards cooperation between the different races.

The newly awakened "Visitors" navigated their way through the Vertical Air-trap Transportation System (VATS) without too much trouble; it was only the first one that they temporarily balked at before Violet showed them that it wasn't harmful. After a few minutes they arrived at the large workshop located near the first couple of rooms, where Sandra had assembled – and Violet had enchanted – the Hauler and wagon a relatively short time ago. For the moment, however, it was relatively empty of projects or supplies; in fact, there was a small open-topped stone box in the corner and three of Sandra's Dungeon Monsters in the room.

One of them was the large Mechanical Jaguar Queen lying down in another corner of the room, which had returned to the workshop after delivering the Elites to the Elven town about a day and a half ago; the other two were a pair of Unstable Shapeshifters, who waited by the edge of the room in their multi-colored amorphous shape that apparently hurt Violet's head if she stared at it for too long.

"What is this place?" Felbar asked, as he – with only the slightest hesitation – walked over to the Jaguar Queen to take a better look at it. To Sandra it only made sense; the Warmaster was used to large constructs as part of their lands' defense, and the large metallic cat was similar – though quite different, of course – enough that it was undoubtedly fascinating to look at. The small, battle-hardened Gnome showed no fear towards Sandra's construct, which was likely the result of his general nature and personality; though, when she thought about it for a moment, it could also be because he knew that he was relatively safe in the dungeon. If Sandra had wanted to kill him, she had plenty of opportunity before now.

The Dungeon Core explained to everyone what the workshop had been used for previously (specifically the Hauler and wagon) – though Violet already knew, obviously – and then went on to describe what she had been using it for...and eventually her plans for the future.

** I've been using it lately for enchanting purposes, because it's far enough away from my Core that I'm not too worried about harming anything vital; I'm still learning to adapt my knowledge to practical applications, and there have been a few...let's just say, "oops" moments that likely would've damaged something if they weren't inside here. **

That last statement was obvious to see – there were a few spots on the floor that she hadn't quite yet had time to repair from an explosion of raw Mana. Sandra had gotten overconfident in her fledgling enchanting skills and had tried to change something in the new Energy Orbs she had been working on; the result was an uncontrolled explosion that practically rocked the room and vaporized one of her Shapeshifters in the process.

Sandra was just glad that Violet hadn't been present, otherwise she would've likely been seriously hurt or even killed; death was something that she couldn't heal the Gnome – or anyone – from yet, and she doubted she ever could. That was the realm of the Creator, and she had unknowingly dealt enough with the entity in the past that she didn't want to jeopardize her existence by trying to reverse full-on death.

She was also glad that she had taken at least a minor precaution and placed her other Unstable Shapeshifter – the original one – at the opposite end of the room. It had been damaged quite a bit in the explosion but fortunately hadn't died; a Repair Drone from the next room was able to patch it up before it succumbed to its injuries. While its death would've resulted in the loss of Mana Sandra had invested in it (which wasn't *that* big of a deal in the long run), the reality of the situation was that the original Shapeshifter was the only one that had access to the forms of the Elite Elves.

Upon creating another Unstable Shapeshifter – after the invasion by the Elites and after the long process of placing defending Constructs through her dungeon again – she found that a brand-new Shapeshifter didn't have the ability to shift into anything. Sandra supposed it made sense, because only the original one had actually gained samples from the living beings in her dungeon; the new one was like a blank slate, without those samples being transferred to it. *Though I wonder if it could procreate and produce offspring with the same samples already inside of it...*

The thought of Dungeon Monster reproduction was immediately shut down by Winxa, however. "Dungeon Monsters cannot procreate because they are formed exclusively by Mana; that Mana will not *reproduce* itself, as it is a finite resource inside of each Monster. I doubt even *you* would be able to work around that simple fact, even given your...unique status...as a Dungeon Core with access to all of the elements."

Sandra couldn't help but be a little glad about that, because the entire reproductive process between amorphous multicolored blobs was not something that she wanted to see. Granted, she could probably force them to change into different shapes that were likely more...suited...for the purpose, but even that thought felt wrong somehow.

Transferring those samples by having the new one touch the original Shapeshifter worked, however. Some instinct told Sandra that the transfer would only work with the one that had acquired the sample in the first place; she would have to test that later when she had a third available and try to copy those from subsequent Shifters. She wasn't exactly sure what difference it made, but again, she had a feeling that "original" samples were the key to how the Unstable Shapeshifters functioned.

All of which made protecting the one that had acquired the samples from the Elite Elves a priority. While she was hoping to acquire more samples in the future, she was limited on what she had to work with at the moment; if those disappeared completely, then having access to all of the different elements in the future was jeopardized.

** And that brings us to the reason we're here now. Echo, Felbar – head over to that stone box in the corner and pick out whatever...calls to you the most. **

Sandra had told Violet not to go into too much detail about the new Energy Orbs that they had created to gradually restore elemental energy; the young Gnome had agreed, as she said it was better that they experienced it themselves. Felbar shared Spirit with Violet, however, and he was instantly drawn to the Spirit Energy Orb around her neck as soon as he woke up; it was only through Sandra's intervention that he agreed to ignore it until later. Echo, of course, didn't have any clue what they were, so she was going into it blind to what was to come.

The two Sandra named walked over to the stone box, evidently confused; when they got nearer to it, though, they both gasped at nearly the same time. The box was filled with dozens of Energy Orbs of various types, though only the Spirit, Fire, Holy, and Air ones called out to the Gnome and the Elf. Without hesitation, they reached down and pulled out their corresponding elements, holding one of each in either hand.

"What—? Is this—?" they both asked, unable to form a complete sentence as they stared in wonder at what they were experiencing.

** Yes, Violet and I devised a way to restore elemental energy without the need for sleep. This is why— **

Before she could finish, Echo was gone from where she was standing, running around the room and activating both her light-bending invisibility and her enhanced speed by reducing the air resistance as she ran. Sandra could still sense her even as she moved because the invisibility wasn't perfect when she ran, and she watched, amused, as the Elf made at least 20 laps around the room before she stopped.

Felbar and Violet couldn't see her as well as Sandra could, but they could feel the wind from her passing; the older Gnome barely paid attention to it as he still stared at the Orbs in his hands, but the younger Gnome stepped back and out of the way in surprise. Luckily, she didn't run into the racing Elf, and pressing herself against the wall seemed to calm down her surprise a little bit.

"This is amazing! I can feel my energy slowly refilling; it isn't enough to completely replace what I consumed while I was running, but maybe...half of it? And given a few minutes or less, I think I'll be completely full again! How did you do this?" Echo asked in between large gasps of breath, looking completely worn out from her run. Before her coma, she probably wouldn't be tired at all, but all of the exercise following approximately two weeks of inactivity was enough to wipe her out.

Sandra tried to explain the concepts of the enchantment to Echo, but the young Elf obviously wasn't following it. The Elven people weren't big on enchantments like the Gnomes were – they preferred to manipulate their elemental energy externally, and usually with devastating results; it was likely that Echo had never actually created an enchantment, in fact, so it was undoubtedly foreign to her.

** Regardless of how they work, the point is this: these Energy Orbs can greatly help **all** of the races here defend themselves against the dungeons surrounding their lands. It's only the first step in my eventual plan— **

"Aha! I *knew* you had some sort of evil plan; are these bribes to have us lower our guard and then strike when we least expect it? Or are you planning on subjugating us and making us your slaves?" Echo asked suspiciously, taking a step toward the exit. Sandra actually chuckled internally at the accusatory tone coming from the young Elf; she could understand where she was coming from, though it was so far from what the Dungeon Core actually wanted that it was ridiculous. She just hoped that some of the amusement didn't transfer over to her response.

** If you would let me finish, you'll see that there is no "evil plan" here. I will admit it is a bit selfish, though it's for the good of everyone if they allow me to help them not just survive but thrive against the dungeons threatening your very existence. **

"What do you mean?" Violet asked, curiosity in her voice. While Sandra had shared some of her ideas on how to help her people – as well as the other races – and given a bare-bones explanation as to *why* she wanted to help, the Dungeon Core hadn't taken the time to explain the finer details. *This is as good of a time as any.*

** When I say it's selfish of me, I mean that in a couple of ways. Ultimately, as you've likely seen and heard me talk about, I love to craft; however, being invaded by the different people around here puts a severe damper on that. The Orcs invaded me first, followed by the Elves; it's only a matter of time before the Dwarves inadvertently learn of my existence and try to destroy me as well. And while your people— **

Sandra said, directly addressing Echo—

** Have agreed to not attack me and hopefully even work with me, the Orcs are likely to attack me if they discover my presence here again and send an even larger force. So, if only for my love of having some peace and quiet to do my crafting, I want to work* ***with*** *the races in their defense against the dungeons. **

"Wouldn't it just be easier to...well...let the other dungeons kill us all off?" Felbar asked unexpectedly. "Then you wouldn't have to worry about anyone bothering you."

It would be like the battle-tested Gnome to point out the easy way to victory. However, Felbar was missing some information that made his question something that she wouldn't even consider.

** While that is true, at least in principle, I wouldn't let that happen if I could help it. While I wasn't a Gnome, or an Elf, or an Orc, or a Dwarf...I was, at one time,* ***Human****; it goes against that part of my nature to allow the complete destruction of a nearby race when there is something I can do about it. And more importantly, while it might help me temporarily – if I were to let that happen – it wouldn't help me in the long run.*

** Why? Well, imagine for a moment if the four races around here were wiped out; the resulting dungeons afterwards would probably be extremely powerful and able to extend their reach even farther out. Eventually they would consume every other race in the world, until there was nothing else to destroy...except for me. **

Sandra explained the concept of Dungeon Core contracts and what she knew of the purpose behind dungeons in the first place – to challenge the people of the world and keep their focus internal, rather than wanting to expand and fight nearby races for land. The contract that would normally prevent the other Cores from attacking her wasn't something that she possessed, so in order to expand into the area her dungeon was located – which was a major driving factor of every contracted Core, apparently – they would have to destroy her.

** And as much as it seems crazy to think so, I believe I was put here by the Creator for this singular purpose: to save you all from extinction. The Creator created you and didn't want any of you to be destroyed and wiped out, which is what will eventually happen if I don't intervene before it's too late. **

They were all silent for a moment, before Echo said, "You sure do think highly of yourself, don't you?" And then she smiled, before continuing. "Look, I can see exactly what you're talking about, at least in Symenora; if there is a person in my land that doesn't think that we're on the decline, then they're deluding themselves. It will perhaps be decades or more before it's really felt, but the end of our people is inevitable without any type of outside help. If what you say is true about the others, then we're all doomed.

"I'm not going to say that you're our savior, but even with access to something like this—" she continued, holding up her Air Energy Orb— "it would greatly delay that inevitability. However, I severely doubt that is going to be enough to save us in the end, but I'm willing to go along with whatever you have planned if it means that my people will survive longer. If it requires being a slave, then so be it."

** For the last time, you're not a slave. I told you that you're free to go at any time, but I would love your help in dealing with your people; I have no way to communicate with anyone I haven't bonded with, so I need a liaison between the Elves and myself.*

** But you're also correct in one thing that you said; these Energy Orbs, even if they provided infinite energy, aren't enough to turn the tide. For the Gnomes, it might mean they could make more enchantments, but there are only so many of them that can operate their War Machines, and the production of those same constructs are at a standstill because many of their strongest Enchanters are no longer available.*

** The Orcs, for their part, are running out of decent weaponry and armor; I had a friend named Kelerim here before you all arrived that is going to do what he can to change that, but he's just one person. Added to that, they have very little in the way of resources in which to arm their Warbands, so they are gradually being beaten back by the Dungeon Monsters because of their inferior armaments.*

** I still have to find out exactly what the issue is with the Dwarves, but from my own observations and from what I've been told, they have almost entirely retreated within their mountain stronghold, allowing the dungeons to expand and hold sway over most of their land aboveground. Given enough time, they'll either be starved out or the Cores will find some way to tunnel underground, breaking* *into their strongholds – and there'll be no end of difficulties they'll face if that happens.* *

"So…what are you saying?" Echo asked.

* *What I'm trying to say is that everyone has to work* ***together*** *to solve these problems; staying separated into different areas just doesn't work for everyone here. It might work for some of the other races of the world, like Humans and even the Beastkin, but it clearly doesn't work here. You're all too specialized to create a lasting, cohesive defense, and it's time we changed that.* *

"What you're proposing won't sit well with our leaders, not to mention the majority of the population – even if it makes sense," Felbar said, surprising Sandra with his comment. "There is a deep distrust, if not *hatred*, of the other races that is instilled in us as a people; I can't speak for any of the others, of course, but I have a feeling they're very similar. Those of us on the border with the wastelands are probably a little more open-minded than the others because we're technically closer to the other races, even if we see them *very* rarely, but even that only goes so far."

Sandra had definitely seen that, especially when the Gnomes and Echo had first met down in the kitchen and dining area she had created. If that was true – and thinking about Kelerim and how he was treated made her think it was – then she was going to have a hard fight ahead of her. Years of negative thinking towards a people couldn't be overcome overnight, if it could ever be overcome at all; it was especially hard when there wasn't any overt threat at their figurative throats. Sure, they would *eventually* all succumb to the ever-increasing assault of Dungeon Monsters, but for the most part there was no *immediate* danger.

Regardless of that difficulty, Sandra had to do something…she might just have to stick to her strategy of being the middleman – or middle*woman* – a lot longer than she planned.

** That's understandable – however, I have to try. And the first step is getting more of these Energy Orbs made and distributed to the Elves, since they are the only ones close to us that won't kill us on sight. After that, we need to somehow get some to the Gnomes, Orcs, and the Dwarves – if we can somehow contact them without starting another invasion of my dungeon. If that is successful – and I'm hoping it will be – then we can move on to something else that will help, and from there something else, and then something else. Eventually, my hope is to give each of the races something that they are lacking, and better equipping them with the tools they need to survive extinction; ultimately, though, I believe cooperation will be the key to continued prosperity. I'm not aiming to be the linchpin that keeps them all alive, because if for some reason I'm not here, then all I've done is delay – like you said, Echo – the* ***inevitable****. **

Everyone was silent for a while, thinking over what Sandra had said. It was asking a lot for them to take the burden of their people's survival on their shoulders, but things had to start somewhere. Progress was already being made with the Elves, but there was a long way to go to get to the point where survival wasn't just a possibility but a certainty.

"So...what's the plan?" Violet finally asked.

** Well, there's a lot that has to get set up for this to work, but for the moment I need your expertise in Enchanting; as for you, Echo, I'm sure that you're eager to get back to your village to show them that you're still alive. But first, the two of you who just woke up after a 2-week coma need some rest before you pass out where you're standing. **

While Felbar looked tired, Echo looked practically asleep on her feet after her run and expenditure of energy. It seemed that although the Energy Orb refilled her *elemental* energy, it did nothing for her *physical* energy. Rather than object, they both nodded in acceptance, and Sandra directed them back to their rooms to get some much-needed sleep. Violet joined Felbar as well, because she had been up for a while waiting for the older Gnome to wake up; when they were all down for the night—*day, actually*—Sandra was alone with her thoughts...so she began to plan.

Chapter 3

The only thing that Sandra needed – if she was going to keep supplying Energy Orbs – was one important resource: Mana. While an influx of ambient Mana was still happening inside her dungeon, her Airborne Mana Absorption Net of Shears (AMANS) was looking a little thin at that point.

Only a few days ago, Sandra had sent over 5,000 flying Animated Shears to their destruction in the Reptile-based dungeon that was bent on attacking the Elven village. They certainly served their purpose in there, but not a single construct she had sent to assault the other Core had managed to survive – including the Shears, which had reduced her AMANS by half. Directly afterwards, she had definitely felt the reduction in Mana absorption; at that point she was *only* getting approximately 250,000 per day from everything, and the increased cost of replacing the constructs that had been destroyed by the Elites had taken most of that since then.

Even then, she wasn't able to replace the constructs in each room with what they were previously; ever since she had advanced her Classification to the next Level, all of her constructs had increased in Mana Cost as well. Now, instead of Steel Pythons and Ironclad Apes, she was having to make do with alternatives like Martial Totems, Roaring Blademasters, and even some Large Armored Sentinels – and less of each, because of their cost. While they were all stronger or larger than their predecessors – and likely much deadlier – the higher production expense meant she couldn't quite fill up each room as much as she wanted.

Over time, she was planning on increasing them bit by bit, especially seeing how relatively ineffective the ones she had defending her dungeon had been against the Elite Elves; she couldn't help but think that if she had more of these improved constructs at her disposal, even the negation of her traps would still be balanced out by the deadlier abilities of her new Dungeon Monsters. Those advanced Constructs were going to be important, because anything "stronger" than her Multi-access Repair Drone – which she was still curious about, since she hadn't had the Mana to create one yet – was unavailable with her current Maximum Mana.

Core Selection Menu	
Dungeon Classification:	Constructs (Adv. Level 1)
Core Size:	20
Available Mana:	6215/19558
Ambient Mana Absorption:	10/hour
Available Raw Material (RM):	14550/49930
Convert Raw Material to Mana?	14550 RM -- > 582 Mana
Current Dungeon Monsters:	5315
Constructs Creation Options:	17
Advancement Creation Options:	2
Monster Seed Schematics:	182 (8)
Current Traps:	36
Trap Construction Options:	All
Core-specific Skills:	5
Current Visitors:	4

Constructs Creation Options	
Name:	**Mana Cost:**
Clockwork Tarantula	25
Reinforced Animated Shears	50
Hyper Automaton	100
Dividing Rolling Force	125
Lengthy Segmented Millipede	500
Iron-banded Articulated Clockwork Golem	750
Roaring Blademaster	1500
Large Armored Sentinel	2000
Mechanical Jaguar Queen	4000
Mechanical Dire Wolf	5000

Martial Totem	8000
Automated Sharp-bladed Digger	10000
Multi-access Repair Drone	16000
Steelclad Ape Warrior	24000
Titanium Anaconda	32000
Steel-plated Behemoth	40000
*Gravitational Devastation Sphere**	15000

Advancement Creation Options	
Name:	**Mana Cost:**
Goblin Foreman	80
Unstable Shapeshifter	16000

There were, of course, two ways to go about affording them: upgrading her Core Size (thereby having a larger Maximum Mana) or using the Advancement System to reduce the Mana Cost of her Dungeon Monsters.

Advancement Options	
Current Advancement Points	37
Advancement:	**Cost:**
--------------	-----
Reduce the Mana cost of Dungeon Monsters by 15% – Cost increases with each purchase (Advancement 0/4)	15
--------------	-----

Upgrading her Core Size was an option that Sandra was reluctant to do at the moment. While it would help her out with increases in everything, none of the other nearby dungeons within her Area of Influence (AOI) were taking advantage of the loophole that allowed them to access her AOI – which meant that they were a higher Core Size than her. That could easily change if she were to increase her own Size; and there was every possibility that *all* of them were just one size away from that. If that happened, the disaster that would befall the local villages would be something Sandra would have trouble preventing.

Then again, it was also possible none or just one would be able to access her AOI – but she wasn't willing to gamble on that a risk that was *currently* unneeded.

Since she didn't want to risk having another dungeon connect to her, she decided to see about using some of the Advancement Points she had earned from destroying the Reptile-based Dungeon Core; it had been a complete surprise that she had unlocked a new Criteria for Advancement, but it also lined up with what she – and Winxa – suspected the Creator wanted her to do. The amount she received for such an act was also unexpected: 30 Advancement Points (AP).

When she added the freshly gained AP to the 4 Points she hadn't spent earlier – as well as an additional 3 AP from bonding more sentients as Visitors – she had a total of 37 AP…which wasn't all that much in the scheme of things. The Advancement option that reduced the Mana Cost was only 15 points, but even with the 15% reduction that would provide, she still wouldn't be able to create the next Construct on her list – the Steelclad Ape Warrior. The issue she was facing was that she didn't know how much the next Advancement of that would cost in terms of AP, since the menu said that it would increase in price…but didn't say by how much.

Winxa, do you have any idea how much the cost will increase if I choose to reduce the Mana Cost of my Dungeon Monsters?

"...hmm...if I remember correctly – and keep in mind that it's been quite a while since the last time I worked with a dungeon that had access to the Advancement system – the cost doubles each time. So, if it costs 15 points now, it'll cost 30 next time, then 60, then 120—"

Ok, I understand – thanks, Winxa. If that was indeed how it worked, then Sandra didn't have enough to make it worthwhile – she was 8 AP short of obtaining the Advancement twice.

At least...she was *currently* 8 AP short.

Looking at the possible ways she might obtain more AP, there were a few options to acquire additional Points – though only a few were obtainable at the moment.

Advancement Points (AP)				
Source	Criteria	Point Value	Lifetime Earned Points	Lifetime Spent Points
Core Size	Receive AP upon Core Size upgrade (does not count for Core Size 1 nor upgrade stages)	1 per Core Size upgrade	19 AP (19X Core Size Upgrades)	19/19 AP
Number of Rooms	Receive AP for each distinct dungeon room at least 4,000 cubic feet in size (20ftx20ftx10ft minimum)	1 AP per qualified room	25 AP (25X Qualifying Rooms)	25/25 AP
Unique Dungeon Fixtures	Receive AP for each never-before-seen fixture in your dungeon	2 AP per fixture	26 AP (13X Crafting Stations)	26/26 AP
Creature Eradication	Eradicate sources of nearby creatures (i.e. lairs and spawning areas)	3 AP per eradication	6 AP (1X Territory Ant Colony, 1X Bearling Lair)	6/6 AP
Sentient Race Elimination	Eliminate members of sentient races	1 AP per 10 eliminations	8 AP (12X Orc, 71X Gnome)	8/8 AP
Sentient Race Bonding	Form a new Dungeon Visitor Bond with a member of a sentient race	1 AP per 2 Bonds	8 AP (1X Orc/Dwarf, 6X Elf, 9X Gnome)	1/8 AP
Dungeon Core Destruction	Receive AP for eliminating another Dungeon Core	30 AP per Core	30 AP (1X Reptile Classification Core)	0/30 AP
?????	*N/A*	*N/A*	*N/A*	*N/A*
(?????) Denotes an unknown, unique Source of Advancement Points. Perform this unknown action to unlock more information.				
Total Advancement Points Earned and Spent			122 AP	85 AP
Total Advancement Points Available			**37 AP**	

Again, upgrading her **Core Size** was out of the question, so that option was ignored. Creating **Unique Dungeon Fixtures** seemed easy enough, but at the moment there wasn't anything that she could think of to build that hadn't been built already; she knew of a few other crafting stations that she could potentially create, but most of them were variations of what she had already set up. The one thing that she thought *should've* been unique enough to qualify was the Enchantment Repository Room she had set up, but she suspected that because it wasn't necessarily "finished", it didn't count yet.

Adding another eight rooms to the **Number of Rooms** in her dungeon was also a possibility, but that would take both Mana and time to complete; it wasn't much of a hardship, however, so Sandra put a portion of her attention to work on adding rooms behind her Home that led deeper underground. She had no distinct purpose for them, and it would most likely take a day and a half to make rooms and tunnels that would meet the minimum size required by the Advancement criteria; despite that, it was a simple way to earn Points that didn't require much effort.

As for the other options, **Sentient Race Bonding** as Visitors was always a possibility but wouldn't likely happen anytime soon. The same went with destroying another Core; she was still recovering from losing all of her constructs during the assault on the Reptile-Classification dungeon and the defense of her own – she wasn't prepared to attack another dungeon anytime soon, nor was she inclined to unless there was no other choice.

Sentient Race Elimination was along those same lines, but she was even more reluctant to kill people unless they were attacking her dungeon – and even then, she would work towards a different solution. She wasn't *entirely* against killing them if they proved to be a threat that couldn't be persuaded to focus their energies elsewhere, but for her it would be a last resort; she wanted to ultimately *help* the people all survive, not do the nearby dungeons' jobs for them. Sure, it was ultimately for selfish reasons – like she had told her Visitors earlier – but that still couldn't change the fact that she didn't want to see any more of them die if it was preventable.

Therefore, the last option she had was **Creature Eradication**. Sandra was reluctant to specifically go out and hunt living creatures for her own benefit, however; it was one thing to defend her Home and dungeon from Territory Ants and Bearlings that were trying to destroy her Core, it was something else entirely actually seeking them out and killing them all in *their* homes. Even though she had just participated in killing thousands of reptilian Dungeon Monsters, she also knew that they were all relatively mindless forms of Mana that were given a shape – so it wasn't quite the same thing in her mind.

When she considered it further – and looked around her AOI to search out the three Bearling lairs and half-a-dozen Territory Ant colonies she identified earlier – she realized that eliminating them might actually be beneficial. If she really was planning on creating some sort of...distribution network...that involved delivering crafted goods to the different races, then anything traveling through the barren wasteland was walking through dangerous territory. The route towards the Elven and Gnome villages that her constructs and others had taken previously had gotten lucky; none of them had strayed too close to one of the creatures' homes, so they weren't attacked. If they had taken a slightly different route, though, things might have been quite a bit more difficult.

Using some of her Animated Shears from her AMANS, Sandra surveyed the surface of the barren wasteland from the air – and was surprised at what she found. There were even more deadly creatures inhabiting the otherwise empty landscape than she had anticipated.

While she could see everything belowground, which was how she knew there were three Bearling lairs and six Territory Ant colonies, everything living on the surface was essentially invisible to her unless she had something nearby to observe it. The other beasts she saw didn't live in underground lairs, which was the main reason she had missed them – and because they camouflaged very well into the surrounding landscape she hadn't noticed them before during her casual exploration.

Consulting with Winxa for more information on them – since she had never seen anything like them before – Sandra identified three more potential hazards for anyone crossing the wastelands. The first was a massive pack of large wolf-like creatures with greyish-brown, stone-made "fur" lying in wait along the face of one of the smaller rocky hills; the Crag Hounds – which Winxa had identified them as – were half the size of the Bearlings but appeared much quicker despite being made at least partially of stone, with long claws that left marks in the hard rock of the landscape.

She hadn't noticed them before because they blended in so perfectly that they were nearly impossible to see unless they moved. Even when she brought the Animated Shears she was directing closer it took almost 10 minutes of staring at the hill to identify three dozen of the Hounds – and she wasn't even sure she spotted them all. There was a smaller pack on the opposite side of the wasteland that she managed to spot; Sandra figured there might even be more, but they were either camouflaged even better than the others or hiding somewhere she couldn't see.

The next creature she found was a horrendously large cluster of Desolate Spiders. Their presence away from dark, hidden places was strange to her; from what she knew of other kinds of spiders, they were ambush hunters that preferred to lie in wait for something to come by or string up a web to catch unwary victims – but staying out of sight most of the time, regardless. *These* Spiders, however, were technically in plain view of anyone that happened upon them, though there were so many clustered together that it would probably be the last thing they ever saw.

From above – and she found it was the same from below, when she brought her Shears down to that level – they were just as invisible as the Crag Hounds; while they were approximately the size of a Gnome's hand, they were also the same colors as the dry dirt and dust of the wastelands. Instead of inhabiting the hills like the Hounds, however, they blanketed the ground with their flat-backed, dirt-colored forms that seemed to fit together when they butted up against each other. When they were completely still – which seemed like their normal state – they appeared like an additional layer of ground, innocuous and safe.

Sandra only discovered their presence when she saw a Bearling unwittingly get too close to the invisible Desolate Spider cluster. In a cascading wave of movement, the ground seemed to lurch forward and envelop the large dangerous beast as thousands of the Spiders bit and stabbed their legs into the tough exterior of the Bearling. For its part, the larger creature swiped and bit at the seemingly unending waves of dirt-colored arachnids, crushing, squishing, and destroying a hundred or more of them.

The result of the "battle" was a foregone conclusion, however; after less than a minute the Bearling slowed down, as whatever the Desolate Spiders were able to inject into its body through their bites took effect. Eventually, the larger beast collapsed on its side – crushing another two dozen of its attackers in the process – where it was further swarmed and covered by hundreds of the horrifically effective cluster of Spiders. Sandra stopped watching after a few minutes as small chunks of the now-dead beast was ripped from its corpse and carried away as the arachnids fed, only to be replaced by others looking for a taste of Bearling meat.

Coming back only an hour later revealed that the carcass of the larger creature was completely gone, as well as the corpses of the dead attackers; as for the victorious Desolate Spiders, they had gone back to where they had lain in wait, practically invisible again. The biggest difference, though, was that there was a large hump in the middle of the cluster; bringing her Shears closer, she found that hundreds (or maybe even thousands, it was hard to tell) of translucent orbs – that she assumed were eggs – had been laid and were being protected by the group. She didn't know how long it would take for them to hatch, but it was obvious that the cluster had already begun replacing those that it had lost against the Bearling. Even though she was just an observer, it was frightening how quickly all of that had been done.

Looking around for more Hounds or Spiders – both of which were extremely hard to identify – Sandra found one more creature that was likely to present a threat to anyone passing by. Unlike all the others, which seemed to rely on packs, colonies, or clusters of themselves, the last beast she found was probably more accurately called a *monster*, as it was both bigger and more frightening than anything else she had seen so far. Winxa didn't even have a name for it, which surprised Sandra, because the Dungeon Fairy – while unable to discuss certain topics – had seemed to have well-nigh unlimited bestiary knowledge in her head.

She found it accidentally when she had brought her Animated Shears too close to the ground, looking for more Desolate Spiders; before she could react, the floor of the wasteland seemed to explode in a shower of dirt, and her construct was enveloped in something she didn't even get a chance to see before it was destroyed.

Racing another pair of Animated Shears to where her previous one was lost, she saw a creature that was about half again as large as one of her Iron-plated Behemoths spitting out the Tiny Copper Orb left behind by the destroyed construct. It was colored similarly to many of the other beasts she had seen inside the wasteland – in greys and browns – but its skin looked scaly and even slightly shiny; with short front legs and long back legs, a bulbous body that looked like a distended bladder, and a frighteningly large mouth filled with hundreds of teeth, it looked like a giant toad minus the sticky tongue.

Looking around for where it had sprung from, she couldn't see a hole anywhere, only a slight depression underneath it. *Where did it come from?* Her question was answered shortly afterward in spectacular fashion, as the...*hmm, I'm going to call it a Rock Toad*...seemed to deflate rapidly, almost like it had been full of air and a large hole was poked into it. It collapsed into the depression underneath it, lying so flat that it looked like a pile of skin with no bones, muscles, vital organs, or even blood inside of it. When it finally settled to where Sandra suspected it had started, the mouth appeared to have been opened completely wide, leaving an oval-like shape flat against the ground that looked like little rocks scattered across the landscape.

Looking at it both at a distance and up close, it was as invisible as the others she had seen – and obviously just as deadly. The jaws of the Rock Toad appeared to be able to swallow even a Bearling whole, which meant that anyone walking over – or even too near – would be swallowed just as easily; Sandra was just glad that the Hauler and wagon the Gnomes had been driving hadn't encountered one of them, otherwise they probably wouldn't have survived. Searching the rest of the wasteland from above revealed the tell-tale pattern of their teeth in four different places – but anything traveling at surface-level would have great difficulty identifying the danger before it was too late.

All of that new information meant one thing to Sandra: danger to the people she was trying to help. She wasn't exactly sure how all of the different creatures she found survived inside the barren wasteland, but if what she witnessed with the Bearling and Desolate Spiders was any indication, they found a way; there might even be some sort of prey that they hunted she hadn't even seen yet, but that didn't really concern her right now. The main thing she worried about was the future dealing with the races around the wastelands – Sandra couldn't have them (or whoever/whatever she sent to help them) dying to the dangers of the "barren" landscape.

What is it my father used to say? "Make twice the profit with just one sale"? Something like that, I think. Regardless of whatever the correct adage was, the meaning behind it applied to her situation: eliminating the dangerous creatures of the wasteland would both make it safer and provide her with much-needed Advancement Points. *Actually, it's almost three times the profit, because I'll get some Mana from their deaths, as well.*

Even though it seemed like the best course of action, Sandra hesitated. The expansion of her Core and Area of Influence as an instinctual need was in the back of her mind, and she worried that she was justifying the deaths of "innocent" beasts and creatures to further her own power. Actually, when she really dug down and thought on it, the current situation wasn't really the problem; she had experienced first-hand how dangerous at least some of those creatures were, and there was every likelihood that they would attack her or hers at some point.

No, it was the *future* that worried her. *Will I begin to think the same thing about the different races around here? That they are a danger to me and my increase in power and Influence? If the Orcs, let's just say, attack me again – will I needlessly justify their deaths as a necessity so that I can help the rest of their race? And would I then destroy the village on the border so that they won't have a staging ground for another attack?*

Those questions rattled around in her mind for roughly an hour before she silenced them with a firm thought. *No, I will not debate every decision I make now in the fear that it will influence my future self.* Sandra was of her own mind, and the instinctual drive to kill everything that the other Cores suffered from was controlled and pushed away, never to show itself...at least, she hoped so.

Once the wastelands were safe for travel, she could concentrate on the one thing she would never compromise on: crafting.

Chapter 4

To help with an assault on the different lairs and colonies, however, Sandra had to put most of her crafting on hold and work on building her AMANS back up – and perhaps even expand it; while she still had nearly 5,000 Animated Shears in it, she was running at half of what she was used to gaining from the ambient Mana absorption. Now that her dungeon was defended with at least an adequate defensive force of constructs – and her traps, of course – she divided her focus again to start building it up again. The problem she had to figure out was how to rapidly scale up the operation again now that they cost five times as much as they used to, while still maintaining her other project (creating more rooms) going on.

Therefore, Sandra had to dig down into the raw numbers, using that same knowledge of math she had learned from her father during their years as merchants. That learning had come in handy more times than she could count in her search for learning crafting techniques and recipes – as well as during her tenure so far as a Dungeon Core – and she was triply thankful for all that he had done to make her the person/floating-glowing-stone she was today.

First, because she had the available AP, Sandra went into her Advancement Options and purchased the option to reduce the Mana Cost of her Dungeon Monsters; this would help her increase her AMANS faster, as well as helping to produce what constructs she was going to need to eliminate some creature lairs later. As soon as she did so, she felt a subtle change in her Core; it was not quite as aggressive as the one that advanced her Classification, however – it was more like a slight alteration of…something. Because she couldn't actually see it she couldn't confirm, but she suspected that there was a change in the enchantment "cage" surrounding her Core. *I'll have to check with one of my Shifters later to see if I notice a difference.*

The change only visually manifested itself when she pulled up her Constructs Creation Options menu and saw that all of her constructs cost 15% less Mana to create – all except the Gravitational Devastation Sphere. Sandra remembered that the particularly destructive construct hadn't been affected by her Classification advancement before, so it was only with mild surprise that it hadn't been affected now. When she pulled up her Advancement Creation Options with her Goblin Worker and Unstable Shapeshifter, she saw that they had also been reduced in cost – which made the Shifter a little bit more affordable for the future at 13,600 Mana instead of its previous 16,000.

The cost was also rounded up, so producing one of her Reinforced Animated Shears now cost 43 Mana; when she added in the lowest-cost Monster Seed that could be used for the construct – which used to be a Tiny Copper Orb at 5 Mana, but was now a Tiny Clay Cube at 15 Mana – the cost shot up to 58 Mana total. When she added in the 80 Raw Materials that were needed to produce the Seed, the cost was still approximately four times the amount they used to be for her previous Shears.

Rather than be disappointed at the cost, though, Sandra looked at it as a challenge; there was no way to produce quite as many as she used to as quickly, but she could still slowly ramp up the production of them until she had as many or more than she had before – it would just take longer.

Getting enough Raw Materials wouldn't be difficult, since she was still hollowing out additional rooms so that she could accumulate the AP from them; however, doing so also took a bit of Mana as well. Right now, she was accumulating approximately 175 ambient Mana every minute – which sounded like a lot – and compared to many other Dungeon Cores in the world, it probably was. When she factored in the cost of around 20 Mana per minute to carve the dirt and stone out of the ground to make more rooms, Sandra only had enough Mana to produce a bit under 3 of her new Reinforced Animated Shears, compared to the 10 or more pre-Advancement Animated Shears with the same amount.

Using some mental math, Sandra estimated that in about 6 hours she could create and send out just over 1,000 of the new Shears, which was a severe drop in her previous production but was manageable. As time went on – and with every 1,000 Shears in her AMANS adding another 33 Mana or so to her per minute total – she would be able to add even more; by the end of a full day, she could be near her original amount of 10,000...if she didn't spend Mana on anything else.

Unfortunately, because there were other things she needed to work on with both her Visitors and to continue to recover her dungeon from the last few days. The situation with Echo was going to be simple, at least, because Sandra was planning on sending her back to the Elven village with the first shipment of Energy Orbs. While her inner Dungeon Core screamed at her that it was a risk to arm the nearby Elves with weapons that could be used against her, she knew she had to start somewhere. On the other side of the coin, it was also a risk to let Echo leave when Sandra needed her so much as a liaison between her dungeon and her race – but she wasn't a prisoner. If she left and never came back, so be it; if the Elf didn't choose to help her and her people, that was her decision.

As for Violet, there were a few things that Sandra wanted her to help with on a few—*safe*—experiments; with Felbar, the Dungeon Core wanted to pick his brain and play around with designing some of the War Machines he used to pilot. From a few conversations with Violet, she was pretty sure he didn't know *how* they were created, exactly, but there was a good chance he could describe what they looked like.

Those experiments and designs were going to require Mana – which would cut into what she could use for strengthening her AMANS. Her treasury behind her Home had been essentially wiped out during the invasion of the Elite Elves a few days ago, with only a few piles of Elemental Orbs left over that had since been used. Some of them went towards the Visitor bonding of those same Elves, while the rest went towards creating various Energy Orbs. If she wanted to continue creating those new enchanted Orbs, she was going to have to make more of the Elemental Orbs, which would be another drain on her limited mana.

As much as she wanted to do everything *right now*, Sandra knew she was going to have to be patient – and to have to split her focus between four different things: building up her AMANS, excavating underground rooms, creating more Energy Orbs, and learning what she could from the two Gnomes. Fortunately, her perusal of the wastelands and surrounding areas had shown no emergencies that she needed to take care of, so she figured she had some time to get what she wanted done.

Therefore, she went ahead and started the process of adding more Shears outside her dungeon; as the first large pairs of Reinforced Animated Shears – they were nearly twice the size of the original and were made of sturdier metal (not quite Iron, but something similar and just about as durable) – hit the air above the Wasteland, Sandra was surprised to find an unexpected benefit. Not only were they stronger and likely deadlier as constructs, but they could also "see" farther than the originals.

Farther, though, wasn't quite the right word; while they could see approximately the same distance, the *clarity* of what they saw was much higher. When comparing the two, a small Desolate Spider at 1,000 feet away was *much* easier to see with the Reinforced Shears than the previous incarnation; Sandra wasn't sure why that made the difference, but she wasn't going to complain.

In fact, by shuffling some things around, she used that advantage of "seeing clearer" by placing all of the new Shears along the outside of the AMANS, to better make out threats that might be heading towards her dungeon. Not only that, but she took a dozen of them and sent them in a route that roamed around the entire border of the wastelands in a constant circuit, looking for anything out of the ordinary; they absorbed a bit less Mana at that distance, but having eyes on the surrounding villages and forest edges made her feel a little safer – for herself and the people she wanted to help, unbeknownst to them or not.

Sandra's Visitors slept for almost half a day, which allowed her to get a lot of work done. At full production, her AMANS would've likely been increased by 2,000 or more of the newer Shears, but she was also contributing to her other projects at the same time. As a result, only about 900 Shears were produced – but at the same time three full rooms were complete, she produced an additional 32 Large Elemental Orbs of different elements, and she was also able to enchant them into Energy Orbs using her Unstable Shapeshifters. She could've produced even more Orbs towards the end of that time, but she decided to start stockpiling some extra Mana for some experiments.

As soon as Echo was up, she was eager to return to her village; after Sandra made sure the Elf was fed, she had over four dozen of the Energy Orbs packed up in a makeshift Cotton cloth bag ready for transport. She also volunteered her Mechanical Jaguar Queen to help with transport, but Echo refused, saying she wanted to be able to return on her own. Sandra was a little hesitant about letting her go all alone after seeing what was *really* out there in the wastelands – as well as noticing that the Elf wasn't completely recovered from her coma – but she wasn't going to insist.

So, just over two days after the Elites had saved the village from an army of reptilian Dungeon Monsters, Echo left to rejoin her people...*hopefully only temporarily.*

*   *   *

Dawn was just breaking over the horizon as Echo left the dungeon for the first time since she woke up from her healing coma. She had honestly been expecting Sandra to offer some sort of other excuse to keep her trapped inside for some reason and had been pleasantly surprised that she was politely but firmly urged to leave. Not that she had a problem with that, of course, since she wanted to get back to her people – but she was not expecting to be given a simple cloth bag full of Energy Orbs and sent on her way. Holding such valuable items in her hands made her a little on edge, truth be told, because such things were likely worth a fortune back in the capital.

Not that she believed that they would actually be *sold*; Echo knew that those in charge would see that they would be distributed to those who needed it most for the defense of their lands, and not for those with the most influence or deepest pockets. Obviously, since she was in charge of them, she would make sure those in the village got the first choice – because they were an important part to maintaining their people's presence on the border. They were also her friends, of course, and she didn't feel bad about making sure they got some preferential treatment.

Echo was entirely conscious that she hadn't fully physically recovered from her experience, but she felt like she was strong enough to at least run back to the village on her own, so she had eschewed using one of the dungeon's monsters to help her back there. It wasn't only for that reason, however; she reached toward her shirt where the Holy and Air Energy Orbs were nestled against her chest, constantly sending additional elemental energy her way. A few minor experiments with them proved that they needed to have actual skin-on-Orb contact to replenish her energy, so they were pressed tightly against the center of her chest where they wouldn't fall out when she was running.

I'm really going to have to find some sort of necklace like the one that Gnome woman, Violet, had. At the moment they were too easy to lose if she got into some sort of altercation with a beast or dungeon monster, and she didn't want to have to carry them in her hands; while Echo didn't have her bow – which made her feel almost naked without her go-to weapon – she knew that she would eventually need her hands free once she acquired one again. She was hoping that Wyrlin – who she was told had picked up her bow after she was bitten by the snake outside Sandra's dungeon – still had it in his possession; apart from seeing her people again and passing out a few of the Energy Orbs to them, getting her hands back on her beloved long-range weapon was what she was most looking forward to.

With a deep breath – and an internal prayer that she wouldn't run out of stamina and collapse as soon as she got to the village – Echo started to run, using her Air-based elemental energy to thin out the air in front of her and push her from behind. Within moments, she was racing away from the dungeon entrance, moving a little more than twice as fast as she could run without elemental assistance; she could've run even faster, but there was no reason to push herself that much if she didn't need to.

Along with increasing her speed, she also initiated her active camouflage, making her form disappear to those who relied on vision to locate targets; it never worked well against those who used other senses to locate her, but it was better than nothing. After about a minute of running, she could feel a slight drain on her elemental energy as she used it, but it wasn't nearly as much as it used to be – the Air and Holy Energy Orbs were greatly slowing down the consumption. Echo smiled as she increased her speed just a little more, enjoying being able to stretch her legs after being inside the confines of the dungeon for so long – even if she wasn't awake for most of her stay.

She took the same route she had used while she had been keeping an eye on the dungeon earlier; it was fairly straight-forward and free from danger – or at least it was a few weeks ago. Echo was still slightly skeptical about all that had happened with the lizards, snakes, and other reptiles that reportedly attacked her village, but she was cautious enough in her surroundings not to completely disregard it. *The last thing I want is to be bitten by another snake*, she thought, which made her shudder mid-run.

Luckily, the journey toward her village through the barren landscape was uneventful; as she got near enough to her home that she could actually see it in the distance, she found that her physical energy was starting to wane dangerously low, so she deactivated all use of her elemental energy usage and walked the last half mile. By the time she was close enough to be spotted by the lookout watching the direction she was coming from – which was relatively new, as they normally hadn't kept a guard on the wasteland's comings and goings in the past – she had somewhat recovered. In fact, she wasn't even breathing hard by that point, but she was still tired.

Her fellow ranger – Wyrlin – was, for a wonder, the one keeping watch; it was nice to see a friendly face after being around strange people in a strange environment. Instead of waiting for her to arrive, the other Elf bounded forward with relief and some unidentifiable expression on his face.

"Echo! You're alive! Porthel told us that you likely were, but I didn't believe him until I saw you walking out from the wastelands like some sort of wraith," Wyrlin told her with a catch in his throat, before enveloping her in a hug that felt like he was trying to squeeze her insides out. To say she was surprised was an understatement; she was glad to see her fellow Ranger, but she didn't think she deserved that kind of response from him. He had never seemed particularly emotional in the past and what he was acting like set warning bells off even in her tired mind.

"It...ugh...good to...see you too," she managed to squeeze out. One of the elemental energies he could manipulate was Earth, and though it wasn't typically used to enhance one's physical body, it certainly felt like it with his sheer strength. "Can you...let me...go?"

Wyrlin immediately released her and stepped back. "Oh! I'm so sorry; I was just happy to have you back. How did you escape—?" he started to ask, but then he stopped when he looked at her face.

"What are you looking at? It's really me – not some sort of imposter." She thought that it was a valid concern, especially after hearing – but not yet seeing – how one of Sandra's monsters could take the shape of anything it came into contact with. Violet had mentioned that it couldn't talk, at least, otherwise Echo would've been worried about a flood of them appearing in the night and taking the place of everyone in her village. Such thoughts were patently absurd, but so was everything else she had seen in that dungeon – which made her shiver at the thought of something like that actually happening, despite the growing heat of the day.

"You...you've changed. What are those marks on your face?" he asked, taking a deliberate step back from her.

"What? What are you talking about?" she asked, now thoroughly confused. She reached up to her face and started to feel around her cheeks and forehead but couldn't feel anything.

"Here – take a look," he said, before a shiny, oval-shaped, vertically placed sheet of water appeared before her face, casting her reflection back at her. She stepped back in surprise at its appearance before she remembered that Wyrlin also had access to Water elemental energy in addition to Earth. Not everyone had multiple elements at their disposal, and the number that did was falling year-by-year; that was one of the reasons she wanted to be an Elite, because they only allowed those with multiple elements into their ranks. She didn't know for certain, but she was fairly confident that Wyrlin also had those same aspirations, though he had never mentioned it before.

Recovering from her surprise, she stared at the reflection in the flat oval of water – and she could finally understand the other Elf's question. On each of her cheeks was a bronze-colored gear that appeared to have some white and yellow accents to them; *where did those come from?* They looked familiar for some reason and it took a few moments of staring at them before she remembered where she had seen them before: on the palms of the Gnome, Violet. Echo hadn't really been too curious about them before, because she thought it was a "Gnome" thing; gears and things like that seemed to be a part of their race, if what she had heard and seen of their war machines was any indication.

But now it appeared as though she had them, too – and it wasn't a coincidence. The one thing they had in common was the dungeon, so it had obviously come from there.

** I'm sorry I didn't tell you about them, but it slipped my mind and didn't really seem important. They are from the Visitor bonding process, and they shouldn't have any negative effects attached to them. **

Sandra's voice in her head startled her so much that she stepped backwards again and tripped over a small rock, landing on her backside with an *oof*. "But why are they on my FACE!" she shouted, partly out of outrage at their appearance, partly from the shock of having the voice of the dungeon she thought she had left behind in her head, and partly from the pain of her rear end landing on a *second* rock.

** Well…when I brought you into my dungeon after you were bitten by that snake, you were convulsing quite dramatically. I couldn't lay the Elemental Orbs on your chest or have you hold them in your hands like I did with Felbar and Violet, so the only other option was to…stick them in your mouth. **

Sandra actually answered her question at the same time Wyrlin was attempting to as well; he didn't know Echo was talking back to the voice in her head, and she realized it would perhaps be best if he didn't find out. Of course, she didn't hear the first part of what he was saying, but she heard the last part. "—know. Why don't you tell me what happened down there for the last 16 days, 17 hours, and 43 minutes."

How does he know exactly when I was taken? The answer was obvious, however; Wyrlin was a master at his craft in the forest as a Ranger, and could easily read the signs of nature, estimating how long ago something passed by within minutes. Though the fact that he had calculated her disappearance down to the minute was strange, plus the fact that he had apparently been keeping track of those minutes as time went by. On the one hand, it probably meant that he cared enough about her that he was extremely concerned for her safety; on the other hand…it was a little creepy.

Regardless of what exactly his motivations were, Echo quickly explained what had happened and how the dungeon itself had *saved* her, not *captured* her like Wyrlin said he thought. When she was done, she looked at her fellow Ranger's face for some sort of reaction, but his face appeared to be set in stone.

"You're a slave to that dungeon, you know that, right? I don't care what Porthel and the other Elites said – those are marks that it owns you," he finally said with a harshness to his voice that Echo had never heard before. "To think, I was worried that it had tortured and killed you; instead, it did much worse – it took away who you are."

Reaching behind his back, he pulled out a familiar bow which had been strung and looped around his shoulder; he looked at her and threw it on the ground with such force that it cracked, making her wince at the anger behind the act. "Here you go, I'm tired of carrying it around for you."

She knew it could probably be repaired, but even using elemental energy in the mending process, it was never as good as it was when it was first constructed. That wasn't really the most pressing issue, though – it was the fact that Wyrlin was angry at her for some reason. "What was that for—?" she had begun to ask, when the other Ranger turned away – completely ignoring her – and started to run back towards Avensglen.

What was that all about? Echo couldn't figure out why he would've had such a strong reaction to the gears on her face. *I was the one that almost died and was in a coma for two weeks, so what's his problem?* It didn't make any sense to her, and she hoped that the others in the village weren't the same way.

So, without much choice in the matter – and because she needed someplace to rest after her already-tiring morning run – Echo slowly walked towards the village she used to call home.

Chapter 5

Sandra had watched Echo's progress from her dungeon, sending her Mechanical Jaguar Queen to follow her from a distance as well as one of her Shears up above – just in case. Fortunately, nothing dangerous was on the route towards the Elven village, so by the time the bonded Elf met up with the one that had found Echo's bow more than two weeks ago she was able to send the larger construct back to its semi-permanent home in Sandra's workshop. The Shears, however, she brought down lower to hear the conversation between the two – and she was a little shocked and saddened by the male Elf's reaction.

She couldn't understand his reaction any better than Echo apparently had, and she hesitated to intervene; some instinct told her that making her presence known any more than she already had probably wouldn't be a good idea if Sandra wanted the Elf to ever return to her dungeon. Therefore, she just watched and let Echo do her thing in the village, hoping for a better result.

Fortunately, the village inhabitants seemed to receive her with guarded open arms; they welcomed her back and were ecstatic over the delivery of Energy Orbs, but they seemed to shy away from the gear tattoos on Echo's face when they saw them. Thinking back to when the Elites had defended them from the reptile force, Sandra couldn't remember them flashing around their own tattoos on their palms; it was quite possible that they deliberately hid them, so the villagers had no idea of their import – other than as a possible "slave" mark.

The Elder of the village took the remaining Energy Orbs and arranged for their transport back to the capital, where they would be put to good use – and then asked when more would be coming, which Echo had no answer for. Sandra hadn't really discussed any type of regular deliveries with her – mainly because the Dungeon Core didn't have a clear idea of how that would work quite yet – so the Elder was left without an answer for the moment. Still...it was a start to a (hopefully) profitable business relationship; the Elves would get Energy Orbs and the Dungeon Core would get cooperation in the future – and hopefully some samples of some rare materials that she could utilize in her dungeon.

After meeting with the Elder, Echo went back to her artificially grown tree-house and went to sleep on her sleeping mat almost instantly; the run out from Sandra's dungeon had obviously taken more out of her than she expected, and she was still recovering from her coma.

Sandra put the whole unfortunate reception of the newly bonded Elf out of her mind for the moment, mainly because there was nothing she could do about it – and trying to do something would probably hurt more than help. *You would think that helping them defend against a hostile force would make them show some gratitude toward me, but I guess the distrust of dungeons goes pretty deep.* When she thought about it a little more, she realized that most of her actions regarding that defense was mostly behind the scenes; most of the fighting was actually done by the Elite group that Sandra had bonded, and none of her constructs had participated – mainly because most of them had been wiped out by those same Elves.

So it was now obvious that the villagers didn't really *know* about everything that had gone on, other than as a source of the Energy Orbs they now possessed a few more of. It meant that Echo was likely facing an uphill battle to convince them that Sandra and her dungeon weren't there to hurt them, which would be hard – especially when the Elf was clearly not entirely convinced of that herself.

Sandra was hopeful that would come in time, though, and it wasn't something that could be forced. Therefore, she turned her attention to her next project that was going to require some of the Mana she saved from her other endeavors; she still kept her excavation of more rooms and the expansion of her AMANS running with two minor parts of her mind, however. They were important to her overall strategy, and she didn't want to handicap them with her...passion project. But first she needed to have a conversation with her other Visitors.

"So...what exactly are your plans, Sandra?" Violet asked as soon as she and Felbar were fed and ready for the day. "Because, as much as I've enjoyed learning about your dungeon, helping to avoid your destruction by negotiating with dangerous Elves, and helping to develop this wonderful enchantment on these Energy Orbs, Felbar is awake and recovering quite well. His well-being was my primary reason for staying, if you remember, and I estimate that in a couple of days he'll be recovered enough to travel back to Gnomeria."

"I'm ready to go anytime, child; I could outrun you—" the gruff older Gnome interjected, before being cut off by Violet. Sandra had noticed that she had become quietly more confident in herself ever since the incident with the Elite Elves, and it showed in how she treated her obvious elder and superior; she wasn't rude or inconsiderate or anything like that, though – but the time she had been in charge had changed her. From all that the Dungeon Core could see...that change was for the better.

"No you couldn't, at least not right now. You still need a few more days to get your strength back up, and then we can head out. Until then, you need to rest those old bones as much as you can," she said. When he looked like he was going to protest, she cut him off before he could even get a word out. "And no, that wasn't a crack about your age, but you have to realize *that you just woke up from a coma*, and even someone younger like me – or even that Elf – wouldn't be up to traveling that far without at least a little more recovery."

That definitely shut him up; it was more than evident that morning that Echo still hadn't fully recovered from her incapacitation, so to expect him to be even further along was foolish. To press the issue would be even more so, therefore Felbar left it alone. Violet looked expectantly at one of her Unstable

Shapeshifters in the workshop, and Sandra realized that she hadn't answered the Gnome's question.

** Well, as far as you leaving for home, I would like to prepare another Hauler and wagon to bring with you; the others already took one shipment of raw materials, but I'm sure your people would appreciate anything additional. There are a few obstacles that could jeopardize your safety in traveling through the wastelands that I just noticed recently; I'd like some time to eliminate the threats before you depart, but I am hoping to have that done by the time you leave in a few days.*

** However, the additional materials and even a load of Energy Orbs for your people is only a temporary measure to help them – as I'm sure you're well aware of. Just like those Orbs Echo brought to her village to help* ***her*** *people, everything I help supply will only delay the inevitable, not prevent or stop it. In the Elves' case, even if they had millions of Orbs at their disposal, they don't have enough of their people to wield them against the dungeons' threat; what they need is help in the form of cooperation, and that cooperation would likely be in the form of additional forces that would come from* ***outside*** *their lands. I'm still working on that problem, but I'm hoping to have a solution at some point.*

** The other races have different problems, but what your people are lacking – if I'm understanding the situation correctly – is a way to* *create more of your war machines. So, I have a question for you both, and I'd like you to answer as honestly as you can: how likely is it that your surviving Master Enchanters will be able to pass on their knowledge of how they are created? And if so, what would be even more important, is how long do you think that teaching will take...and do you think it will be in time to save your people? **

They were both silent for a while as they looked at each other in contemplation. Finally, Violet ventured to answer, though she was obviously a little hesitant. "Yes, I believe that if the remaining Master Enchanters dedicate themselves to only teaching, then—"

"No," Felbar said loudly, cutting the other Gnome off. "Sorry to burst your bubble, child, but I worked side-by-side with most of them before I was sent off to babysit the operation in Glimmerton, and I can tell you that they don't have enough time. I know you'd like to think so, but if they take any time away from creating and repairing what they were already struggling to keep up with, then we're all dead within a decade or two, if not sooner. It's a little-known fact outside of a few circles, but the consensus – at least when I was there a year or so ago – is that there are not enough of the Master Enchanters available to make a difference. With the severe lack of potential Enchanters that could even *learn* how to create them, there are already plans in place to...*delay the inevitable*, as Sandra said."

That...doesn't sound good.

** What plans are you talking about? **

Felbar sighed heavily, as if he didn't want to even think about it; luckily, he wasn't disinclined to answer. "Instead of War Machines that us Warmasters could pilot, they were going to focus on large stationary heavy defenses and portable weapons that could be maneuvered around with a small crew. While the heavier defenses I agree with – I wish we had some of them during the attack on Glimmerton, for instance – the portable weapons that they want to make will be largely ineffective. Pushing a cart around with enchanted ballistae, static sawblade defenses, and various minor elemental attacks won't help much against a dungeon monster that can just move out of the way.

"Sure, it'll probably kill quite a few of them that are stupid enough to attack it, but the reason we were so successful in our piloted War Machines was because we could improvise, easily retreat if we needed to, and easily maneuver through trees to hunt down monsters on their own turf. The larger cart-based weaponry is hard to get through dense forest, takes a team of at least three to operate, and if they are surrounded they are virtually guaranteed to be overrun and destroyed. There are a few smaller portable weapons that a single Gnome could use, but they aren't powerful enough to drop some of the larger monsters out there; as much as it pains me to say it, we just don't have the physical capabilities to carry heavy loads, move quickly, or defend ourselves using primitive armor and weaponry."

By "primitive" Sandra assumed he meant things like swords and shields, which, when she considered it, made perfect sense. Unless they were facing something their same size or smaller – which was perhaps only about 10% of the Dungeon Monsters they were likely to face outside of an actual dungeon – then they were useless without their enchanted "gadgets". In fact, the one thing they actually had going for them because of their small size was their ability to move quietly and unobtrusively through her dungeon; there were times when Violet – and even some of the other Gnomes that had survived the fall of Glimmerton – had moved so naturally silent through her rooms and hallways that she was surprised a few times when they showed up somewhere she hadn't been expecting them.

But that didn't really translate well when they were trying to take down a giant turtle, a ferocious bear, a horde of goblins, or a charging unicorn. The piloted War Machines were what helped the Gnomes as a race keep the number of monsters in their land down to a reasonable level, and if they lost those then they were doomed, despite whatever they tried to make up for their loss. It appeared as though the leadership knew that fact – even if most of the population didn't – so Violet's thought and dream to become a Master Enchanter seemed like it would never happen. By the look on her face, the Dungeon Core could see that realization had hit her as well.

Unless Sandra helped to change that eventual outcome.

** So, what I'm hearing is that your people are facing a crisis right now, one of which you won't be able to recover from without...time. **Time** to teach, **time** to repair or create more War Machines, **time** to let future generations grow up to become full-fledged Enchanters – all of which won't happen because of the threat that the dungeons surrounding your land pose. But what if I was able to give you that time? It would only be a short-term solution – like I hope most of my solutions will be – but it might be just enough to give you all that **time** you need. **

"A fancy speech is all well and good, but what exactly are you talking about?" Felbar asked gruffly – but with a hint of curiosity and hope mixed into his voice as well.

** I'm talking about making your War Machines here— **

"I told you before, I don't know how to enchant them; I was just an Apprentice and don't know all the secrets of how they were made," Violet interrupted her.

Felbar added his opinion, as well. "And although I can operate one of them better than just about anyone else, even *I* don't know how they're made. They require someone that has the Spirit and Natural elemental energies at their disposal; while I can remember what the Spirit enchantments looks like, I'm not sure I could reproduce them with any particular talent."

** Ok, then I have one more question for you, Felbar, before I reveal my idea. I don't want this to seem insensitive, but...why you? What makes Warmasters so special that only you and others like you can pilot the War Machines? **

Felbar bristled at that for a moment, as if Sandra was questioning his worthiness or something. After a moment, though, he seemed to realize she was asking because of ignorance, not because of any doubt in his abilities.

"We Warmasters specialize in manipulating the Spirit-based enchantments that directly control the movements of the War Machines. By infusing small amounts of Spirit energy into particular enchantments in a specific order, we can cause the constructs to do just about whatever we want; it takes years of practice and coordination to properly control them without causing them to fall apart in the process, and *that's* why Warmasters are so special."

"That's true," Violet agreed. "They actually maintain the vital Spirit-based enchantments from their energy infusions, though it doesn't necessarily recharge them – more like putting patches on the rune to keep it operating longer; occasionally one would start to break down because of time or physical damage to the construct itself – which I and some of the others in Glimmerton had to repair with a direct replacement of the enchantment rune. The other, non-Spirit enchantments on the War Machines themselves, however, had to be replaced once every couple of days, otherwise they would start to fail. For instance, many of the Natural enchantments on them made the wood and steel parts pliable enough to bend and flex without breaking, which takes a surprisingly large amount of energy to maintain – especially when they are used in constant combat like they usually were.

"For other enchantments, like the Hauler we built for the others to bring home, the energy is constantly recycled through the enchantment, but after a while even those start to break down without additional infusions of energy or rune replacement. The one they took, for instance, could probably function for a few months before it started to lose power, eventually ending with it breaking down until it wasn't usable anymore."

All of that was excellent information, and Sandra was more encouraged every moment. She had suspected that they had worked that way, but of course the *how* was the hard part; it was one thing knowing the principle behind their operation, but how it got to that point was something else entirely.

** I think I understand. Well, if we don't know how your Master Enchanters do it, maybe we'll just have to figure it out ourselves. **

"What? You can't be serious; it took dozens of Master Enchanters decades or perhaps centuries to perfect the techniques they use. I highly doubt you'd be able to duplicate what they did in such a short time," Violet remarked with severe doubt edging her voice.

* *Oh, I'm not going to try to duplicate exactly what they did – I couldn't hope to do that. However, I think I can figure out a way to get them to work, even without knowing exactly* ***how*** *they went about it. What will help immensely is if you can teach me all that you* ***do*** *remember from the enchantments, as that will give me a place to start. And to do that, the first step in the process is to go down to the Enchantment Repository.* *

Violet and Felbar looked at each other and shrugged. "I guess it couldn't hurt; if she really can figure out how to get them working, then I'm on board with it. Besides, it's probably about time to recharge the Stasis Fields on those pillars," Violet mentioned, before heading out the workshop door.

* *While that is true, there's something about those Preservation Barriers...er, Stasis Fields...that I want to experiment on.* *

The Gnomes stopped at that. "When you say experiment, I hope you don't mean, 'try a whole bunch of different enchantments and hope they don't blow up', do you?" Felbar asked, more than aware of Sandra's accident earlier where one of her Shapeshifters was destroyed.

** No, of course not. I need someone with steadier hands and more experience, so **Violet** will be doing the enchanting. **

Instead of relaxing, that only caused them to tense up even more. "That...isn't encouraging. However, if it's a relatively safe experiment like the one where we created the Energy Orbs in the first place...then I guess I can do it."

Excellent! Now all I have to do is figure out a way not to blow her up...

Chapter 6

The problem with Sandra's Rune Repository Pillars – which she had known about from the beginning – was that the Preservation Barriers (or Stasis Fields, as the Gnomes called them) surrounding each Pillar, which helped to preserve enchantments for teaching purposes, needed to be replaced at least once a week. Due to their size, the Barriers that were needed to stop the passage of time ate through the energy infused into them quite rapidly; they could always be replaced without disrupting the preserved enchantments inside (which had already been tried and had been successful), but if they were forgotten about – or, say, Sandra was undergoing a Core Size upgrade and it took longer than expected – then the Barriers would fail. If that happened, then whatever enchantments that were previously preserved on the Pillar would be lost.

But Sandra envisioned something that would be available for any Visitors to her dungeon that wanted to learn about enchantments – for as long as Sandra's dungeon existed. She knew well enough how hard it was to record such knowledge back when she was Human, how guarded Enchanters were with their techniques, and the risk there was in not being able to pass it down to future generations due to an unexpected death. The Gnomes were going through that last problem right now with the deaths of most of their Enchanters; without enough to go around to keep their land safe, they couldn't teach their knowledge to their younger generation. If they died before they could do that, then that information would likely be lost to the ages...just like the Gnomes would be, if Sandra didn't do something about it.

In order to preserve that knowledge, the Dungeon Core needed to make the Enchantment Repository Room (ERR) one that could maintain itself even if she weren't there anymore. If, for instance, she were destroyed – which she didn't want to think about but would be a fool to consider as something impossible – then all that work would be undone without anyone to maintain the Barriers. Sandra was aiming to change that.

When her guests arrived at the ERR, Felbar was fascinated by it; he hadn't gone on much of a tour yet, so hadn't been far enough down to see the room. Violet had already given him the lowdown of what exactly it was but seeing it in person was a whole new experience.

Sandra had earlier created a few Large Elemental Orbs – two Spirit and one Natural – and placed them inside the room; she asked Violet to place a small Preservation Barrier over one of the Spirit and the Natural Orbs to see if the Barrier could preserve what was to be done with them...and then asked her to create the enchantment that would turn them into Energy Orbs. The creation of all those enchantments only took a fraction of what Violet was capable of, and Sandra could tell that she was already being refilled by the Energy Orbs hanging around her neck as she asked Violet to enchant the last Spirit Elemental Orb outside of the small Barrier.

As she asked the Gnome to step back, and across the room, Sandra had one of her Large Armored Sentinels she had standing still near the wall walk forward and pick up the separate Spirit Energy Orb that was newly created. She wanted to try an experiment with a smaller Barrier, with the hopes that the energy involved wouldn't be too destructive if something went wrong.

Bringing the Energy Orb in contact with the edge of the Barrier, Sandra indeed obtained the reaction she was expecting; just like the Orbs would do with a person and restore their elemental energy, so too did the Barrier Enchantment absorb the energy given off by the Orb to replenish what it used to maintain itself.

"That's…I never thought of that! That means you could maintain these Fields for years, possibly even centuries if you had enough—"

The invisible field surrounding the two static Energy Orbs started to become visible as it glowed with a soft grey luminescence; in a matter of seconds, however, it went from a barely visible tinge to an alarmingly bright, piercing light that hurt to look at. Sandra instructed her Sentinel to remove the Energy Orb it was holding from contact with the Barrier and the brightening stopped – but didn't disappear. Instead, over the next few minutes, the glow gradually lessened in intensity to the point where it didn't hurt to look at anymore; still, it was an "angry" enough glow that approaching it at the moment didn't seem like a good idea.

"What...happened?" Felbar asked, looking highly confused.

Violet, on the other hand, was studying the barrier and the Energy Orb in the Sentinel's hand. It was hard to tell exactly without comparing it to another unaltered Elemental Orb, but Sandra could've sworn that the Energy Orb was a little smaller than it had been just a few moments ago.

** I was worried about that; I was expecting it to work, but I suspected that it wasn't going to be that easy. This is what I need your help on, because I believe if we solve this problem, then making those War Machines will be* ***a lot*** *easier. **

While Sandra had some ideas on how to do that, she was hoping that Violet would be able to provide another perspective – and she was not disappointed. "I...think I see the problem here. Whereas our bodies have natural limiters on the amount of elemental energy we can absorb, enchantments do not. That is why knowing exactly how much energy to pump into a new enchantment is vital, otherwise you risk overloading what it can handle; if that happens, it could do something innocuous like unravel with a few sparks, all the way up to a deadly explosion. It's also why small infusions to an enchantment are possible – like how the Warmasters operate their War Machines – but anything larger isn't recommended to even try, as it might cause the runes to break and explode, especially if they're worn.

"However...there might be a way to limit the amount of energy being siphoned off of the Energy Orb, allowing just a certain amount to be transferred over to the original enchantment to 'recharge' it without damaging it in any way. Since the enchantment on the Orb is self-sustaining, repairing itself in the process of converting what you call Mana into energy, then I don't see why the same couldn't be applied to this situation."

That actually made sense, and it had been sort of what Sandra had been thinking of, but she couldn't really figure out the process needed to get there. Now that Violet had worked it out in her head the basis of what they needed to do, the Dungeon Core had an epiphany – and it was one that would change the way she looked at enchantments from then on.

** That's it! If we construct the Stasis Field with an additional inverted* ***Strengthen*** *rune, then it will use the energy it has inside of the enchantment to constantly repair itself, just as it does with the Energy Orbs! Of course, doing so would eat up the energy at a greater rate – which is where the Energy Orb comes in; it could easily replenish any of the energy that is used to maintain the enchantment rune structure.*

** ...But then we still have the problem with transferring too much energy to the enchantment. While it would repair itself using some of that incoming power, eventually it would become so bloated that* *it would explode in spectacular fashion – with potentially catastrophic effect due to it being a stronger enchantment.* *

Sandra thought that they had solved the problem, but it turned out that they had only switched it for another, worse problem. Violet looked stumped, and Felbar appeared to finally understand what the issue was; he wasn't ignorant – far from it – but he also wasn't brought up as an Enchanter, either.

"What if there was some sort of actual manipulable 'limiter' to how much energy is transferred? It sounds as if you solved the problem of recharging the enchantment, but now you need some way to 'control the flow', I guess you could say," Felbar asked when no one said anything.

But Violet was already shaking her head. "I don't think I've heard of anything like that; I may not know *how* to create a lot of enchantments yet as an Apprentice Enchanter, but I'm sure I would've at least heard of something along those lines," she said sadly.

Something about what Felbar said tickled a memory in Sandra's mind, however. Blocking out all external stimuli – going so far as to even halt progress on the AMANS and room excavation – she delved into her memories, trying to figure out what exactly had occurred to her. After almost a minute of searching, she very nearly gave up…when she finally remembered.

She was young – only about 14 at the time – but she was already well on her way, learning about as much Enchanting as she could; given that many crafters didn't like to talk to children or even young teenagers, she considered that an accomplishment in and of itself. One stubborn woman, however, refused to teach her how she created a **Limiter** enchantment rune, which she had made a fortune with by applying it to thin sticks of finely crafted wood she called "wands" for some reason.

They were popular in the Hero community, though, because they helped those who could manipulate their elemental energy much in the same way the Elves did; because there were many Heroes that were not quite as *efficient* at "casting spells", the Limiter Wands would help regulate the amount that was needed for a particular spell. They were all custom made to a particular spell, because the actual **Limiter** enchanting rune could be altered minutely during its creation to suit whatever it was being used for.

For instance, if a Hero liked to manipulate their Fire elemental energy to throw out fireballs towards monsters, the Limiter Wand would help ensure that a precise amount was used with each cast; that way, every fireball they sent out could be the size of their head, or the size of an apple, or even the size of a house if they wanted – but they'd of course need to have the capability of doing that in the first place.

The beauty of it was that it required the person casting the spell to send the elemental energy *through* the **Limiter** rune, and there was no backlash if too much was provided in the first place – which was perfect for their situation. If they were somehow able to integrate the versatile rune into the enchantment rune sequence, then the Energy Orbs could be used to recharge and essentially power...any enchantment.

Of course, there was a catch; because the woman who made the **Limiter** enchantments wanted nothing to do with Sandra, her young self had needed to sneak into her workshop and observe in secret. She felt bad about doing it now, but at the time she had been so obsessed with learning the secrets of all types of Enchanting that she wasn't thinking about the fact that she had broken the law by trespassing where she shouldn't have been. When Sandra had been found only a short time after watching the woman perform a single enchantment, she had run before she was identified – and made her father leave the large town in the middle of the night.

The result was that she knew *how* the rune was created but had only the vaguest idea how it was changed to set the "limit" – and that was only from comparing the completed rune enchantments of the one she saw made and one she saw later on in her life. How it was fine-tuned from there she had no idea, so it would likely take some experimentation.

Luckily for Sandra and Violet – her resident Apprentice Enchanter – the **Limiter** enchantment rune sequence was created from Spirit energy, so it would mesh well with what they were already working with. Though, when she thought about it a little more, she realized that *any* of the elements would work for the utility-type enchantment, because it didn't actually use elements itself – it only regulated whatever passed through it. Having a similar element to the ones used for the enchantment cage around the Energy Orb would help to ensure proper connection of the rune sequence. Once they figured it out with the Spirit element, then Sandra could apply it in different ways using her Unstable Shapeshifters.

"Figuring it out" would probably take a while, as such minute changes affecting energy transfer would be hard to measure immediately.

** I actually think that it can be done. I know of an enchantment called a **Limiter**, but there's an issue… **

Sandra went on to explain a little bit about how she knew of it – leaving out the part about her trespassing – and told them how it would take a bit more experimentation to fully understand how it worked. Violet was actually enthusiastic, because she would be learning a new enchantment that could turn out to be extremely versatile; when she saw that Sandra had brought her Unstable Shapeshifter and had transformed into a Violet Copy in order to show her how the runes were made, she lost some of that enthusiasm.

"At least you have some semblance of clothes on, but do you seriously have to copy me every time?" she said, seeing herself walking through the entrance to the Enchantment Repository. Felbar's eyes opened wide as he looked between the two of them, and Sandra realized he hadn't actually had a chance to see her Shifter in action quite yet.

** Sorry, I could switch to Felbar or one of the Elite Elves if you prefer, but I only brought these clothes down with my Shapeshifter. **

"No, that's fine – the last thing we need is a naked Felbar or Elf running around down here," Violet sighed dramatically, smiling at the other Gnome's discomfort. "Besides, you've done it enough that I'm starting to...not get used to it, but maybe ignore the fact that I'm staring at myself. Go on, let's get this over with."

Sandra used the Shifter's Spirit energy to create what she remembered of the two enchantments on the wooden Rune Repository Pillar, because the one she always remembered seeing was made on those wooden "Limiter Wands"; once it was on there, it stayed *almost* complete but not quite, due to the function of the Stasis Field around it. It was a crude representation of what she remembered seeing – because Sandra wasn't quite as adept at enchanting as she'd like – but she made sure to spend special attention on the very slight differences in them that she remembered.

The rune itself was a series of eight concentric circles that grew smaller as they all closed in on the same point; from there, eight wavy lines crisscrossed the circles in a strange pattern, leading from the center and out to the edge of the largest circle.

The slight difference that she had noted from her remembrances came from an alteration of one of the wavy lines, where there was an extra "hump" in the wave – and that was it. Whether having an extra "hump" meant the enchantment would let *more* or *less* through, Sandra didn't know, nor did she know the magnitude of that difference.

Violet, however, didn't seem to care; cooped up in the dungeon for so long with not much to do made her look upon the slightly different enchantments as a challenge. Which was fine with Sandra, because she wanted to steal Felbar away so she could get his input on how the War Machine she eventually wanted to make would look.

Therefore, she left the Apprentice Enchanter to work on experimenting with the new enchantment. Her method of research was quite simple, actually, and would only be *slightly* dangerous; Violet created a tiny Preservation Barrier the size of her hand and used altered Energy Orbs to test the viability of the **Limiter** rune alterations she made – by bringing them into contact briefly herself. To further increase the safety of the experiment, Sandra created multiple Tiny Spirit Elemental Orbs and had them sent to her; with less Mana inside the Energy Orb, there was less that could ultimately be used to overload the enchantment.

Once she'd gotten her started, Sandra checked in every once in a while with the Apprentice Enchanter, but she had most of her attention on Felbar. After making his way up to the workshop again with the Unstable Shapeshifter (unshifted) in tow, the battle-hardened Gnome showed that he had a deft hand with a stick-shaped chunk of coal and a wooden board; within a few minutes, the basic shape of one of the War Machines Sandra had seen being used in Glimmerton was pictured, giving much more detail than she expected. While she had her memories to go on of what they looked like, it was much easier to consult with someone who actually used one in action.

It was a shame that the ones that were destroyed had been carried off the field of battle afterwards by the reptile army; Sandra supposed that there might've been some reason the Dungeon Core had done that, though she thought it was because it wanted some of the material they possessed for use as a Monster Seed. It would've made the process of constructing one much easier if they had been left alone, but she was making do quite well.

Most of the parts of the wooden-and-steel construct Sandra could make just by using some Raw Materials and Mana; other parts – just like portions of the Hauler and wagon she had made previously – she had to create using the forge inside the workshop. Fortunately, Felbar knew about the physical construction of the War Machine like the back of his hand, even if he didn't know about the enchantments that made it move. The work progressed quickly as it was assembled by a large crew of Sentinels Sandra borrowed from one of her rooms, and by the end of eight hours it was basically complete...in all of its 12-foot-tall and 5-foot-wide glory.

It was a marvel of ingenuity and deadliness, a headless person-shaped construct that reminded Sandra a little of her Automatons; a sharp-spiked hammer on one arm was matched with a double-bladed axe on the other, making it capable of smashing or slicing a variety of different monsters. Some of the details regarding the pilot seat was still needing to be done, but she had held off on it until she could figure out how to enchant the entire thing.

As Felbar and Violet headed off to bed after a full day of working on Enchanting – the Enchanter had made progress but was still stymied by a few things – and constructing a Gnome War Machine, Sandra took a break herself and looked over what else had been accomplished during the day. Seven of the rooms she had been excavating were already finished, and the last one would be finished in a few hours; her AMANS had increased by another 1,100 Shears, which brought her total up in the air above her dungeon to 6,715 – which was a noticeable improvement over what she had before.

She also checked on Echo to see how she was progressing in the slightly hostile Elven village, and nothing much had changed; apparently being "home" relaxed her tired body enough that she slept through the entire day and was likely to sleep through the night, so Sandra resolved to check up on her in the morning.

Another check through the wastelands and surrounding villages showed that nothing else was really going on, so Sandra spent time trying to figure out the enchantments for the War

Machine. After just over four hours of thinking it through, mentally trying out countless options based on her extensive knowledge of Enchanting, and even cautiously attempting a few things on a small 6-inch tall model she had made of the War Machine...she determined that it was currently impossible.

Based on what she remembered seeing on the Gnomish War Machines before they were destroyed during the battle with the Ancient Saurians, Sandra was fairly confident that she could copy most of the runes she remembered that dealt with movement and material pliability; she hadn't seen any of the runes from inside the pilot's chamber which allowed them to control everything from there, but even that she could imagine what it looked like and *probably* figure it out. No, the real issue was that the original enchantment had to be done *all at once* with an extensive enchantment rune sequence that required precise skill, extreme care, and more elemental energy than both Gnomes and her two Shapeshifters could supply *combined*.

Actually working it out herself helped her understand exactly what the problem was that the Gnome homeland was facing; even if they could teach the exact way to create the enchantment, those who could learn how it was put together didn't have the necessary elemental energy to actually do it. Even the Master Enchanters needed to work *together* to supply that much energy, so unless they had dozens of Apprentice Enchanters collaborating on a single, complex rune sequence that would likely take years to learn how to create properly – which sounded like a disaster with that many trying to mesh it all together – then there was no way it was happening. Sandra began to see why the Gnome leadership thought they were doomed.

Now, working on the smaller model she had created, Sandra thought that something quite a bit smaller than the War Machine might be plausible – like maybe something a little bigger than a Gnome; as it was, however, there was no chance of getting something like what she had built to work...at least, not yet. In the future...perhaps...but right now? No.

She knew that even if she managed to create something small enough, she still had to work with Violet to pull together all of the thoughts she had about getting the rune sequence to function properly; while she wasn't going to try to duplicate what the Master Gnome Enchanters did, the same principle of enchanting the entire construct all at once still applied. Once the enchantment was in place, only then could individual enchantment runes be replaced and repaired—

Wait...

That thought sent a jolt of inspiration through her mind, though it wasn't fully formed quite yet. She was beginning to see how it *might* be done, but it was going to take a bit of trial-and-error to see if it was more than just a feeble hope. The reason – as far as she understood it – for the original sequence having to be done all at once was because everything had to be tied into the central enchantment; the purpose of that was to regulate the energy consumption of the construct while it was being controlled

– otherwise anything the pilot did to manipulate the runes via infusions of elemental energy could become unstable.

If that happened, the same thing Violet was experimenting with could happen; the vast amount of elemental energy contained in the War Machine – and based on what she had calculated earlier, it was indeed *vast* – could cycle through every enchantment sequence, creating a feedback loop that could lead to an explosion of vast proportions.

At least, that's what she assumed after Violet and Felbar had tried to explain what they knew about the enchantments on the large Gnome construct. It was a bit technical and Sandra wasn't quite sure if she had understood it correctly, but as far as she could tell that was the basis behind the whole theory. But if she eliminated the potential for that type of catastrophic result – by utilizing a **Limiter** rune, perhaps – then the entire enchantment sequence could be put together piecemeal.

Now it's doubly important that Violet figures that rune out.

Chapter 7

Violet spent the next two days working on the **Limiter** rune, growing more and more frustrated at her lack of progress. Sandra and Felbar even tried their hands at it, but weren't getting anywhere, either; they had hit a mountain of a bump in the road that seemed insurmountable, but the Dungeon Core knew that it was only a matter of time. While they were working on it, the older Gnome was recovering nicely from his coma – to the point where he would possibly be able to travel long distances within the next day or so.

Echo came back once during that time at Sandra's request to pick up another bag of Energy Orbs; the rest of the time the Bonded Elf spent either inside the village sleeping or going out to hunt in short sprints, using her hastily mended bow. The hunts seemed to tire her out, but Echo persisted in going on them despite the fact that she missed about a third of her shots; the repair to her bow had altered it slightly, throwing off her aim – which Sandra could clearly see even from a hundred feet up in the air.

I have to see if I can make her a better one down in my dungeon, she thought – after seeing the Elf miss for the third time that day. The residents of the village had fortunately warmed back up to Echo after the initial frosty reception, and if they didn't treat her with quite the same affection as they had before, at least they weren't openly hostile – unlike the male Elf that had broken her bow. Sandra soon learned that his name was Wyrlin, and that he had been trying to convince the Elder that Echo was a danger to the other villagers, the village itself, and the Elven people as a whole.

Luckily, the Elder – and anyone else he approached – seemed disinclined to listen to his angry ramblings (probably because Echo was supplying Energy Orbs for her people via the dungeon); after a few days of no one listening to him, the Elf took off into the north-eastern woods one afternoon and didn't come back. Sandra watched him leave and followed him for another few miles into the trees, but he eventually hit the boundary of her Area of Influence and disappeared. She assumed he was heading farther into the Elven lands to warn those about the new "dungeon slave", but he was taking a strange route; when she mentioned it to Echo, she didn't even want to discuss it and only said that she was glad he was gone.

Since Echo seemed content to live inside her village and come back to the dungeon every once in a while to deliver more Energy Orbs – which was essentially what Sandra was wanting – the Dungeon Core left it alone; there was no reason to invite trouble when there was no point to doing so.

In spite of the worry about Wyrlin and the lack of progress in the **Limiter** rune – there was something that they were missing, but none of them could understand what it was – Sandra and her dungeon were doing quite well. In the two days the Gnomes were experimenting with enchantments, her AMANS had managed to accumulate and surpass 10,000 Shears; at that moment, it was currently sitting at just under 11,000 – and still growing.

Sandra was starting to see a marked decrease in how much they were funneling back to her Core as they continued to spread out, however, so she decided that she might bump it up to about 12,000 and see if that was a good balance. Theoretically, she could continue to expand until she filled up her entire Area of Influence, but she had already seen that anything farther out from where her Shears currently roamed didn't provide nearly as much ambient Mana every hour. Whereas she was getting approximately 2 Mana per hour from a good portion of the Net above her dungeon (the outer edges of it she estimated to be about 2/3 of that amount), the Shears she had roaming around the border of the wastelands were maybe bringing in 2 Mana per *day*.

Sure, after a few weeks every Reinforced Animated Shears that she created would pay for themselves; with just over a half million Mana being funneled into her Core every day, however, she thought it was a good place to stop. One reason was because she was starting to feel a major strain on her mind at having it split up and doing multiple things at once; another reason was because she was ready to start cleaning up the land around her dungeon and make it safer for future travel.

After creating her eighth additional room a while ago, Sandra had quickly used the AP she earned from the project to unlock the additional reduction in the Mana Cost of her Dungeon Monsters. That helped to speed up production of her Shears a little since it brought the total cost of each one to an even 50, though it also required her to excavate more rooms for the Raw Materials to produce them. Therefore, in addition to the eight rooms she had excavated, she added another ten to that total; looking at everything from a distance underground, her neatly spiral-shaped dungeon looked like it had a very long tail.

With the influx of Mana inside her Core, and with her AMANS and excavation projects wrapping up, Sandra was ready to start assembling a strike force that could wipe out the creature-based threats around her dungeon. It was about time, too, because she had observed a gradual migration of the new ones she had discovered; since they weren't confined to a cave lair like the Bearlings or a colony like the Territory Ants, the groups of Spiders and Wolves were able to place themselves where they wanted. Apparently, where they wanted was the pathway that Echo used to reach Sandra's dungeon, as well as the winding route that the Gnomes had used to leave with their wagon.

It was almost as if they could somehow sense where their potential victims had been traveling, so they moved to intercept them when they came back; it made sense, unfortunately, as Sandra had heard that many natural predators tended to congregate where they knew prey was likely to frequent. Therefore, Sandra warned Echo not to journey back to the dungeon until she made the way safer, which the Elf readily agreed to.

Getting her army ready for the first assault – which would be a large group of Desolate Spiders – Sandra felt like she was going on a shopping spree where everything was on sale. She pulled up her Constructs Creation Options and saw that the new 30% total reduction in cost was already making quite a difference.

Constructs Creation Options	
Name:	**Mana Cost: (30% Reduction)**
Clockwork Tarantula	18
Reinforced Animated Shears	35
Hyper Automaton	70
Dividing Rolling Force	88
Lengthy Segmented Millipede	350
Iron-banded Articulated Clockwork Golem	525
Roaring Blademaster	1050
Large Armored Sentinel	1400
Mechanical Jaguar Queen	2800
Mechanical Dire Wolf	3500
Martial Totem	5600
Automated Sharp-bladed Digger	7000
Multi-access Repair Drone	11200
Steelclad Ape Warrior	16800
Titanium Anaconda	22400
Steel-plated Behemoth	28000
*Gravitational Devastation Sphere**	15000

Advancement Creation Options	
Name:	**Mana Cost: (30% Reduction)**
Goblin Foreman	56
Unstable Shapeshifter	11200

While she couldn't yet afford to create a Titanium Anaconda or a Steel-plated Behemoth, the previously out-of-reach Steelclad Ape Warrior was now only 16,800 Mana; she was very excited to finally have them back, because they were both better suited for crafting and versatile in combat. The only problem, though, was that each one she produced was going to be expensive in terms of both Mana and Raw Materials; while she had previously unlocked a few options that would be able to contain the construct, they were expensive to create.

Monster Seed Origination				
Name:	Raw Material Cost:	Mana Cost:	Min. Mana:	Max. Mana:
Small Dragon Glass Sliver	40000	14000	5000	20000
Small Faceted Sapphire Sphere	24000	7000	3500	17000

The Small Faceted Sapphire Sphere was the least expensive of the two options, but when she added all the costs up, she was going to have to use a total of 23,800 Mana and 24,000 Raw Materials to create a single Steelclad Ape Warrior. The Mana itself wasn't that big of a deal now that she was receiving that much practically every hour, but the Raw Material cost meant that she was back to excavating more rooms. Fortunately, every two hours of excavating gave her enough to produce another Monster Seed, so the only thing holding her back now was time.

So, the next day saw Sandra alternatingly doing multiple things again, though her AMANS project wasn't one of them. Excavating more rooms only took minimal concentration for a part of her mind, so she didn't feel the strain as much as she had before; almost as soon as she stopped the constant creation of Reinforced Animated Shears for the Net, she had felt like a weight had been lifted off her mind. The two other things she concentrated on were easy enough to focus directly on, so she didn't have to divide her focus again.

First was the creation of her creature eradication army; it consisted of four Steelclad Ape Warriors (which were just *slightly* larger than the original Ironclad Apes, but were made of a shiny steel material), a dozen Mechanical Jaguar Queens, a dozen Mechanical Dire Wolves (which, like the Jaguar Queens, were basically large wolves made from stronger metal than their predecessors), a single Multi-access Repair Drone (it looked nearly identical to the regular Repair Drone, so she wasn't exactly sure what the difference was yet), and...300 Dividing Rolling Forces.

The last entry into the lineup was something Sandra put in as an impulse, mainly because she knew she was going up against the Desolate Spiders. The Dividing Rolling Force was about half again as large as the original Rolling Force and made from a metal that was a bit heavier, denser, and could withstand a little more damage; the largest difference, however, was that the construct could *divide*. Not just in half, but into at most six different parts of roughly equal mass. That didn't seem like a benefit, but it was the dividing action that made it spring into the air a couple of feet, where it could propel forward if it had enough momentum, or slam down into the ground from normal gravitational force.

It would've been even more effective if the separate parts were sharp, inflicting cuts on an enemy, but the blunt force they enacted on a target was brutal enough. After they sprang apart, their divided parts would slowly gravitate toward each other and reform into a perfectly round ball again, ready to fight some more. Through some quick experimentation in her dungeon, however, Sandra found the downside to the new Rolling Force; if more than half of the divided segments were destroyed, the entire construct would cease to function and be destroyed shortly thereafter. If there were at least three of the segments still "operational" when they came back together, then it would form together again into a smaller ball – that was able to be repaired by a Drone if necessary.

Still, Sandra was planning on using them effectively against the Spiders, because having a lot of extra targets to attack would hopefully let the other constructs do their thing without too much hassle. As much as she didn't like to think of her constructs as "expendable", losing the new Dividing Rolling Forces wouldn't be too much hardship; she was just glad that none of them could be poisoned by the Desolate Spiders, so she was hoping they would survive with few casualties.

The other thing that Sandra was focusing on between creating constructs for her threat-eradicating army was building another Hauler and wagon. Even though Violet and Felbar were dedicated to figuring out the **Limiter** enchantment rune, she could tell that they were anxious to get home. Now that the older Gnome had pretty much fully recovered, getting back to their homeland was a priority; Sandra would miss them and their help, but they weren't prisoners or anything – and having another representative to vouch for Sandra and her dungeon to the Gnome leadership was always good.

When the Dungeon Core told the two Visitors about her project, she was proven right in her assumption that they wanted to leave; they doubled their efforts with their enchantment experiments, saying that they wanted to do as much as they could before they left. Sandra definitely appreciated it, so she made sure to include as many materials as she could in the wagon they were going to take back to Gnomeria – which included blocks of Titanium.

The new metal she gained access to – because of the Elite Elf Porthel's broken sword – was extremely useful for crafting weapons and armor, and it would also be useful for the Gnomes in the construction of whatever defenses they could. Although it was approximately as strong as Steel, it was less dense; this made Titanium lightweight with a better tensile strength (meaning it could bend more without breaking) and it resisted metal fatigue from repetitious use, which helped to prevent cracking. It was also able to withstand higher temperatures – it had a melting point that was even higher than Iron – and it was thought that because of that, it could handle being the focus of certain enchantments for longer periods.

Not that you couldn't use just about any enchantment on any material, but Sandra knew that some were better suited for certain ones; for instance, if you had an enchantment that would light something like the tip of a sword on fire when it was activated, it probably wouldn't work very long or successfully on something made of wood or a softer metal with a lower melting point.

Sandra was excited to use Titanium herself in her crafting, but she hadn't had the opportunity to experiment yet. Once the wasteland was "safe" and the Gnomes had left, she was planning on digging into a lot that had been neglected from the recent emergencies. In fact, her Core was practically vibrating from excitement at the thought of having a little peace and quiet to get back to her crafting.

The next morning, her construct army was complete, the wagon was essentially filled to the top with materials, the Hauler that would bring it home was enchanted by Violet (the doing of which Sandra watched intently and learned some valuable tips from), and the Dungeon Core was actually able to start stockpiling Elemental Orbs and other Monster Seeds for future use with her excess Mana. She had already finished all of her stages towards the next Core Size upgrade – which took nearly 240,000 Mana all told – but she had already determined to hold off on doing so; since she didn't have to worry about accumulating more Mana for that, once her current self-imposed obligations were taken care of, she was...free. Free to craft and free to plan more for the future.

Of course, that morning when Sandra was about to strike at the first massive clutch of Desolate Spiders getting a little too close to the route Echo usually took to-and-from the village and the dungeon, the problem with the **Limiter** rune was finally solved...in spectacular fashion.

*   *   *

Violet was getting thoroughly frustrated with the strange rune that Sandra had shown her on the wooden pillar in the Enchantment Repository Room. There were eight concentric circles and what she assumed were eight wavy-looking access lines, which would theoretically help to designate the "limit" of energy being funneled through it. However, the only thing she had to go by was a slight difference in one of the lines from the Core's examples, and Violet thought that it would be easy to figure out the difference, using even more slight differences to see how they would change the performance.

As it turned out, they didn't have any effect at all.

In fact, the original rune – which Sandra helpfully called a **Limiter** – didn't do a single thing that she could tell. She had tried incorporating it into the original enchantment over the Energy Orb, tying it to the tiny Stasis Field she had created, and even kept it completely separate – all with no discernable difference at all to the amount of energy being transferred. At first she thought that Sandra was just mistaken, and the rune was nonsense, but some innate Enchanting instinct told her that it was correct – but she was missing something, some vital piece of information to get it to work.

She had tried altering the circles little by little, then changing the positions of the access lines themselves, then straightening them all out and shaping them one-by-one, and so on and so forth. She had essentially given up the day before, but she was stubborn enough to keep trying for some sort of result even when she thought she had tried everything.

Felbar had even joined in on the experiments, because the **Limiter** rune was fairly easy to create; even old War Masters could learn new runes, it seemed, because he picked it up within minutes. She had enchanted his very own tiny Energy Orb for his use and had even set up another tiny Stasis Field for him – which was easy enough for him to see, since he also had access to Spirit elemental energy. Despite his earlier enthusiasm, though, he had just about given up and was playing around with different ways of creating the rune sort of how Violet herself was, hoping that it would finally do something.

"Have you...tried creating the rune with your Natural element? That might make a difference," Felbar asked her, which made her jump since it had been at least an hour since either of them had said anything.

"Of course not, because Sandra said that it was created from Spirit only – so I doubt it would have any effect, either. I can *almost* feel like it should be working with the one I have, but there's something preventing it that I can't see," she answered, having done everything she could with the Spirit Energy Orb, **Limiter** rune made from Spirit elemental energy, and the Spirit-based Stasis Field. *Though now I'm beginning to wonder if he has a point; have I been going about this all wrong?*

Before she could try it herself, Felbar answered. "It probably can't hurt to try...hopefully...so I'm going to test out my Fire element to see if that works; if it doesn't, I'm out of ideas – not that I had many to start with," he said, before creating what she could only assume was the **Limiter** rune using his Fire element. She couldn't see or manipulate it, so she had to assume he had done it; he had been creating the other one out of Spirit over and over for about a day and a half, so she had faith that it had been done correctly – or as correctly as they could assume, given Sandra's spotty recollection of it.

Felbar had only lightly connected the rune to the Spirit Energy Orb he had been using, because he didn't quite have the Enchanting skill to weave it into the rune sequence around the Orb; when he brought it close to the Stasis Field, Violet held her breath...and let it out in disappointment as the Field started to brighten slowly like it usually did when they connected the Orb and the Stasis enchantment. *I guess that wasn't it either.*

"Oh, well – it was worth a try, Felbar," she said, failing to keep the disappointment she was feeling from her voice. "I'm going to try a couple of other things, but then I'm giving up for now; at least we have this rune that we can take back, and maybe one of the Master Enchanters still around will know what to do with it."

"That's fine; I can't wait to get back – these old bones can't take the cold of this dungeon for this long," he said, putting the tiny Energy Orb next to the others on his neck as he leaned back against the wall. They had found that *two or more* Energy Orbs could increase the regeneration rate of elemental energy, so it was a common practice for them to do so when they were feeling a little drained from all the Enchanting. "In fact, I'm going to heat this little area up if you don't mind using a trick my father taught me."

Violet was barely listening as she looked at her own experiments – trying to see a different way to test what she had already been testing – so she just grunted out an affirmative. The next moment, she was practically blown onto her back from a wave of heat and force coming from Felbar's direction. A scream was abruptly cut off as she looked up to see Felbar stumbling towards her on fire, before he collapsed on his face – unconscious or dead.

Before she could even react, two of Sandra's healing constructs were there, having moved from their position in the corner of the room; they had been stationed there since the beginning, mostly in case something disastrous happened – kind of like what just occurred. She crawled over to Felbar's unmoving body, seeing burns all over his skin, which was easy to see because all of his clothes had been burnt off.

Within moments, though, the burns started to heal rapidly, the angry and blackened skin flaking off as new skin was revealed underneath. Violet sighed in relief as she saw Felbar's back moving up and down as he started to breathe deeply again, which meant that he was certainly still alive. She had seen the healing constructs work miracles before, and now was definitely not an exception.

It took another few hours for the old Gnome to fully recover from the ordeal, get some clothes, and shove his face full of food to replenish what had been lost during the healing. When Felbar – now completely healed, though his entire body was now completely devoid of any hair – was finally able to explain what happened, Violet sat back and stared at him in surprise, because he had just solved the problem.

That's...so simple.

Felbar had used a simple temporary enchantment on the floor of the room that would warm the immediate area around him by 10 degrees; when it had enveloped his body, it interacted with the Energy Orbs he had on his chest. Normally, that would've just resulted in the enchantment absorbing energy at a rapid rate, which would make it increasingly hotter and hotter until he moved the Orbs away. However, because he had the **Limiter** on one – and it was obviously touching the Fire Energy Orb – it acted as a catalyst that kicked the rune into working. Instead of the expected trickle of energy leaking through, the **Limiter** was apparently cranked all the way up; the energy in the tiny Spirit Orb was expended all at once, as well as some of the Fire Orb.

The tiny Spirit Orb was entirely fine, but Felbar's Fire Orb had been reduced by a quarter, or perhaps even a third; Violet could only be thankful that the relatively minor heating enchantment was relatively safe in the first place, otherwise the heat and flames would've been...*deadly*. Fortunately, it hadn't been and Felbar was alive – if a bit shaken from the experience. Not only that, but Violet thought she had figured out how to use the rune, though it would still take some *very* cautious experimentation to control it.

Spirit energy was also thought of as "living" energy, found in almost everything that was considered alive; this made a difference in this case, because it was apparently the catalyst for initiation. Going back to Sandra's description of how Humans would cast their spells through the enchantment, the Spirit element was applied by the living Human; it was probably a failsafe built into the rune so that it wouldn't be activated by stray elemental energy. When they "initiated" it, only *then* would the **Limiter** activate to do what it was supposed to do.

All of that ultimately meant that every enchantment that they were hoping to power – like the Stasis Fields – needed a Spirit Energy Orb for "initiation" and one supplying the actual energy. In Felbar's case, the tiny Spirit Orb started the process with the **Limiter** rune and used his Fire Orb as energy – and consumed a good portion of it in the span of a few seconds. In any further experiments, Violet knew she needed to supply at least a Spirit Orb to start the process, and a second one to act as the power source.

Felbar rested for the remainder of the day from his harrowing experience, but Violet was now eagerly waiting to experiment some more now that she *thought* she figured it out.

** Just be cautious, Violet. Felbar was very close to dying there; I know it was an accident – even if you may have learned something from it – but that doesn't mean you can be reckless. Just in case, I'm placing an additional two Repair Drones inside your workspace, bringing them up to four; two was **barely** enough to save Felbar, and I don't want you dying because I didn't have enough help for you...but that doesn't mean you should throw all caution to the wind. **

"I know, Sandra; don't worry, I'm planning on being extra careful from now on, especially seeing what happened to Felbar," she told the dungeon, safety a very conscious thought on her mind. "Did you know that the rune could extract the energy at a *faster* rate than usual? I thought it was only to limit the amount already coming out?"

** I didn't – which is why I want you to be extra careful. I don't know what other unexpected things will come from this whole experiment. **

"Me neither, Sandra, me neither. But I hope a lot of good comes from it as well."

** That's my hope as well. Well, I've got some deadly beasts to kill that are inhabiting my wasteland, but I'll be keeping an eye on you, nevertheless. My Drones have instructions to heal you on the chance that you need it, but I'd rather they not be needed – if you catch my drift? **

"I do, I do," Violet said, walking back into the Enchantment Repository Room. "You go have fun, and I'll call if I need you—actually, can you create a whole lot more Orbs of different sizes?"

** Already on the way. Good luck. **

"Thanks – you too."

** Oh, I don't need luck; I'm going to absolutely annihilate these things and make it safer for everyone to travel through these lands. **

Sandra said that with such conviction and confidence that Violet had to chuckle a little. As she settled down in her little corner of the room she had designated as her workspace, she rubbed her hands together and smiled in anticipation.

Hmm...where to start, where to start?...

Chapter 8

"Annihilation" turned out to be putting it mildly.

Sandra's force of Ape Warriors, Jaguar Queens, Dire Wolves, Dividing Rolling Forces, and one Repair Drone poured out of her alternate dungeon entrance connected to the workshop one after another until they were gathered outside in – if she did say so herself – an impressive display of might. When they were all assembled, she immediately sent them towards the massive Desolate Spider cluster that was now fully moved to the pathway Echo used to travel towards her dungeon. It was now clearer to Sandra than it had ever been that she needed to eliminate the deadly creatures of the wasteland if she wanted to maintain a relatively safe environment.

She sent her Dividing Rolling Forces in first, bringing them to within a dozen feet of the leading edge of the cluster; with what looked to be a perfectly choreographed action – but in reality was just that the Rolling Forces decided that it was the right time – they all sprang apart. More than a thousand heavy slices of the constructs shot into the air, their forward momentum launching them up and over the first ranks of Spiders. When they reached the apex of their vertical arc, the pieces of Rolling Forces rained down on the backs of unsuspecting Spiders; their weight alone was enough to snap their thin stone-covered bodies, cracking them like a chunk of iron dropped on an egg.

It didn't take long for a response, however, as the Desolate Spiders swarmed over the slices of Sandra's constructs within their midst. Watching from above with two dozen Reinforced Animated Shears, she lost sight of them as they were buried under thousands of Spiders trying to bite or stab them with their sharply pointed legs. Sandra could sense that three of her Rolling Forces had been destroyed, but not from the incessant arachnid attacks; from what she could tell, quite a few Force slices had impacted something harder than Spider shell – like a sharp protruding stone jutting from the ground – which severely dented and mangled them, causing the few remaining segments of those constructs to dissolve into the ground and disappear, leaving behind their Monster Seeds.

While the horde of Spiders were – for the most part – ineffectually trying to damage her Dividing Rolling Forces, her other constructs attacked with brutal efficiency. Steelclad Ape Warriors leapt into the air and slammed down on small clusters of Spiders, flattening and killing dozens within seconds as they flailed around them with their fists. The Mechanical Jaguar Queens and Dire Wolves crashed into the arachnid forces like a wave, stomping down with their paws and crunching the Spiders apart with their jaws. Within 30 seconds of the attack starting, over a thousand of the enemy had already died, while none of her larger constructs were harmed seriously…except for one unlucky Ape.

Venomous bites and stabs with pointy Spider legs did absolutely nothing against her metal-formed Dungeon Monsters…but that didn't mean they were invulnerable. Enough blunt-force damage could hamper or destroy most of her constructs, while others had other vulnerabilities; her Apes, for instance, were animated by a glowing "core" inside their well protected chests. One of her Steelclad Ape Warriors was swarmed by hundreds of Spiders at the same time, and a half-dozen managed to squeeze their way inside the few gaps in the Ape's torso; within seconds, the deadly arachnids had bitten, stabbed, and destroyed its vulnerable power source, killing her construct.

Seeing that happen, Sandra made sure the others were aware of that happening and to avoid being overwhelmed; while they couldn't exactly acknowledge their receipt of that information, she saw them retreat and jump away when too many were surrounding them. After that, the rest of the battle was relatively anticlimactic; thousands of Spiders died in just under 10 minutes to Sandra's forces, leaving heaps of smashed, oozing corpses spread out over hundreds of feet of wasteland.

Other than the Steelclad Ape Warrior, which she had already replaced and was sending to join her extermination force, she had lost three dozen of her Rolling constructs. A few were from the initial impact at the start of the battle, but the others were from another vulnerability she wasn't previously aware of; apparently, if the slices of them were kept apart for long enough – for at least two minutes was what she determined – then not being able to reform into a single construct would be just about the same as losing half of their pieces. The press of Spiders had been so thick in some places that some pieces couldn't get to each other, resulting in their loss.

Checking on Violet, she found that the Gnome had made some progress with figuring out the **Limiter** rune; Sandra was still a little saddened on *how* the method of getting the rune to work had been discovered – with the whole Felbar being charred to a crisp – but Violet seemed to have no obstacles towards her experimentation. *Hopefully within the next few days we'll be able to start actually* ***applying*** *the rune to help power a number of things.*

The deaths of all the Desolate Spiders had also supplied a massive amount of Mana – nearly as much as a full day of ambient Mana absorption from her AMANS. She used some of it to replace the Ape and Rolling Forces that had been destroyed, but the rest she fed into more Elemental Orbs. She would've rather used them to create Monster Seeds that could contain some of her more Mana-expensive Constructs, but she was a little short on Raw Materials; she was still actively making some rooms to help provide those, but her excavation was only so fast.

Fortunately, as much as it would be disgusting, there were now thousands of corpses that could be "recycled"; Sandra had already thought ahead and created a small army of Hyper Automatons, the advanced form of her Tiny Automaton. The new Hyper Automatons were only slightly larger than the original and appeared to be made of the same soft metal material – but they made up for those similarities with something else: strength and speed. Whereas the older ones walked slowly around, their stiff-like legs making their pace a toddling amble; the Hyper ones, however, had fully jointed legs and could *run* – and run fast.

They weren't the fastest of Sandra's constructs by any means, but they could move quickly for their size. Not only that, but they could lift and carry things that seemed impossible; a few experiments with some blocks of iron showed that they could lift something that weighed up to 100X their own weight – sort of like she had heard some insects could do.

As a result, they were the perfect transportation service for corpses big and small; they could work together to lift and carry something larger, but even on their own they could drag something twice or three times their size. As 200 of them ran out of her dungeon and towards the battlefield that wasn't much of a battle, she saw each of them use their hands to grab three or four Spider legs and start to drag them back towards her dungeon at a run. A few times some of the legs got ripped off in the process and the Automatons had to grab another, but within about 10 minutes the first of the corpses were dropped off inside her entrance and she immediately started to absorb them.

New Monster Seed Origination Material found!

Paralyzing Spider Venom
While the Paralyzing Venom ***cannot*** *be directly used as a Monster Seed, it can be combined with specific other materials to create a whole new Monster Seed.*

What? That is...interesting.

She wasn't exactly sure what that meant, but the informational notification looked very similar to when she obtained the Territory Ant Eggs from the colony near her Core.

Winxa, is this starting to make any sense now? I can't even imagine how I could use Paralyzing Spider Venom or a Territory Ant Egg to create a whole new Monster Seed.

The Dungeon Fairy had been relatively silent and unobtrusive lately, and Sandra was beginning to worry about her guide. Upon reflection, however, it was obvious that Winxa was feeling a little lost because her Dungeon Core was figuring out things all by herself – and didn't necessarily need her help. The question perked her up a little bit, even if she didn't really have an answer that satisfied Sandra.

"Like I said before, I have no idea; you could always try combining it with some of your other materials, but as you said, I can't imagine what you could create. It could be that it's for something that you *can* do but haven't figured out yet."

That definitely didn't help. If it was true that it was for something she didn't even know she could do, then that just meant a whole lot more experimenting – which she didn't currently have time for. Pushing that to the back of her mind – and to the bottom of her list of things to work on/experiment with after things calmed down a little – she continued to absorb the Spider corpses that were delivered, as well as gathering up the Monster Seeds from her destroyed constructs. She was starting to rebuild her treasury near her Home up again, and they were welcome additions to the growing stacks of Orbs and Cubes.

She also converted a lot of the Raw Materials she was receiving from the battle's aftermath into crafting materials, including stacks of Iron, Steel, and Titanium bars; creating wood or cloth and storing it away wasn't always the best for those kinds of materials, so she stuck with things that could exist for years and years without deteriorating. She knew that as soon as she got to the point where her treasury was at an "acceptable" level – it was never going to be at a perfect amount, because she could always use more – she was going to start unlocking more materials via her Organic/Inorganic Material Elemental Transmutation Menu.

There's almost always more to do!

Speaking of more to do, Sandra had already started her extermination force towards their next target; since they didn't need to rest – and the Repair Drone only needed a few minutes to repair some damage to a few constructs from the battle with the Desolate Spiders – they were well-equipped to keep going. Next on the list was a Bearling lair that was located just off the pathway the Gnomes had taken to leave a few weeks ago; they fortunately hadn't been attacked at the time because most of the Bearlings had been gone – off hunting somewhere, Sandra assumed. Now, however, they were a threat to future travel.

There were two dozen of the Bearlings in their cave, and they somehow detected her constructs before they got within 100 feet of their entrance; they poured out of their lair, and immediately went on the attack – only to get pelted by heavy metal pieces as Sandra's Dividing Rolling Forces split and launched themselves at the larger beasts. Unlike the damage they did to the Spiders, the results were less than spectacular; a few of the large fur-covered creatures seemed dazed as they were hit on the head by multiple slices of her constructs, but for the most part they shrugged off the attack.

Their counterattack, though, did some horrendous damage to the Rolling Forces; with ultra-sharp claws that could cut through stone, hundreds of her constructs' pieces were swiped at with large paws that gouged out large chunks of them – if not sliced completely in half. She lost half of her Rolling Forces in the first few seconds of battle as they lost many of their components, causing them to be destroyed and dissolve into the ground.

Luckily, Sandra wasn't counting on them to make much of an impact; just like they were against the Spiders, they were primarily there as a distraction. As another few dozen were sliced apart, her other constructs fell upon the Bearlings and systematically tore them apart while bashing in their heads. The Ape Warriors leapt and slammed their heavy Steelclad bodies on the backs or necks of the dangerous beasts, snapping bones and causing heavy damage with their fists. The dozen Mechanical Dire Wolves acted almost like pack hunters, picking off those Bearlings at the edge of the melee; they would surge forward essentially as one and latch onto different parts of the beast with their powerful jaws, and then literally rip them apart.

It was – Sandra had to admit – quite disgusting.

The Jaguar Queens weren't much better, though they pounced and sliced open vulnerable spots on the Bearlings' bodies – using their claws that were probably sharper than the beasts' own claws – letting them bleed out and weaken before they went in for the actual kill. It was an effective strategy, mainly because they were so quick and could avoid being caught...most of the time. One of the Jaguar Queens didn't scurry away fast enough and lost a leg from a sudden paw swipe from a Bearling it was attacking. It collapsed to the dirt, unable to move effectively on only three limbs – and its skeletal metal head was crushed in between a Bearling's jaws.

A Dire Wolf also lost a back foot as it was sliced apart while trying to grab onto a Bearling, but it managed to drag itself away from the fight – where Sandra's Multi-Access Repair Drone got ahold of it and started to restore the amputated appendage.

By the time they were done, all but two dozen of her Rolling Forces had been lost; from her main attackers, though, only the one Queen was destroyed – though there were a ton of little injuries that would take a few hours to fully repair. To cut that time in half, Sandra created and sent another Repair Drone along with the other replacements, using the Mana from the Bearlings' deaths. Overall, it was a very successful operation.

One thing that she noted during the battle – and which disgusted her even more – was when she saw one of her Steelclad Ape Warriors pick up a dismembered Bearling leg (from the Dire

Wolves' handiwork) and use it as a makeshift weapon to break the leg of another Bearling, before tossing it away when it was destroyed in the process. *Does that mean...they can use weapons?*

"I don't see why not; many other Dungeon Monsters – such as some of the Bipedals, Giants, and Goblins – can use weapons," Winxa responded unasked to her mental question. "Most come equipped with them when they are created, but there shouldn't be any reason why they couldn't pick up another one somewhere and use it. And the name change does kind of hint at that, doesn't it?"

Steelclad Ape *Warrior* did indicate that it was different from the previous Ape – so that was what it probably meant. While the Ironclad apes could pick up a hammer and use it to craft, they weren't made to use weapons in a fight; they could certainly use them, but they didn't have the necessary experience to use them properly. It was like giving a wooden switch to a toddler; the Ironclad Apes would use a master-crafted longsword like a stick and smash things with it, instead of using the sword how it was intended. *Perhaps these **Warriors** are different.*

On that thought, Sandra used her Hyper Automatons that were heading towards the new battle site to carry four Steel longswords she had crafted a while ago, along with four Steel warhammers; she wasn't sure based on the little she saw if they were skilled enough to use a sword effectively, or if they just liked to bash things.

It turned out it was the latter, as they all immediately picked up a warhammer and stood upright with them positioned against their shoulders. Sandra thought it was strange to see them wielding weapons like that, but after a few minutes it started to look normal – as if they were meant to be armed the entire time. With their decision made, a group of Automatons brought the longswords back to the dungeon, along with two Bearling corpses; it took approximately 60 of her little constructs working together to lift and carry each intact body, and the remaining few assisted each other in carrying…limbs that were ripped off.

With the extra Raw Materials from the Bearlings' bodies, the Mana she gained from killing them, and the Seeds left behind by her all deceased constructs, Sandra was able to increase the amount of stored Monster Seeds and material even more – to the point where it surpassed the most she had ever possessed. She had so many, in fact, that there was hardly room for her older Tiny Automatons – which helped to transport all of the Monster Seeds she created – to maneuver anymore. *I think that is sufficient…for now*; she could always expand the room and add more later, but there was currently enough stored in there to replace all of the constructs in her dungeon at least once over.

Instead, the overflow she had from the last battle she used on adding more constructs to her extermination force. That turned out to be a good idea when she sent them against the nearest Crag Hounds, as the stone-furred wolf-like creatures were fairly resistant to the slicing attack of the Jaguar Queens, as well as not allowing the Dire Wolves much purchase with their jaws to rip them apart. Well, that, and there were many more than Sandra expected to be on the side of one of the mini-mountains – almost double the amount that she had actually seen, in fact. They really camouflaged themselves well, and many of them were hiding *under* the ones she saw on top.

If it weren't for the extra two Steelclad Ape Warriors she sent to reinforce them, her entire force might've been lost; the Crag Hounds were as deadly as the Bearlings with super-sharp teeth and claws – but they were also three times faster and more agile, despite being essentially covered in rock. Sandra's Rolling Forces did absolutely nothing against the Hounds and were completely ignored; her Jaguar and Wolves managed to do a little damage, but they were outmatched and outnumbered, and more than half of them fell before the Apes came to save the day.

They swung their Steel Warhammers like an extension of themselves, hitting the Crag Hounds so hard they were practically obliterated. The first one she saw get smacked by one of their weapons surprised her, because she had thought that only their fur was stone-like; it turned out that their fur, skin, and at least three inches of flesh were also made of stone, leaving only the middle of their bodies vulnerable to serious damage. Fortunately, they weren't strong enough to withstand a super-strong Ape Warrior bashing them apart with a warhammer specially made for that kind of thing, so they didn't last long against her powerful constructs.

Despite their ability to kill them quickly and efficiently, there were only 6 of the Ape Warriors against ten times their number; all but 2 of the Apes were destroyed when they were overwhelmed, joining the 21 Jaguars and Wolves that didn't survive. Sandra's Repair Drones were able to save the rest – which were all damaged in some way – so it wasn't a complete loss; the construct that took the least casualties was her Rolling Forces for a change – because they were completely ignored.

The amount of Mana she received from the Crag Hounds' deaths was equal or more than the Bearlings, however, and it was more than sufficient to replace every single one that was lost, though there wasn't much left over. She had to use some of her treasury of Monster Seeds to do so, but they were easily replaced later when the corpses of the Hounds arrived at her dungeon. She also received another bonus from absorbing them – and more questions.

New Monster Seed found!

Raw Crag Hound Meat

You now have access to:
Slice of Raw Crag Hound Meat
Origination Raw Material Cost: 400
Origination Mana Cost: 100
Monster Min. Mana: 120
Monster Max. Mana: 720

New Monster Seed Origination Material found!

Crag Hound Stone Carapace
While the Crag Hound Stone Carapace ***cannot*** *be directly used as a Monster Seed, it can be combined with specific other materials to create a whole new Monster Seed.*

The fact that the outer fur, skin, and flesh was called a carapace confused Sandra, because she thought that was for things like turtles or even spiders – which raised the question: was the Crag Hound misnamed? The fact that it came up described that way in the notification said that it wasn't, but it was a confusing mystery. Added to that, it was *another* origination material she didn't have any clue how to use in any way, joining the Ant Egg and Spider Venom. Something tickled the back of her mind when she thought of it all, but the more she tried to drill down into it, the less it made sense.

The Crag Hound Meat was a nice surprise, because it gave her some variety from the Bearling meat. It was more expensive Raw Material and Mana-wise, which she hoped meant that it was *better* – but only one of her Gnome visitors would probably be able to tell her that when she cooked one up.

When her extermination force was fully replenished – with even a few extras – she turned towards eliminating the others around the wasteland, not even stopping at night because she could see well enough by the light of the moon above. While she didn't control them all directly, she transferred her knowledge from the previous battles to try to cut down on casualties – which worked for the most part. Everything was easily replaced when her constructs were destroyed, and soon there were only some of the so-called Rock Toads left aboveground.

They were the easiest to kill out of all of the dangerous beasts, it turned out; she had one of her Apes trigger its attack –

and then her construct practically ripped it apart from the inside. The Toad didn't last long against a Steel-made Dungeon Monster, and apart from hundreds of scratches and a few dented places on its body, her Ape was largely unhurt – and required less than a minute from a Repair Drone to be back to normal.

Just like the other creatures she had brought back, this one had something extra to it – and she was finally able to learn its real name.

New Monster Seed Origination Material found!

Solitary Broat Mass
While the Solitary Broat Mass ***cannot*** *be directly used as a Monster Seed, it can be combined with specific other materials to create a whole new Monster Seed.*

The Territory Ant Colonies took a slightly different approach, because they couldn't be destroyed without digging down sometimes hundreds of feet below the surface. Instead, Sandra stored her victorious extermination force inside her Workshop – which was getting a little crowded – and sent in over a hundred Lengthy Segmented Millipedes. Her newer version of the Segmented Centipedes were ten times the length of the original, but not much different, otherwise. They were more than enough to wipe out each colony she identified, however, and by the end of the second day of her extermination focus...the wasteland was essentially empty of threat.

Chapter 9

Flushed with success at freeing the wastelands from all visible threats, she was finally able to turn back to her dungeon and focus on more important matters – and Sandra considered crafting to be much more important. She had accumulated quite a bit of Mana and Raw Materials from the entire venture; not only that, but she had also gained what she was seeking from the beginning: Advancement Points (AP).

It was just after dawn out in the world when Sandra contacted Echo in the village to let her know that travel was now "safe" again in the wastelands; she couldn't ever be entirely sure because of many of the dangerous beasts' penchant for camouflage, but her constructs had done a good job scouring the barren lands looking for potential threats. If there *were* any more creatures out there, they were very well hidden.

Before she arrived, Sandra took stock of her current situation. Her creature threat extermination force was currently slowly roaming the area around her dungeon; it had expanded greatly since its first inception, and now it was something she was confident could go up against just about anything it came up against. There were now a dozen Apes equipped with Steel warhammers, three dozen each of her Jaguar Queens and Dire Wolves, 500 Dividing Rolling Forces, 200 Lengthy Segmented Millipedes, and 4 of her new Repair Drones wandering around basically at random – though staying together as a cohesive unit.

She made sure they stayed far out of sight of any of the remaining villages on the border, but even then they were able to cover quite a bit of territory.

They also absorbed and funneled ambient Mana to Sandra; it wasn't nearly as much as her AMANS, but it was enough to be significant. In fact, when she did some quick calculations, she found that she was gaining approximately 25,000 Mana every hour from everything, which equated to 600,000 per day; she couldn't help but think that if she were focused on upgrading her Core Size, she could be at 30 or beyond in no time. Now that she had a significantly powerful – and sizable – force of constructs, she was tempted to do just that...but decided to hold off until she was sure she could help protect *all* of the nearby villages at the same time, if that became necessary.

As far as resources went, Sandra spent about an hour the night before taking inventory of her treasury. She felt a little like a greedy moneylender that liked to obsessively count all the gold pieces in their vault, but she knew it was a good idea to know what she was sitting on rather than hope that it was enough for the future. As much as it might've been "fun" to count every single thing in her now-full treasury, she only counted the most important things.

- 1600 Large Elemental Orbs (200 of each element)
- 30 Tiny Faceted Sapphire Spheres

- 12 Small Faceted Sapphire Spheres
- 10 Small Dragon Glass Slivers
- 50 Large Steel Orbs
- 100 Large Iron Orbs
- 150 Average Steel Orbs
- Approximately 1,500 smaller Monster Seeds of various sizes
- 120 Titanium ingots
- 300 Steel ingots
- 500 Iron ingots
- 1,000 ingots of various other metals (Copper, Tin, Nickel, Lead, Bronze, Silver, Gold)

Her treasury represented millions of Mana and Raw Materials-worth of Monster Seeds and crafting materials, and it filled her treasury room up. She was now confident that – in case of another emergency – she had the "funds" available to bail her out; it would most likely hurt her again to dig into her reserve, but she also knew that it might be the only thing that could save her.

Even with all of that filling her treasury room, Sandra still had an overflow of Mana – both from the deaths of the deadly creatures and through her continuous ambient Mana generation from her AMANS. As a result, she was able to unlock some of the materials she hadn't been able to before in her Organic/Inorganic Elemental Transmutation Menu.

Organic/Inorganic Material Elemental Transmutation Menu				
Transmutation Options	Elemental Orb Required (Size/Qty)	Mana Required	Additional Seed Material (Size/Qty)	Unlocked (Y/N)
Precious Gemstones				
Citrine	N/A	N/A	N/A	Y
Hematite	N/A	N/A	N/A	Y
Onyx	N/A	N/A	N/A	Y
Sapphire	N/A	N/A	N/A	Y
Topaz	N/A	N/A	N/A	Y
Ruby	Fire (Large/6)	268000/500000	Copper (Large/5)	N
Emerald	Natural (Large/6)	0/1000000	Bronze (Large/5)	N
Diamond	Holy (Large/6)	0/10000000	Steel (Large/5)	N
Moonstone	?????	0/20000000	?????	N
Dragon's Eye	?????	0/50000000	?????	N
Magistone	?????	0/100000000	?????	N
Fruit-producing Tree Seeds				
Apple	N/A	N/A	N/A	Y
Pear	N/A	N/A	N/A	Y
Peach	N/A	N/A	N/A	Y
Plum	N/A	N/A	N/A	Y
Apricot	N/A	N/A	N/A	Y
Orange	N/A	N/A	N/A	Y
Lemon	Air (Large/5)	50000/50000	Redwood (Large/4)	N
Lime	Natural (Large/5)	60000/60000	Yew (Large/4)	N
Coconut	?????	0/100000	?????	N
Elderfruit	?????	0/1000000	?????	N
Ambrosia	?????	0/25000000	?????	N

Sandra was able to unlock Citrine, Hematite, Onyx, and Topaz gemstones; the others on the list she was working on but hadn't had the Mana for quite yet. She was also able to grow Ash and Pine trees for their wood, which also provided the Seed Material for Plum and Apricot fruit-producing trees – which she then unlocked. She currently had Redwood and Yew maturing in her growing room along with her new acquisitions, which would contribute to unlocking Lemon and Lime tree Seeds; she had already paid the Mana for them, so all she was missing was the materials.

She had previously unlocked all that she could from the other categories in her Menu, so all she had left to work on were the remaining fruits and gemstones, but she still needed to figure out the requirements for several of them. Experimenting with the mystery materials and Elemental Orbs for her locked transmutations was definitely something that she wanted to pursue, because the potential of having rare and superb materials to use with her crafting was a huge draw. However, there were a few things that she wanted to do before that, including looking at what she could use her Advancement Points to purchase – which turned out to be quite a few Points.

Advancement Points (AP)				
Source	Criteria	Point Value	Lifetime Earned Points	Lifetime Spent Points
Core Size	Receive AP upon Core Size upgrade (does not count for Core Size 1 nor upgrade stages)	1 per Core Size upgrade	19 AP (19X Core Size Upgrades)	19/19 AP
Number of Rooms	Receive AP for each distinct dungeon room at least 4,000 cubic feet in size (20ftx20ftx10ft minimum)	1 AP per qualified room	45 AP (45X Qualifying Rooms)	33/45 AP
Unique Dungeon Fixtures	Receive AP for each never-before-seen fixture in your dungeon	2 AP per fixture	26 AP (13X Crafting Stations)	26/26 AP
Creature Eradication	Eradicate sources of nearby creatures (i.e. lairs and spawning areas)	3 AP per eradication	72 AP (5X Territory Ant Colonies, 6X Bearling Lairs, 4X Desolate Spider Clutches, 4X Crag Hound Packs, 5X Solitary Broat Spawn)	6/72 AP
Sentient Race Elimination	Eliminate members of sentient races	1 AP per 10 eliminations	8 AP (12X Orc, 71X Gnome)	8/8 AP
Sentient Race Bonding	Form a new Dungeon Visitor Bond with a member of a sentient race	1 AP per 2 Bonds	8 AP (1X Orc/Dwarf, 6X Elf, 9X Gnome)	8/8 AP
Dungeon Core Destruction	Receive AP for eliminating another Dungeon Core	30 AP per Core	30 AP (1X Reptile Classification Core)	30/30 AP
?????	*N/A*	*N/A*	*N/A*	*N/A*
(?????) Denotes an unknown, unique Source of Advancement Points. Perform this unknown action to unlock more information.				
Total Advancement Points Earned and Spent			208 AP	130 AP
Total Advancement Points Available			**78 AP**	

Advancement Options	
Current Advancement Points	78
Advancement:	**Cost:**
*Choose **1** Dungeon Monster from another available Classification (Repeatable)*	5
Give your Dungeon Monsters the option of having a chosen accessible elemental attribute in addition to their base element – Cost increases with each purchase (only works on Monsters capable of using/applying their element) (Repeatable)	10
Reduce the Mana cost of Monster Seeds by 15% – Cost increases with each purchase (Advancement 0/4)	15
Reduce the Mana cost of Dungeon Monsters by 15% – Cost increases with each purchase (Advancement 2/4)	60
Reduce the Raw Material cost of Monster Seeds by 15% – Cost increases with each purchase (Advancement 0/4)	15
Reduce the Mana cost of Dungeon Traps by 15% – Cost increases with each purchase (Advancement 0/4)	15
Extend your Area of Influence by 10% – Cost increases with each purchase (Advancement 0/10)	50
*Advance a current Classification **1** level to acquire access to stronger and larger Dungeon Monsters – this also includes any "Advancement Unlocked" Monsters – Cost increases with each purchase (Advancement 1/3)*	150
Select a second available Classification to hybridize your Core (This option is only available once)	150

Sandra had received quite a few AP for eliminating all of the creatures inside the wastelands; when she added it to the 20 additional rooms she had created at the end of her dungeon, she had a total of 78 AP to spend. There were a few that she could rule out as unneeded or too expensive at that time, such as adding additional usable elements to her Dungeon Monsters (which wouldn't really work for her constructs), reducing the Mana cost of traps in her dungeon (most of them were easily replaceable and she saw no need to spend *more* on them at the moment), extending her Area of Influence (it was quite extensive already and covered everywhere important), advancing her Classification (it was too expensive and she was still trying to afford all of her constructs from the last advancement), and choosing another Classification (it was plainly just too expensive, nor was it really needed yet).

The remaining options, though, were all things that could be beneficial in different ways. Purchasing the third reduction of Mana cost for her Dungeon Monsters would allow her access to the Titanium Anaconda, as well as making the rest less expensive – but Mana right now wasn't that much of a problem, especially with her AMANS at full strength. The same went with the reduction of Mana cost and Raw Materials needed for Monster Seeds; in the long run it would save a lot of each resource as she created them, but she was currently sitting fairly pretty with both of those things. Still, they were definitely a possibility.

She decided to hold off on that for now, and instead looked at what Dungeon Monsters were available from the other Classifications. The benefits of having access to other Monsters from different Classifications was already being shown with her Unstable Shapeshifter – if not the Goblin Worker she had first purchased. It was entirely possible that having other choices of things to create might work in her favor, though she didn't really have a goal in mind.

When she was searching through the hundreds (or possibly thousands) of choices before, she had been looking for something that could be used by Violet to help enchant; now, though, she was covered fairly well in that department. Nevertheless, she started to peruse the possible choices while her six Unstable Shapeshifters – she had expanded her crafting crew as well – were busy alternatingly creating Energy Orbs. As a side note, she had found out that she was correct about the sample transference; it would only work with the original one that had obtained them in the first place. Therefore, the subsequent Shifters she created had to obtain the forms for the Elite Elves from that specific one, though she made sure to grab samples from Violet, Felbar, and Echo directly.

By the time Echo came back to the dungeon a little later in the morning, there were over 200 of the Orbs there for her to bring back to the village and her people. It would've been even more, but 400 Energy Orbs (50 of each element) had been added to the Gnomes' wagon to bring back to their own people, along with all of the other materials.

The Elf appeared to have fully recovered from her forced coma, though she didn't look as happy as Sandra thought she would've been being outside of her dungeon. It was probably because her people still hadn't shown the same "warmth" towards her as they had before, though at least none of them had been outright rude like Wyrlin; however, the village Elder was becoming more and more insistent that Echo get more of the Energy Orbs from Sandra – or "*your* dungeon", as she liked to say to the young Elf. It was getting to the point where it was bordering on unfair harassment, but fortunately the Elder hadn't risen to drastic lengths quite yet – and was likely to be mollified with the latest shipment.

"Thanks, Sandra – this will get Elder Herrlot off my back for a while...at least, I hope so. As much as I appreciate these for my people, sometimes I wish you had never created them," Echo said as she picked up the two large – and slightly heavy – bags full of Orbs and slung them over her shoulder.

** Why is that? Don't these help your people? **

Echo sighed heavily as she settled the two cloth bags so that they sat along her back more comfortably. "Oh, absolutely – there's no denying that they are literally miraculous," she said dully, which contrasted completely with the words she was saying. "But I'm worried that my people will see them in a light different from what you expect; I don't even think the original ones I brought to the village have even reached the capital yet, but I have a feeling they will engender...unhealthy...competition between the Elite Elves to get one – or more – for themselves. I can already see the desire and – dare I say it – *greed* in Elder Herrlot's eyes as she keeps asking for more."

** Are you sure it's not because she just has her people's best interests at heart? Now that they found a viable way to fight back against the Dungeon Monsters and dungeons, I would think that would be normal. **

"Yes, I can see that – and I'm sure some of it is exactly what you say. However, I suspect that the Elder has taken a portion of the Orbs I've brought to her for herself, before sending the rest on to the capital. Whether it's for her own use – and I'm well aware that having more than one in contact with your skin will speed up the restoration of elemental energy – or for some other purpose, I couldn't tell you. It wouldn't surprise me to know that she's hoarding them as a bargaining chip to have her transferred from the village, which I've heard rumored was a punishment of some kind – though no one seems to know what that punishment was for. Regardless, the scarcity of the Orbs, which she is contributing to, could be bad for...you."

That didn't make any sense to Sandra at first, but as she thought about it from her own experiences as a merchant...horror overcame confusion as she thought she understood. Scarcity of a demanded product caused the price of it to rise, which was one of the first things she had learned while she was a very young girl. That wouldn't normally be a factor in the current situation, because she was giving everything away – not charging for it; not only that, but it was doubtful that the leaders in charge of the Elven nation would charge for it either, negating "price" as a factor altogether.

However, when it came to objects that "enhanced" someone's power, those kinds of things were considered priceless anyways. Sandra remembered a tale about an Enchanter that had spent 40 years researching and experimenting with various enchantments he had learned over the years, before finally creating one of his own inside the facets of a precious gemstone; rumor was that the enchantment somehow *increased* someone's available elemental energy by a significant amount when they held the stone. The story went that he made a total of eight gemstones – one for each element – before it was somehow discovered what he had done.

The gemstones were stolen from his workshop by a group of powerful Heroes working for someone even more powerful and the Enchanter was forced to flee. The nameless Enchanter was inevitably found and held captive, where he was told to create more of what he had made; for some reason the man had refused and asked to be released, stating that he couldn't make any more. Rather than risk letting him go and potentially finding a way to make more, the Enchanter was killed, his identity lost to the ages – along with any knowledge of the enchanted gemstones' whereabouts.

Most thought it was a myth; even if it was, the story held an important lesson to anyone who really dug into it. Power (whether politically, physically, socially, or economically) was attracted to power, and the already-powerful want nothing other than the chance to be even more powerful. Even the Elves, who needed the Energy Orbs to protect their people, were obviously not immune to this lesson – if what Echo said was true about the Elder.

The same thing was likely to happen even in the capital, though Sandra hoped it was on a lesser scale – but now she didn't think it would be. She was originally banking on the fact that their people were in danger of extinction to curb most of those greedy impulses, but she was wrong; once the people who wanted the Orbs – and couldn't get them from those in charge – found out about their existence, then (as Echo had said) the "unhealthy competition" between the Elites could end up with them trying to steal or even *kill* to possess them. What was even worse, objectively, was if they found out the source of the Orbs: Sandra.

The Dungeon Core could only imagine large groups of Elves coming to her dungeon to demand more Orbs; even if she gave them hundreds of the enchanted creations, it would never be enough. There would be every possibility that they would try to invade her dungeon and try to force her into being some sort of Energy Orb-making factory, where they would control the distribution of whatever she produced. They would also likely cut off all Sandra's access to the other races, and her plans to help the Gnomes, Orcs, and Dwarves would be denied.

Of course, there was no way she would *ever* allow something like that to happen – but then Sandra would ultimately have to kill more people, which was something that she would prefer to avoid.

What have I done?

All of that was conjecture, though, unless Echo was proven right about the Elder. Sandra hadn't really been paying attention because she had other stuff she was trying to take care of – like eradicating her deadly creature problem in the wastelands – so she had no clue whether the Elf was correct; confirming those suspicions would be difficult and probably dangerous for Echo, so there wasn't a need for the bonded Elf to risk herself. *The truth will come out eventually.*

The only way to fix those potential problems was either to stop production completely and hunker down or to ramp it up, "flooding the market" with so many Energy Orbs that scarcity wasn't a problem anymore. Sandra hated to have a target on her back and have to defend against greedy Elites looking for her creations, so she disregarded stopping production completely. Not only that but doing so would ultimately end up hurting the Elven people more, taking the Elites away from the front line against the dungeons.

Therefore, she needed to ramp up production and distribution; the first was easy enough, but the second was going to take some strategizing – and unfortunately, Echo was no help when Sandra asked her about it. The Dungeon Core also expanded on her options to see if the Elf had an opinion about the situation – and that was when a third option was brought up.

"I don't have any access to any of the messengers that journey in between the Avensglen and the capital; there are only a few towns and villages on the pathway back, as most of our people have retreated back to the city for protection. Short of going myself – which is always possible – I'm not sure how to get them there without going through the Elder," Echo said when Sandra was done explaining the situation.

The Elf was silent for a few moments as she contemplated something. "I don't know if your 'flooding the market' idea will necessarily work – those in charge like the Elder will just accumulate larger amounts, making them even more powerful; unless you can make *millions* of the Orbs, then the 300,000 Elves that aren't part of the Elites or ruling houses will probably never see them. Granted, it's more than likely that those who are doing the majority of our defending will obtain what they need, but if they become overconfident and start to actually *push* back against the dungeons...there's a good chance many of them won't come back. If that happens, then we'll lose some of the few Elites still out there that have a chance of stopping our inevitable demise.

"What *you* need to do – as crazy as this idea is coming from me to a *dungeon*, of all things – is expand your...territory, or whatever you call it until you can actually reach the capital. That way, *your* Dungeon Monsters will be there to distribute your Orbs to everyone, not just those in charge – but to those who could use them to increase their own fledgling abilities so that they could also help in the defense. From my perspective, it'll be much easier to ensure our survival if we have 300,000 Elves that can defend themselves from Dungeon Monsters, rather than just the 300 Elites that we have."

That number was news to Sandra, who had known that the Elves were in trouble – but she wasn't aware of how deep in trouble they were. She couldn't even imagine only having 300 Heroes around when she was Human; she wasn't even sure if there was an accurate accounting of them anywhere, but she could only guess that there were tens of thousands of them, if not hundreds. With only a few hundred, though, Echo was right – if they lost even a dozen of them to overconfidence and pushed back before they were ready, then their survival was in jeopardy.

But…expanding my Area of Influence? There were risks in that as well, not in the least allowing access to it to any lower-Sized Dungeon Cores in the area – of which there were likely a few. Most of those towards the capital were probably quite a bit developed if they were actively pushing against the defenses the Elves had in place, so that wasn't really a worry; Sandra's concern were those smaller towns and villages along the way that weren't in danger…until she came along and messed that all up. She was still torn up about what happened with the Gnome village because of her expansion, so she was hesitant to cause any more issues like that.

Nevertheless, the "Dungeon Core" part of her existence was excited at that prospect. Expansion and becoming powerful were natural instincts of her particular incarnation, it seemed; even if Sandra was able to curb most of those impulses because she wasn't contracted, that didn't mean they weren't there…only *contained*.

** I have to agree with your assessment of the situation, Echo – but I'm not yet prepared to expand quite that far. The repercussions of such an act, as much as I'd like to do it, are currently too great; for now, I'll keep providing as many of the Orbs as I can easily produce,* *as long as you deliver them. In the future, though, I'll see what I can do – unless another solution presents itself.* *

"That's fine with me, just don't be surprised if you have some of the greedier and seedier examples of my people show up here looking for handouts within the next few months. At least *some* of what I'm bringing will help my people, if not all of it; from what you've provided already – even considering if half of it is taken and squirreled away – our people will survive for years or decades longer than they probably would've. And for that, you have my thanks – even if some think you're a bad influence on me and the Elven people in general, I feel that you're honest in what you've been doing, and generally want us to live and survive."

With that, Echo hitched the two bags on her back again as they had shifted slightly over the last few minutes and headed out of Sandra's dungeon. Watching the Elf make her way through the barren – and hopefully relatively safe now – wastelands, it was more than obvious that she had fully recovered; even loaded down with two heavy bags, she was able to run fairly quickly towards her village.

I'd like to think that what I'm doing is for the good of their people, but the scenarios I thought of earlier might still come to pass. If that happens, then I may have just hastened their extinction – rather than prevented it.

Chapter 10

Regardless of the results of what she was doing with the Elves, Sandra wasn't planning on worrying about them for a while at least. It was going to take some time for the original shipments of Energy Orbs to even make it to the Elven capital, after all; the possible visits by the "greedier and seedier" people Echo had mentioned probably wouldn't happen for months, by her guess – which meant that she had some time to work on a solution.

Speaking of solutions, as soon as Sandra started to shuffle through the screens and screens full of possible Dungeon Monsters she could purchase with her Advancement Points, Violet (with very cautious help from Felbar) finally perfected control of the **Limiter** enchantment rune – and as a bonus had discovered how it could be easily altered in the future when it was part of an enchantment sequence. That alone was impressive considering it had only been about two days since Felbar's beneficial accident, but she had also begun to figure out how to use it in practical applications.

"So, I think that I can integrate the new rune into the enchantment sequence surrounding the Energy Orbs – the Spirit and whatever else we need to use for the power source – thereby altering the amount of elemental energy it puts out. I can then tie it to the Stasis Field enchantment – without disrupting it, don't worry – and regulate the power output so that it stays consistent to maintain the Field without overloading it. You see, it has to do with the specific frequency modulation inside the Field that—"

** Whoa, you're losing me there. I may know a bit about creating these enchantments, but the highly technical aspects of them are still quite new to me. Though it pains me to say it, perhaps if you try explaining what you're saying like you would to a small child? **

Violet smiled at Sandra's interruption and said, "That *was* me trying to explain it to a small child. I'll try to do a little better, though.

"Anyway, like I was trying to explain, the **Limiter** rune is much more versatile than any of us had first assumed. Not only does it dictate the amount of energy passing through it – from very small amounts to extremely large amounts, as seen with Felbar's accident," Violet continued, looking apologetically in the older Gnome's direction. In his case, he still looked a little haunted from the experience, but he was hiding it well; Sandra thought it could be because his hair was starting to grow back, which was covering up a little of the physical evidence of his accident that was still left.

"What this obviously means – when we look at the Stasis Fields for example – is that we can dictate the precise amount we want the power-providing Spirit Energy Orb to feed into the enchantment. Not only that, but there is a built-in feature that...hmm...how to explain this...*copies* the precise amount of energy being drawn out from the Stasis Field – or any enchantment, for that matter – so that it matches what is being fed to it. Therefore, as an example, if a Field uses up one Spirit Energy unit per day, the **Limiter** rune will match that with an equal amount supplied; if for some reason that were to change, say to *three* the next day, it would match that as well.

"Ultimately, it all depends on how you set the original rune sequence up; you can set it up to resonate—match—the power input/output directly, or you can do it manually with a simple application of elemental energy that matches the **Limiter** rune element. Just like Felbar used small infusions of Spirit energy to make a War Machine move, this new rune works in a similar fashion; by altering the access lines on the rune itself – which can be done even after it's created – you can regulate the energy you want to transfer to the enchantment.

"As an example for that, we'll use the simple enchantment that Felbar used the other day," Violet said, mouthing "sorry" to the older Gnome – who started to look a little nervous. "It was intended to warm up the space around him a little bit but was obviously overloaded. With precise control, however, the new rune can change the temperature even by minute amounts – so that you can alter it to be *very* hot or even a milder warmth than the original enchantment by suppressing the energy used in its original creation, and of course anywhere in between."

That was great news, because it meant that some of the plans she had for the War Machine were likely to work out beautifully. However, something about what Violet said sparked an idea in Sandra's mind.

** Does that mean the **Limiter** rune could be used with Energy Orbs that, say, you're using right now to provide faster energy regeneration? **

Violet didn't even have to think about that for more than a few moments. "Yes, I'm sure that it could, though it would take...*tying*...it to a specific person for it to work. Everyone has their own specific energy 'aura', which can act like an enchantment in some ways; by tying it to the 'aura' like I would do for an external enchantment, I think that would work the same way. Then, by manipulating the access lines, a person could change it so that they receive more from the Orb than they normally would; of course, this would also consume the Energy Orb much faster than normal as well, but it could be done."

That was intriguing, though it didn't really help in the current situation, especially as using more than one Orb at a time helped Violet to regenerate her elemental energy quite quickly already. Violet seemed to dismiss the idea of doing something like that probably because of the same reasons, but as something for the future it was an aspect of the Energy Orbs that might be useful.

** How long do you think the Stasis Field would stay operational with one of these setups attached to it? **

Sandra was hoping she would say something like 10 to 15 years...and was severely disappointed. "Well, seeing as the enchantment without anything extra lasts approximately a week, I would assume that with a Spirit Energy Orb powering it that it might last...a year? I can't be more precise than that, but I'm going on my own experience with the Orb and how much it replenishes my own energy compared to how much it has been consumed in the process."

The Dungeon Core could definitely see a difference in the Spirit Orb Violet had around her neck – it was her original one, in fact. It wasn't a huge difference, but in approximately 5 days it was perhaps 20% smaller. Of course, this was with almost constant use by Violet and the Stasis Field would consume a bit less...

With a little mental math on her own part with some guesstimates thrown in, Sandra had to admit that Violet was probably right; even if she was off by a lot and it lasted *two* years, it wasn't quite as long as the Dungeon Core wanted if she was hoping her Enchantment Repository would outlast Sandra herself if something were to happen to her Core.

** What's the likelihood of using two – or even more? **

The Gnome was already shaking her head before Sandra even finished her question. "Wouldn't work – or at least not without *a lot* of time to experiment, and to follow up with it over time. You could set them to automatically regulate the input/output, but with two or more doing it, they would *all* contribute the energy needed – which would end up in disaster after a short time as it overloaded the Field enchantment. The same goes for anything else; two or more Energy Orbs connected to the enchantment would cause it to fail the same as if it didn't have a **Limiter**.

"That's not to say it isn't possible, but you'd have to manually adjust the amount being fed into it from each rune sequence to balance out the output; this might work in the short term, but if it's allowed to continue unchecked, if the energy amount being fed into it was just a fraction too much or too little, over time it would eventually fade or overload, depending on the outcome. It could take years, but then you'll have the same problem as now.

"A year of maintaining this Stasis Field is incredible, however – something that I wouldn't have thought possible even a few days ago. Replacing the Limiter Energy Orb enchantment is easy enough at that point."

On anything else, Sandra would have to agree – going from 1 week to 52 weeks of power was *quite* the improvement. It didn't solve her problem of sustaining the enchantments even if something interfered with that replacement; for instance, what if in the future she went for a Core Size upgrade and it lasted a *few months*, rather than a few days. She could wake up and find that it had all been undone because she took a prolonged vacation from the outside world and was stuck in her own mind.

No, there had to be something else Sandra could do. She was disappointed about not being able to place two or more – as

Violet had coined it – Limiter Energy Orb enchantments to power something; the extra quantity of power would make all the difference. It was just a shame that she could only make Large Elemental Orbs—

Wait…that may not be the case.

It was true that, according to her Monster Seed Origination menu, she could only make up to Large Elemental Orbs for the purpose of being Monster Seeds, but did that mean she couldn't create something larger on her own? She could make walls of Steel and bars of Iron without having them be Monster Seeds, so why not condensed Mana Elemental Orbs.

She hadn't even thought of it before because she didn't really consider Mana to be a "material" like Iron, Cotton cloth, or even an Oak plank of wood; it didn't really have a physical state of substance *except* when it was condensed into an Elemental Orb, so she never really played around with it other than when she first discovered how to create their Tiny versions – and had unlocked the others just by spending Mana to create their Seeds.

Can I make…an even larger Orb?

Right now, the Large Elemental Orbs were approximately a third the size of one of Violet's hands, which allowed her to hold two in her hand relatively comfortably. Sandra wanted to see if it was possible to make one at least twice the size of a Large Elemental Orb – so she went back in her mind to the day she created the very first one: a Tiny Fire Elemental Orb. If she remembered correctly, she had pulled out 50 Fire Mana and brought it forth into a spherical shape before she mentally condensed it into a much smaller sphere – and just like that, it was done. She had then created Tiny examples of each element but had never bothered to actually *create* anything larger.

After telling Violet to hold off on adding anything to the Stasis Fields, Sandra switched her focus to the farthest room she had excavated behind her Home; she was going to try something that could be dangerous and she didn't want to risk the safety of anyone or anything in her dungeon. Even if it exploded (which she severely hoped it didn't), there was quite a lot of space in between the last room and anything vital.

Sandra knew that the Elemental Orbs she could create as seeds cost 50, 100, 400, and finally 800 Mana for the largest; what that meant was that she needed to use 1600 Mana to create one twice the size of her Large Orb. Without further ado, she pulled out 1600 Fire Mana from her Core and had it float in the middle of the room; it was actually quite a large sphere with at least a 4-foot diameter, but she knew it would shrink down when she condensed it.

Within seconds, she remembered why she was happy enough to unlock the other sizes of Elemental Orbs – because it was *hard*. The Mana wanted to squeeze out of her mental grip at every opportunity; whenever she thought she was condensing it all together as one, a large hump of Mana would slip out of her control and stick up where she wasn't expecting it. She equated it with trying to shape a massive ball of clay with your bare hands, except your hands weren't big enough to fully reach around the entire sphere – and every time you pushed *in* one place, it would make another section push *out*.

It was frustrating, but after nearly ten minutes of straining at the mass of Mana and almost giving up, she started to see a solution. The problem was that Sandra was trying to push it all in at the same time, obviously, so she figured she had to cut down on how many *sides* she was focusing on; since she was working with a sphere, she currently needed to concentrate on hundreds or thousands of spots on her project all at once.

Therefore, she made a cube.

It was strange and a little foreign at first – since she was accustomed to handling orbs and spheres – but in less than a minute Sandra got a handle on the large mass and formed it into a relatively equal-sided cube. As soon as it was in the shape she wanted, she pushed in on each side and condensed the Mana down; she found that it was *much* easier to concentrate on only six areas at once, though she had to admit that it was a little harder to keep pressure on each face of the cube to ensure it stayed the same shape.

Regardless of that difficulty, in less time than she had ineffectually spent on the original sphere, Sandra shrunk the Fire Mana down into a tight little box that was a little larger than twice the size of a Large Elemental Orb. The strain she had first experienced when making the Tiny Elemental Orb was there on her mind but was surprisingly a lot less than she had been expecting.

She wasn't sure if it was because her mental and Mana-manipulation capacity was a lot more than it used to be or from the new shape of her creation; nevertheless, she was very happy it wasn't trying to rip her mind apart.

With a final push that condensed the cube even further, Sandra felt the pressure she had been maintaining on the Mana completely disappear as what she had made locked into place and fell to the ground, her control over the mass of Fire Mana now absent. A strange...*ripple*...went through her mind and her Core, which was followed up by some welcome surprises.

	Skill Evolution
***Advanced* Elemental Monster Seed Origination (Core-specific Skill)**	**The *Advanced* Elemental Monster Seed Origination skill allows the Dungeon Core to condense Elemental Mana into condensed *objects*. These Elemental *objects* can be used as Monster Seeds or in other unique applications. Requirements: Mana. (Skills are permanent and remain even after a Classification change)**

New Monster Seed created using your *Advanced* Elemental Monster Seed Origination
skill!

<u>You now have access to:</u>
Tiny Fire Elemental Cube
Origination Raw Material Cost: 0
Origination Mana Cost: 1600
Monster Min. Mana: 300
Monster Max. Mana: 800

<u>Currently locked:</u>
Small Fire Elemental Cube
Average Fire Elemental Cube
Large Fire Elemental Cube

Skill Evolution?

Winxa seemed surprised – shocked even. "I've only heard of that whispered around the other Dungeon Fairies as a rumor; I never thought I would hear about it firsthand!"

Yes, but how did it happen? And what is it?

"It comes from applying your skills in different and unique ways, stretching the bounds of what it should be capable of normally. Typically, Dungeon Cores that have Core-specific skills only use those skills as they are described; if they work the way they are supposed to, there usually isn't any reason for the Core to experiment and try to get it to do something else – that kind of ingenuity just isn't encouraged, especially with a contracted Core. You, on the other hand, obviously have the kind of thinking that is *exactly* what the Skill Evolution needs to activate.

"As for how it works, it should work similarly to how the old skill worked, though usually with improvements. Like I said, Skill Evolutions were more of a rumor in Dungeon Fairy circles, so your guess is probably as good as mine," Winxa said with a shrug and a smile.

That wasn't particularly helpful but based on the description of her *Advanced* Elemental Monster Seed Origination skill, she could see that instead of it just being a small "orb", it now said "objects". Then there was the fact that the large red cube that she had created was called a "Tiny Fire Elemental Cube" – despite the fact that it was bigger than the largest Elemental Orb she could create. Sandra was just glad that she could unlock and access the larger sizes of Cubes; while she could theoretically create them on her own, she'd rather not have to struggle with handling and condensing that much Mana all at once.

Monster Seed Origination				
Name:	Raw Material Cost:	Mana Cost:	Min. Mana:	Max. Mana:
Tiny Fire Elemental Cube	0	1600	300	800
Locked Seeds:	**Unlock Requirements:**	**Mana Cost to Unlock:**	**Min. Mana:**	**Max. Mana:**
Small Fire Elemental Cube	2 Tiny Fire Elemental Cubes	3200	300	1600
Average Fire Elemental Cube	4 Small Fire Elemental Cubes	12800	300	6400
Large Fire Elemental Cube	2 Average Fire Elemental Cubes	25600	300	12800

She couldn't quite unlock the largest of the Fire Elemental Cubes, but the others were more than easy enough to do. However, before she did that, she needed to get back to Violet with the solution to their longevity problem. By her simple calculations, if a Large Orb was going to last for a year, then with twice as much Mana inside a Tiny Cube it should last for 2 years. Following that same logic, a Small Cube would last for 4 years, and an Average Cube would last for *16 years!* The Large Cube – which she of course couldn't produce quite yet – would be even better at 32 years, but the 25,600 Mana it would take to unlock and create more of them was too expensive—

Or…was it?

She did have some AP to spend, and she had been going back-and-forth on what to spend it on. Some quick glances at the multitude of Dungeon Monsters she could purchase for her use hadn't shown anything that stood out quite yet, though she had only been half-heartedly perusing the lists; Sandra would still have some left over even if she spent the Points on something else, so she could still find a few new Monsters later. The only thing that she had to reconcile in her mind was whether it was worth it to unlock the Advancements she was considering; after some consideration, she decided that it *was* worthwhile in the long run, not just for the project with the RRPs, but for the future as well.

As a result, Sandra spent 45 of her AP to purchase the two Advancements that reduced the Mana Cost of her Monster Seeds by a total of 30%. After another strange alteration in her Core that felt like a small tickle that time, she pulled up the cost of her new Cubes – and mentally smiled when she saw that the Large Fire Elemental Cube now cost only 17,920 Mana – down from the previously unobtainable 25,600. Better yet, she still had 33 AP left to spend from the 78 she just had, so there was more than enough to still get 6 Dungeon Monsters if she chose to do that.

Without hesitation, Sandra brought forth 1,600 Spirit Mana and worked to condense it into a small cube, which she found was much easier and faster than her original Fire Cube – probably because of experience and knowing what to expect. She had to wait a little to acquire enough Mana to unlock the larger sizes, which was easy enough with what she currently had and another hour of accumulation. In just under two hours since she started with her experimentation, she now had what she wanted – a way to ensure the Rune Repository Pillars and their Preservation Barriers/Stasis Fields would last for *decades.*

To say that Violet was surprised was an understatement, as one of her constructs delivered a Large Spirit Elemental Cube that was half of her size – and about a third of her weight. "What? How? Where?" she asked, too shocked to form coherent questions.

** I was able to create these Large Spirit Elemental Cubes to help provide the longevity needed to keep the Fields intact for approximately 32 years, if your guesstimates are correct. It'll take a little bit for me to make more, but by the end of the day I'm hoping to have this entire room filled with more RRPs – and their Stasis Fields, of course. Let's see if your theory works!* *

Sandra was excited to finally see everything they had been working on come to fruition. As much as she enjoyed crafting with materials – mundane or otherwise – she was most passionate about Enchanting, and with these final components in place her Enchantment Repository would be set up and complete! When it was, she was hoping that with enough practice, she would be able to finally transfer all of the knowledge she had in her mind to the pillars, creating a place where anyone could learn how to enchant everything she had knowledge of – as well as add new ones that were discovered.

The process of enchanting the new Cube took a little bit for Violet to figure out because of its sheer size, but a half hour later saw it finished – with a **Limiter** rune inserted into the enchantment sequence. As a test, Violet created a small Stasis Field and had Felbar help her move it into position; with the amount of Mana/elemental energy that the Cube possessed inside of it, an accidental overload of one of the larger Fields would be...*catastrophic* might be putting it a little lightly.

Holding their breath, they pushed it up against the small Field – and nothing bad happened: no explosions, overloads, or indications that it wasn't operating perfectly. Through her experimentations over the last few days, Violet had "attuned" herself to the flow of energy pouring out from the Energy Orbs and into the enchantments; as such, she was able to sense the tiniest trickle of energy coming from the Cube, keeping the enchantment intact – and stable, which was more important.

Without further ado, they cautiously moved the new Cube with its accompanying Large Spirit Energy Orb (for operating the **Limiter** rune) next to the nearest RR and connected it to the Stasis Field there. They immediately stepped back out of the way and Sandra had one of her Steelclad Ape Warriors step up next to it; her construct was ready to remove it in a hurry if something went wrong. Fortunately for everyone, it worked exactly the way it was supposed to.

Success!

Now that she had a viable proof of concept in the setup around the RRPs, as soon as the Repository room was complete, it would be time to work on the War Machine sitting immobile and unenchanted up in the workshop above. Afterwards, she could work on getting the Gnomes back to their homeland and start the process of—

As seemed usual, just as Sandra was thinking things were looking up, a new problem presented itself.

Chapter 11

"What did you think was going to happen if we weren't there anymore?" Violet asked. "You may have gotten rid of *one* of the dungeons, but I thought you were taking over for us," she continued, after being told of the issue that had just come up. Of course, the Gnome was still helping to enchant the Large Spirit Cubes that Sandra was providing, because that project had taken priority over almost anything else as far as the Dungeon Core was concerned – though this...development...was going to have to be addressed very soon.

Sandra couldn't believe she had completely forgotten about the *other* dungeon that was near the Gnome village that had been destroyed. While the Reptile-based Core had been destroyed in response to the attack on the Elven village, the Undead that were roaming the forest on the opposite side of the Gnome lands had been small and fairly non-threatening. At least, they *were* non-threatening; at some point that Sandra must have missed, the Core – which was currently allowed to create more Dungeon Monsters without fear of them being culled by the Gnomes – had upgraded its Core Size and expanded its Area of Influence. She suspected that it had happened during the whole invasion of the Reptile dungeon and subsequent attack on her own, so it had been easy to overlook.

But now the Core and its AOI had grown again, to the point where it could reach where the ruins of the Gnome village were; in fact, with its current territory, it could fill most of the open land around the area with its Dungeon Monsters without fear of them being destroyed, bringing in more and more ambient Mana for the Undead Dungeon Core. This in turn would allow it to upgrade its Core again and again, eventually growing so large that it could start to attack the Dwarves to the north.

Granted, it wasn't growing nearly as fast as the Reptile-based Core had; the dungeon that Sandra had destroyed had accumulated Mana quickly from the deaths of all of the Gnomes, as well as from absorbing all of the Monster Seeds looted from the destroyed village. While it was growing slower, it would still be as much of a threat to the people near the wastelands if left unchecked – which was exactly what had happened.

** I didn't even think about it, in all honesty. I wasn't made to thin out the nearby Dungeon Monsters, you know; nevertheless, I have to do what I can to stop it from expanding even farther than they already have. **

"Can't you just go in and destroy them like you did with the other dungeon?" Felbar asked. "With what I've seen you capable of, I'm sure it probably wouldn't be that hard."

The older Gnome had a point; compared to where she was when she attacked the Reptile-based Core, she both had more Constructs at her disposal *and* they were of a better quality – stronger, faster, and deadlier. It was obvious from her eradication around the wasteland that they were more than capable of doing so – as long as she was cautious and didn't lose them to traps inside the Undead dungeon. Sandra knew from personal experience both in her own dungeon and the one she had invaded that those types of defenses were more likely to destroy her constructs than any Monsters they went up against.

However, she debated on whether or not that was the right move to make. The dungeon was only following its instincts and wasn't "technically" a danger to any of the other villages, though it was slowly expanding into the territory owned by the Golems near the Dwarven lands. While it couldn't pass *through* the Golems' Area of Influence, if it expanded past them, then there wouldn't be any stopping them from reaching the Elves.

The Reptiles had been "lucky" that the Beast Core near the Elves had been further south, so they were able to skirt around the edges to reach the village; the same was looking to be true with the Undead-Golem area, as the Undead dungeon was further east than the other. It was so far east that Sandra saw that it was barely within her own Area of Influence, though it appeared that she would be able to have her constructs reach it and delve through its dungeon without any issues.

*Did the Creator put me here to destroy **all** of these Dungeon Cores in the area? If that's true, where would it stop? If I upgrade my Core Size and reach even more dungeons, do I destroy them too?*

Sandra didn't have an answer to that, though she could tell Winxa did – but couldn't tell her. The Dungeon Fairy's face was flushed, and she held her mouth forcefully shut, for all intents and purposes looking like she was about to burst with the need to vocalize her opinion. The Dungeon Core told her to calm down and breathe, all while reminding her not to say anything; Sandra was nearly positive that if Winxa tried to say something, it would probably be the end of her. While she wasn't sure she would actually *die* – because the Creator didn't *destroy* things – the Fairy would undoubtedly be knocked out and somehow confined to her own realm in the future, therefore unable to help Sandra out. Not only that, but it was quite possible that she would be punished as a result of that, though the Core had no idea what kind of punishment that would entail.

With a great visible effort of willpower, Winxa managed to hold in what she was about to say and immediately opened a portal to wherever it was she lived and disappeared through it. Sandra could hear the beginning of a frustrated yell coming from the portal before it closed behind the Fairy, and she couldn't help but chuckle a little at it – despite the fact that Winxa had almost "died". She understood the frustration, but there was nothing she could do about it; she just had to shrug it off and hope that the Dungeon Fairy pulled herself together and came back soon. Sandra had gotten so used to her being there to answer questions – even if they weren't always satisfactory answers – that she felt like she was missing a part of herself with the Fairy's absence.

As to what exactly Winxa was trying to convey to Sandra was a mystery, as there were too many things to consider. *Should I just destroy this one Core, should I destroy all of them around my AOI, or should I just keep expanding and getting stronger, eventually destroying* ***every*** *Core I come up against?* That last seemed like a daunting – yet possibly doable – task, though she was positive that solution wasn't what she was there for in the first place. With the fact that she could receive Advancement Points from destroying other Cores, she knew that the intention was there, but...*where do I stop?*

After almost an hour of contemplating it, she still didn't have an answer – and Winxa hadn't come back quite yet. Sandra eventually concluded that she had to take some sort of action against the Undead dungeon one way or another, even if she hadn't come up with a final decision. Therefore, she gathered her roaming extermination force of a dozen Steelclad Ape Warriors equipped with warhammers, 30 Mechanical Jaguar Queens, 30 Mechanical Dire Wolves, 800 Dividing Rolling Forces, and 4 Multi-access Repair Drones and sent them to the east. From her dungeon, she also sent out a small team of her Hyper Automatons to gather up any dropped Monster Seeds left behind; not for her own constructs – hopefully – but from the foreign Undead she was about to destroy.

The first Undead Dungeon Monster they encountered was a small shuffling skeleton with glowing red orbs inside its sunken eye sockets. It was just about the size of a Gnome – or Goblin – if it was missing all of its flesh, and it seemed to be animated by some invisible force; just like her own constructs, the little skeleton was made to move because it was formed from Mana, which allowed normally inanimate objects (like her metal-made constructs and flesh-stripped bones) to move as if they had a life of their own. Which, when Sandra thought about it, they essentially did.

As had been her strategy thus far, Sandra sent her Rolling Forces in first; as the small skeleton turned towards her forces with its hands outstretched in front of it – like it wanted to scratch and dig into her constructs with its bare hands – it was pelted by dozens of Force pieces one right after another. The divided construct slices had enough momentum and weight behind them that bones cracked underneath their impacts, demolishing the Undead before it could do more than look at the incoming force. All of her constructs came out of the mini-fight unscathed, and the few dents on her Forces weren't even enough to disable a single one – but they were repaired by Sandra's drones anyway.

That...was easy.

Of course, that small skeleton seemed to be the easiest and smallest of the enemies her eradication force encountered over the next hour as she methodically swept them across the open field near the Gnomes' destroyed village of Glimmerton. There were larger skeletons that walked on two legs that could've been Orcs, Elves, or even Humans that could move faster and appeared stronger; her Rolling Forces took them down almost as easily as the first, though it took more of them to do it.

A singular skeleton towered over the rest, however, and it was an anomaly in comparison. It was twice the height of a human and wider than even Sandra's Behemoths, and it had bones that were extremely thick and dense. When her smaller rolling constructs hit the massive undead...*ogre, maybe?*...they bounced off the bones ineffectually, doing *themselves* some damage; Sandra was used to that from her attacks against the Crag Hounds, so her other constructs were going to finally have a chance to fight.

The Undead Ogre Skeleton – which was what she chose to finally call it in her mind – lifted up something that she hadn't seen it carrying previously: a massive femur bone that it wielded like a club. It brought it above its head and quickly whipped it down onto the ground, flattening and destroying dozens of Rolling Force pieces in a single smash of its club. Just as it was lifting it back up to continue its devastation of Sandra's small constructs, a dozen Dire Wolves arrived and surrounded the huge skeleton.

They attacked as one, biting onto the thick bones of the Undead Ogre Skeleton before trying to pull it apart. It seemed to be effective as one of the bones in its leg was pulled away...momentarily; as soon as it got about a foot away, whatever force animated the looming figure pulled it back into place – along with the Wolf still holding onto it. A few others had similar results within the first few seconds of their attack, but then the Ogre swept its bone club around it, sending Wolves flying in all directions. None of them were destroyed, fortunately, but half of them had their bodies smashed in so much that they could barely pick themselves off the ground.

The Mechanical Jaguar Queens had even less luck, as they usually relied on their sharp claws to slice up and eviscerate the flesh of their enemies; as the Ogre Skeleton didn't have any skin or flesh, they were only able to make cosmetic scratches on the hard bones. They were fast enough to avoid being hit by the Ogre's stone club, at least, but they fell back anyway when the Steelclad Apes joined the fray.

One of her Apes leapt towards the massive Undead with its warhammer upraised to smash it to bits, but it was knocked out of the air by an unexpected swing of the bone club in the Skeleton's hand. A hazy dark cloud had seemed to envelop the Undead Ogre just as the Ape attacked, and it persisted long enough for Sandra to see that the enemy Dungeon Monster had somehow increased its reaction speed. Her 11 other Apes attacked at the same time, only to have 6 of them knocked away like the first, the sides of their bodies crumpled in so badly that they couldn't move. One of them was hit so hard that the internal glowing power source that characterized its vulnerability was punctured and destroyed, leaving behind its Monster Seed – which was immediately picked up by one of the accompanying Hyper Automatons and brought back towards her dungeon for reuse.

Five of her Ape Warriors, however, managed to close in on the Undead Ogre Skeleton and went to work with their warhammers. Even bones that were thicker and more dense than normal ones couldn't stand up to the weapons of her constructs; a few impacts from the heavy hammers were enough to start shattering the skeleton, in fact. As a few vital bones were destroyed in its legs, it collapsed on the ground, the hazy dark cloud enveloping it dissipating at the same time.

With its legs literally cut out from underneath it and its reaction speed back to normal, the Ogre quickly fell to the repeated blows of the Apes. After approximately 30 seconds, the bones fell apart from each other, dissolving into the ground and leaving behind an unusual-looking black orb as a Monster Seed. When one of her Hyper Automatons picked it up, Sandra immediately recognized it as Onyx; judging by its size, she thought it was an Average-sized one, which was a bit worrying.

Sandra couldn't create an Average-sized Precious Gemstone, even with her special Advancements; if the Undead dungeon followed the same rules as she did, then an Average Faceted Onyx Sphere cost 28,000 Mana – not to mention 96,000 Raw Materials. Her Advancement brought that down to 19,600 Mana, which was 42 more than her maximum, but she also only had about approximately half of the required Raw Materials. If the Dungeon Core could afford to create one, then it had to be at least a few Core Sizes more than Sandra herself.

"That's not necessarily true; I've heard of some skills for other dungeons granting the ability to use elementally connected Monster Seeds that would normally be out of reach," a voice from Sandra's Home startled the Dungeon Core.

Winxa was back and hovering near Sandra's Core, her face composed and thoughtful – entirely unlike how she appeared earlier. The Fairy must've come back during the middle of that fight with the Ogre and Sandra had missed her arrival.

Welcome back; you seem to have...recovered. And what do you mean "elementally connected"? And what skills are you talking about.

"Thank you, I feel much better now," Winxa said. "As for what I mean, do you remember the Sapphire you found from those Ancient Saurians? Sapphires are normally 'elementally connected' to Water-based Dungeon Cores, just as Onyx is affiliated with Nether Cores, Emeralds with Natural Cores, and so on. Some Core-specific skills allow them to take advantage of the elemental connection to produce those Monster Seeds relatively cheaply, though they would still need to be able to pay the Mana cost for the Dungeon Monsters themselves. It's quite possible that this Undead Core – as well as perhaps the Reptile Core, based on what it was able to create – has this skill, though it seems strange that two dungeons so near each other have the same – or at least similar – Core-specific skills."

That's...not good. It almost seemed unfair to Sandra that they would have something so useful like that when she didn't, but then she looked at her own Core-specific skills and abilities – and had to acknowledge that they would probably consider a lot of what she could do as unfair. Regardless of whether their skills were unfair or not, it meant that she had to worry about the other Core sending out some powerful Dungeon Monsters.

Why weren't there any of these powerful Undead out here before? Is it just because the Core upgraded its Size?

Winxa seemed to consider that for a moment before answering. "Normally, dungeons reserve their most powerful Monsters for their dungeon for protection, so you wouldn't necessarily see many roaming the land around it – mainly because they get culled so often that it would be a waste. My guess is because there wasn't any culling going on lately that the Core finally decided to let some of their protection go out to join in the absorption of ambient Mana. If they didn't have to worry about being invaded and destroyed, then it makes the most sense to take advantage of that."

Sandra was inclined to agree with that; if she didn't have to make sure she was protected, she would've sent most of her constructs out into the wastelands, absorbing Mana as they went. There were only so many that were needed inside her dungeon to get the maximum ambient Mana from it, so it did make "financial" sense to her; if they were just sitting around doing nothing, then they weren't contributing to making her more powerful. It was like having merchandise that you could sell if you sent it out into the market, but instead of doing that, you kept it in your hidden hole-in-the-wall store that didn't get many customers. Of course, having that "merchandise" in her "store" helped to fend off thieves, so there was a balance that needed to be established.

While the Repair Drones fixed up her damaged constructs after the battle, Sandra got to work replacing the ones that had been destroyed, including 56 Rolling Forces, one Steelclad Ape, and one of the Dire Wolves that ended up being too damaged to survive after being hit by the bone club. She put the completion of the Preservation Barriers/Stasis Fields on the RRPs on hold for the moment, mainly because Felbar and Violet needed a break; they had managed to finish three enchantments from the Large Spirit Elemental Cubes that she was able to produce before and during the attack against the Undead, but it was already getting later in the day. They needed to rest after all of the excitement of finally figuring out a way to power the Fields for long periods of time, and Sandra thought that was a good idea – there was no reason to risk Violet accidentally messing up an enchantment.

The Dungeon Core had been watching what she was doing, however, and thought that she *might* be able to do it with her Unstable Shapeshifter. The problem was that if she messed up incorporating the **Limiter** rune into the enchantment sequence, it might not just blow the Shapeshifter itself up, but half of her dungeon as well. She knew she needed to start small and keep practicing until she was sure of her skill before she did something like that, so for the moment she was going to leave it to someone more experienced.

Instead, she used all of her incoming Mana over the next few hours to create some Martial Totems to add to her eradication force. Based on the Undead nature of what she was facing, she wanted something that could act similarly to her Steelclad Ape Warriors; the bites and clawing of her Jaguars just weren't doing much, and though her Wolves could rip things apart, the evidence from the last fight showed that they weren't going to be much help against bones that were animated with Mana. That's not to say they wouldn't do any good at all; in fact, they would probably both be good against the decaying zombies she had seen previously walking around the forest. The Martial Totems, however, would help against any more skeletons they encountered, especially the massive Ogre Skeleton, as she had already seen that the newer Totem could pound stone into dust – so it was likely it could destroy bone just as easily.

Approximately four hours after the battle with the Ogre, Sandra was ready to proceed against the Undead forces. The open land around Glimmerton was empty of Dungeon Monsters, but the few glimpses she had through the trees with her Shears showed that there were many more inside the trees to the northeast. Sandra hadn't sent them in too far because there were still some strange mist-like Monsters floating around the perimeter that seemed to see her flying constructs, and she didn't think that there was any reason to risk them being destroyed.

The sun was starting to set as her Rolling Forces led the way into the trees, crunching fallen leaves scattered over the forest floor as they busted through a few smaller skeletons near the outskirts. Soon enough, her entire band of constructs was inside the trees, which quickly grew closer together – with the result of dividing her force into smaller groups.

She encountered her first zombie-like creatures, some smaller Gnome-sized Monsters with decaying flesh, open wounds that didn't bleed, and generally unrecognizable features. Her rolling constructs did the job just as efficiently against these as against the skeletons of the same size, though it took more to smash its body apart; soft, decaying flesh prevented a lot of the bone-shattering impacts, but hundreds of them occurring around the same time was enough to practically dissect the zombie.

Just like the skeletons, the size and strength of the zombies increased as they slowly worked their way inside the trees, making sure to cover every square foot on their progress towards the dungeon itself. Sandra left a pair of Shears hovering around every 100 feet or so to ensure that the area her constructs cleared was still empty and hadn't been replaced yet; she didn't want to clear everything out, just to come back and find them all returned with brand-new ones.

Strangely enough, the mist-like Dungeon Monsters she saw had completely disappeared from sight. They were along the perimeter of the forest earlier, but now she didn't see a single one; not only that, but the frequency of zombies was starting to lessen the farther her extermination force traveled – which she thought was strange. *I would think that the dungeon would be **more** protected the closer we got to it—*

As her force poured through the trees, the forest opened up into a small clearing about 100 feet long and 50 feet wide. In the middle of the clearing – and behind it – was a frightening host of Undead that appeared ready for a pitched battle.

Well, there they are.

Chapter 12

Sandra had to remind herself that just because the other Dungeon Cores around her were driven by their insatiable instincts, that didn't mean they were stupid and ignorant. The Reptile Core had been surprised by the presence of her constructs and her interference; despite that, it still locked into her location as the reason for its incomplete success at wiping out all of the Gnomes and tried to destroy her by sending its army of reptiles. When that didn't work, it protected itself the best it could and went after easier game, following its instincts to kill things: namely, the Elves. It was only through fortunate circumstances – and a little luck – that she had been able to actually destroy the other Core at all, as well as ensuring that the Elves survived.

But this Undead dungeon wasn't currently suffering from the unquenchable thirst for death and murder – there weren't any people within its Area of Influence, nor did it most likely have any idea that the Dwarves were relatively nearby, if out of reach. Therefore – and this was only what Sandra suspected after the fact – it reacted to Sandra's attack on its territory by assembling its own army to combat her forces. It was probably more than obvious that even solo Dungeon Monsters – like the Ogre Skeleton – weren't going to be able to stop her large band of constructs, so the host of Undead that greeted them was the result of that fact.

There were some basic skeletons in the bunch, but most of the Undead horde was comprised of more-powerful Monsters –

including two massive Undead Ogre Skeletons. There were a few regular zombies, but there were also some beast-like ones as well: a dozen large rotting bears, a few dozen smaller wolves that were grouped up into three different packs, and even a pair of zombie creatures that looked similar in size to Sandra's Iron-plated Behemoths.

Those were all bad enough, but there was even more than she had seen since she first scouted the forest a few weeks ago. There were what she suspected were some sort of ghouls; she had heard about them before from Heroes back when she was alive as a Human, but never expected to see one herself. It looked vaguely humanoid but misshapen in form, almost as if it had extra bones in places it shouldn't; it was completely naked without any form of reproductive organs and its skin was so pale that it was essentially white, which really accentuated how thin the creature was. To set it off from looking like any type of person, it had sharp teeth that were as long as its fingers; speaking of its fingers, its digits were also tipped with razor-like nails that could rend flesh from the bone with ease. Fortunately, she didn't have to worry about that with her constructs, but it was also said that they were extremely strong in comparison to how they looked – strong enough to bend metal, if the rumors were true.

In the air were the white mist-like Dungeon Monsters that Sandra had seen earlier which had prevented her from sending her Shears in to investigate the forest. They had a vaguely oblong form, but they were insubstantial enough that it was hard to really get a good look at them; despite that, the air around them almost seemed to crackle with a temperature drop, as if the misty Undead were sucking all of the heat from the air.

Next were some Monsters that appeared to be pale and featureless corpses – that were wearing full suits of plate armor. It was either made of some sort of black metal she had never heard of before, or it was painted; either way, it was so dark that it was hard to look at them and accurately determine their features. The open-faced helmet showed only a blank face devoid of anything resembling eyes, nose, or mouth – like a blank canvas without anything on it. If that wasn't unnerving enough, they were also holding massive claymores in their hands that were practically as tall as they were, made from the same metal as their armor – and they looked as though they could use them.

There were also a half-dozen tall robed figures that almost seemed to exude darkness from their shadowy forms; they were situated near the back of the Undead host and didn't look that impressive at first glance. However, even watching them through one of her Shear constructs, she mentally shivered as she stared at one for half a second – and she knew that they were probably the most dangerous of the bunch.

And then everything seemed to happen all at once.

Her constructs weren't under any type of leash, because – as she had noticed before – they fought better when she gave them general orders and didn't try to control them directly. As such, they didn't hesitate to attack the assembled Undead host with some of the strategies that had worked for them against the skeletons and zombies they had encountered thus far. The enemy didn't just wait for them, of course; they immediately streamed forward and hit her incoming constructs with their own devastating attacks.

Her Dividing Rolling Forces targeted and slammed into many of the smaller skeletons, breaking them apart and destroying them. Some of her rolling constructs bounced ineffectually off of a few of the beast-like zombies, and even more broke themselves upon the two Ogre Skeletons stomping towards her eradication force as they slammed into their thick bones. Sandra watched as the Rolling pieces that survived the original assault *tried* to reassemble into a single construct, but many of them were broken, smashed, or just plain trampled by the incoming tide of Undead behind them. All told, perhaps two dozen of the weaker enemy skeletons were destroyed by them; in comparison, 800 of her Rolling Forces met their end in the first few seconds of the battle.

Her dozens of Mechanical Jaguar Queens and Dire Wolves raced ahead and immediately latched onto the humanoid-shaped and wolf-like zombies and sliced/tore them apart quite effectively; when they encountered the bears and massive "behemoth" variety, however, they were quickly overpowered. Razor-sharp claws and teeth from Sandra's big cats ripped chunks of flesh from the monstrosities, but ultimately didn't seem to do anything more than annoy the enemy; the decaying and rotten appendages on the larger beasts seemed to be held together by a stronger force than their smaller brethren, which resisted most of the tearing and ripping her Dire Wolves tried to inflict on them.

Not only that, but the bears and behemoths seemed to be physically much, much stronger and faster than she would've thought; a quick backhanded swipe by the bear tossed one of her Queens away so hard that it smashed up against a distant tree, snapping its spine and killing it in the process. The behemoth wasn't quite as quick, but a speedy shuffle-step by its enormous legs caught a Dire Wolf or two underneath its feet, pinning them in place while at the same time deforming the metal of her Mechanical construct like it was clay. Overall, her Jaguar and Wolf constructs were doing quite a bit of damage to the larger zombie creatures, but it was going to take some time for their constant attacks to do enough to take one of them down.

Time, however, wasn't something that they were going to have a lot of – especially when she considered the rest of the battle. Her Steelclad Ape Warriors had jumped straight into the fray against the two Ogre Skeletons – backed up by the Martial Totems she had just recently added to her forces – and started to smash apart the enemy Dungeon Monsters with great success. Even after the hazy dark cloud enveloped both Ogres and sped them up, her Apes managed to break quite a few of their vital bones, while only taking minimal casualties. The Totems were exceptionally well-suited for cracking and pulverizing the hard and thick bone of the massive Skeletons, though one of them practically folded in half – despite being made of something similar to Iron – when it was hit by an oversized bone club.

If it were just a matchup between her Apes/Totems and the Ogres, her constructs would've won handily; unfortunately, there were other Undead in the small clearing that negated any advantage they had. While her constructs were attacking the skeletons and zombies – probably because Sandra had prior experience fighting them and they ultimately took their cues from her – they were in turn attacked by the new Undead she hadn't fought before.

In the end, it was a slaughter…and it was an unusual – and disheartening – experience being on the *receiving* end of such an outcome.

The undead she thought were Ghouls of some sort jumped on the backs of some of her Apes and latched on with their ferocious strength; they immediately went to work scoring rents into the Steel forms of her constructs with their claws and teeth. Given enough time, it appeared as though they would be able to tear through and get to her Steelclad Dungeon Monsters' "power sources" to kill them – but her Apes didn't even survive that long. While a few Ghouls were punched off by the powerful fists of the nearby Martial Totems or a swing of a nearby warhammer wielded by other Ape Warriors, they were not the only threat.

The faceless undead that were wearing full suits of armor stomped up next, swinging their enormous claymores with deadly efficiency. One massive sword swipe was enough to lop off an Ape arm or leg – or if they were really lucky, a head – or even partway shear through one of her Martial Totems. Within a minute of the fight starting, half of her Apes and Totems that she had brought were down if not out from the unexpected assault...though they didn't give up easily.

The undead inside the armor were just as susceptible to impact damage as anything else, perhaps even more so; half of them were destroyed in her constructs' counterattack as powerfully swung warhammers and Totem fists slammed into the – remarkably sturdy, Sandra couldn't help but notice – black-colored armor, breaking the bones of the undead creature inhabiting it, even if the armor wasn't damaged overly much. In fact, it almost looked like they were turning things around, when the last two unknown Undead entered the battle and took their toll on her forces in new and unexpected ways.

First, the mist-like Dungeon Monsters floating through the air descended on the combatants, primarily targeting her Ape Warriors. Sandra wasn't exactly sure what they would or *could* do, though; they didn't seem to have any real form, so she didn't think that they had any way to inflict damage on her constructs. Her assumption was proven right as they came into contact with her Steelclad constructs and didn't seem to do anything with their touch; in fact, upon the first contact, the mist seemed to recoil in pain. A rime of frost appeared on her Dungeon Monsters where the mist creatures touched them momentarily, but even that didn't seem to slow them down.

It was only when the Undead mist floated around her Apes for a moment and then stopped when it seemed to find something of interest that she became a little worried. Quicker than she had seen them move before, Sandra watched the strange mist creatures condense their forms and shoot forward into the tiny joins of her Ape Warriors' bodies; in less than a second, they were inside and gone from view – and then her Steelclad constructs started to fall to the ground one-by-one, like a puppet that had its strings cut. As they dissolved into the ground, leaving behind their Monster Seeds, she saw the mists appear where her constructs died – though they were severely reduced in size, or else gone completely.

The loss of her 8 remaining Apes in the matter of seconds was bad enough, but the introduction to the last Undead Dungeon Monster was what put the final nail on the coffin of her eradication force's destruction. The shadowy hooded figures hadn't done anything so far during the battle, but now that her constructs were being wiped out they apparently decided to join in. Raising arms out to their sides, Sandra saw their robes slip off of their hands, revealing dry-looking, desiccated skin – though not rotting like a zombie's flesh – tightly covering thin, fragile-appearing bones. From what she could see, its physical appearance looked more like a dried-out animated corpse without much strength behind it, but she quickly found that it wasn't there to get into a fistfight.

Billows of pure darkness emanated from their hands until there was a growing cloud of...whatever it was...floating in front of each of them, darker than even the current night-time environment of the forest. They blocked out Sandra's view of the hooded figures, in fact, but other than that the dark fog-like substance didn't look very threatening; if it was designed to blind her constructs, she doubted it would have any major effect on them – because many of them didn't use *physical* eyes to see. It was also why the darkness of night didn't really affect them, because they didn't necessarily need light to see by.

After 20 excruciating seconds of her remaining constructs getting slowly destroyed by the other Undead, the now-significantly larger clouds shot forwards in the blink of an eye, splitting up and surrounding all of her remaining Martial Totems, half of her Jaguars and Wolves, and even two of her Repair Drones that were trying to fix some Apes that had been smashed across the clearing either by an Ogre's bone club or the flat of one of the armored Undeads' claymores.

She couldn't see what the clouds did – even when she ineffectively tried to look through the "eyes" of one of her Mechanical Dire Wolves surrounded by one – but she didn't have to wonder long. After 15 seconds of total obscurity, the dark clouds dissipated, leaving behind her constructs – or what was left of them.

The best she could guess from the holey and weak sections of metal she saw on her Dungeon Monsters, the robed Undead figures had manipulated Nether-based elemental energy and sent a devastating spell towards her constructs – not unlike what many

Human Heroes and Elves did. The difference was that the spell they cast was extremely potent, much more potent than anything she had heard of or seen before; she wasn't sure if it was designed to eat away at metal specifically, or if it just sped up the aging of whatever was inside of the cloud, but the results were essentially the same. Those constructs that were enveloped in the dark fog spell were practically falling apart and collapsing in on themselves as they tried to continue fighting.

With that final blow to the formerly cohesive and powerful eradication force Sandra had assembled, she knew the battle was lost – though she doubted she would've "won" even if those last two Undead hadn't been there. The fight wasn't going her way almost from the beginning; she thought she had a group of constructs that could tackle virtually anything and prevail – but she was sadly mistaken.

As the spell-weakened constructs were quickly finished off, the last few Jaguars and Wolves were surrounded and systematically destroyed. Sandra tried to save her remaining Repair Drones by having them flee, but they weren't very fast compared to the surviving Undead Ghouls; they were quickly hunted down by the fast-moving creatures and literally ripped apart – only for the Undead to be brutally killed themselves when her constructs exploded in a fiery conflagration of metal shards. *Hmm…I forgot about that.*

Brief thoughts of the damage her Repair Drones could do if they had been destroyed in the middle of the Undead army flashed through her mind as she watched the destruction of her last constructs. Even one of the two Reinforced Animated Shears she had watching the battle from above was caught by one of the mist-like Undead. It didn't have a "power source" like her Apes, but that didn't seem to matter; it was almost like the Mana involved in her construct's creation was eaten away rapidly and it was done so quickly that it didn't have a chance to fly away before it dissolved in the middle of the air.

Watching that happen from her other pair of Shears – which she had flee as soon as she could – she saw the already smaller-sized mist creature shrink even smaller as a result of the attack on her construct; she could only assume that some of the mist was consumed in the attack, but she still didn't have enough information about them to know for sure.

With disappointment and frustration mounting, she brought the only surviving construct from her eradication force out of the forest and set it to watch the trees, waiting for the Undead to come pouring out and head towards her dungeon. After a few minutes, however, none of them showed; Sandra realized that there was no point for them to come out from the safety of the trees, because the Undead Core's Area of Influence only reached about a half-mile into the barren wasteland she called home.

But that won't last long.

While the Undead Dungeon Core had lost quite a few Dungeon Monsters before and during the battle, it was nothing compared to the constructs that Sandra had lost. Not just in terms of the Mana used in their actual creation, but more importantly the Monster Seeds they had left behind. While contracts normally prevented Cores from attacking each other's Dungeon Monsters for the sake of looting their Seeds, that didn't apply to Sandra and her unique situation; therefore, all of the Monster Seeds dropped by her constructs were now in the possession of the Undead Core.

After doing some quick estimations of how much those Seeds would be worth if the Dungeon Core decided to absorb them all for their Mana and Raw Materials, she figured that it might be enough to pay for another Core Size upgrade – depending on what their current size was, of course. Sandra had no way of actually knowing, of course, but she figured that it was probably only a few Sizes larger than her own; if that was the case, then the Mana from those Seeds was more than enough to provide for an upgrade. Even if it was already a much higher size, they would still contribute quite a bit towards that goal.

What have I done? In trying to prevent the Undead Dungeon Core from growing and expanding its influence, thereby threatening more people, Sandra had inadvertently *helped* it do just that. *Every time that I try to help, it just seems like I make things worse.*

With that depressing thought on her mind, she turned her attention back to her dungeon to inform Winxa about her failure – and the repercussions that would likely stem from it.

Chapter 13

"So, you're telling me that you made it worse?" Echo heard the small female Gnome—*Violet*—say as soon as she walked into Sandra's "workshop" near the surface, which the Dungeon Core automatically translated for her. It was strange to hear the Gnome speak something that sounded completely foreign to her and then hear a translation that Sandra provided for it in her mind, but she was growing used to it.

The Elf was coming back for the day to pick up another shipment of Energy Orbs for her people; though, as soon as she walked into the dungeon she was curtly told by Sandra that it was going to be a little bit. Apparently, something had happened to slow down production – which was honestly fine with her; she was getting tired of the looks the other villagers were throwing her way when they thought she wasn't paying attention. She wasn't sure if it was because some of them held the same views about her as Wyrlin did or if it was for some other reason – either way it was...uncomfortable.

*It's strange to think that I'm more comfortable **here** than with my own people.* She knew that what the dungeon was providing to her people – Energy Orbs, to be exact – was literally life-changing, and in spite of the danger to the Dungeon Heart/Core, she appreciated what Sandra was trying to do. Echo just wished that she wasn't the one in the middle handling all of the deliveries and negotiations between her people and the dungeon.

As far as she was concerned, she wasn't cut out to be any type of negotiator or political liaison – she'd much rather be out in the forest hunting down beasts for food or culling Dungeon Monsters to protect the village.

However, after the first day or two of hunting with her mended bow – which took some getting used to in order to shoot semi-accurately – she was advised by Elder Herrlot not to endanger herself in the forest when there were other hunters that could do the job perfectly fine, especially since they all now had Energy Orbs of their own. It was painfully obvious that her *duty* was to be a delivery woman/dungeon contact and not a Ranger anymore, which irked her to no end; her present circumstances didn't particularly lend itself to becoming an Elite in the future, which was what she always hoped to become. Regardless of her feelings, however, she knew she wouldn't shirk her duties even if it wasn't ideal to her own personal development.

To get away from such depressing thoughts, Echo left the village as soon as the sky was light enough to easily see her way through the wastelands, which was why she was back at the dungeon only shortly after the sun had come up. Even though Sandra had said that the area was clear of any threats – which was remarkable in and of itself – she had no desire to travel by the darkness brought on by night-time; she'd rather be able to spot any danger way before she actually encountered it, which was always made much easier if she could actually see clearly.

"What are you talking about, Violet? What did Sandra do this time?" Echo asked half-jokingly. Despite the "righteous" attitude that the dungeon seemed to affect most of the time, the Elf was more than aware that some – or possibly most – of her activities seemed to come with serious repercussions. The issues that would eventually arise from her production of the Energy Orbs aside, she also was informed that the destruction of the nearby Gnome village was caused by something the Core had inadvertently done – even if Sandra wasn't *directly* responsible.

The Gnome whipped around at the sound of Echo's voice, her eyes wide in surprise. Just past her, the Elf could see Felbar leaning against the nearby wall showing no sense of surprise at her appearance; it was plain to see that she had already been noticed by the grizzled older Gnome, so her question hadn't startled him.

"Whoa! Where did you come from?" Violet asked, before waving off her own question. "Never mind, I'm assuming you came for more of the Energy Orbs, but we only have a dozen or so ready for you. We've been busy with other...projects," she explained distractedly, her vision looking off into the distance like she was thinking of something.

"What other projects are you talking about? And what was it that Sandra did?" Echo was half-expecting the dungeon to explain it for the Gnome, but the Core was uncharacteristically silent other than the automatic translations in her mind.

"We were working on improving the Fields on the enchantment pillars down below, but that isn't really important right now," Felbar chimed in. "What *is* important, though, is that Sandra 'accidentally' just gave the Nether dungeon near Glimmerton a whole bunch of dungeon loot that it can use to...expand itself, or whatever it is that it does. While the nearest Gnome town is likely safe – as it's a few days of quick travel away – it's going to start to threaten the Dwarves to the northeast of here. Not that I care *overly* much about them, but when I was assigned to our village I was put in charge of culling the monsters around there – and this feels like an extreme failure on our part."

"Yes, just like those reptiles attacked *your* village, the undead monsters from the dungeon will be attacking the Dwarves within the next month or two, if what Sandra said is correct," Violet added.

Now that got Echo's attention; just like Felbar had said, she didn't particularly care about the Dwarves – other than the fact that she didn't want *anyone* to necessarily die from monster attacks like the Gnomes had – but the mention of the Nether dungeon was something else entirely. As it wasn't just any sort of a Nether dungeon, but an *undead* dungeon to boot, she felt her natural instincts flare up and all she could think about was destroying it. It was the same reason she had been so adamant about getting help to destroy Sandra's dungeon, because she thought they were undead monsters at first.

The Elven people had an instinctive hatred of the undead, and many Elites had been lost over the years when they dropped everything else to destroy their particular dungeons when they were found. Echo couldn't explain what it was that drove her or her people to do such a thing, mainly because it was so ingrained in her psyche that it was almost normal and natural to think that way. She wasn't aware that there was an undead dungeon so close to her village; she was pretty sure that if she or the others were aware of it, they would've sent a team to try to destroy it as soon as they could – even if they trespassed on Gnome lands.

"We have to destroy it – undead dungeons are abominations that need to be eliminated as soon as possible," Echo automatically said, the words tumbling out of her mouth before she could stop them – not that she would stop them even if she had a choice. It was something she believed in with every fiber of her being.

Violet and Felbar stared at her with strange looks on their faces. "That was apparently what Sandra was trying to do—" Felbar started to say, before the Dungeon Core herself cut him off with the first non-translation message Echo had heard since she walked in.

** That wasn't necessarily what I was trying to do; I was only trying to cull the Dungeon Monsters outside of the dungeon enough to delay its expansion. I hadn't quite yet decided on whether or not to destroy the Core, but that seems like a moot point right now. I messed up and made it worse, and I'm not even sure that I could destroy the Core even if I wanted to. **

Sandra went on to describe what had happened to her own force of monsters she had sent there to destroy the undead, and how they had been thoroughly eradicated.

"We never saw some of those other undead she claims to have seen; I only remember killing thousands of skeletons and zombies in my time there culling them in my War Machine. As for those Specters – the mist-like undead she was talking about – all it took to kill them was a quick temporary Fire-based enchantment on one of my weapons and they were destroyed quite easily," Felbar added when the dungeon was finished talking.

* *Wait a minute, you put an enchantment on your weapons? Why?* *

Sandra seemed completely confused by that, but it was so natural and obvious to Echo that she answered for the Gnomes. "It's because the undead are vulnerable to certain elemental attacks. Holy-based attacks work the best, of course, but Fire works quite well in a pinch; others like Natural, Air, Earth, and Water are nearly useless against something that is already technically dead, but they can be used in various ways to at least inflict damage. However, for undead monsters such as that Specter Felbar was talking about, they are resistant to most *physical* forms of attack, though the touch of iron can 'hurt' them if they are in constant contact with it.

"Then there are others that are resistant to *anything* other than Holy-based attacks, which was one of the main reasons I was hoping to become an Elite with my ability to manipulate Holy elemental energy. Destroying Nether dungeons – and especially undead-based ones – is something I desperately want to be able to do one day," Echo explained.

The Gnomes nodded along with her explanation and Violet added, "I thought everyone knew that, which was why I hadn't thought to tell you."

Sandra was silent for a while, leaving Echo and the others staring uncomfortably at each other. While she didn't necessarily dislike the other races, the distrust between the Elves and the others was deeply ingrained and taught at a young age; she put a lot of that aside after she was saved from death by the dungeon and the subsequent interaction between them all, but whispers of it were still there. Therefore, she still wasn't entirely used to being around the small people, and it was obvious that they felt at least a little of the same.

** Yes, well, I don't have much knowledge about the undead from my previous life. I mainly concentrated on crafting; while there were some enchantments that pertained to killing the undead, I never had time to study the actual Dungeon Monsters themselves. I didn't realize that some of them could only be hurt by elemental attacks, and I was unprepared with how ineffective my constructs would be against them.*

** I can only blame myself for not asking about it; Winxa turned out not to have much knowledge on the subject of the undead, as she had never been put in charge of an Undead Classification Dungeon Core before. As much as I don't like admitting my abject failure in this instance, I would appreciate all of your help to fix this problem. **

To Echo, that sounded much more interesting than picking up and delivering Energy Orbs to her people; even though she knew they needed – or at least *wanted* them – she'd much rather be doing something...productive. Something that would make a difference, at least – and destroying an abomination in the form of an undead dungeon would definitely classify as that.

"I would love to help, though I don't know exactly how I can," Echo said, having some doubts about her effectiveness in delving through the dungeon by herself. Even if she was accompanied by hundreds of Sandra's constructs, she knew that such an endeavor would be extremely dangerous – the hundreds of lost Elites over the years who participated in such an act could attest to that.

"I don't think she means for you to go *yourself*; rather, I think Sandra wants your knowledge of the undead to help her defeat them with her constructs somehow. While Violet and I have *some* knowledge of the undead – and obviously more than the dungeon does herself – you seem to have a greater understanding of their dangers and weaknesses," Felbar said.

** Exactly. And as you're the only one here that can manipulate Holy elemental energy to cast spells and other effects, it will be extremely useful to have that type of knowledge. Violet and Felbar can help me with some of the enchantments that I know of that might be beneficial, but I have almost zero knowledge of how to manipulate elemental energy in the way that you and the Elves do. **

Echo was very confused. "And how would that knowledge help you? I thought your constructs couldn't manipulate energy in that way, and even if they could I've been told that controlling the elements in the way that we do is unique to each race. So, unless I'm going with whatever force you send, I'm not sure that it would do any good." The prospect of going to the undead dungeon with the intent of destroying it was both frightening and exciting at the same time, and she didn't want to be left out of it if she had a choice.

** It's true that my constructs can't manipulate energy like that; it'll probably take some time and effort on your part to educate me how it's done, as well. However, we'll have some time before things start to get too dangerous for the Dwarves or anyone else, so I'm* *hoping to have the opportunity to finish up my other projects and get a course in basic spellcasting.*

** As for you going with them, I wouldn't have it any other way...but it won't exactly be in the way you think. **

Out of the corner of her eye and against the far wall of the workshop, Echo saw the creepy-looking Shapeshifters start to shrink and take on another form. Within seconds, she was looking at six exact copies of herself – *naked* copies, to be exact.

Her mind shut down for a few seconds as she stared at herself in multiplicate; when she was able to think again, she saw that Felbar was determinedly looking in the opposite direction of her doubles, while Violet was smiling at her. *I think she's enjoying this for some reason!*

"Uh...what...?" was all Echo was able to get out, just before the Shapeshifters dropped her form and expanded into their former multi-colored amorphous blobs.

** Sorry about that – it was probably a bit of a shock. I just wanted you to see what I was talking about; not only will "you" be going, but* ***many*** *of you will be accompanying my constructs on the way. **

Echo was still recovering from the shock of seeing so many of herself in duplicate, so all she could do was nod in acceptance. What she had just seen went against the laws of nature in her opinion – and could be dangerous in the future for a multitude of reasons – but she figured it would perhaps be okay because it was ultimately going to be used to eradicate an undead Nether dungeon. She wasn't sure if the ends justified the means in this case, but her instinctive hatred and abhorrence of the undead overrode any real hesitation.

"Very well," she finally said haltingly, her throat dry and causing her voice to crack. "When do we start?"

Chapter 14

Putting the failure and subsequent consequences of that failure behind her, Sandra threw herself into training, crafting, and various lines of development. Everything was hinging on an estimated timetable of three months, which was a guesstimate of the time the Undead Core would need to expand its Area of Influence enough to endanger the Dwarves – and possibly even stretch far enough to attack Sandra's dungeon. That time was based on how the other Core had previously operated with its Dungeon Monsters, sending them out to accumulate ambient Mana, as well as guesses at its Core Size and how soon it would be able to upgrade itself; it was also contingent on the ability of Sandra to thin out and cull some of its undead numbers outside of the dungeon, while at the same time ensuring she didn't fall into a trap like last time.

She wasn't about to let the Undead-based Dungeon Core have free rein to grow as quickly as it could; whether it was based on the need to delay its expansion as much as possible or through some innate need for revenge against those that completely destroyed so many of her constructs, Sandra had the desire to—*safely*—kill as many of the undead as she could. Her Shears she placed around the border of the wastelands and in the Gnome lands had already seen skeletons and a few zombies roaming the open areas again, and it would be prudent to cut down on their numbers before they grew out of control.

So, using a small portion of her treasury – and the Mana she had accumulated during the night before – Sandra assembled another eradication force; this time, however, it was comprised entirely of Dividing Rolling Forces. They had proven to be more than capable of destroying many of the skeletons and even most of the zombies they had encountered and were fast enough to flee if something stronger and more dangerous came along – like the Ogre Skeletons or bear-like zombies. Having 1,500 of them all roaming around as a quick strike force, they could rapidly kill something and then escape before another horde of undead came to wipe them out.

With the Mana cost of their creation and Monster Seeds at just under 150,000 Mana and 120,000 Raw Materials, it was a bit of an investment; however, the loss of a couple of them every now and then was much better in her eyes than the loss of even a single Ape Warrior if it was caught off guard going against the Undead. Besides, the Hyper Automatons she had gathering up Monster Seeds and bringing them back to her dungeon would negate most of those losses – and it turned out that her Rolling Forces could move *much* faster when they didn't have to wait for any of the other constructs with them.

As soon as they were assembled and took to the field, they practically swept through the roaming skeletons and small zombies in a matter of minutes. They would throw 200 or so of their number against even a larger skeleton – Human or Orc-sized – and completely pulverize it in a few seconds, while the others continued on and targeted the next. A few times some of the pieces of her constructs were damaged in the process, but the original Rolling Force it came from was usually able to continue; when it became too damaged, it would be destroyed and leave behind its Seed – which would be picked up by the following Automatons that were already gathering up the ones left by the undead that were killed.

The other Core was initially slow to react to the lightning-fast attack on its Dungeon Monsters, to the point where the area outside the forest was completely wiped out of all Undead. When her Forces entered the trees and started to pick off random zombies, she started to see less and less of them; rather than progress towards the center and encounter the same powerful army she had before, she continued to have her constructs roam around the inside perimeter of the forest, picking off the few stragglers roaming around.

At one point, one of the mist-like Specters – or at least that was what Violet called them – had swooped down to attack a group of her rolling constructs; after it enveloped about a dozen of them in its misty form, she could see her Dungeon Monsters succumb to its unusual attack just like her Shears had. However, she could also see that its attack also consumed a sizable portion of the Specter as well; therefore, she ordered another hundred of her Rolling Forces to attack the Undead mist.

The results were interesting; as the Rolling Forces split apart and flew through the Specter – since there was nothing physical for them to hit, they only came into contact briefly before exiting out the other side of the misty form – they "ate" away at the undead bit by bit. A few of the Force pieces were destroyed in the process, but most of them didn't touch it long enough to have much effect; on the flip side, five to six hundred heavy metal pieces – that had at least some traces of Iron in them – flew through the Specter and practically shredded it. When it was only a small fraction of its original size, the undead Dungeon Monster dissipated and left behind a Large Nickel Orb.

It was good knowing that they could be killed, but the Specter also ended up destroying 15 of her Rolling Forces in the process; that wasn't too much of a hardship because her Automatons would soon pick up all the Monster Seeds and bring them back to her dungeon, but too many of those fights would quickly diminish her Rolling Forces. It was for that reason that she had them retreat and stick to the forest's perimeter and open land nearby; being able to avoid them was much easier out in the open, though if it came down to a fight she knew she could eliminate the Specters by throwing all she could at them.

After a few hours, individual undead started to roam again in the areas her Forces had previously cleared as they were slowly replaced. It made sense, actually, because the reason the Core didn't keep all of its Dungeon Monsters together in one group was the same reason Sandra had her AMANS spread out over thousands of feet of open air; grouped up together, they accumulated much less ambient Mana than if they were spread apart. Whenever they would venture out from the safety of the deep forest, she would immediately order her constructs to kill them, before retreating to safety themselves.

With that taken care of – at least for the moment – Sandra focused on the proposed solutions regarding the *entire* Undead Dungeon Core problem. It was unfortunately no longer a question whether or not she was going to have to destroy the other Core; it was already too powerful and there was very little hope that she would be able to perpetually prevent it from upgrading its Core Size enough to threaten the Dwarves – and possibly others that might be present even beyond her own Area of Influence. It was sadly better to eliminate the problem now rather than have to worry about it in the future.

She thought that it would only be a simple matter of enchanting some of her Steelclad Ape Warriors' warhammers and learning from Echo how to cast spells, but it wasn't going to be that easy. Not because it wouldn't work, but because there was some unexpected pushback from the Gnomes she was going to ask for help with the enchanting.

"I want to help with the culling of them outside of the dungeon; it's still technically my duty, and I *need* to do it. If you get my War Machine working, we'll do whatever you want – which includes finishing the rest of your Enchantment Repository with the new rune on the Fields," Felbar told Sandra as soon as her attention was back from her Rolling Forces. It was unmistakably an ultimatum – and one that she would normally be all for if the circumstances had been different.

** I told you what I saw there; you can't deny that it'll be extremely dangerous. How about we take care of the Undead-based Dungeon Core **first**, then we can concentrate on your War Machine? **

Her plea fell on deaf ears, though Sandra could tell that Violet was wavering and would probably fold if pushed far enough. However, the entire ultimatum appeared to be Felbar's idea and he wasn't budging; the Dungeon Core almost decided to try to do it herself and not rely on their help, but the fact of the matter was that she hadn't even come close to perfecting the incorporation of the **Limiter** rune yet. Without seeing the relatively complex sequence constructed a few more times – as well as lots of subsequent practice with her Shapeshifters – she wasn't sure she could reliably create it. The last thing she wanted was to accidentally make a mistake and blow up half of her dungeon because she thought she could do it without help…so she decided to be the one to fold to their – not wholly unreasonable – demands.

The learning and teaching coming from Echo was going to have to wait until she was back, anyway, because she was gone after taking the few Energy Orbs that had been completed. She was supposed to tell the Elder that she was going to be in and out of the village for the next few days, but would be bringing more shipments when she could; Echo was going to need to stay close at hand so that she could be there to instruct Sandra on the basic art of energy manipulation. While it was vaguely similar, she felt that at its heart, it was entirely different from Enchanting.

Meanwhile, before they could get started with that, Sandra took a look at the War Machine and conveyed her earlier ideas about how to get it enchanted in a way that didn't require it to be done all at once. Violet instantly rejected the idea as impossible at first, but as the Dungeon Core explained it further, she could start to see that the Gnome was warming to the concept she was trying to convey. After describing what she envisioned for nearly half an hour, the Apprentice Enchanter finally nodded and said, "I...think that might work."

The problem she had identified as needing to be overcome was linking up all the enchantments as a cohesive whole; the Master Gnome Enchanters could create an entire enchantment sequence that would cover the entire War Machine, but they didn't have that luxury. Instead, they were going to have to create 10 different smaller enchantment sequences (2 for each leg, 2 for each arm, 1 for the torso, and 1 to link them all together) that would work in the same way.

The individual Natural-based enchantments on the War Machine that allowed the normally inanimate material – like wood and steel – to stretch, bend, and move to the will of the pilot Violet knew quite well; she had been tasked with replacing and maintaining them in her time there in the village. It was the Spirit-based enchantments that she didn't have as much knowledge of, since those were what controlled everything; the Master Enchanters of the Gnomish people had created an intricate network of interlinked sequences that were easily manipulated by the pilot. It was this that they needed to replace and still have it function in essentially the same way – but it was going to take some trial and error experimentation to get it to work.

Sandra had already made a much smaller model of the massive War Machine to assist with the process, so Violet dove straight into working on it. Starting with a single lower leg and foot, the Gnome used a variation of **Transform**, **Flex**, **Movement**, and **Conform** runes in an enchantment sequence made with Natural elemental energy to manipulate the materials used in its construction; at the same time, she interwove a Spirit enchantment comprised of various **Activate** runes connected to those Natural runes which would trigger the motion the pilot wanted to achieve. On the small model, it was a lot to fit into the small leg section – but Violet was able to somehow connect it all together in a single enchantment sequence.

Of course, that was a gross oversimplification of the entire process which ended up taking a few hours just for that single lower leg. She had to make sure she had the foot joint properly aligned with the enchantment so that it would flex properly – ensuring that the War Machine didn't stomp around flat-footed and trip itself up – as well as making sure the lower leg portion could bend and absorb the sheer weight of the entire War Machine while it walked.

The upper leg took a little less time even though it encompassed the all-important knee joint, but it was probably because Violet was becoming a little more comfortable with the process. When it was done, there were two different enchantments on the right leg, currently unconnected to anything; despite that, Felbar was able to experiment and independently insert an infinitesimally small amount of Spirit energy into various portions of the leg, making it move how he wanted...sort of. It wasn't perfect by any means, and there was a section that had a touch too many Natural runes in the sequence – which almost caused the leg to bend in a way that stressed the material and nearly broke it – but once those were fixed, it worked remarkably well.

The major problem with it was that Felbar was forced to devote all of his concentration to the separate enchantments just to have the leg move naturally. Two enchantments seemed to be about the limit for his focus, however, because when Violet finished up the left leg with similar enchantments, he wasn't able to manipulate both legs at the same time. Instead of a fluid movement with each leg as he tried to make it walk forward, it was more of a jerky stop-and-start motion that caused the model to fall down more often than not. Fortunately, the linking enchantment sequence that would be created after all of the other enchantments were in place would help bring it all together to make it easier to control – or so she hoped.

By the time Violet was done with those two legs and Felbar had experimented with making it walk – and was in general pleased with it, despite the difficulty in trying to manipulate four different enchantments all at once – it was already dark outside. After they went to sleep for the night, Sandra could finally work on some other things.

Not that she had been idle while the Gnomes had been working. Apart from ensuring her Dividing Rolling Forces were maintaining their eradication of roaming Undead, she had been spending her Mana on replacing what she had needed to use from her treasure to create said Forces – and used the rest to help with some crafting. She was finally starting to work with the Titanium she had received from the Elites, and it was turning out to be a little more difficult than she had expected.

The main reason was because Titanium had a higher melting point than even Iron did, so the furnace she was using needed to be turned almost all the way up. When it got that hot, even her Steelclad Ape Warriors were affected by the heat emanating from the furnace, so it made getting whatever she placed in there hard to get out; not only that, but the Iron tools that she had created to take her pieces in and out of the heat would get so hot that they would sometimes fuse to the Titanium itself.

After some frustration, she found that she needed to coat her tools entirely in a thin layer of Dragon Glass – which took a bit of experimentation and even more Mana to execute – to protect them from the heat. The drawback with using the Glass, however, was that it made the tools a bit slippery to hold as well as grip whatever she was working with, and even with creating sharp ridges on the coating it was still difficult – but not impossible – to handle. As for her Apes' hands and arms warming up and softening because of the extreme heat, she actually had to craft something entirely new – which was exciting and productive in and of itself.

Sandra began with finishing the process of tanning more Raw Bearling Hide she had started a few days before when she had some downtime; she wanted to experiment with a new process using some of the salt she had acquired earlier to see if she could finally make some decent leather. By adding a small amount to the boiling process, it helped to eliminate many of the particulates that caused them to rot and putrefy afterward. Once they were done and stretched over racks to dry, she then used something she recently gained access to but hadn't been able to use until now: Cedarwood Oil.

She found a use for one of her rooms to create a new workstation, one where she could make a Steam Distillery. First, she crafted a large drum using sheets of Steel, which she had her Ape heat and shape until it was a four-foot-tall, three-foot-wide open-topped vessel; into the drum she had some other constructs place leaves, berries, and some bark from the Cedar tree she had in her growing room, along with enough water to just barely cover the mixture. Then using her ability as a Dungeon Core, she had her Ape place a Steel dome top on the drum and perfectly sealed it so that it was completely air and water-tight – except for a hole leading out from the apex of the dome. From there, she created a simple arched Steel tube made from folding a thin sheet of Steel around a piece of stone she created, before sealing up the ends; using her cheating Core abilities to seal the tube to the top of the drum dome and had it arch over to another – though much smaller – Steel drum.

When that was set up, she then created a dual-element trap for the process; Fire Mana was used to heat up the outside of the larger Steel drum, while Water Mana was used to add nearly frozen water to the outside of the Steel tube and surrounding the outside of the small drum. She tied the entire trap to the Steelclad Ape Warrior she had working in there, so that it would activate when it was close enough to the crude – but serviceable – Steam Distillery. Before she finished, she also created a much smaller version of the entire contraption for use after the initial step was complete.

When her Ape activated the trap, the heat from the Fire Mana caused the water/Cedar mixture to boil, creating steam laden with Cedarwood Oil to flow upwards through the Steel tube up above. The nearly frozen water caused the steam to rapidly condense, falling as a liquid down the other side of the tube into the smaller drum. The liquid was a mixture of water and Cedarwood Oil, so once enough of it was produced she unsealed the smaller drum, had her Ape take it to the smaller Steam Distillery contraption and pour it into the larger of the two drums there.

This was where she had to alter the traps a bit, because she needed to have the temperature be just high enough to boil the water away, while leaving the Oil behind. After a few unsuccessful attempts, she finally found the correct heat temperature to get the job done; after all – or at least most – of the water was boiled away, she was left with some Crude Cedarwood Oil.

New Origination Material found!

Crude Cedarwood Oil

While Crude Cedarwood Oil cannot be directly used as a Monster Seed, it can be used as a material for use in the dungeon or other purposes.

It was a lot of work for just Cedarwood Oil – and Crude one at that – but she didn't think she needed to refine it any more, especially for what she was going to use it for. Creating some of her new Oil, she had some other constructs near her tanning room use it on the hides stretched across the racks. The substance had two major benefits: one, it would moisturize the hide during the drying process, preventing cracking – especially with her earlier use of salt during the boiling process; and two, it would make the final Leather she made softer and more pliable.

The Leather she had been using up to that point was relatively stiff and would rot after a while if not taken care of, but with the Oil to seal the moisture inside while protecting it at the same time, she was hoping this Leather would qualify as "finished".

Fortunately for all her hard work, she was rewarded with long-sought-after success.

New Monster Seed and Origination Material found!

Basic Bearling Leather
While Basic Bearling Leather can be directly used as a Monster Seed, it can also be used as a material for use in the dungeon or other purposes.

You now have access to:
Basic Bearling Leather Scrap
Origination Raw Material Cost: 75
Origination Mana Cost: 25
Monster Min. Mana: 25
Monster Max. Mana: 125

Finally! The Leather she created was classified as "Basic" and that was fine with her; she knew there were other ways to finish off the material that would make it even softer and supple, or even change it so that it could defend someone wearing it even more – but she was happy with what she made. All of those things could come later; the important point was that she could now use Leather as a material – which she used to help protect her Steelclad Ape from slowly melting when it got too close to the furnace with the Titanium warming up inside of it.

Using a basic glove pattern she knew from memory, she cut out a pair of gloves from her new available Leather that would fit her construct; however, she also added more Leather to the normal hand opening, creating long sleeves that would go all the way up to her Ape's shoulders. When it was finished, she hoped it would protect the hands and arms – the most important parts she needed for crafting – of the construct, but she knew that she was going to need something even more.

To protect it from even more heat, Sandra created a shallow stone bowl that was long enough to contain the entire glove. In that stone bowl, the Dungeon Core turned to the boiling vats used to boil the hides used in the making of the Leather. One of the byproducts of that process left behind in the vats was a sticky "glue" that was made from the prolonged boiling of the hides, from the random connective tissue that was removed from the actual skins. It was a little difficult to remove from the vats – because it was very sticky – but once she collected enough of it, she managed to fill the shallow stone bowl with the substance. Before it could dry, she had her Ape stick the gloves into it, coating the outside of them well and good.

Then, in another shallow bowl of the same size, she created very tiny granules of Dragon Glass – almost powdered, in fact – and then dipped the glue-covered gloves inside the bowl. Soon enough, when the pair of gloves were completely covered in the black Dragon Glass, she had them laid aside and allowed to cure. A few hours later, the glue had bonded to both the Glass and the Leather, creating an outer covering that would hopefully protect anything wearing them from the intense heat created by the forge.

Sandra controlled her Ape and tested out her new creation cautiously; after just under a minute of the glove being near the forge, it showed absolutely no ill effects from the heat. A less cautious test had her actually placing her Ape's entire hand inside the blazing hot forge and was rewarded for a similar result – though its body started to soften from being that close. The only drawback to the gloves that she could see was that they were a little stiff from the added glue and Dragon Glass, but the strength of her construct made that almost a non-issue.

After she was done and happy with her crafting of a brand-new unique pair of gloves, Sandra belatedly realized that she could've just done what Human Blacksmiths who worked with Titanium did, which was use enchanted clothing that would absorb the heat of anything over a certain temperature it came into contact with. She even thought she knew how to make the simple enchantment sequence and with a little practice could probably duplicate it…but that just wasn't quite as fulfilling as creating something new like she just did. It could be that she was too used to not having access to enchantments for her crafting purposes to rely on them or because she wasn't quite confident in her Enchanting abilities yet; regardless of the reason, she was much happier finding a more *mundane* way of achieving the same result – and it gave her some ideas for future uses of some of her materials.

Doing all of that took most of the day and partially into the night, but now that she could work Titanium without worrying about her Ape's hands and arms melting, Sandra bent her efforts to practicing with the new metal. She had only seen small amounts of Titanium worked while she was learning all she could about Blacksmithing, mainly because it was a rare material; despite not seeing it being handled very often, she had learned that it was relatively easy to work with.

She found that it was similar to working Steel in some ways, while the heating properties of it was more like Iron, but it was also more malleable than either of them when it was soft from the heat. She almost felt like she could shape it with her own hands…so she did – or at least with her Ape's hands. With the extreme strength of the Steelclad Ape, she was able to pinch, bend, and even *fold* the metal. *Now* ***this*** *is something you can't do with enchanted clothing like the Human Blacksmiths use;* the enchantment on those would cool the metal so quickly with only a touch that they would be useless in something like what she was doing.

When the metal was hot enough – nearly to its melting point – it almost acted like clay, where she could literally shape it into anything she wanted; however, the size and stiffness in her new gloves prevented her from doing anything that required detail, and anything more than basic shapes was hard to accomplish. Still, the heat-proof gloves did allow one thing she wasn't expecting when she created them – she didn't have to rely as much on the Dragon Glass-coated tools to handle the metal. Her Ape could actually physically hold it now, and she didn't have to worry about it slipping out of its grip.

Sandra spent the next few hours crafting weapons from Titanium, starting with some smaller knives and working her way up to a longsword; what she really wanted to do was to make a warhammer for her Steelclad Ape Warriors to use, because she could already tell that the new metal was definitely stronger and weighed slightly less – meaning they could swing them faster and harder. They wouldn't have as much weight behind them, but she didn't think that would matter too much; most of the damage they inflicted on their targets was due to the strength of the Apes themselves wielding the weapons.

She wasn't able to test that quite yet, however, because the day was just starting – and there was a lot of work to be done.

Chapter 15

The first day of "learning" how to manipulate elemental energy didn't quite go as well as Sandra had hoped it would. She used the term loosely because it was just so foreign to her that it was hard to comprehend what she was supposed to be doing, so not much "learning" was done. It wasn't that Echo was a bad teacher or anything, but she apparently assumed that Sandra had a knowledge of some *basic* concepts that she actually didn't – like how to hold energy outside of her Shapeshifter's body when it wasn't being used in an enchantment.

Normally, all she had to do to use the elemental energy inside of her shapeshifting Dungeon Monster was to pull it out and immediately feed it into the enchantment she was creating; she never pulled more or less than she wanted – even if it was a mistake to use so much in an enchantment – because it was practically natural to her at that point. She likened it to what she did when she created almost anything inside her dungeon: Dungeon Monsters, Monster Seeds, and even traps automatically pulled out what was needed to create them, and she didn't have to measure it out.

In fact, the only experience she had in handling raw Mana like that was when she was creating her Elemental Orbs and Cubes. Thinking that would be a good place to start...she immediately found that it wasn't anything similar to what needed to be done. There were a multitude of reasons, from a different way she needed to pull it out from her body to how she needed to concentrate on it to keep control of it rather than letting it dissipate, but the end result was that she was unable to do much of *anything* that first day.

To be fair, though, she was making progress.

At the end of the first day of alternating between her Unstable Shapeshifters because of their tendency to only keep their form for an hour at a time, Echo was nearly pulling her hair out trying to understand why Sandra couldn't do something so simple. Then, just minutes before the Dungeon Core could tell the Elf was about to give up for the day, she was finally able to look deep inside her Shapeshifter and yank out a large chunk of just over 500 Holy energy. Ecstatic and self-congratulatory, Sandra almost immediately lost control of it; floating untethered to anything, the bright white blob of energy floating in front of her Shapeshifter ignited in an even brighter light – which blinded everyone in the workshop and caused some seriously intense pain, at least she assumed so by their screaming.

Sandra immediately left her Shapeshifter – which was also blind but was fine when it lost its "Echo" shape and returned to its amorphous form – and threw out a huge blanket of over 5,000 Nether Mana, surrounding and smothering the bright light emanating from the Holy energy. She was momentarily worried when it didn't appear that even that much Mana would be enough because the floating energy/Mana combination started to expand;

after a few seconds, however, it shrunk back down and settled into a more stable floating form.

The screaming had fortunately stopped, and three of Sandra's Repair Drones were nearby to heal them of their blindness; she had them stationed in the workshop at all times, for just such a reason – or something equally destructive. A few minutes later they were all healed up from their temporary blindness and Sandra apologized for the accident – but she was also encouraged because she had made progress.

"I think you need to work on exactly how *much* you are bringing out from your body; a little goes a long way, you know," Echo said testily, before heading off to bed. Sandra had improved her room down below with her better leather for the bed itself and Finely Woven Cloth sheets for her, but as the Elf – and the Gnomes, who had made even more progress on their War Machine model (it was *almost* finished) – left in a disgruntled huff complaining about working conditions to get some sleep, the Dungeon Core knew she needed to find some way to make it up to them. When she saw Felbar scratching at something underneath his clothes as he walked away, Sandra had an idea.

Using another one of her excavated rooms, she divided the space into two equal halves with a stone wall that stretched nearly to the ceiling. Then in each divided area she created a large stone basin that was almost the entire length of the room at 20 feet and just under 10 feet wide; building it up so that it was over 6 feet deep towards the center of the basins, she created a series of steps a foot and a half wide that ran around the perimeter, getting deeper the closer to the center it went. When that was done, she added another narrow set of steps outside of the basins leading from the entrance of the room to the top of each basin.

When that was done, Sandra used her Mana to fill both basins in with water until they were close to full, the water perfectly contained inside the large stone tubs that were assembled without any joins or cracks. Next she created some traps that only involved Air and Water Mana, with only about a quarter of her maximum Mana used to complete it. With the Water portion of the trap, she made one pool stay consistently warm – almost bordering on *too* hot – and the other slightly on the cool side. Some of the Air portion of the trap caused little bubbles to erupt from the bottom of the hot pool, floating up to the top and agitating the water; she also took one of the traps she had seen in the Water-based Reptile dungeon and downgraded it severely – and switched the element. All along the edge of the stone steps inside the water, she had delicate air jets shooting out, creating a nice relaxing pressure against the water that slowly swirled the water around until it looked like a very safe whirlpool.

In addition, at the entrance/exit she also placed a hot Air trap that would blow powerfully downwards, so that anyone stepping out of the pools could walk over to it and get themselves dried off fairly quickly, with little slots in the stone floor that the water could run off into. Lastly, she concentrated on the room and its natural light source; while she couldn't shut it off completely, she could dim the lighting so that it was much softer than it was before.

Looking at her handiwork, she was pretty proud of what she had created; it didn't quite match the bath houses or hot springs she remembered from when she was alive as a Human, but it was close enough. In reality it was better, because it was controlled by Mana alone and had some extra characteristics to it – like the hot air dryer – that she hadn't seen before. She didn't really have any type of soap at the moment but given enough time she could maybe make some, though it wouldn't smell very pleasing. Regardless, she had made a place where her Visitors could bathe and relax if they wanted to; she couldn't smell them, of course, but weeks stuck down in a dungeon – at least as far as the Gnomes went – probably didn't bode well for personal hygiene when there wasn't anywhere for them to wash.

She tied the entire thing to a small Hyper Automaton who acted as a catalyst for the dual-element trap, who could trigger the entire trap just by walking over a specific spot. When it was triggered, she estimated that it would last for just under two hours – which was plenty of time to get clean or even just relax.

Amazingly, she got all of that done within two hours and it was just barely dark outside; her Visitors had gone to bed early after the whole "blinding" incident – which she couldn't blame them for – so now Sandra had most of the night to work on other projects. The first thing she did was finish her experimental crafting with Titanium, creating a single warhammer made exclusively from the metal; after giving it to one of her Apes, she found that it could indeed swing it faster and it didn't appear too much lighter than the Steel ones it was using earlier.

The Titanium, however, was stronger and would hold up to the abuse it would likely see in battle; a few of the warhammers she had given her previous eradication force – before it was destroyed, of course – had started to show some damage and dents, though none of them had been rendered ineffective. If Sandra equipped them with the new warhammers, though, they would probably be able to fight longer with the weapons before they failed under the extreme abuse they'd be under. That was, of course, before she enchanted them.

She wasn't exactly sure how to go about that yet, but she had plans; Sandra needed Violet's help initially to get started because of the Dungeon Core's inexperience, but she was hoping she'd be able to take over the enchanting after that with her Unstable Shapeshifters. There were a few things she thought she could add to the weapons to make them more powerful – and suited to taking out the Undead Dungeon Monsters – though it was going to have to wait until the War Machine was done.

Speaking of that, since she was on a Titanium kick lately, Sandra started replacing all of the Steel components on the Gnome construct with new Titanium parts. It was actually fairly easy since the structure was already there, she just absorbed the Steel sections one by one and placed the new metal in its place. That took another couple of hours of quick work, and by the time it was done the inoperable War Machine was stronger and lighter – all it needed was the enchantments to make it operate. The main thing that Violet was missing was the linking enchantment, which she was planning on working on the next day with Sandra's input.

With the itch to craft with Titanium scratched, she turned to creating the Elemental Cubes in elements other than Fire and Spirit, which took another hour of intense concentration and most of her Mana; she didn't have quite enough to unlock the larger sizes quite yet, but it was enough for her to at least have access to the smallest of them at the moment.

She was knocking things off her list one-by-one and she was feeling extremely productive; she was occasionally glad that she was a Dungeon Core sometimes because she didn't have to sleep – she got so much more done than she would've otherwise. Of course, that was before the thought that she was only in her current position because she had actually *died* and didn't actually have a body to get tired – and that kind of made it a wash.

Next on her list was to complete the Lemon and Lime Fruit-producing Trees on her Transmutation Menu, as well as finally acquiring Redwood and Yew as usable wooden material; the trees required to unlock the two new fruits had fully grown a couple of days ago, but she had neglected to follow up with them. After acquiring the two woods by absorbing a portion of the trees, she opened up the Menu and started to select the Lemon option...before she paused in shock. Some of the mysterious requirements were now visible and some of the verbiage was slightly changed.

Organic/Inorganic Material Elemental Transmutation Menu				
Transmutation Options	Elemental Source Required (Size/Qty)	Mana Required	Additional Seed Material (Size/Qty)	Unlocked (Y/N)
Fruit-producing Tree Seeds				
-----	-----	-----	-----	-----
Lemon	Air Orb (Large/5)	50000/50000	Redwood (Large/4)	N
Lime	Natural Orb (Large/5)	60000/60000	Yew (Large/4)	N
Coconut	Spirit Cube (Small/4)	0/100000	Ironwood (Large/6)	N
Elderfruit	Natural Cube (Large/5), Holy Cube (Large/5), Spirit Cube (Large/5), Air Cube (Large/5)	0/1000000	Elderoak (Large/10)	N
Ambrosia	?????	0/25000000	?????	N

She looked at all of her options under the other categories and found that they were similar – with the new "Elemental Source Required" as one of the new Elemental Cubes she had just discovered. In addition, the "Additional Seed Material" showed one of the now-accessible materials that had been revealed with the addition of the Cubes, such as Ironwood for a Coconut requirement; Ironwood was now available to unlock because it needed Titanium as an Additional Seed Material.

Organic/Inorganic Material Elemental Transmutation Menu				
Transmutation Options	Elemental Source Required (Size/Qty)	Mana Required	Additional Seed Material (Size/Qty)	Unlocked (Y/N)
Metals				
Titanium	N/A	N/A	N/A	Y
Platinum	Spirit Cube (Average/3)	0/5000000	Fire Clay (Large/6)	N
Orichalcum	Nether Cube (Large/7), Water Cube (Large/7), Earth Cube (Large/7), Fire Cube (Large/7)	0/20000000	Ball Clay (Large/5), Fire Clay (Large/5), Kaolin Clay (Large/5)	N
Mithril	?????	0/50000000	?????	N
Fibrous Plant Seeds				
Bamboo Seed	Natural Cube (Small/3)	0/75000	Yew (Average/2)	N
Ramie Seed	Natural Cube (Average/3)	0/100000	Ironwood (Large/3)	N
Clays				
Ball Clay	Earth Cube (Tiny/3)	0/25000	Steel (Small/3)	N
Fire Clay	Earth Cube (Small/3)	0/40000	Steel (Average/3)	N
Kaolin Clay	Earth Cube (Average/3)	0/50000	Steel (Large/4)	N
Non-Fruit-Producing Tree Seeds				
Ironwood Seed	Natural Cube (Average/3), Earth Cube (Average/3)	0/500000	Iron (Large/7), Titanium (Large/7)	N

Elderoak Seed	Natural Cube (Large/4), Holy Cube (Large/4), Spirit Cube (Large/4), Air Cube (Large/4)	0/1500000	Steel (Large/10), Gold (Large/10), Titanium (Large/10), Platinum (Large/10)	N
Magewood Seed	?????	0/5000000	?????	N
Ancient Silverpine Seed	?????	0/10000000	?????	N
Precious Gemstones				
Topaz	Earth Orb (Large/6)	0/400000	Tin (Large/5)	N
Ruby	Fire Orb (Large/6)	268000/500000	Copper (Large/5)	N
Emerald	Natural Orb (Large/6)	0/1000000	Bronze (Large/5)	N
Diamond	Holy Orb (Large/6)	0/10000000	Steel (Large/5)	N
Moonstone	Spirit Cube (Large/5), Air Cube (Large/3), Holy Cube (Large/3)	0/20000000	Titanium (Large/15) Platinum (Large/15)	N
Dragon's Eye	Fire Cube (Large/8), Earth Cube (Large/6), Nether Cube (Large/4), Natural Cube (Large/2)	0/50000000	Dragon Glass (Average/5) Platinum (Large/20) Orichalcum (Average/10)	N
Magistone	?????	0/100000000	?????	N

This is...unbelievable! It appeared as though with enough time – and enough Mana – she could unlock nearly everything on the Transmutation list. There were a few of the more incredible options that were still a mystery as far as what they required, but there were plenty of other things to work with already. Some of the things she now had potential access to were things she never thought she would see, let alone work with, such as Orichalcum and Elderoak; others were so legendary that she had largely ignored them previously because they seemed so far out of reach...but not anymore.

As much as Sandra wanted to funnel all of her Mana for the next few months – or perhaps years – into unlocking *everything,* she still had obligations she had to take care of first. To that end, she went ahead and unlocked the Lemon and Lime Tree Seeds – like she had originally been doing – and then planted them inside her growing room. They were already "paid for" earlier, so it didn't require any more investment on her part.

After that, Sandra spent the rest of the night working on her Enchanting skills with her Shapeshifters, making more of the Large Elemental Orbs for them to work with, and planning out the linking sequence that was going to be needed for the larger War Machine in order for it to work. Upon some reflection of what was likely going to be needed, she made some alterations to the body of the War Machine; she wanted to make sure that the Gnome construct stayed powered for a long time without having to worry about replacing faded runes that were out of energy. As a result, she hollowed out two square areas of the wood-and-metal contraption that were just big enough to put a Large Energy Cube into.

Since there were Spirit and Natural elements in the enchantment sequence, it only made sense that they would need both Energy Cubes to power them; while the Stasis Fields over the RRPs could only take a single Cube because there was only Spirit energy within them, Sandra assumed that the two connected to the War Machine's enchantment sequence wouldn't interfere with each other, since they were two completely different energy sources.

At least, she hoped so, because if they ended up amplifying the amount of energy being pumped into the enchantment, then she didn't want to be anywhere within a mile of the War Machine when it exploded.

*Hopefully the model will tell us if it will work or not; if **that** explodes, however, I may need to rethink my strategy.*

Chapter 16

"Wait...you want to...what?" Violet asked, shock running through her at the implications of what Sandra was saying.

** I want to power all the enchantments with Large Energy Cubes, so that the War Machine can run for a lot longer. It should theoretically stay operational and won't have to be serviced to replace the runes very often. And, if it works like I'm thinking of, the additional elemental energy feeding the various rune sequences will allow them to be used to their fullest potential. That is, if you don't think having two Cubes attached will cause any problems? **

She had briefly thought about adding a smaller Energy Orb to the War Machine to help with the linking rune sequence, because it was what used most of the energy for the entire enchantment. The additional energy feeding into it would help maintain the entire sequence structure for longer periods, especially since it wasn't likely to be as efficient as the ones made by Master Enchanters; the division of separate enchantments all over the construct meant that more was needed to tie it all together. She was planning on having to maintain the Natural runes and replace them as they wore out, but with what Sandra was proposing, there wouldn't be any problems at all making sure it was all operational for a long time.

"I don't believe having two different elemental Energy sources will have an adverse effect, because they shouldn't interact with each other. As for their 'fullest potential', are you saying what I think you're saying?"

** Absolutely; without having to worry about depleting the Natural rune sequences too quickly, Felbar should be able to move much faster than he was previously able. Essentially, the only limit will be how much the materials the War Machine is made of can withstand what is being done to it. **

Normally the War Machine pilots were limited to only moving at a certain speed to ensure that the energy in the runes weren't depleted too quickly; it was only in an emergency that they could and would speed their constructs up to escape potential disaster. There really wasn't a limit to how *fast* the Machines could move, but the wood and metal material it was made from could only handle so much stress before it started to break down. Slower movements negated most of the wear-and-tear they would experience over time – as well as using much less energy –but the potential was always there to move *much* faster.

Violet and Felbar had already noticed that the larger War Machine had been altered quite a bit while they were asleep; there were some strange areas around the base of the torso that Sandra explained as compartments for Energy Cubes, but that wasn't the only change. The steel it had been made from before had been replaced with Titanium, which was much stronger and a little more lightweight, making the entire construct better able to withstand the stress it would be under if its enchantments were pushed to the limit. It was just a shame that the wooden parts of it were made of sturdy oak instead of something harder and more durable, but there were no special trees nearby that could provide that type of strength, even in the other races' lands – or so she'd heard.

"I can definitely see that you've been busy; you're also right – the War Machine can move much faster, though the oak the body is made of won't be able to withstand that kind of work it sounds like you want it to go through." More than half of the Machine was made from wood to reduce the weight of the entire construct, which prevented too much stress being put on the legs and lower joints; it also prevented it from being too top-heavy, which could result in the War Machine falling over when quick movements were made.

Twisting and turning the wooden torso was important for combat, otherwise the construct would be extremely limited in how it could attack and defend itself. That was why Violet thought it was a valid concern about the oak being put under too much stress; while wood actually bent and flexed better even than Titanium, it also tended to show wear-and-tear faster because of that for some reason. As she should've known, however, Sandra seemed to have an answer for that, too.

** I'm going to be working on that soon; I'm planning on having access to some Ironwood within the next few days, so I should be able to replace all of the oak as well. **

That was great news, but it also meant that it would delay the completion of the War Machine and consequently their departure for home. She felt it was imperative that they get back to their lands to let everyone know the current status of everything going on near the wastelands, as well as the news they had learned about the other races. While Jortor and the others had departed and were likely already halfway back to the capital, they didn't have all of the information. More importantly – at least to Violet – was the need to get back to a place where everything felt...normal.

Not that the Dungeon Core hadn't done what she could to make them more comfortable, such as giving them a place to sleep and providing food to eat – even if it was a bit limited in variety (meat and fruit only went so far). Violet was starting to dream of a delectable vegetable stew served with hot, steaming bread that had a crispy outer crust and soft delicious inner portion—

Anyway, despite all that, being enclosed in what was essentially a furnished cave wasn't something that Gnomes could get used to; she missed being able to see the sky whenever she wanted to and was tired of it being slightly cool wherever she went inside the dungeon – bundling up with some extra clothes (that Sandra also provided) wasn't really enough to make her comfortable.

Then there was the fact that when they had to...defecate...they had to go to a private corner in another room and do their business; the ability the dungeon possessed to completely absorb and get rid of their waste was beneficial, but it was just another thing that made the whole place...strange. Violet was more than ready for some normalcy and to really step back and evaluate all that she had personally learned from her experiences so far. Not only that, but she would try to kill one of those massive lizards that attacked her village with her bare hands if it meant she could take a bath. She would even settle for a dip in a freezing cold lake at that point – and would throw Felbar in as well, because she was pretty sure he stunk more than she did...or at least that was what she was telling herself.

The Elf hadn't appeared yet, but Violet honestly couldn't blame her for not being eager to go in the morning. Echo was obviously frustrated by the lack of progress trying to teach Sandra how to manipulate elemental energy in order to cast spells, and after the painful blinding light from yesterday the Elf was probably reluctant to suffer through something like that again. Violet vividly remembered how much it had hurt when the light seemed to burn through her eyes and into her head – and she had been on the other side of the room; she couldn't even imagine what Echo had experienced being so close to the light's point of origin.

For herself, however, the Gnome was excited to get to work. They were very close to finishing the War Machine model's enchantments and today would likely see if everything would work properly together. They still had the linking enchantment to do – which Violet had to admit intimidated her a little – and to test out if two different-element Energy Orbs could be used on the same enchantment to power. They had finished everything else the day before and Felbar had tested each enchantment individually…now they just had to put it all together.

Violet listened as Sandra communicated in detail her vision of what needed to be done to tie all of the enchantments together, and it was certainly a daunting task. Not only that, but it was going to be different from what Felbar was used to when controlling a War Machine; it was necessary that it be different because it wasn't all on the same enchantment sequence like the Master Enchanters back home could make, but it would also take some adjustment on the veteran Warmaster's part.

In fact, it wasn't until she was really designing the enchantment sequence in her mind that she realized what the biggest difference was: there was no need for the pilot to supply Spirit energy at all. Instead of activating each of the rune sequences with an extremely small amount of energy from the pilot, it would all be controlled by the linking enchantment – which would in turn be powered by a Large Spirit Energy Cube. What it also meant – and what gave her a moment's pause at the implications she suddenly saw stemming from it – was that *anyone* could pilot the War Machine, not just those Gnomes with access to Spirit energy. It would still require them to learn how to manipulate the new runes to get them to work, but with the improvements they were making, the training time could be drastically reduced. Even *she* could probably do it, though it would likely take a while to get to the point where she wouldn't make it fall down with every step – not that she wanted to pilot it in the first place.

In short, the simplification of the overall enchantment rune sequence made it accessible to all.

"Alright, then – let me see what I can do. I don't know if this will work, but if it does – it could change everything," Violet said, keeping her rambling thoughts about the enchantment to herself. She could tell that Felbar noticed a change in how everything was created – *how could he not* – but he wasn't entirely in the know on all the technical details; some of it was a bit advanced even from *Violet's* perspective, so the differences were a slight mystery even to her.

Reaching inside of herself, Violet pulled out a trickle of Spirit and Natural energy and got to work visually designing the rune sequence. It was a trick she had learned back home from her parents to learn the structure of an enchantment without providing it with enough power to actualize. It was a good way to practice something without worrying about it exploding or backfiring in any way, but it was also energy-consuming if you did it for too long. Fortunately, her Spirit and Natural Energy Orbs around her neck in a thin leather-string cage was enough to offset the expenditure.

Violet looked down at them and was surprised to see that they were almost half the size as they were when she first made them; she had been using so much elemental energy lately that it made sense, though. She could tell that the maximum amount of energy she could hold had increased as well, though it was hard to gauge by exactly how much.

If she were to guesstimate and give her capacity a number, she would say that when she arrived at Sandra's dungeon she could hold 500 each of Spirit and Natural energy; after just a few weeks of constant enchanting, however, she had probably doubled the amount of Spirit energy she could access (to approximately 1,000 or more) and increased her Natural energy by half (to approximately 750). The difference was because she had been using Spirit energy much more in her earlier experiments, though with the War Machine she had been primarily been using Natural elemental energy.

The hardest part of designing a brand-new enchantment sequence was that she could never be sure it would work unless she actually tried it with the required elemental energy, but the visual model she made floating in front of her allowed her to place everything just how she wanted during the design process. Whether or not it would work was something else entirely, of course, but she was slowly learning that she could *feel* when it would do something as she stuck specific runes in place – good or bad, though, was up in the air.

For this linking enchantment, she designed thin sequences of simple **Transfer** runes with alternating Spirit and Natural elemental energy that would connected to a specific place on each existing enchantment on the model War Machine. These sequences led back to an area behind the model on the workshop's stone floor and a nearby waist-high stone block – as well as a sturdy leather harness with a lead fused to the block – which would act as a kind of center where commands could be given; the lines linking the arm, leg, and torso enchantments almost looked like small blood vessels that led back to a heart – or perhaps a brain would be a more appropriate analogy.

It was this area – which would be in the pilot's enclosure on the larger War Machine, but had to be separate on the smaller model – that would act as the control center; commands given from there would be *transferred* to the linked enchantments, which would in turn control the movements of the construct. In the Machines that she was used to, the entire system was all one enchantment, which helped to equalize the energy drain during use and made the operation of the construct "sip" at the overall energy infused into the rune sequences; this new system would practically "gulp" in comparison, but the Energy Cubes would easily provide that energy.

The way commands were given was a unique combination of **Pressure Feedback**, **Convert**, **Activate**, and **Control** rune sequences layered on top of each other with the two different elements. If that wasn't difficult enough to deal with, there were also a total of five of these command enchantments that would control different parts of the War Machine: one for each arm and leg, and a fifth that would control the torso. The arm controls would be placed on the stone block while the legs were on the floor; the torso would be controlled by the leather harness and would mimic the movements of whoever was piloting the construct.

For the purposes of the model, the linking sequence "command center" was connected from the stone and leather materials through a series of very thin copper wires that were fused to the back of the model; the metal was remarkably flexible but it was so thin that she needed to be fairly precise with her enchantment development to ensure it infused the material. On the larger War Machine the linking enchantment would be mostly internal, fortunately, so they didn't have to worry about that so much – but it made the testing process a little harder...but also safer.

Violet spent over two hours working on visually building the linking sequence – while blocking out everything around her – before she was satisfied that it would...do something. She let the non-powered enchantment fade from her view and looked around the workshop as she got accustomed to the world again; she felt like she was waking up from an out-of-body experience after finishing the design and she realized that she had just spent more time in that phase than she ever had before. She felt drained despite her elemental energy levels being near full from the constant regeneration from the Energy Orbs, but she had a feeling she had gone through her entire capacity more than once.

The way she was feeling was completely at odds with how the Elf looked, who had apparently shown up at some point while she was working. Echo appeared to be rested and refreshed, if a little flushed for some reason; she even had what appeared to be a genuine smile on her face, which was a little strange to see on the normally surly or sarcastic Elf. Felbar was nearby and talking to her, and he had a small grin as well.

"...I'll be sure to let her know; she's been working really hard to finish these enchantments on the War Machine, and I'm confident she'll be pleased to hear about it. Truth be told, I think I need one as well—" Felbar was saying to Echo, before he saw Violet looking in their direction and cut himself off. "Ah, you're done! There's a pleasant surprise waiting for you when you're ready for it," he continued, still grinning from ear to ear.

She had no idea what he was talking about, but she wasn't about to let herself get distracted. The design for the linking enchantment was fresh in her mind and she was ready to test it out, for better or worse. "I'll check it out once I'm done with this – I don't want to lose it."

Turning her attention away from the others, she picked up the two tiny Energy Orbs with **Limiter** runes she had created earlier – one Spirit and one Natural – and placed them on the two little slots carved into the back of the War Machine; once they were in and secured with a simple metal flap, she started the process of creating the linking enchantment – for real this time.

After playing around with them so much during the design phase, the process went faster than she thought it would; as she quickly used her Spirit and Natural elemental energy to first create the **Transfer** sequences, she started to worry that she wasn't going to have enough to complete it all despite being full. Building one control module after another, she breathed a sigh of relief as she found that she indeed had enough, though it was close with her lower quantity of available Natural energy. When she filled the last rune of the enchantment sequence, Violet started to tremble as she held it steady for a moment, before carefully connecting the entire thing to the two tiny Energy Orbs.

The entire sequence she had created – as well as the prior enchantments she had created on the model – flared brightly for a moment and she thought she had made a mistake somewhere; in less than a second, however, the light faded, and everything seemed to stabilize. Violet found that she had collapsed to her knees at some point from the strain of holding everything together, so before it could get any worse she took a deep breath...and let the enchantment finish.

The rune sequences seemed to sink into the materials she had used for them, from the stone and leather harness, to the copper wires, to the wood and metal of the model itself. The Apprentice Enchanter waited for something to happen and readied herself to scoot backwards out of the way...but nothing happened. In fact, she wasn't even sure it actually worked, until she reached a hand over to the right arm control module and placed her fingers on it.

The arm on the model shot upwards, until it was pointing towards the ceiling with its battleaxe attached to the end of its "hand". Violet slowly moved her fingers down the control module and watched as the arm came down and moved side to side as she continued to adjust her fingers. She felt a smile of her own slowly creep across her face as she realized what it meant.

I did it! It worked!

There was still a lot of testing that needed to be done, of course, but it was a very good sign that nothing had blown up or seemed to have any other issues so far. As she looked over to the applause of both Felbar and Echo, she felt a strange sensation pass over her.

** Congratulations, Violet! Or should I say Journeyman Enchanter Violet – at least that's what your name says on my Visitor list now. I didn't want to bother you before because you appeared to be determined to finish the enchantment – and what an enchantment it is – but like Felbar mentioned, there is a surprise for you I think you will like. And you deserve to take a much-needed break after that! **

"Nice job, Violet! I can't wait to practice with it while you get washed up, and don't worry – I'll be partaking later," Felbar said excitedly.

Washed up? What does he mean? Violet was so exhausted from the enchantment that she walked in a daze out of the workshop as Sandra told her where to go. She had no reason to argue, but she had enough presence of mind to let the Dungeon Core know something important. "I…don't believe that I'll be able to complete the enchantment on the larger War Machine by myself; that smaller model almost wiped me out all by itself, and I'm worried that the other will be impossible with my current energy levels."

** Don't worry about that; I had figured that it was going to require more than just one to complete it, even if it is simpler than what your Master Enchanters create. I saw what you did to put it all together, and while I'm pretty sure I couldn't duplicate the entire thing right now with my fledgling skills, I do have some access to some more Journeyman Enchanters that can at least help with portions of it, you know. **

It took Violet a moment to understand what Sandra meant by that, but then she realized she meant her Shapeshifters. *Well, if that is what it takes, then I guess that's what I have to put up with—*

She unknowingly walked into a dimly lit room that felt warm for once, and she stopped when she saw a series of steps leading up. Blinking in surprise and confusion, she walked up the left-side steps at Sandra's direction and as soon as she saw what it was she felt her smile come back full force.

** I made some crude soap from mixing up fat from Crag Hound meat and the ashes from some burnt trees and leaves, before adding in some different fruit juice scents from crushed Oranges, Peaches, and Apples; it's pretty basic, but at least I'm hopeful that it doesn't smell like rancid flesh – which is what Echo said the unscented soap smelled like. Enjoy and relax as long as you like...you deserve it. **

As she stripped down and slid into the almost too-hot water, feeling the air bubbles and jets shooting at her from various directions in a way that seemed to loosen up her muscles. *I think I'll even forgive Sandra for using copies of me to enchant the War Machine.* Reaching for one of the square blocks of soap laid out along one edge of the hot water pool, she smelled oranges as she lathered herself up, scraping off weeks of dirt as she rinsed. When she was as clean as she thought she was going to get, she sat on one of the steps inside the water, relaxing completely for the first time since their village was attacked.

I think I could get used to this...

Chapter 17

Things seemed to be coming together nicely; Violet – now a Journeyman Enchanter for some reason Sandra didn't quite comprehend – had created the linking enchantment successfully; Felbar was currently practicing with the model with some success, though he was having to learn a whole new control scheme; and Echo was refreshed and forgave Sandra for blinding her the night before.

Of course, as seemed the norm when things were going well, the Dungeon Core felt a drastic change somewhere.

Winxa, it looks like I was right – the Undead Core just expanded its Area of Influence.

"Well, you knew it would happen eventually, so it shouldn't be a surprise," the Dungeon Fairy said. "How close is it to the Dwarves now?"

Sandra looked at the other Core's AOI and confirmed what she had felt initially; the distance they overlapped seemed to have increased by at least two miles – which was a fairly significant increase, and more than she was expecting. Even though she couldn't see every part of the Undead Core's range, she estimated that it was at least halfway through the nearby Golem Core's area; it was possible that along the far edges of the smaller Core's territory it would be able to attack the Dwarves. All of that she relayed to the Dungeon Fairy, who looked a little worried.

"Such an increase in its Area of Influence likely means that it hit Core Size 30 with its recent upgrade; if you remember, every 10 Sizes tends to have some extra benefits, and apparently a significant increase in its AOI was what it received," Winxa mused. "Unless, of course, it somehow found the Advancement system and is increasing it that way, but this appears to be too much even for that all at once."

That wasn't something Sandra wanted to even consider, because that would most likely make everything that much harder. It was bad enough if the other Core was already 10 Sizes above her, because that would likely mean that it had access to some nasty Dungeon Monsters; if some Advancements were placed on top of that, she worried for her chances of success.

What I really want to know, however, is how the Undead Core seemed to be able to direct its Dungeon Monsters while it was upgrading its Core Size – and how it seems to upgrade so quickly. Whenever ***I*** *go through an upgrade, I'm next to useless and it seems to take forever – especially the higher my Core Size became.*

"It probably isn't actively giving orders, but instead gave detailed, specific instructions to them before undergoing the process. Just like you can get the flying Shears around your Core to make random patterns to give you something to look at while you're upgrading, you can make those instructions even more detailed conditional parameters. For instance, you could have them do their little dance down here, but if your dungeon was invaded they could break off and fly off to defend a specific room.

This was basically what was happening with the other Core, though its orders were almost certainly designed to maintain a spread of its Monsters to achieve the highest Mana absorption rate, and to react to what you might do in pre-planned ways," Winxa replied, matter-of-factly. The fact that she could lay out a whole plan for her constructs while she was unavailable during an upgrade (or otherwise) was something that she'd have to keep in mind.

"As for the speed at which it seems to upgrade, it could be due to a number of factors. It could have a Core-specific Skill that increases the speed at which it upgrades and perhaps even reduces the amount of Mana required to do so; it could've already started the upgrade before you thought it did and finished in the normal amount of time; or – which I think is most likely – is that single-element Dungeon Cores require less time to upgrade than multi-element ones at higher Core Sizes. I've rarely stayed with Cores past Size 20, and those that I remember doing so had multiple elements; I'll have to check with the other Dungeon Fairies to see if that theory is true or not, but I suspect it is."

That's not good if it's true. Though, it would certainly explain how quickly this Undead Core has expanded, as well as the rapid expansion of the Reptile-Classification Dungeon Core I was forced to destroy. Thanks, Winxa.

Sandra briefly thought about trying to warn the Dwarves at that point to watch out for Undead, but she dismissed it after she realized they would still have a major communication barrier preventing such a warning. Besides, when she looked at their village and their efforts against the Golems – animated dirt-and-stone figures of different sizes, as well as even a few that she hadn't noticed before that appeared to be made of gravel – on one side and Goblins on the other, she saw that they were well equipped to take care of any Undead they found.

From the looks of them, the Dwarves seemed to be equipped with superior weaponry and armor – which was only to be expected with their Master Blacksmiths – that practically glowed with elemental energy. As opposed to the Orcs who used energy to enhance themselves, the Elves that manipulated energy outside of their bodies to cast spells, or the Gnomes that enchanted everything they could lay their hands on, the Dwarves used their energy in the process of crafting their armaments. The armor and weapons then used the energy from the ones using them to empower themselves; it was similar to enchanting in some respects, but the energy was *infused* in the crafted metal instead of through enchantment runes and thereby stronger – and more limited at the same time.

From what she understood, if the energy was completely drained from the armor or weapon – and by extension the Dwarf – then the metal would start to degrade and fall apart, rendering it useless. So, while their armor was stronger and could withstand impacts better than all but the most powerful enchantments, as soon as the energy ran out the Dwarves would be next to defenseless. In the same light, while their weapons were lighter-weight in terms of swinging them around, as well as being sharper and packed a punch when hitting Dungeon Monsters, once they ran out of energy...that was pretty much the end of the fight.

Enchantments, while less powerful in general, were much more versatile and didn't rely on the energy of the user to exist; and if they ran out, they usually didn't take the material the runes were enchanted onto with them as they deactivated. She could see the benefits in having energy-infused metal, though, because it made the wielders quite powerful, especially when she watched one of the dwarves out culling Goblins instantly light the edges of his double-bladed axe on fire as he lopped off an arm and then a leg from a surprisingly large and strange-looking one.

"It was probably a Hobgoblin, which are a bit larger than your normal run-of-the-mill Goblin," Winxa answered her question when she told the Fairy about what she saw. "And the Dwarves can also use their energy to produce effects like that fire you saw in their weapons and even their armor, as long as it matches what elements they have access to. You can usually see a slight tint to the metal depending on which element each piece of their armament was crafted with, not unlike those gear tattoos you formed on all your Visitors."

Now that she was really looking, Sandra could definitely see that the armor and axe the Dwarf was carrying had a noticeable reddish tint to it, especially when she looked at some of the others she saw that were fully equipped. She saw some green, brown, blue, and even a very slight hint of yellow in one of them, which she assumed was for Natural, Earth, Water, and Air; she didn't see any black, white, or grey, but they might be out in the forest culling where she couldn't see them. Regardless, Sandra thought they were well equipped to kill any Undead they saw with their access to various elements, though if they were forced to fight too many for a prolonged period of time they could have some issues.

It was only when the Undead Core upgraded again that they would be in danger of direct attack. Though, unless they expanded their AOI by another few miles, then the Dwarves' actual village – if not the surrounding open lands – was safe for the time being even with another upgrade; Sandra and her own dungeon, because of the specific placement of the Undead Core and her relative proximity to it, *might* be in danger of being attacked. She wasn't overly worried despite the danger, because her dungeon and traps should be more than powerful enough to destroy whatever came her way.

She wasn't going to take that for granted, of course, as evidenced by the way those Elite Elves almost destroyed her Core. Luckily she had some time before that became a real possibility so she planned on adding some improvements to what she had...but she doubted that the Undead-based Core would even attack her unless she provoked it – there wasn't a lot of benefit in doing so. The Reptile-based Core had attacked her because she had directly intervened between it and the Gnomes, taking away some of its "meal"; if the Undead Core did the same to the Dwarves, that would likely happen again, but she was hoping to destroy it before it got to that point.

The major danger was in the wastelands now, as the AOI of the other Core had greatly expanded inside of it; most of the previously clear route to the Gnome lands was cut off except on the extreme southeastern side near the former Reptile forest, making travel that way dangerous. It was looking more and more like Violet and Felbar were going to have to wait until the necessary deed with the Undead Dungeon Core was done before they went home.

Her Rolling Force eradication group of constructs had wiped out all of the skeletons and zombies that had ventured out of the forest over the last few days and had even taken to hunting the few Undead they found within the first few hundred feet within the trees; it was now obvious why there hadn't been much in the way of reinforcements because of the Core's Size upgrade, but with that changed Sandra started to see more skeletons coming out into the open. Now that they had even farther in which to roam, they were even more spread out – which made her forces have to split up in order to keep up with them.

She added another 500 of her rolling constructs to keep up with the culling, but with nothing that could really be done about the Undead for the moment, Sandra turned her attention back to ways to accomplish the ultimate task of destroying the Core. While she started to funnel her incoming Mana into the Ironwood Seed Transmutation option – which required 500,000 Mana in addition to the resources it needed – she started to work with Echo again on learning to manipulate energy outside of her body.

Fortunately, the breakthrough from the night before was apparently all she needed to finally make some progress. Taking it very cautiously, she learned how to bring out just a few Holy energy units from her Shapeshifter; after a while she started to get a feel for how much energy she was bringing out, though trying to compare it to Mana was for some reason trying to compare a candle flame to a bonfire. Elemental energy was much less...dense, she supposed...which was probably why she had yanked out so much the day before when she expected it to be a lot less.

Regardless, within a few hours she was able to take out and put back any amount of energy she wanted – though not all, as was evidenced when her Shapeshifter started to lose its form when she tried to take the entire amount out. Fortunately, Sandra was able to shove it all back in before she lost control of it, otherwise the Holy energy might've caused more than some painful blinding. After that, she stuck to very small amounts – at least until she could figure out how to manipulate it properly to do what she wanted with it.

Luckily for her, that was the easy part. It turned out that once she had the energy pulled out from her body – which was initially very difficult – the actual manipulation was startlingly familiar to what she did with her Mana. The major difference was that it was done from a singular perspective instead of through her normal dungeon senses, so it took particularly focused concentration to perform the simplest of tasks in comparison. That was even considering that she wasn't using it to create traps that had triggers and multiple moving parts, but instead were powerful manifestations of the elements.

"How did you...do that so easily?" Echo asked, astonished, after Sandra had created a bubble-like shield of Holy energy around her Shapeshifter. Now that she finally had control over the energy, she started to manipulate it in ways that were only limited by her imagination.

** Now that I can finally use this energy, I found that it is remarkably similar to the Mana I've been using; my Mana is a lot more...potent...I suppose you could say, but I've been using it ever since I became a Dungeon Core, so it's natural to me, I guess. **

The only thing Sandra needed help with was devising ways to use the energy effectively for attacks. Most of her traps inside her dungeon were of a defensive nature, despite their deadliness, so going on the offensive was something else entirely. She usually had her Dungeon Monsters for that kind of thing, and while she was starting to learn a little bit about tactics from watching many battles over the last few weeks, it didn't really include spell-casting – especially with Holy and Air as elements. She had a few ideas from watching the Elite Elves tear through her dungeon, but they also looked more complicated and energy-consumptive.

"Well, if that's the case, then this will go much smoother than I anticipated," Echo said with a relieved smile, though her astonishment was still showing on her face. "Who would've thought that the easiest part of the whole process was going to turn out to be the hardest for you..." she muttered under her breath.

For the rest of the day and into the evening – with a few breaks in between sessions – Echo started to teach Sandra all of the different ways she knew of to use Holy and Air elemental energy. It was actually very informative because her ability to manipulate the energy so easily was both a benefit and a curse, apparently. It was like having a large lump of easily moldable clay in her hands, but she had no idea what to do with it; she might have a vague idea of what a specific type of pot looked like, but without a picture to go by or specific instructions sometimes her efforts would be a shot in the dark rather than a guaranteed success.

That was the main difference she found between using her Mana for traps or other things in her dungeon and the elemental energy she was handling with her Shapeshifter; Mana was easily quantifiable, structured, and ordered, while elemental energy was a bit more fluid and almost wild. It was another reason she liked Enchanting so much, because while it used the same energy she was manipulating now, it was used in a structured rune or rune sequence to achieve a desired result.

Therefore, while she could manipulate it fairly easily, other than a few things like the Holy-based bubble shield and using her Air energy to create a miniature whirlwind that could slice up her skin if she put her hand in the middle of it, everything else was just a guess. When Echo began telling her details – and a few demonstrations – of various spells she knew, the way they were made became much easier to comprehend. For instance, with the Lightstrike spell, it seemed obvious after the fact that she needed to compress the energy together, elongate the entire mass so it looked like a long stick, and then form a sharp tip on one end before mentally "throwing" it forward – but it was a mystery before Sandra was given some nudges in the right direction.

Despite Echo being able to use Air and Holy energy, that didn't mean she was anywhere near an expert in their use; she could easily demonstrate the way she became "invisible" and left echoes of her form using her Holy element, as well as how she used Air to speed herself up, but the other spell knowledge she had was relatively basic. Describing it, however, allowed Sandra to experiment and figure them out – and even to help teach the Elf how to do those certain things even better. It was a learning experience for both of them, and it was greatly beneficial all around.

The rest of that day Felbar continued to practice with the War Machine model; he was having a slightly harder time than Sandra had expected, but when she remembered what his normal piloting consisted of it made sense. With the older constructs, the older Gnome would wear a special suit that was able to tie into the entire enchantment, conveying via small energy infusions the movements he wanted to perform with the War Machine itself. It took specialized training to properly control it all and required him to provide those energy infusions at the same time, though he could manually move parts of the construct by focusing on certain parts of the enchantment itself.

The new control modules, in comparison, were almost completely different in design. Sandra watched him occasionally jerk his own body around and infuse extra energy into the enchantment, which only served to degrade the runes as they acquired just a touch too much energy – and it didn't help him control it any more than that. He was slowly learning how to operate everything differently from what he was used to, but it was clear that his previous – and *instinctual*, by that point – training was interfering with his practice. Over time the Dungeon Core knew he would get it, but she was just glad he was training with the model instead of the real thing, otherwise it could be dangerous for everyone.

Violet came back after a while, looking relaxed and ready to go again. She also worked with Felbar to replace runes that were getting worn out from the mistaken energy influxes, as well as adjusted a few that weren't quite perfect by replacing them altogether. Nothing was seriously wrong, fortunately, and by the end of the day the entire enchantment was working as flawlessly as possible.

The next few days was a repeat of mostly the same. Felbar continued to practice with the model, getting more accustomed to the new control scheme enough that Sandra actually brought some of her smaller constructs nearby for him to practice with "live" targets. Violet worked on completing the enchantments for the

Titanium arms and legs on the larger War Machine, continuing with the torso when Sandra replaced it with Ironwood midway into the second day.

New Origination Material found!

Ironwood Tree Seed
While Ironwood Tree Seed cannot be directly used as a Monster Seed, it can be used in specific applications to create a whole new Monster Seed.

New Monster Seed and Origination Material found!

Ironwood Wood
While Ironwood Wood can be directly used as a Monster Seed, it can also be used as a material for use in the dungeon or other purposes.

You now have access to:
Tiny Ironwood Wood Chip
Origination Raw Material Cost: 500
Origination Mana Cost: 250
Monster Min. Mana: 250
Monster Max. Mana: 600

Ironwood had a distinctly darker color than any of her other wood types, and while it was a little heavier than the Oak that was being used before, it was *very* durable. It also cost a bit more resources to create, but Sandra had plenty saved up or constantly coming in to supply that need. One side-effect that Violet instantly noticed when enchanting the Ironwood was that it seemed to take to the enchantment sequence faster; when she began to put all the runes together, the wood seemed almost to suck it into itself, locking it in place with a solid foundation. With neither of them ever having seen Ironwood enchanted before, they weren't sure if it was beneficial or not, but once the enchantment was there it appeared to be somehow *strengthened* – which might make it less likely to be damaged in combat, which happened occasionally with normal wood.

Her new status as a Journeyman Enchanter didn't seem to affect Violet too much, though Sandra could see some extra confidence in her bearing as well as her Enchanting efforts. She had also increased her energy capacity enough that she could complete all but the linking enchantment by herself, which was an enormous feat in and of itself.

Echo taught all that she could to Sandra and her own "copies", so her Shapeshifters changed into the other forms of the Elite Elves to practice with other elements – with some limited success. The most beneficial manipulation of the other elements was the ability to throw out a small Fireball spell, which was essentially a smallish roiling ball of super-hot flames approximately the size of one of the Elves' fists. She found that she could launch it only about 20 feet before it dissipated, and once it hit something it would flare up for a moment a little larger and then disperse.

Of the other elements, she had some ideas of how to use them – but couldn't find the proper method of their creation. After she accidentally killed one of her Shapeshifters by creating a nasty Nether void of some kind that consumed almost two-thirds of its body within a matter of seconds, she gave up until she had some better instruction.

After Echo was done teaching – and learning – she went back to the village with another shipment that Sandra had managed to squeeze in when she had the time and Mana. When she came back the same day, the Dungeon Core was surprised; however, a couple of hours spent in the hot pool down below was evidence enough why she returned so eagerly. That, and she was interested in learning about Enchanting – and Sandra eagerly tried to teach her what she could.

It was actually good timing because she was also finishing up her Enchantment Repository Room. After a lot of practice making the Energy Orb and even Energy Cube enchantments, Sandra had learned how to finally incorporate the **Limiter** rune into it; she had also practiced making the Preservation Barriers/Stasis Fields that Violet was so good at, so that she could enchant brand-new Pillars herself – as well as replace the ones that were starting to run out of elemental energy with ones that incorporated the new Cube.

She, of course, experimented with *much* smaller enchantments first, but once Violet looked at them and approved of them – and Sandra felt somewhat proud of that – she finished off the rest of the Repository. Once she had completed Pillars for most of her materials – at least the ones that really mattered – she spent some time transferring as much of the knowledge she could remember of Enchanting onto them. It was at that point that Echo started to be curious about the process, and Sandra took the time to teach her.

The teaching of which was just about as successful as Sandra's first day learning how to cast spells. Enchanting was an extremely foreign concept to the Elf, but the Dungeon Core could see that there would eventually be some progress – though it would probably take a while; Sandra thought that Echo might eventually be able to create them (because the Elves *did* create some enchantments, though not nearly as many or as well as the Gnomes) but doubted she'd have the same instinctual feel of them that the smaller race seemed to have.

Eventually, with all the training and development of skills, the production of enchantments and upgrades to the materials on the War Machine, and the completion of the Enchantment Repository Room, they were ready to finish the final step: the complex and energy-consumptive linking enchantment.

Fortunately, Sandra had prepared for that.

Chapter 18

“Is she okay?” Echo asked Sandra as Violet collapsed to the stone floor. Felbar rushed over to the girl and placed her on her back instead of being in a tangled heap; Sandra knew she was fine because none of the Repair Drones nearby had even twitched when she fell. As for the Dungeon Core herself, she thought that if she had a body she’d be on the floor, too.

** Yes, she’ll be fine; she’s just exhausted after that intensely powerful and intricate enchantment. My Shifters took over what they could but controlling so many of them at once was much more…difficult…than I had anticipated. **

“Difficult” was a major understatement. For something as intricate as Enchanting, Sandra had needed to personally control each one to create the lines of linking rune sequences that led to each of the existing enchantments, as well as contributing what she could to the actual control modules – which wasn’t a lot because a few sections of the sequences were a little more intricate than she could easily do. Then, once she did a section with one Shifter, she would have to mentally instruct it to hold it in place while she went on to another. The mental strain of doing that wasn’t quite as intense as when she divided her concentration in the dungeon to complete multiple tasks – but it was amplified by the sheer number of Shifters she had doing it.

Who would've thought that controlling 20 Unstable Shapeshifters at the same time would be hard?

Sandra had done it, however, and so had Violet – though it had apparently taken all of her elemental energy to do that, even with a dozen mixed Spirit and Natural Energy Orbs hanging around her neck. Like she had told Echo, she needed some rest and she'd be fine; Sandra, on the other hand, was already starting to recover from the strain and she looked at the enchantment on the War Machine to see if it had taken properly – and was pleased at the result.

Her Shapeshifters had done a great job of maintaining each section they were responsible for, and they all amazingly meshed together without any hiccups; Sandra had to mentally congratulate herself for a job well done with so many "hands in the pot", but she acknowledged that it was almost like one – since they were all Violet's form doing the enchanting. Nevertheless, it was done, and she didn't see anything different from the one on the model—

What the—? That's not possible...

Sandra's attention was pulled away from the workshop and her dungeon as she felt a change somewhere else. She briefly thought that one of the Cores around the Orcs, Elves, or even the Dwarves had expanded its Area of Influence, but she just as quickly identified the culprit: the Undead Dungeon Core. Its AOI had expanded again, and just as she had feared it just barely overlapped her entire dungeon.

Winxa – how did it upgrade again so soon? I thought we had at least another week or two before this happened!

The Dungeon Fairy appeared to be at a loss and somehow scared; Sandra suddenly realized that she had practically shouted at Winxa – and it wasn't in a nice tone, either. Feeling bad but unable to apologize right away (because she *was* angry, though more at herself than the Fairy), she waited for a reply as she explored what she could of the Undead Core's new AOI. Looking towards the Dwarves, she saw that it stretched nearly to the forest's edge, only about a mile or less from being a serious threat to the village.

"I...I don't know. I know of no way that it could do that since you've been culling it so thoroughly; even if it *had* found the Advancement Menu, such a rapid increase wouldn't explain it," Winxa finally said in a small voice.

Taking a mental breath and trying to relax – the proximity of the Undead Core's Influence was putting her on edge – she finally apologized to the Dungeon Fairy.

** I'm sorry for yelling, Winxa – I just don't understand why— **

The answer to that came streaming out of the woods just then. Thousands of small rat skeletons emerged from the trees and spread out all over the open land, their little forms constantly in motion as they stayed separate from each other; they swept across the Gnome village and beyond, filling the open spaces, before bleeding into the wastelands. Eventually the flow of rat bones stopped coming; looking at the land from above, she could see that all of them had at least 20 feet in between them as they ran around in circles that slowly tightened towards their centers. Sandra couldn't understand what they were doing, until she backed up even further and caught a glimpse of her AMANS.

That sneaky little...

She'd been played, there was no doubt about it. The flow of simple skeletons and zombies really hadn't stopped gradually coming into the open land where her eradication force was systematically destroying them one by one. Sandra only had them venture a little ways into the forest, where she had found essentially the same thing – though there were stronger varieties the further in she went. She hadn't thought anything of it at the time, because she figured culling the greater quantity of weaker Dungeon Monsters would slow down the growth of the Core as opposed to trying to eliminate anything harder was the way to go.

Obviously, she had read the situation wrong. The explosion of growth could definitely be explained away by thousands of rat skeletons running around in circles in parts of the forest that she didn't really have access to because of the floating Specters. There was still a goodly sized area beyond the actual Undead dungeon that she couldn't even reach yet with her own AOI, and if that was filled with skeleton rats – who she *just* saw could also climb up and down trees – then they could act similarly to her own AMANS.

Sandra should've known that something was up after the trap that had destroyed her first force, but she had been distracted;

it wasn't a great excuse, of course, but it was the only one she had. It was *her* fault that the Undead Core had expanded so quickly; it had obviously seen her floating Shears and understood what they were being used for. Not only that, but she had been *too* cautious about exploring the forest and pushing towards as full of a cull as she could, so she had missed the signs that not everything was as it seemed. She had no one to blame but herself, and now things were going to start getting out of control unless she did something quickly.

The Undead Core had obviously been planning on revealing its skeletal rat army for some time, because as soon as her Rolling Forces started to smash them to pieces, another much larger – and more dangerous force emerged from the trees. She noticed that it was comprised of the same Undead as the group that had surprised her almost a week ago, though with greater numbers. They immediately headed for her eradication force, overtaking them within minutes; outnumbered and practically useless against such a group, she had her rolling constructs use their greater speed to keep destroying skeletal rats and stay out of the way of wherever the larger Undead were going.

Before they could get far, however, a veritable cloud of Specters shot forward and quickly descended from above, enveloping her Rolling Forces. There followed a short and bloodless battle that saw all of her over 2,000 constructs destroyed – but taking out over a hundred of the mist-like Undead at the same time. Normally she would consider that a fair exchange, but when all of the nearby skeletal rats picked up the dropped Monster Seeds in their fleshless jaws and carried them back to the forest, she knew she had lost big in that exchange.

As for where the larger Undead were going, it was obvious by their unerring direction that they were headed straight for Sandra's dungeon.

** Echo, get below – there's a huge force of Undead heading this way! Felbar, take Violet down as well, I can't have you up here when they invade. **

Echo hesitated, looking at her bow that was propped up against the nearby wall; she brought it everywhere with her – even to the baths down below – and Sandra was meaning to talk with her about creating a brand-new one for her. That wouldn't help right now, of course, but she wanted to thank her for her help with teaching Sandra about casting spells and for delivering the Energy Orbs to her village.

** That's not going to do much good against these Undead, Echo; you're better off getting below where it's safe. **

The Elf reluctantly nodded and grabbed her bow, slipping it around her shoulder by its string. As she was running past the Gnomes, however, Felbar reached out to Echo and grabbed her by the arm. "Please, would you take Violet with you? I'm staying here to help defend this room."

** What are you doing, Felbar? It's not safe up here— **

"There's no way I'm letting those vile monsters get a chance to destroy this War Machine, especially now that it's complete," Felbar said, cutting Sandra off. "And I'm pretty sure you don't want to lose all those supplies in that wagon over there, so you're going to need my help."

He...had a point – or at least a half-point. The wagon she could absorb and create the supplies – if not the wagon itself – immediately somewhere else, like one of the empty rooms she had created earlier. The War Machine, though, would be...painful for her to destroy; she couldn't take the risk that one of the undead could figure out how to use the Gnome construct, especially now that it didn't require someone with a certain elemental energy to control it. With all of the hard work put into it – especially all the enchantments – losing it would feel like she had just bought a foal, raised it until it was a full-grown and trained horse, and then been forced to sell it before she had a chance to ride it.

Time was running out before the Undead arrived, however, and Sandra couldn't afford to argue anymore.

** Fine, stay or go – that's your decision. I would prefer it if you were safe down below, but if you feel the need to help I'm not going to* *stop you. Once the girls are through the doorway to my VATS, though, I'm sealing it until the danger has passed; all access to the safer rooms below will be cut off, so if you need to retreat you'll be stuck here. Are you still sure you want to stay? **

Echo had already picked up Violet and easily carried the Gnome through the doorways to the VATS, not even bothering with seeing if Felbar was coming. "Yes, I'm staying. Now...is there any way you can have one of your constructs give me a boost?"

She had two of her Steelclad Ape Warriors stationed in the room to help with any crafting via the forge in the workshop or anything else that needed their assistance, and one of them quickly ran over and practically tossed the Gnome into the pilot's enclosure. Steadying himself, Felbar reached up to close and secure the Titanium gate covering the front of the War Machine before strapping himself into the leather harness. When he was secure and correctly placed, it lifted him slightly off the floor of the enclosure, allowing him to literally run in place; his feet would touch the control modules under them, and because of the **Pressure Feedback** runes there it would translate his movements to the construct.

Felbar's hands went to the wooden protrusions in front of him, fingers immediately finding where they needed to go to control the arms – and subsequently the weapons permanently attached to the ends. With a great jerk the entire construct moved…and promptly fell on its back. The Gnome seemed shocked for a moment, but then he started to chuckle.

"Uh…that was a lot more sensitive than I expected. Hold on—" he said, before manipulating the controls to turn over the War Machine. In seconds he had gotten the construct to its knee joints and then back to its feet shortly thereafter. "Ok, I think I've got a handle on it now."

Sandra watched as Felbar cautiously walked forward, followed by some simple movements to test everything out. When it appeared as though he was moving everything well enough, the Dungeon Core left him to his own devices – backed up by the 20 Unstable Shapeshifters in their unshifted forms that were still inside the room. Since they had been Enchanting for nearly an hour, they didn't have a lot of "Shift-time" left, but every little bit might count.

Looking around her dungeon, she saw that everything was as prepared as it was going to be – all except a quick change to the very first room. A quick check of her available Mana showed that it was currently a little over 17,000 and she pictured rubbing her hands together in anticipation as she eliminated the Nether-based trap already there. The lessons she had with Echo and all of the enchantments being done lately had given her some ideas, and she thought she had more than enough resources to put them into play.

Using Holy and Fire elements together, she tied a brand-new trap to a single Martial Totem she left in there, moving the others further down the dungeon. An earlier experiment trying to enchant one of her constructs ended in failure, despite Sandra thinking it might work because they could enchant Elemental Orbs and Cube; however, Winxa said it was due to the enchantment being separate from the Orbs and Cubes, not actually a part of them. She'd never had the opportunity to actually use one of her Dungeon Monsters as the *trap* before, so she figured she'd try.

First was a dual shield made from Holy Mana that surrounded her Martial Totem. One layer of the shield mimicked the same thing Echo did to become "invisible"; the other was the same bubble of protection that she had first made when trying out her casting abilities. The protection bubble would prevent both physical and Nether-based effects from reaching her Totem – at least until the Mana charged in it was used up (which should take a while, because she was pumping a lot into the trap). In addition, when the construct's protection bubble was struck, it would flash with a painfully bright light and emit a small Lightstrike "spear" in the direction the attack came from, up to 5 feet away.

That wasn't where its main offensive power came from, though; using Fire Mana, she created a field in front of the Totem that would move along with it wherever it went in the room. When the six-armed construct punched forward, its fist would launch a small ball of fire wherever it was aiming; it wasn't a very large ball of fire and would probably be just an annoyance to some of the undead, but then again the Martial Totem could punch *fast*.

She wasn't sure how long that Fire Mana field would last under repeated blows by the construct, but it was sure to inflict some major damage before it ran out. Even when it did, the Holy shield would likely still be operational, and the Totem could definitely dish out some major damage with its fists still. After making sure the trigger to activate the trap was set just inside the entrance to the room – and hoping that it actually worked, since she didn't really have a chance to test it – she turned to see what else she could do before the Undead arrived.

Unfortunately, a quick look showed that they were relatively close to her dungeon. There weren't a lot of Specters left after most of them had been destroyed in their suicide attack against her Rolling Forces, but those that were left immediately shot upwards towards Sandra's AMANS when they got within 100 feet of the entrance. The center of her Shears net was primarily her pre-Advancement ones, and hundreds of them fell out of the sky before Sandra could react, only to dissipate and drop their Copper Orb Monster Seeds before they hit the ground.

Knowing that a major source of her Mana was in jeopardy, she immediately had the rest scatter, flying to the southwest and out of range of where the Undead Core's AOI could reach. As a test, however, she kept a few dozen of her newer Reinforced Animated Shears and had them dive straight towards a single one of the black-robed spell casters that had so devastated her first eradication force. It was her hope that since it stayed towards the back and out of direct physical combat that it would be more vulnerable to physical attacks.

While they might indeed have been vulnerable, her Shears never got the chance to test their resistance. When they got within a foot of the creepy Undead casters, a shield of darkness appeared out of nowhere around the robed form, reflecting the impact from dozens of Shears like it was nothing. Most of her constructs were destroyed when they hit the shield at full speed from above, but two of them managed to hit at an angle and were embedded in the ground. She tried to get them to move afterwards and dig themselves out, but a black sludge seemed to coat them where they hit the caster's shield; within seconds, they were eaten away by the mystery substance, leaving Sandra relatively blind other than a single Mechanical Jaguar she had in one of the nearby hills.

To rectify her inability to see what was happening, she took another dozen of her newer Shears and sent them high up into the air above her dungeon, where they could look down from almost a mile; the act caused the Specters to try to reach them, but they fortunately couldn't reach that far. It wasn't the best view, but at least she could see in general what was happening.

She expected them to immediately stream into her dungeon entrance and she prepared herself...but they all stopped before they actually entered. It was kind of eerie, actually; the lead elements of the Undead horde were five feet from the entrance, and yet they all seemed frozen in place. After about half a minute approximately half of the horde broke off and started to move;

Sandra thought, *this is it*...but all they did was rush over to the other entrance to her dungeon in the old Bearling lair connected to her workshop. Once they were there, they stopped five feet away from that cave opening as well.

What is going on?

"What do you mean? What happened? Are they inside already?" Winxa asked, sounding a little more confident than just a few minutes earlier when Sandra angrily yelled at her, though she was still a bit reserved in her appearance. The Dungeon Core explained what was happening, but the Fairy didn't have an answer.

"Again, this is something I'm unfamiliar with. Core on Core fighting has never been a thing before this – literally *couldn't* have been a thing because of the contracts – so I'm not sure what it's doing."

Sandra was no strategist herself, but she was beginning to see what was happening. First, the Undead Core had tricked her by hiding all of those skeletal rats; when she went to destroy them as they emerged, it sacrificed a portion of its horde to destroy her eradication force. Then when it got close enough to her dungeon, it made her AMANS retreat out of range, but it also had the side-effect of reducing the amount of Mana she was receiving from them by almost a quarter because of the distance from her dungeon entrance. Not only that, but it also cut down on her surveillance directly above her, though she could see from a significant distance away.

Lastly, the Core had obviously seen the outline of her dungeon from down below the ground and camped all of its Monsters right outside of her entrances – *why would it do that?* The only explanation that made sense was one that just showed how devious the other entity really was; by guarding the only ways in and out of her dungeon, she couldn't field an army of her own to destroy them. Everything she sent out would be immediately destroyed, as nothing would be able to work together to take the Nether-based Dungeon Monsters down. The Undead Core didn't need to invade her dungeon to attempt to destroy Sandra; all it had to do was keep her bottled up while it went about its business.

Sure, she might eventually wear the Undead down by a constant stream of constructs thrown out the entrances, but she could already see reinforcements coming from the trees in ones and twos. There were a few tricks that Sandra had up her sleeve, of course, but she felt like she was always one step behind the other Core; *what else will I have to defend against after I destroy these Undead?*

She mentally spoke too soon, because emerging from the forest near the Undead dungeon was a gigantic, horrendous-looking abomination.

Well, I guess I know what I'm going to have to do now...

Chapter 19

Fifth-shield Gerold agilely stepped out of the way of a slow and clumsy strike by the Dirt Golem in front of him...only to be slammed from the side by its other appendage. He went flying through the air a dozen feet before he crashed to the ground, tumbling a couple of times before he smashed into a nearby tree. The young Dwarf heard cracking and worried that either his body or his armor was damaged, but looking up from where he had fallen, he breathed a sigh of relief when he saw that it was only the tree itself that had suffered the ill effects.

Picking himself up from the ground, he was surprised to find that he hadn't lost hold of his battle-axe even through his flight and subsequent acrobatics. His full-plate armor also looked pristine – like it should – though he could feel that absorbing the impact and protecting Gerold had drained him of a little elemental energy. It was probably only about 5% of what he had available, but the day was just starting; if he wasted all of it now because of stupid mistakes, then he'd be useless halfway through the day.

The Dirt Golem was already heading in his direction, so the Dwarf readied himself, determined not to fall for that kind of sneak attack again. This was his first solo outing to cull the dungeon monsters outside the village of Nurboldar, and he winced internally when he imagined what Second-shield Bregan would say about his performance so far. His mentor would doubtless chastise him to no end, pointing out his mistakes, and berating him until he shaped up. Despite the abuse from the veteran Shield he had withstood over the last month of training, Gerold knew that it was all done to make him a better fighter – and to help him not die when fighting his first monster.

I'm not doing such a good job of that so far, am I?

"Come on, Gerold – get your act together," he mumbled to himself. The Dwarf stepped forward with his shield strapped to his left arm and his battle-axe in his right hand, trying to exude the confidence he knew he should feel; it was difficult, however, especially when there wasn't the safety net of his mentor there to help if he messed up. Nevertheless, Gerold knew that the 8-foot-tall Dirt Golem shouldn't present that much of a challenge – or at least the ones he had killed before hadn't been in the past.

Giving himself a little shake to get rid of his nerves, Gerold stepped towards the Golem, while at the same time funneling a trickle of his Water elemental energy to the edge of his battle-axe. He did the same with his Nether energy, mixing the two until it made the edge an interesting combination of black and blue that crackled with power.

Quickly dodging another obviously clumsy strike from the Golem as he closed with it, he saw the other arm of the vaguely person-shaped monster come flying towards him out of the corner of his eye and ducked by practically throwing himself to the ground. The dirt appendage passed a beard hair's-length over his head, and Gerold swiftly straightened up and counter-attacked. With a sweep of his Water-and-Nether enhanced axe, he sliced completely through the thick right lower "leg" of the Dirt Golem; the Water instantly turned the dirt it touched to mud, making it softer and easier to cut through, while the Nether did something equally important: it prevented the wound to the monster from "healing".

Regenerating or *Reincorporate* might be a better word for how the Golems could normally use their unique abilities to reattach sliced-off parts of themselves by absorbing and reforming whatever got chopped off. It wasn't instant, of course, but even if you completely dismembered a Golem, after a few minutes the different parts would slowly come back together and reform the monster – though usually it lost a portion of its original size in the process. If a Dwarf didn't have access to elemental energy to prevent that from happening, then constantly dismembering the Golem was the only method to really destroy it; that process worked, of course, but it took a while.

Gerold's Nether element applied to his battle-axe, however, sealed the ends of the "wounds" he inflicted with necrotic energy, preventing the pieces from rejoining. There were other methods with other elements, of course – including Water if he really needed it – but using Nether energy in that matter was the best and most efficient course of action for him.

The Golem – now missing a leg that was chopped off just above its dirt "knee" – toppled forward onto its arms and remaining knee, and Gerold narrowly missed being crushed by half a ton of dirt by stepping out of the way. He knew that just because it was missing a leg, that didn't mean it wasn't still dangerous; a quickly flung-out arm in his direction from the Golem was proof of that, which he easily blocked with his shield, though he had to take a step back to maintain his footing from the impact.

The Dwarf continued his attack by stepping forward and using his axe to slice off the lower half of the arm that just hit his shield. Now missing a portion of the arm keeping it upright, the Golem fell forward again onto its chest – but it also kept up a flailing assault on Gerold. Fortunately, the attacks by the intact and amputated arms were mistimed and awkward and he was easily able to avoid them completely; he almost took a foot to the face when the entire Monster seemed to shift itself and a leg came flying at him, but he ducked under it and sliced it off.

After that, it was just a matter of finishing the Golem off by removing the arms and the featureless protrusion on top of its shoulders that he assumed classified as a head, before cutting the torso in half. Once all that was done, the dungeon monster completely made of dirt melted into the ground, leaving behind a small gold sphere as Loot. Gerold sighed as he picked it up and stuffed it in a small pocket behind his breastplate, wishing that it had been steel instead; gold was a metal that was practically useless in Blacksmithing weapons and armor, as it was just too soft to make anything that would last. He had heard that other races prized it because of its shiny appearance and even traded it for goods and services, but to Dwarves it was little better than dirt.

Overall, what he picked up as Loot out in the forest didn't really matter – unless it was somehow something really rare –

because that wasn't what the Shieldmen (of which Gerold was a relatively new member) were there for. There was plenty of metal to be found in their mountain homes, so collecting Loot was only a secondary purpose; their real purpose was to cull the Monsters from the surrounding dungeons so that the village of Nurboldar could grow food on the extensive farm it possessed. Such areas of land not already overrun by monsters was extremely rare these days – other than Dwarven mountain strongholds, of course – which was why they were at the back end of nowhere trying to grow food that didn't take to the environment very well.

That was in part because they were so close to the wastelands that were dry, barren, and dangerous. It rarely seemed to rain, and even when it did it was fairly light; if there hadn't been a major river nearby that years ago had been partially diverted for irrigation, then they wouldn't have been able to grow much there. There were only two other places around their entire land that could grow food outside of the mountains, but Nurboldar was by far the largest of them. While certain types of food could be grown and animals could be raised for their meat inside their strongholds, it didn't provide a lot of variety – and the most important ingredients to one of their staples was only able to be grown outside.

All of which was why Gerold felt honored to be assigned to the farming village – though it wasn't like those in charge had much choice. The ranks of the Shieldmen were getting thinner and thinner over the years as fewer and fewer of the Dwarven population were willing to leave their comfy and safe mountain strongholds to brave the dangers of either farming or culling dungeon monsters. It wasn't a glorious position, but Gerold felt like he was really making a difference – *and I should probably get back to it.*

He was about to venture further into the forest when he *felt* something strange and yet familiar at the same time. Gerold immediately recognized it as something related to the Nether element he had access to; he had always been uniquely sensitive to the darker elemental energy for some reason, though he didn't know why he was different from most other Dwarves. Some of the older generations were concerned that it boded an ill omen, but Gerold and his family had dismissed it at superstition – though it *had* prevented him from having any friends outside of his immediate family.

Luckily the Shieldmen didn't care about things like that, so Gerold was happy to leave the mountains and be out where things like his particular affinity to the Nether element didn't matter so much. In fact, it seemed like it was coming in handy that day, since he could sense some where there shouldn't be any coming from the trees near the forest's border with Nurboldar's farmland. As he turned around to investigate, he followed the traces of Nether with his senses, finding that it was moving around fairly quickly; despite that, within 15 minutes he had found the source – or at least he thought he did.

Some rustling of leaves was the first thing that alerted Gerold to the presence of something, and he jumped back in surprise when a small rat emerged from beneath a tree root and stared at him. He assumed that it was staring at him, though it was hard to tell – *because it was missing all of its flesh, including its eyes!* Essentially, it was a skeleton of a small rat walking around, though he figured it could be a large mouse; however, the shape was enough like some of the rats that had infested the long-abandoned tunnels back home – that he used to explore as a kid – that he couldn't picture it as anything else.

Reacting instinctively, Gerold swung his battle-axe at the frozen skeletal rodent and split it right down the middle. He knew it shouldn't have been a surprise to see it dissolve into the ground and leave behind a small copper sphere as Loot, but the presence of something undead – that really shouldn't be there – threw his mind for a loop. He knew what it was, of course, because there were at least two dungeons that had undead monsters around the Dwarven Kingdom, but he had never seen one in person before; now that he had, though, his mind struggled to comprehend what it meant.

There must be a new Nether dungeon around here! Gerold hadn't ever heard of two dungeons being so close to each other before, but the fact that he had only seen a very small dungeon monster likely meant that the dungeon was new and didn't have much stronger than that. He briefly wondered why he couldn't sense it since it should be fairly close by; then again, he had never been near a Nether-element dungeon before, so he didn't know if he *could* sense them.

Regardless, he knew that he had to let Second-shield Bregan know about it right away, because having *another* dungeon nearby could cause some trouble if they needed to start culling that one as well. Either that, or they might decide to destroy it, though they hadn't done it before to either the Goblins or Golems because the risk to the farm was too high if they failed. The Shieldmen were strong, but they definitely weren't invulnerable – they were as likely to fall to traps and overwhelming dungeon monsters as anyone else. It was decided that culling and keeping them contained was the best option based on their own numbers – but a smaller dungeon should be relatively "safer".

Again, it wasn't *his* decision, so he started to jog out of the forest, intending to head straight for the village and let Bregan know what he had seen. However, as soon as he got to open land and traveled past the last trees, he was hit by an overwhelming miasma of Nether...that was coming straight from the wastelands in the distance. He couldn't believe that he hadn't felt it before then because it was so strong; in fact, its presence to his senses was so deep that he felt inexplicably drawn to it. Against his volition, his feet immediately turned towards the source of Nether he identified, and he left the village and the other Dwarves behind.

He was halfway to the barren wasteland when he forcibly stopped himself and took a deep breath. *What am I doing? I have to go warn Bregan and the others about this!* Unfortunately, the seductive pull of the Nether-based elemental concentration in the distance was too much for him to resist. *I should probably just check it out and give them a full report; if there's an undead dungeon in the middle of the wastelands then they need to know that. Besides, seeing a small skeletal rat doesn't really say much, does it?*

Gerold used that rationale to start jogging again, and as he stepped into the dry, broken land he could feel himself getting closer and closer to the source of what he was sensing. He didn't see a single beast or monster anywhere, though, despite hearing that the wastelands were dangerous and infested with groups of creatures that could kill a dwarf in minutes, if not seconds.

Finally, following the draw of the concentrated Nether element ahead, Gerold carefully climbed up a small craggy hill and reached its apex; as soon as he did, however, he ducked back down and hid himself behind an outcropping when he caught a glimpse of what he was sure was the source he had heading towards that entire time.

Below him in a broken valley of dust, desiccated wood branches, and broken stone, was a veritable army of undead – and they scared the armor off of Gerold. There were skeletons and zombies of all shapes and sizes, but there were also some undead covered head-to-toe in black armor, robed figures that seemed to pulse with Nether energy for some reason, and even some misty-like undead monsters floating in the air. That was bad enough – especially with their sheer numbers, which had to top 8 or 900 by that point in two equal groups – but what really frightened him was a huge...thing...in the middle of the two groups.

Gerold couldn't even look at it long, because it was disturbing to look at. The best way he could describe it was if you took the bloodless corpses of hundreds of various people and beasts and shoved them together into a massive blob, which apparently moved by either rolling or *oozing* over the ground. It was just a guess, though, because it was frozen in place, just like the other undead he saw; they seemed to all be facing the same way, either towards a small uniformly dug cave about 500 feet from him or a second larger, naturally created cave which was just below and across from his location.

Ok...I think I've seen enough...I should be going now—

Before he could inch himself back down the mountain and hopefully not call attention to himself, Gerold glanced up and saw a trio of the mist-like undead above him descending in his direction. Looking back down at the other monsters, he saw that those nearest to him were now looking in his direction, though fortunately none of them were moving – only those undead above his head.

Judging by the speed they were moving, there was no way he could outrun them – even if he could run quickly in all of his armor; the most he could maintain was a slower jog, but that wouldn't do much to get him away. Therefore, knowing he had no other choice, he unstrapped his battle-axe from his side and readied it and his shield to defend, using his Water element to coat the edge of the axe and the face of the shield with ice. He was pretty sure that his Nether element was going to be useless against monsters made exclusively with it, so Water was going to have to do.

As the first one reached him, Gerold swung his axe upwards and cut all the way through the mist-like form of the monster; he was expecting some sort of resistance, so he ended up unbalancing himself and falling backwards. It was a good thing that he did, because as he fell on his rear end, he looked up to see that the undead mist was still coming for him even after it paused, reformed, and was plainly reduced in size from his attack. He was used to having to completely dismember Golems to kill them so it wasn't that much of a surprise, but it would make it much harder to kill them if it kept on like that.

He got his axe and shield back up just in time to defend himself...but the mists all stopped before they reached him. Before he could wonder why, he saw them float off downward towards the other undead – which he just realized a lot of noise was coming from. He could hear the impact of what sounded like something hard smacking against flesh, the crack of bones, and the screech of metal as it was ripped apart. Finally looking down there, he was shocked to see what looked like some sort of warzone between two different races that he'd only heard stories of when he was a child.

Except, instead of the Dwarves fighting against Elves, Orcs, or Gnomes – or even the fabled Humans – it was a war between strange metal-like creatures and the undead. *Actually, that's not quite true*, he thought, after seeing what he assumed were Elves streaming out of the natural cave near him, though he had never seen one in the flesh. There was plenty of flesh to see now, however, as he saw nearly twenty of them rushing out without a stitch of clothing or armor of any kind; not only that, but either he was being extremely racist, or they all looked exactly the same. It was said that it was hard to tell them apart because they all tended to look alike, but he thought that this situation was taking that stereotype a little far.

Accompanying them were large silvery metal monkeys wielding what appeared to be warhammers, strange thick metal poles with three sets of arms that floated just barely above the ground, and even – he had to rub his eyes to check if they were working properly – a horde of *Goblins* rushing out and getting in the undead monsters' way. That was about all they were doing, because they died very quickly and didn't appear to have much in the way of offensive capabilities, but they certainly were a distraction.

The robed figures caught his attention again as they started to move their arms; Gerold could feel the Nether energy building in them as the area around their hand started to darken. Before whatever they were trying to do could be accomplished, however, dozens of bright flashes shot out from the Elves, striking the undead figures and interrupting them. More and more spears of light hit them, and he saw one and then another get pierced as it penetrated its shield of darkness; within seconds they were down, leaving behind their Loot as they dissipated.

But there were at least a dozen more that he could see – on this side of the broken valley, at least – and they continued to try to build their Nether energy up in what he assumed was some sort of attack. Suddenly, Gerold heard a whistling coming from above and behind him, and he readied himself for another attack by the misty undead; when he looked back, however, all he saw were some strange metallic shapes hurtling towards him out of the sky. He squatted down and braced himself behind his shield for the impact, but when nothing hit him he looked up to see that they were actually aiming *over* his head – and striking the dark-robed figures down in the battle.

They didn't seem to do much good at first, but as the Elves continued their light-slinging attacks he could see some of them penetrate the dark shield surrounding the undead, taking them out one-by-one. That ultimately didn't seem to matter, though, as the rest of the skeletons, zombies, and armored undead started to swarm over the initial assault by the metal creatures and goblins. He even saw one of the Elves get picked up and ripped in half by a massive skeleton wielding a huge bone club, but after the initial blood and insides that spilled out, Gerold could've sworn that the entire body melted into a weird multi-colored ooze before dissipating – and leaving behind some Loot that he couldn't identify from where he was.

"What in the world is going on?" he whispered to himself as he watched the insane battle playing out. He originally thought the metal creature/Elven/Goblin team would come out ahead, but then he saw the group of undead near the other cave rush over to reinforce the ones closest to him. In addition, the gigantic, disturbing, horrific mass of melded-together bodies was rolling over – *at least I know it* ***rolls*** *to move* – towards the fighting.

When it got closer, a strange black glow surrounded the smaller undead fighting; it didn't seem to do anything at first, but when he saw one of the metal monkeys smash a skeleton apart that had the glow, the undead broke into pieces – which then quickly started to put itself back together. Gerold thought it was similar to how the Golems he was used to killing "healed" themselves, though this was at a much faster rate.

With the ability to regenerate, the battle took an even greater toll on the odd team of combatants; the Dwarf thought it was all over and he looked back down the hill he was on to look for the best way down – he wanted to flee before the undead remembered he was there. However, another strange noise coming from the large cave stopped him.

Emerging from the cave was a 20-foot-tall wood-and-metal machine of some sort; on the front of the strange contraption was a small metal grate, which – unless his eyes were still playing tricks on him – held another, paler Goblin...and it seemed to be controlling the machine. One of the arms on the contraption was fused to a mighty-looking warhammer, while in the other was a massive double-bladed axe; looking closer, Gerold's Dwarven senses kicked in and he immediately determined that they – and the rest of the metal on the machine – were made *entirely* of titanium, which was astonishing in and of itself.

The weapons were crossed in front of the large contraption, however, and it appeared to be carrying some sort of metal ball. Gerold watched as the machine took two giant steps out of the cave, just barely out of range of the rampaging undead that were barely being held back by the metal creatures, Elves, and other Goblins. Before it could be overwhelmed, the two arms on the contraption quickly lifted up into the air, tossing the metal ball nearly 15 feet; the Goblin-controlled machine stepped its right leg back, turning the entire thing so that it was looking to the side.

With the piercing sound of metal striking metal that reverberated throughout the broken wasteland valley, the massive contraption swatted the large ball out of the air with the flat of its double-bladed axe, sending it over the heads of the undead closing in. Gerold watched the ball fly through the air – with one side slightly dented from the impact with the axe – and land just feet from the front of the gigantic corpse blob. The group of undead from the other cave were just passing by it when the disgusting abomination rolled a little more forward; the gigantic undead just barely touched the metal sphere...when the world seemed to explode.

On second thought, *implode* would probably be the better word. After an initial flash of light that almost blinded him, a weird vortex of glowing energy had taken the place of the metal ball. Gerold could see blue and black prevalent inside of the glowing vortex and he could sense the Nether energy in it – more than he had ever felt before, even compared to all of the undead in the valley. It felt more *raw* than what he sensed from the undead, so he thought that also might have something to do with how powerful it seemed.

For almost five seconds, everything seemed to freeze, though Gerold could see out of the corner of his eye that the Goblin and its machine had retreated back into the cave and was now nowhere to be seen. After those five seconds, however, the vortex started to pull at everything around it; the corpse-blob next to it was the first to get sucked in, shrinking at the same time as it was absorbed faster and faster. In less time than the Dwarf thought possible, it was completely gone, having been sucked completely inside the raging vortex of energy.

It wasn't done yet, however; undead up to 30 feet away were picked up off their feet or pulled out of the air and were immediately sucked into the vortex and disappeared. Then those farther out at 40, 50, and then 100 feet were pulled in and destroyed one after the other. It wasn't just the undead monsters that were sucked into the maelstrom of energy, but rocks, loose dirt, and desiccated sticks were also pulled in; when the range of the vortex reached 150 feet away – which in reality took less than 10 seconds from when it first started – Gerold watched and felt unsteady as the ground started to tremble.

Below the vortex, the ground in which it was sitting broke apart and was sucked in as well, leaving a bowl-shaped crater in the stone and dirt. That only seemed to increase the speed of its expansion, as it started grabbing at all of the rest of the undead now starting to flee. Not only that, but it also indiscriminately picked up and destroyed the remaining metal creatures, Elves, and Goblins still out keeping the undead horde back. Soon enough there wasn't a single dungeon monster left out in the broken valley as they were all pulled in and destroyed.

But the expansion didn't stop.

"Oh, no..." Too late, Gerold realized he should've moved from his perch on top of the nearby hill earlier. He could feel himself being picked up, so he held onto an outcropping near the apex of the craggy hill to prevent himself from being sucked into the vortex. His battle-axe was ripped off his belt and he looked back to see it fly straight toward the energy maelstrom, disappearing in seconds; as his hands started to slip, he could feel his armor strengthening him as it enhanced the strength in his fingered gauntlets. Even that wasn't enough, however, because he was still slipping – and his elemental energy was being drained quickly.

He knew it was over when he felt the last of it give out and it felt like he got punched in the head; if the backlash of using too much energy in such a short time wasn't bad enough, his armor – that took weeks of work for the Master Blacksmiths back home to design and create – disintegrated around his body, including his fingers. Gerold immediately lost his grip on the outcropping and felt himself being quickly sucked towards the vortex. Closing his eyes, he tried to shut out everything in an attempt to block out what he expected to be a tremendous amount of pain.

He was spared that particular pain, however, as he felt the powerful pulling abruptly cease; the next thing he knew, he was falling towards the scooped-out ground underneath the vortex. Gerold opened his eyes just as his head collided with something hard below him...and then there was just darkness.

Chapter 20

"Is he dead?" Felbar asked, climbing out of the War Machine.

That seemed to be a question that came up a lot in Sandra's workshop – or at least what remained of it.

** No, but he's definitely unconscious and I believe bleeding internally. He doesn't have long before it's too late; I'm going to have to form the Visitor's bond on him to heal him with my Repair Drones. I have a feeling it'll put him in a coma like you and Echo were, but at least he'll— **

She was going to say, "be alive" but she was stopped when she saw one of her Repair Drones moving toward him from the other side of the now half-destroyed workshop. Actually, upon looking at it closer, she realized that it was the one Multi-access Repair Drone she had in the room, unlike the two others that were of the previous version. She was already getting a Large Water and Nether Elemental Orb ready to perform the bond – she had seen the blue and black tints on his armor before it disintegrated – but she stopped her Ape when she saw the Drone moving.

The construct approached the fallen Dwarf that her Steelclad Ape Warrior had gingerly brought inside the workshop from where he had fallen outside. Technically, the outside was almost *inside* already, as half of the workshop's roof had been torn off and sucked up into the Gravitational Devastation Sphere. Despite the new open top, it still counted as a room in her dungeon – just one now with a very large entrance. The previous entrance/exit in the Bearling lair was basically gone, having been hollowed out along with the tunnel leading there from the workshop. She was just glad that it hadn't expanded any further, otherwise Felbar and the War Machine would've been crushed as they were pulled into the Gravitational Sphere outside.

Sandra was also glad that it had shut itself off before it killed the Dwarf, though it was still up in the air if she'd be able to heal him in time. That didn't seem to be a problem, though, because the Multi-access Repair Drone had its arms with the pads on the ends on the Dwarf's head, pumping healing energy through his body and fixing him up. *So...I'm guessing that's what "multi-access" means? That it can heal...anybody?*

There wasn't really anything that she could do to speed that process up, so Sandra spent some time evaluating exactly what happened because of that...unique...construct that seemed to suck everything into it. She had obviously already seen that her workshop and other entrance had been essentially destroyed along with all of her constructs that she had sent out to push back and distract the undead horde; what she didn't know, however, was what exactly happened to everything that was pulled into the Sphere when she activated it.

** Felbar, I'm going to try and discover what exactly happened out there; if the Dwarf wakes up soon, try to...reassure him that he's safe. With your language barrier, I doubt you'll be able to communicate that well with him, but hopefully he'll be thankful that he's not dead. **

"Sure, I can try to do that – but who's going to reassure me that what I just witnessed isn't something that I should be afraid of in the future?"

** What are talking about? Oh...you mean the Gravitational Devastation Sphere? You don't have to worry about that; I can only use it every 60 days and it won't activate if it goes more than 300 feet past my entrance. So, unless I'm being attacked like I just was by those undead, I have no reason to use it. Also, based on what kind of destruction that thing did, I'm not sure I'd ever* ***want*** *to use it again. **

That didn't really seem to reassure the old Gnome, but there was really nothing that Sandra could say to convince him. She was telling the truth, though; seeing the utter devastation she caused was making her rethink her decision to use it in the first place. Bringing back her remaining Shears in her AMANS so that it was floating over her dungeon again – since there weren't any more Specters trying to destroy them nearby – she brought a dozen down to survey the damage up close.

It was actually quite remarkable how much of the ground had been ripped away in such a uniform way; there were places where buried boulders were pulled out of the ground and left holes in the dirt behind, but for the most part all of the packed dirt was scooped out in a roughly semi-circle shape. Anything small within approximately 500 feet of the exterior of the Sphere's destruction was sucked up, leaving the landscape around clean-looking without any rocks, pebbles, or dirt clods anywhere. The hill where the Dwarf had been hiding was half gone itself, and Sandra was surprised that he had managed to hold on as long as he had.

Why was he here in the first place? She was actually a little thankful that he was there, because he provided a much-needed distraction that allowed the vanguard of her construct, Shapeshifter, and Goblin fodder force to spread out from the cave entrance enough to stand a chance. While his presence was beneficial for her in the end, it still didn't explain *why* he was there at all.

Unless...

She quickly tasked the Shears she had keeping an eye on the Dwarven village check on their status; a quick peek showed that they were fine, and a few minutes of looking around the forest nearby showed nothing there, either. If the Undead Core had managed to send some of its Dungeon Monsters there, the presence of them might have alerted the Dwarves to what was happening near her dungeon...*maybe?* It was a working theory, but until she got some better information that was the best she could come up with.

With everything there looking like it was as normal as could be, Sandra resumed her perusal of the battlefield – while at the same time producing Rolling Force after Rolling Force down by her Core. She immediately sent them out in a constant stream with orders to scatter and hunt down skeletal rats; the previous mistake she made earlier was keeping them all together in a group, because that seemed like the best method at the time – strength in numbers and all that. However, it was already proven that her constructs were faster than pretty much anything but those Specters when they were determined enough, and they could also easily destroy the rats by themselves one-on-one.

She couldn't let the Undead Core continue to accumulate so much Mana without any opposition, so destroying as many of those rats as possible was essential to reducing that amount. In fact, to offset what she was using to produce the Rolling Forces, every fifth one she created she added another pair of Shears to her AMANS to replace the over 1,200 that she had lost during the battle. She had to dig down deep into her treasury to keep up with what she was spending, but the current situation was exactly why her father always stressed keeping as much in savings at the bank as possible. This was a rainy-day scenario if she ever saw one, and everything she knew about Dungeon Cores told her that it would take the Undead one causing so many problems a while to recover from the loss of so many of its Monsters.

A quick glance inside the workshop showed that the Repair Drone had finished its work and the Dwarf looked much healthier – but was still asleep for some reason. Sandra was really hoping that he wasn't in a coma, but she figured only time would tell.

After exploring the destruction while continuing her construct production below, she finally came to the spot underneath where the Sphere had done its thing earlier. At the bottom of the carved-out semi-circle of dirt and stone was another sphere-shaped object; initially she thought that the Devastation Sphere had survived, but it was smaller and multi-colored as well – unlike the large plain-looking metal ball the Sphere had been.

Looking closer at it brought no more explanation of what it was; the only thing she could see was that it was apparently *very* heavy, as it was starting to crack a small stone underneath it with what appeared to be sheer weight alone. Sandra watched as the stone finally burst apart and practically disintegrated, but when the strange sphere slammed into the packed dirt below it seemed to settle a little. She could still see that it was pressing down into the dirt with great weight, but the fear that it would continue dropping through the ground – and her dungeon below it – was relieved at the sight.

Apart from that, though, there was nothing left. Curious about what the sphere really was, she had her remaining Steelclad Ape inside the workshop come out and bring it into her dungeon; at least, that's what she intended, but when her construct came to pick it up, the sphere barely twitched despite the Ape's not-insignificant strength.

** Felbar, do you think you can use the War Machine to move this thing? I'll keep an eye on the Dwarf. **

The Gnome nodded, using some stacked empty wooden boxes that Sandra had left over from filling the wagon – which was still intact and waiting to go back to the Gnome homeland – to climb his way up into the massive construct. When he stomped off, making the ground shake a little as he moved, Sandra looked at the Dwarf and wondered why he hadn't woken up yet. *Why does it seem like everyone likes to be unconscious here, at least lately?* First, Violet collapsed into unconsciousness after creating the linking enchantment – and now there was a Dwarf lying in the middle of what was left of the workshop.

Violet, however, was already awake and asking about what happened—

Wait! I feel stupid for not putting it together before now.

Violet had expended pretty much all of her elemental energy in the process of creating the enchantment, so her unconsciousness made sense because Sandra actually saw her do it; the Dwarf, on the other hand, hadn't actually *done* anything – but his energy had been drained completely, nonetheless. That much was obvious by the way his armor had disintegrated off of his body while he was being pulled into the Sphere, but the Dungeon Core hadn't really put it together until now.

Her remaining Unstable Shapeshifter – the original one, with the samples taken from the Elite Elves – was still alive in the workshop mainly because Sandra hadn't wanted to lose access to those forms. The other Shifters had been destroyed in the attack against the Undead, but she made sure to keep it back, figuring that an extra Elf tossing out Holy-based spells probably wouldn't that much of a difference. As a result, it was available to help her because her Ape was still outside, acting as a guide to Felbar on where the strange object was located.

Sandra shifted it into Echo's form and had it grab a Water and Nether Energy Orb – which matched the tints on his now-destroyed armor – that were packed away in the Gnome's wagon, figuring that she would replace them later; they weren't doing much good there, anyway, so she figured they might as well be used. The Shifter then walked over and placed them on the bare skin of the Dwarf's chest, where his shirt was open; almost immediately, the transfer of elemental energies started, and the stirrings of movement came from their unexpected visitor.

He wasn't exactly awake yet, but she was hopeful that it wouldn't be long. In the meantime, she watched as Felbar in the War Machine approached the spherical object with a little hesitation; she couldn't blame him – the destructive power of the original sphere was so great and admittedly quite scary that seeing anything of the same shape would probably make Sandra hesitate as well. Regardless, he was next to it within a minute, after having navigated his way out of the workshop through the open top – apparently he could jump relatively small distances if he wanted to (and by "relative", she meant half of the War Machine's height of 20 feet) – and he cautiously attempted to move the sphere with his warhammer arm.

It moved more than it had with the Ape…all of an inch before settling back down in the packed dirt again. Using a little more force, Felbar smacked it with the warhammer, getting it to move roughly a foot before stopping – and slightly bending the shaft of the Titanium weapon in the process. As for the strange sphere itself, it showed not even a single mark on it even after being thwacked with enough force to shatter stone.

"Uh…this thing is really heavy; I don't want to destroy all our hard work smacking it like this."

** Don't worry, I'll be able to easily fix any of the minor damage and it shouldn't affect the enchantments at all. Maybe try kicking it? **

As Sandra had suggested, Felbar kicked it with the War Machine's foot, which actually worked fairly well – though it left significant dents in the solid Titanium of the construct's foot. Still, it was relatively minor damage in the scheme of things, so he kept on kicking it and alternating his feet. By the time it got up the curvature of the hollowed-out space left by the Gravitational Devastation Sphere – which was difficult, because it kept wanting to roll back down – and tipped over the edge into her workshop, the War Machine's feet were basically unrecognizable lumps of battered metal. Still, they were functional, and Sandra knew they could be fixed with a little effort.

The floor of her workshop – which had been heavily reinforced stone to handle even the War Machine as it stomped around – didn't fare so well when it was hit by an extremely heavy sphere dropped essentially from the ceiling. Not only did the stone crack, but it practically shattered and disintegrated into dust underneath the multi-colored ball; the only reason it stopped moving was that when it hit the dirt below, it settled into a hole three feet deep. When the sphere itself was only approximately two feet across, that meant it had gone so deep that it wasn't even visible from the surface of the workshop anymore.

The destruction of the floor wasn't the only side-effect of the heavy ball falling down from the ceiling; the impact also shook the ground so violently that some of the ceiling that hadn't fallen previously cracked off and fell inside the room. In addition, the jolt finally woke up the Dwarf, with what Sandra assumed was now with a little of his elemental energy restored.

Chapter 21

Gerold struggled to wake up from the incessant nightmare that he was being sucked into a strange vortex before falling from a great height and smashing into the ground. He wasn't sure how many times he dreamt the whole weird and frightening sequence over and over before he started to panic in his mind; he couldn't wake up from it no matter how much he tried, and he was beginning to think he was dead, and this was his eternal punishment.

Miraculously, one of the times when he dreamt he was smashing into the ground again...he woke up. It was a gradual awakening, but he could definitely tell he was awake – though when he opened his eyes and looked around he immediately wished he was back in that seemingly endless nightmare cycle. Above him was a tall ceiling made all from one piece of smooth stone, though there were a few cracks running through it; such a thing was nearly impossible to achieve even by the Master Stonemasons like his father was back at home. For one, it required that there be a large enough stone to carve out like that in the first place; for another, there wasn't even the slightest sign that it had been worked at all – there were no chisel marks or repair joins where potential faults in the stone may have been found.

All of which meant one thing to Gerold – he was looking at the ceiling of a dungeon; that was the only explanation he could think of after listening to his father lovingly talk about stone for most of his life, and how he had once heard that dungeons could craft with stone and dirt without having to use tools at all – which was "so unfair" and all that. He remembered blocking out most of what he had lamented about, but the main concept behind what he was going on about was definitely something he remembered.

Moving his head to the side, his fears were only confirmed when he saw a large multi-colored blob of some unknown material sitting in the corner of the strange room he was in, though he couldn't look at it long or his eyes went all funny. In the other corner was something even stranger and he thought shouldn't even exist in a dungeon – a forge. Being Dwarven, Gerold knew instinctively what it was and the sight of it he supposed should have made him more comfortable, but it had the opposite effect.

Just as he turned his head the other direction, he saw the massive Goblin machine fall out of the open ceiling, slamming down on the stone floor and cracking it in the process. Its feet appeared to be damaged and it stumbled upon impact, though it was able to catch itself before it fell on its front. Gerold felt paralyzed as he stared at it, seeing that it was even larger this close to him than he had first thought; it had to be at least 20 feet tall and looked capable of slicing him apart with its double-bladed axe even in his armor.

The thought of his armor and his own battle-axe brought the memory of what happened crashing down on the Dwarf; Gerold felt intense despair at the realization that his weapon, his armor, his *livelihood* even, had been completely destroyed. There was no way he'd be able to convince the Master Blacksmiths back home to create another set for him; it was rare that any Shieldmen got a replacement for their armor, and those that were lucky enough to survive their destruction were usually First or Second-shield ranked. For a Fifth-shield like him, the possibility of being re-armored was almost nil.

It's probably better just to die here than to go back to Nurboldar and Bregan in shame over losing my armor. If it were just my weapon, there might be a way to have another one made, but without protection I'd be doomed to die in my first fight.

His new disregard for his own life actually helped knock Gerold free of his temporary paralysis and he sat up, wanting to face his death on his own two feet rather than lying on his back. As he was sitting up, however, he could feel something fall off his chest and run down into his lap.

Two glowing orbs – one a light blue and the other a deep black – had rolled down to settle just above his legs; not knowing what they were and if they were there to harm him further, he immediately grabbed them to throw away. One touch, though, was all he needed to dismiss that idea, as they called to him and seemed to fill him with strength.

Or, more accurately, *energy*.

For the first time since he woke up, he realized that his Water and Nether elemental energy levels in his body weren't completely empty; either he had slept for longer than he realized and gotten some of it back, or the two orbs he was holding was helping to recharge them. After a few seconds of looking down at them in his hand in confusion and then wonder, it was more than obvious that it was the latter – which was an impossibility, as far as he knew.

Speaking of impossibilities, he had been so distracted with his whereabouts and the strangely wondrous orbs he was holding that he hadn't noticed that he didn't feel even the slightest amount of pain. His memory of the last few seconds of being sucked up into the vortex and then falling towards the ground far below were a little hazy but dropping over a hundred feet from the sky onto hard dirt and stone had to have damaged him a little. He distinctly remembered his head being hit hard and the hollow sound of cracking bones somewhere on his body before he blacked out; reaching up to his head and neck – followed by the rest of his body – with his hands each holding one of the colored orbs still, he couldn't find a spot that felt injured or even sore.

How...what...?

His thoughts were interrupted when he heard a noise coming from the Goblin contraption and he tensed up, chastising himself for losing focus – he had completely forgotten the danger he was in after being distracted by pretty orbs. He quickly got to his feet and faced towards the machine, bracing himself for an attack even though he knew he would probably die with one sweep of its axe or pounding of its warhammer. Instead, he watched the metal grate on the front of the contraption swing open, revealing the Goblin inside, which immediately jumped down and out of the massive machine.

It only took him a few seconds to realize that it wasn't actually a Goblin, but what couldn't be anything other than a Gnome. First of all, *he* didn't have the right color of skin, but also because he started talking to nothing in the air in some sort of gibberish – but Gerold figured it was Gnomish or another language, because he had never heard a Goblin speak before. Even if he had heard one say something, he doubted it would sound so...normal.

The Gnome looked older and battle-hardened, at least judging by the scars he could see – and the intense stare coming from his eyes, despite being shorter than even the Dwarf. Still, jumping down 10 feet from the chest of the machine he was obviously piloting didn't seem to be much of an effort for the little person, which just went to show that the look of old age could be deceiving.

Even given the Gnome's smaller stature, Gerold wasn't confident he could win in a fight; still, he kept his body ready to defend itself as the smaller person walked by him with seemingly no care as to the Dwarf's defensive stance. He watched as the Gnome made his way over to a large wooden wagon and picked up two orbs that looked very similar to the ones Gerold held in his hands; they appeared to be negligently discarded earlier, which was strange to the Dwarf considering that they seemed to be so powerful.

Before he knew it, the older Gnome was in front of him offering the glowing orbs to him in either hand. Gerold looked at him and then the orbs in confusion, wondering what this was all about; with some obvious gestures that indicated that the Gnome wanted him to take the orbs followed by some words that meant nothing to him, the Dwarf said, "You want me to take these? Why?"

The Gnome seemed to be listening to something in his head as he looked blankly past Gerold, before he nodded a couple of times in acknowledgement. Then, strangely, he pulled up his shirt and revealed a very strange bronze-colored tattoo of what looked like a gear on his chest, accompanied by flecks of grey and red. It looked strangely familiar – the flecks, not the gear – and it took him a moment to realize why. Second-shield Bregan had Fire and Spirit as the elements he could access, and his armor reflected that with tints of red and grey, which was crazily similar to what he was seeing on the tattoo.

"I have no idea what that is, but do those colors mean you can use Fire and Spirit?" he asked, forgetting for a moment that they had a language barrier.

The old Gnome looked away like he was listening again, before he nodded again, pulling out a necklace that was hidden before behind his back at the same time. Gerold saw that two of the glowing orbs were tied loosely to a leather string – one red and one grey, exactly what he had assumed it would be. *I still have no idea what is going on here, though.*

It didn't look like the Gnome or anything else there meant to hurt him, however; they had ample opportunity to kill him before he woke up, and with that Goblin—*Gnome*—machine he would've been dead in moments if it had attacked. Therefore, with a shrug he took the again-proffered orbs, which was a little awkward considering that he already had one of each in his hands; he wasn't sure if it was happenstance or by plan, but he now had matching pairs – two blue in his left and two black in his right.

An unexpected pain came from his hands and traveled all the way up his arms, before suffusing the rest of his body; it was so great that he screamed out and dropped to his knees as a bright light coming from his hands nearly blinded him. The pain then ramped up to heights he had no idea it could reach, causing him to start to black out…but then everything stopped abruptly.

The cessation and lack of lingering pain made him fall to his hands as he tried to make sense of what had just happened. Gerold realized he was breathing heavy as he hung his head, so he tried to slow his breathing down and take stock of the rest of his body.

* *Well, now…that was new.* *

Gerold whipped his head up and looked around at who had spoken to him – and in his own language, at that. It was a distinctly female voice and it didn't match what he had heard the Gnome say before, so he looked for someone – or some*thing* – else.

"Who said that?" he asked, quickly getting to his feet – and was amazed to find that all traces of the unimaginable pain he had just experienced was completely gone, now just a fading memory that he had trouble believing was real.

** I'm sorry for the pain, it really shouldn't have been that...intense. I'm not sure exactly what happened—actually, that might explain it. **

As the voice was talking, Gerold realized he didn't hear it with his ears – he heard it in his *mind*. He brought his hands up to his head in an automatic response, but before he could touch it he paused; looking at his palms, he saw the same bronze-colored tattoo on each hand, though one had black flakes and one had blue flakes. Not only that, but the orbs he had initially been holding were no longer being *held* – but were instead embedded *inside* his palms in the center of the bronze gear.

He opened and closed his hand over and over, expecting some sort of resistance, but despite most of the orb being in the middle of his palm with just the top showing, it didn't seem to hinder any of his finger or hand motion. He could still feel the slow regeneration of his elemental energy coming from them, though he had to admit that it felt more...natural? Almost like he was missing a part of himself and was now...complete.

** That is interesting; I can see a very small trickle of my Mana being fed through the Visitor's Bond into the Energy Orbs, somehow replenishing them as they transfer you some elemental energy. It's barely even noticeable to my natural ambient Mana regeneration, and I would doubt it would consume more than a single point of Mana over a whole day; if it's doing what I think it's doing, I think as long as you're within my Area of Influence, those Energy Orbs embedded in your palms will continue to supply energy for as long as I exist.*

Violet, are you getting this? I don't know how this happened, but if we can harness this for other applications, we might be able to—

"WHAT IS GOING ON?! WHO ARE YOU AND WHAT DID YOU DO TO ME?!" Gerold shouted, which immediately silenced the voice in his head and even made the old Gnome take a step back. Everything was silent for a few moments, before the voice came back, though instead of the former excitement it instead sounded apologetic.

** I'm sorry, that was very rude of me, especially after all that you went through. Again, I apologize for the unexpected pain and I assure you that I didn't intend for all that to happen.*

** Anyway, my name is Sandra and you're standing in the workshop attached to my dungeon. I know, I know, it's probably hard to* *believe – but it's true, and I'll take you on a tour later if you want it. In the meantime, I want you to know that you're not a prisoner and the Visitor's Bond – the tattoos on your palms – only allows me to talk to you and prevents my Dungeon Monsters from attacking you and the traps I have set up throughout from activating accidentally. You're free to go at any time, but I do have some questions for you if you don't mind. **

"Free to go? Go where? If I go back to my village I'll be shunned and sent back to the mountains as a failure; having lost my weapon, shield, *and* armor on my first solo day of culling the Golems, I can't show my face back there. And all because of whatever it was that *you* apparently did, it will be better if they just think I died – that way my family will be able to remember me as brave in falling in the line of duty instead of being incompetent," Gerold angrily muttered, his voice rising gradually so that it was practically a shout by the end. The fact that he was talking to a voice in his head that was purporting to be a dungeon had barely penetrated enough after he realized it was most likely its—*her?*—fault that he had lost everything, been nearly killed, and then had the most horrific pain go through his hands and body.

** I'm also sorry that you lost your armor and axe – but what were you doing here in the first place? This place is so far from your lands that you couldn't possibly have seen what was going on from there. As much as I tend to take responsibility for a lot of things* *around here that may or may not actually be my fault, there was no way I could've planned for your presence here so close to my dungeon. **

That question made Gerold's anger subside as the real reason most of that had happened became clear: it was his fault that most of what had been done to him because his curiosity forced him to follow his sensitive Nether sense. The pain and "bonding" or whatever it was came directly from the dungeon, obviously, but he probably wouldn't have even been in that situation if he hadn't made the conscious choice to venture out into the wastelands. As his mind cleared a little, he felt himself telling the voice – whether it was a dungeon or not was still yet to be determined – about what led him to be on top of that hill and watching the battle play out.

She—Sandra, she said her name was—seemed interested in his claim to be able to sense Nether energy even from a distance and asked a few more questions about what he was doing in the forest before he made his way to where he was now. She also expressed concern that he had seen one of those skeletal rats so close to the forest's border.

** I'm concerned because it means that the Undead Core knows about the existence of your people, whereas it was likely that it had no previous knowledge of the Dwarves at all. From what I can see of its Area of Influence, I doubt that it knows your exact location,* *but if it isn't stopped soon it'll expand far enough to either reach your village or else be so close that it will be difficult for your people to move around the land anymore.* *

"Even if I was there, we don't have the Shieldmen to fight something like that; the few reinforcements we have from the stronghold *might* be enough if they could make it here in time, though it would probably end up with more casualties than we can afford to destroy the dungeon. I have a feeling that they'd rather just abandon Nurboldar and try to find someplace else to farm," Gerold said with a touch of melancholy. He had just barely started on his duty to the village and the Dwarven Kingdom, and already it looked like it was over for the relatively quiet existence of everybody there. He knew Second-shield Bregan would be disappointed, because the village was supposed to be a place he could train newcomers and semi-retire in a place that didn't see much fighting. *Heavy* fighting, that is.

* *I'm working towards destroying it myself, but I've had a few setbacks lately; the use of the Gravitational Devastation Sphere – while definitely being more destructive than I had originally thought it would be – has actually given me an opportunity to fight back. It's going to take some time and constant attrition against the other Core to get to the point where I can eliminate it, though, so it might not be in time to stop it from reaching your people.*

** On that note, however, I have some ideas...**

Gerold listened to Sandra talk, growing more incredulous as the minutes rolled by and the dungeon mentioned some unbelievable things – as well as an invitation. "Before I commit to something like what you're proposing, I want to see exactly what you're talking about. Let's go on this tour you mentioned before; I think I trust you enough not to kill me outright by this point, but what you've said is too hard to believe without seeing it with my own two eyes."

Less than a minute later, Gerold found himself following one of the strange steel-made apes that he had seen before, hoping he hadn't been too trusting and made a poor decision. *Who would've thought I'd* ***ask*** *to go deeper into a dungeon, especially since I'm unarmed and unarmored.* Regardless of the craziness of it, he found himself looking forward to seeing if everything the voice said was true.

Chapter 22

The Dwarf was surprisingly receptive to the whole situation of Sandra being a dungeon, considering what had just been done to him. The tour that the Dungeon Core brought him on went even further to impress upon him her intentions towards the races surrounding the wastelands, as well as her desire to help them where she could.

Sandra technically didn't have time for the whole sight-seeing thing with the newly Visitor-bonded Gerold, but she knew it was going to be imperative that she establish the correct type of relationship with him – and by extension, his people – right from the start. Fortunately, even though most of her focus was on showing him her crafting stations, the Growing Room, the Enchantment Repository Room, and even – with plenty of personal protection in the form of nearby constructs – her Home room, she was able to split her attention to more...important matters.

Like maintaining her current Mana advantage over the Undead Core.

Her Rolling Force constructs were already "rolling" over the scattered skeleton rats, destroying dozens of them every minute. The number of her own were still building little by little, and they were already topping 800 scattered everywhere over a portion of the wasteland and the open land near the Gnome village. While they were making fairly good progress wiping out every rat they found, she had to have her rolling constructs come together in groups of 20 to take out the larger walking skeletons they were starting to encounter. Eventually, she upped that number to 50 when some of the weaker zombies started to make an appearance closer to the forest, and anything venturing into the forest had at least 100 grouped together.

Having that many together was a risk, but they were also able to work together to destroy all but the most powerful zombie beasts that occasionally made an appearance. The Ogre Skeletons were the only ones of that kind that she avoided entirely, but everything else fell under the onslaught of her constructs. As time went on, she planned to send the larger groups into the forest, sweeping through it to destroy all of the weaker Undead they could find, only leaving the stronger ones alone.

She knew from personal experience that it really didn't matter how strong or powerful one of her Dungeon Monsters were, because they all essentially funneled the same amount of ambient Mana to her. Now, something like that gigantic abomination of jumbled-up corpses that had joined the Undead forces around her dungeon might be able to reach more because of its size, but she didn't think it was that significant of a difference. It was why her Shears – and in comparison, the skeletal rats – worked so well because they accumulated nearly as much as a Monster that was 10 or 100 times the Mana cost. So, the other Core might have 50 or so powerful Undead that were slowly accumulating Mana, but without the smaller, cheaper ones running around, its overall growth would be slower.

Over time, of course, those powerful Undead could multiply until that was all there was out roaming around the Undead dungeon's AOI, but Sandra was banking on that not happening for a while. She had the advantage now – but she had to make sure she maintained it.

To that effect, she had already emptied out about 2/3 of her treasury, keeping the Rolling Force and Shears production going, while also trying to replace the constructs – and Unstable Shapeshifters – she had lost during that chaotic battle above her dungeon. The problem she was quickly running into, however, was a lack of Raw Materials. She was seriously considering cannibalizing the wagon of Gnome supplies for more, but while she was looking at it she remembered the heavy sphere that Felbar had helped to bring into her workshop – and therefore into her dungeon.

Without thinking, she tried to absorb it – but nothing happened. At least, she thought that nothing happened, but when she looked at her available Raw Materials...she was completely full. Peering back as the sphere stuck in the hole it had made in the floor, she saw that a sliver of it had been carved out from the top, exactly where she had been looking at it in her effort to absorb it. *What the...? How is that possible?*

Winxa, disregarding for her own safety, created a portal that led from her home to the workshop, where she peered down at the sphere and her mouth opened in a "O" shape as she took it in. "Wow, you've really got something here."

What are you talking about? What is this material?

Sandra still had no idea what it was and absorbing that little sliver's worth of Raw Materials revealed no new type of material – which she had been half-expecting.

"Well, keeping in mind that I'm not an expert in gravitational physics—" the Dungeon Fairy began.

Uh…what?

"—I'd say that this strange ball consists of everything that was sucked up into your Sphere construct when you activated it," she continued. "No wonder you're limited to only using this every 60 days and within a few hundred feet of your entrance; if something like this was able to be used by a Dungeon Core of a less…hospitable…nature and able to be brought near a village or fortified town…well, I don't think I need to tell you what would happen."

How is that even possible? That vortex thingy sucked up so much dirt and massive rocks, not to mention all of the undead and constructs I had out there, that there's no way that it would fit in there.

"Well, consider if that material was like your Mana in a way; when you created your Elemental Orbs, you took a large quantity of it and then condensed it down until it was much smaller. This is essentially the same thing, though the force used to condense this material was at a hard-to-imagine level compared to what you used on that Mana. What you see here is the result of so much material smashed together that it obviously made it really heavy, as I can see by the hole it made," she further explained.

Logically, what Winxa said made a lot of sense; in reality, Sandra had a hard time picturing how such a thing was possible. Nevertheless, it would definitely explain how just a little sliver of it could give her approximately 50,000 Raw Material, as well as being the reason why it hadn't been a "new" material. If she was right, then the strange sphere was made from dirt, stone, desiccated branches, a whole assortment of metal-based Monster Seeds, and some Sapphire and Onyx gemstones. There was always a possibility that there was something different in there, but it would require eating away at the multi-colored ball for a while to discover it.

Thanks, Winxa, she told her, before said Fairy opened another portal and disappeared back down near Sandra's Core.

"You're welcome," she said when she appeared. "Whew, that's the last time I go near the surface – it's way too dangerous. You should warn a girl," she muttered, smiling at Sandra's Core.

Rather than wasting her time arguing with Winxa and telling her that she had nothing to do with the Fairy going up there in the first place, Sandra used her time more wisely and started to make enough Monster Seeds with the new source of Raw Materials to last a while. With her Rolling Forces adding to the amount of ambient Mana she was receiving from her AMANS already (which was also growing slowly back up to the level it was before) she was flush with that particular resource – so she spent it on building up another force that she hoped would eventually be sent to start destroying the Undead outside of the other dungeon. From there, with some additional reinforcements, it would be on to the dungeon and Dungeon Core itself – to end the threat once and for all.

There was still going to be a bit of time before that happened, of course, and some other preparations that had to be made – which would hopefully start the next day. Now that the War Machine was finished and working excellently – *I still have to fix the mostly cosmetic damage tonight, though* – Violet was going to be free to help with designing some more enchantments that were sure to be useful.

For the moment, though, she was still resting and Felbar had joined her and Echo down in the dining area for a late lunch/early dinner. From their conversation, the two Gnomes were talking about turning in early and getting a fresh start in the morning. As for the Elf, Sandra could see she was restless and itching to do something; unfortunately, it was still a little dangerous to go outside because it was always possible the Undead would come back – though it was unlikely. She'd have to figure out if there were something she could have Echo help with, though she said she might go back down to the Enchantment Repository and study the enchantments there some more.

By that time, the grand tour of the dungeon was almost done with Gerold; she made sure everything else was running as smoothly as they could be before she turned her full attention back to the Dwarf. Earlier, he had met the others – Violet and Echo – in the kitchen they were still lounging around in and had seemed a bit disconcerted with the Elf for some reason; Sandra thought at first it was because he had some sort of racial prejudice against Elves – which seemed all too prevalent – but when she saw the brief blush on his face the Dungeon Core knew exactly why. Seeing nearly 20 naked "Echos" outside fighting against the undead must've been a little much for him.

It's a good thing that they can't really communicate verbally – the last thing we need is for him to say something about that. Clothing for her Shapeshifters had seemed like a waste since she figured many of them would die anyway; she wasn't expecting *all* of them that she sent out to die, of course, but she didn't think modesty had any place out there in a battle between Dungeon Monsters.

Other than that, the tour had been relatively normal until the very last room she showed him, which contained her distillery. "Wait, you distill spirits here? Whiskey?" he asked, his eyes wide and pleading as he took in her relatively simple still. "How about brewing? I'd kill for a nice ale right now," he continued, looking around the room.

** No, not really; I was using this for steaming some Cedarwood to obtain some Cedar Oil and hadn't really had a use for it. Besides, I don't possess any of the required material for that...and I have to admit that – as extensive as my crafting knowledge is – it didn't really extend to the creation of hard spirits or beer. **

"Not *beer*—" he said, putting specific emphasis on the word— "but *Ale* – they're two completely different things." Sandra really didn't have enough knowledge to contradict him, so she took him at his word. He was silent for a moment as he stared at her distillery set-up, before seeming to come to a decision.

Gerold's voice was soft and a little despairing at the same time as he continued. "I don't know if you have much knowledge of our land, but it isn't a secret that we're running out of available land aboveground to grow things. Much of it used to be used for food, but we've learned to cultivate other sources that can be grown in our mountain strongholds to supplement our diet; instead, we raise some livestock out here for our own purposes and have some sent back home, but most of what we actually grow on the farms near the village is used for another purpose: alcohol.

"Yes, it sounds funny even to me when I say it, but we have yet to find a way to grow wheat, barley, and hops underground consistently. We Dwarves can live without alcohol, of course – but that's not really *living*, is it? In fact, the shortages of anything good to drink has been attributed to the drop in both our population and the number of us willing to actually leave the safety of the mountains to fight back against the dungeon monsters out there. We've kept a fairly stable supply line out to the few farms we have left, but without the biggest farm near Nurboldar being there – if those undead overrun it – then that'll be another massive blow to our people's morale."

** How do you know so much about the whole situation? Is it common knowledge to all of the Dwarves? **

Gerold laughed shortly, before saying, "Oh, no, not at all. My mother is on the King's council back in Grandhall, one of the biggest mountain strongholds still existing today. She tended to tell bedtime stories that were politically and economically based, so I kind of grew up with that stuff."

Hmm...now ***this*** *is an interesting development.*

** So, what do you think about my invitation from earlier? Do you think your people would be willing to live here in safety while we attempt to destroy the dungeon threatening them? At this point I can't guarantee that even if we succeed in eliminating that threat that the Golem and Goblin dungeons won't take advantage of your absence, but I'll do everything in my power to try to get your land back if that happens. I don't particularly want to spend all my time and Mana destroying Core after Core, however, so if there is a way to maintain the status quo that has already been established I will try that route first.*

** As far as your farm and what you need for your...alcohol...goes, you've already seen that I can grow things down here that aren't normally meant to be grown. Perhaps we can come to some sort of* *arrangement that will allow that to continue, as well as possibly brewing and distilling your drink.* *

Gerold definitely looked interested, though he tried to appear as if he was thinking it over. Despite looking quite different from a Human, years of working with her father as a merchant let her see signs in his face and posture that indicated she had him hooked. Now all she needed to do was complete the transaction, getting as much as she could out of him – and his people, of course. She generally didn't like to take advantage of those with a less-than-stellar negotiating ability (like Gerold obviously had), but the Dwarves had something she wanted. All she had to do was wait for him to initiate the conversation—

"What kind of *arrangement* are you talking about?" he asked when she didn't elaborate.

There it is. Sandra had initially proposed that the Dwarves in the village come take refuge in her dungeon while she dealt with the Undead Core with nothing expected in return; now that she was proposing putting in some work to continue their farming and even start crafting beer—*Ale, apparently*—and other alcoholic drinks, she wanted to get something in return. Secretly, she was excited to learn about new brewing and distilling techniques from them – but Gerold didn't need to know that.

** I can safely house all of the Dwarven villagers and even your Shieldmen here, provide a place to grow your food and ingredients for your spirits and whatnot, and even create a large distillery and brewery so that you can create it here instead of having to deliver it back to your strongholds and hope that you'll get some product in the future. Not only that, but I can even provide a quick transport system for your people to bring everything that is produced here back to the rest of your population – and I'll even throw in some Energy Orbs for whoever wants them.*

** Like I also said, I* ***will*** *eliminate the Undead Core threatening your people, but whether or not it comes too late to save the land your village is sitting on from being overrun by the other dungeons nearby is another matter; regardless, I'll pledge to do everything I can to get it back to you.*

** And I'll do all of that for two relatively simple things; the first is a promise to cooperate in the future with the other races on something important. I already have a tenuous agreement with the Elves and I'm working on getting help from the Gnomes, but I need all the races around here to be on board or it won't work. The second...well, the second thing is something that only your people can provide. **

Now he started to look a little worried, especially after hearing all that Sandra was laying out to him. Gerold had looked down at his hands at the mention of Energy Orbs, but now his eyes appeared to be unfocused. "I...*think* my people might agree to some sort of future cooperation – if it isn't something that will endanger our people or strongholds, but what is it that only my people can provide? You want to rule our Kingdom? Do you want to make every Dwarf your slave? I can't think of anything else, since it seems as though you can just...create everything you want to here. What could you possibly want?"

** Oh, it's nothing material, I can assure you of that. No, what I want is something completely different...I would like to learn how your Blacksmiths make your armor and weapons absorb your elemental energy to make them more powerful. And unless you know precisely how it's done it'll probably entail having one of your Master Blacksmiths come here to teach me. **

Gerold's face seemed to lose all of its color and his mouth opened and closed repeatedly. "Uh, well," he finally managed to get out. "I'm...not sure about that. The secrets of their production are passed down from Blacksmith to Blacksmith and very few outside of their little community know how it is they're made. *I* certainly do not, and I'm almost positive no one in the village knows, either – not even Second-shield Bregan. As much as I think your help would both be much-appreciated and may even be highly beneficial, I can't see a way to convince any Master Blacksmiths to give up their secrets—"

** You know, if I learn how to make some, I can make you some replacements for the ones you lost earlier. **

His mouth shut with a snap at her words, and Sandra could see something in there that just sealed the deal: hope. Gerold had mentioned that he likely wouldn't ever be getting replacement armor or axe for the ones that were destroyed by the Sphere, and she was dangling that *hope* of…being whole again…in front of him. She wasn't deceiving him, of course, and she would absolutely create another full set of everything for him – nothing soured a relationship like deception, even inadvertent deception. What he didn't realize was that – because of her unique access to quite a few different techniques as a Dungeon Core – she was fairly confident she could not only create some of the special armaments once she knew how it was done but could *improve* on them as well.

"I'll see what I can do. It might take a while to convince them to share that knowledge, and I may have to lean on my mother and her political influence, but I will do my best. If you can convince all of the other Shieldmen in Nurboldar that it's the best for everybody, that will certainly go a long way towards bringing a Master Blacksmith here."

** That is all I needed to hear. I trust you to see that through, but you have to take things one step at a time. You've got another task before that could ever happen, you know. **

"Don't remind me; convincing everyone from the village to abandon everything and move into a *dungeon* because of a threat they undoubtedly aren't even aware of is going to be tough," he said, before shaking his head. "Actually, tough isn't the right word; *impossible* is more like it."

** I have no doubt you'll figure it out, because it's their lives on the line if they don't listen to you. Or, to be more accurate, it's all the* ***alcohol*** *they're going to miss out on if ignoring you seems to be the way they're going. It's up to you to do it, though, because I have no way of communicating with them. Let me know how I may be of help, as limited as that will probably be. **

"I will; I just have to figure out what kind of help you could possibly provide other than sending your monsters—" he started despondently, before he tilted his head to the side. "Actually, I think there might be something you could do..."

Chapter 23

Sandra knew that Gerold wasn't going back to the village right then, however, because of two very important reasons. One, it was nearing the end of the day and it was already starting to get dark; two, the fatigue from being horrendously injured and then miraculously healed finally hit him all at once. She could only guess that he had been fighting the fatigue while he was still adjusting to where he was and exploring the potential refuge for his people; once that was all over, he practically sleep walked up to the dining area to get something to eat, before flopping down on the bed Sandra had hastily created for him in a nearby empty room.

The thought of beds made her realize that she hadn't even asked how many Dwarves were in the village; she had seen at least 50 of them out in the fields and around some of the buildings from afar, but she knew there could've been twice that many still inside those buildings and she wouldn't know it. Not to mention the Shieldmen who seemed to house themselves separate from the villagers, which were hard to get a count on because they were constantly moving in and out of the immediate area as they culled the Dungeon Monsters in the nearby forests.

Regardless of the numbers, before they arrived – she had no doubt the village Dwarves would eventually escape to her dungeon for protection once they had visual proof of the threat – she had to prepare places for them to sleep and, well, live. It was one thing having a place to lay down their heads to sleep and that might be enough for Echo, Violet, and Felbar at the moment; they had other things they had been doing like enchanting, working on the War Machine, teaching Sandra how to cast spells, and delivering Energy Orbs to the Elven village. The Dwarves, on the other hand, wouldn't likely do any of that; the villagers' jobs had been farming and things related to farming, while the Shieldmen were used to culling and killing Monsters.

If Sandra was going to help them farm – and she had already decided she was going to start doing that, even if no Master Blacksmiths ever came to teach her (though for *how long* she would do such was dependent on that eventuality) – she needed to start finding a place they could do that. Before she did any of that work, however, there were more important matters to attend to.

Namely, figuring out a way to destroy the Undead dungeon.

Her Rolling Forces were still slowly making their way around much of the open space and just inside the trees, destroying everything they were easily able to. More Undead were slowly coming out from where she sensed the dungeon was, though, and the new ones she was seeing were tending to be just a little too much for her constructs out in the field to easily handle – or reach. Specters were suddenly the popular way to go for the Core, mimicking the way her Shears stayed above the ground and consistently moved around; they were obviously much more expensive than skeletal rats so she didn't see hordes of them, but it was probably only a matter of time before the sky above the trees was filled with mist-like Monsters.

Other than that, she saw the more-powerful zombie beasts, a few random Ogre Skeletons, and scattered sightings of the ghouls she had seen before. Her Rolling Forces proved to be able to kill one of the latter, but it required all 100 of the ones she had in groups to sacrifice themselves in their bombardment to do enough damage to them. The first skirmish she had between her constructs and the ghouls proved that they could be injured, but it took *a lot* more hits before they went down, and the Undead itself was quite adept at quickly slicing through the pieces of her Forces with its sharp claws. After that, she knew it would be better to leave them alone and hunt safer targets.

However, she estimated that by the time the next day dawned that there wouldn't be many more that she could eliminate. To top it off, there was still approximately 3 square miles of the other Core's AOI that she couldn't even reach, as it was now too far past the dungeon itself to access. If the Undead Core was smart – and Sandra had seen enough evidence so far to assume that it was – then that area she couldn't reach right now was likely packed with monsters.

Even if they were only those rats, it was enough space to let the Undead Core accumulate massive amounts of Mana – and there was nothing she could do about it. By the amount of "new" Undead (she assumed they were newly created, instead of just being sent out from the defenders already stationed in the dungeon) she saw, Sandra thought this was indeed the case.

She was still filtering through all of that information as she looked around the entire Area as night set in. Her Visitors were already asleep – or feigning sleep, in the case of Echo – so Sandra had some time on her hands to figure out what she wanted to do. She already knew that she wanted to enchant some Titanium warhammers that her Steelclad Ape Warriors would be carrying into the fight against the Undead, but she wasn't sure where to go from there. Since that was really the only construct that could reliably wield a weapon, the Dungeon Core was at a loss for what to do to enhance her existing Monsters.

Of course, she had her Unstable Shapeshifters, which could wield their elemental energy and cast spells like the ones that had been so effective against those robe-wielding Undead. After consulting with Echo who seemed to know quite a bit about them despite never actually seeing them before, she discovered that they were called Liches. Apparently, they were the most despised of the Undead – as far as the Elves were concerned – because they were originally purported to be the reanimated remains of Elves that had turned towards using "necromantic"-type spells as their focus. Whether that was true or not, Echo was almost spitting with obvious hatred and barely restrained violence when she mentioned them earlier.

Nevertheless, the ability to cast spells from a distance – and relatively powerful ones, at that – was a great addition to her forces. She was already adding quite a few of them to her eventual army that would eventually be sent to the area around the dungeon, as well as inside when the time came, but there were a few downsides to using them. The first one was the most obvious one – their time limit; they could only hold their shape for an hour before they had to revert to their normal form, which had proven not to really have any offensive capabilities when it was a multi-colored blob. Other than possibly suffocation if it were allowed to envelop an enemy, but that really wouldn't do much to Undead Monsters that didn't have to breathe in the first place.

Second, giving them some sort of armor to protect them or weapons to attack with if they ran out of elemental energy was technically possible, but there was no real easy way to bring them along; she'd have to assign some sort of transporters for the sole purpose of carrying their gear, because the Shifters themselves couldn't carry more than something small in their blob-like appendages they could extend – and poorly at that. Not only that, but she had also found that if the Shifter was wearing something in, say, Echo's form, if the "shift" time ran out before it could remove the clothing it was practically shredded as the Unstable Monster ballooned up into its "normal" shape. Sandra wasn't sure if something a little more durable than just cloth would act the same as well, or if it would hurt the Shifter as it suddenly became too large for its protection.

The third thing – and it was the most worrisome of the entire situation – was that she wasn't sure if she could even have her Shapeshifters cast spells while in the other dungeon. During the battle outside her dungeon entrance, it was proven that they could take orders and cast spells that Sandra knew how to easily create without her having to directly control each and every one – which would've been virtually impossible in that type of situation, regardless of how much practice she'd had at it lately – so that wasn't necessarily the issue. The problem was that during her assault on the Reptile-based dungeon not so long ago, her response time and ability to give detailed orders to them was severely hampered by their presence in a foreign dungeon.

Sandra wasn't sure if they would – or even *could* – react to threats in the way that she wanted them to; her other constructs seemed to have a natural battle instinct to them that worked pretty well, but there were times when death came to them in the form of a trap that they basically stood still for, despite the danger. Whether those two things would apply to dozens of "Echos" traipsing through the other dungeon was something she couldn't even test without going there directly.

So, either she was going to have to find some way to ensure they did exactly what they were supposed to, or Sandra was going to have to find some other potential "weapons" to use. Those "weapons" would, of course, come in the form of Dungeon Monsters – and not necessarily her constructs. They were already proven to be powerful against creatures and Monsters that could bleed with their various slicing weapons – such as her Shears, the Millipede's mandibles, her Blademaster, the Jaguar Queens, and even her Sharp-bladed Digger (which was similar to the original, but could turn much faster and had very sharp edges on the "buckets");

however, against the Undead, many of their strengths were disadvantages because they couldn't do enough damage to something that didn't bleed.

That didn't mean there weren't Dungeon Monsters out there that might be better suited to eliminating the Nether-based Undead.

Therefore, Sandra brought up her Advancement Menu to see how many Advancement Points she had to spend on a little shopping spree. She was surprised to see that she had acquired a few more AP from somewhere; a quick perusal showed that they came from another Crafting Station, which she immediately assumed was the Distillery she had created. Not only that, but her "Bathing Room" and her Enchantment Repository (which was finally as complete as it was going to get) apparently were considered Unique Dungeon Fixtures; she briefly wondered why her growing room, her dining room, and even her VATS weren't considered unique fixtures if that was the case. The only thing she could think of was that they weren't "unique" and were seen somewhere else in a dungeon in the past, though that seemed...well, not *impossible*, but unlikely.

Advancement Points (AP)				
Source	Criteria	Point Value	Lifetime Earned Points	Lifetime Spent Points
Core Size	Receive AP upon Core Size upgrade (does not count for Core Size 1 nor upgrade stages)	1 per Core Size upgrade	19 AP (19X Core Size Upgrades)	19/19 AP
Number of Rooms	Receive AP for each distinct dungeon room at least 4,000 cubic feet in size (20ftx20ftx10ft minimum)	1 AP per qualified room	45 AP (45X Qualifying Rooms)	45/45 AP
Unique Dungeon Fixtures	Receive AP for each never-before-seen fixture in your dungeon	2 AP per fixture	32 AP (14X Crafting Stations, 1X Bathing Room, 1X	26/32 AP

			Enchantment Repository)	
Creature Eradication	Eradicate sources of nearby creatures (i.e. lairs and spawning areas)	3 AP per eradication	72 AP (5X Territory Ant Colonies, 6X Bearling Lairs, 4X Desolate Spider Clutches, 4X Crag Hound Packs, 5X Solitary Broat Spawn)	39/72 AP
Sentient Race Elimination	Eliminate members of sentient races	1 AP per 10 eliminations	8 AP (12X Orc, 71X Gnome)	8/8 AP
Sentient Race Bonding	Form a new Dungeon Visitor Bond with a member of a sentient race	1 AP per 2 Bonds	8 AP (1X Orc/Dwarf, 6X Elf, 9X Gnome, 1X Dwarf)	8/8 AP
Dungeon Core Destruction	Receive AP for eliminating another Dungeon Core	30 AP per Core	30 AP (1X Reptile Classification Core)	30/30 AP
?????	*N/A*	*N/A*	*N/A*	*N/A*
(?????) Denotes an unknown, unique Source of Advancement Points. Perform this unknown action to unlock more information.				
Total Advancement Points Earned and Spent			214 AP	175 AP
Total Advancement Points Available			**39 AP**	

Advancement Options	
Current Advancement Points	39
Advancement:	**Cost:**
*Choose **1** Dungeon Monster from another available Classification (Repeatable)*	5
Give your Dungeon Monsters the option of having a chosen accessible elemental attribute in addition to their base element – Cost increases with each purchase (only works on Monsters capable of using/applying their element) (Repeatable)	10
Reduce the Mana cost of Monster Seeds by 15% – Cost increases with each purchase (Advancement 2/4)	60
Reduce the Mana cost of Dungeon Monsters by 15% – Cost increases with each purchase (Advancement 2/4)	60
Reduce the Raw Material cost of Monster Seeds by 15% – Cost increases with each purchase (Advancement 0/4)	15
Reduce the Mana cost of Dungeon Traps by 15% – Cost increases with each purchase (Advancement 0/4)	15
Extend your Area of Influence by 10% – Cost increases with each purchase (Advancement 0/10)	50
*Advance a current Classification **1** level to acquire access to stronger and larger Dungeon Monsters – this also includes any "Advancement Unlocked" Monsters – Cost increases with each purchase (Advancement 1/3)*	150
Select a second available Classification to hybridize your Core (This option is only available once)	150

All of that meant that she had a total of 39 AP to spend – and she was suddenly glad that she hadn't purchased the Advancement that would reduce the Raw Material Cost of her Monster Seeds, because that would've given her much less to work with. As it was, she had enough AP to acquire 7 new Dungeon

Monsters, though she was hoping to find something that might work before she spent almost all her accumulated Points.

Obviously, what I need is something that will directly oppose the Undead – who are Nether-based – so I think I'll look at some options that are primarily Holy-based. There were quite a few to choose from, especially when she extended her search to include multi-element-Classifications, but she eventually narrowed it down to those she thought *might* have potential.

Dungeon Monster Selection (Base)			
Unicorns (Holy)			
Glowing Lemur	Mirrored Lynx	Bright Unicorn	Radiant Pegasus
Lustrous Bicorn*	Translucent Quadricorn*	Sparkling Pegacorn**	Resplendent Septicorn***
Angels (Holy/Spirit)			
Innocent Angeling	Devoted Cherubling	Transcendent Angel	Pure Cherub
Celestial Authority*	Revered Virtue*	Sacred Archangel**	Immaculate Seraph***
Divine Beasts (Holy/Air)			
Soaring Serpent	Climbing Cockatrice	Gliding Griffin*	Tenacious Thunderbird*
Hovering Hippogriff**	Kiting Kitsune**	Meandering Manticore***	Aetherial Dragon***
Phoenix (Holy/Fire)			
Charred Salamander	Smoldering Firebird	Burning Sundog	Flaring Phoenix
Rising Phoenix*	Scorching Behemoth*	Searing Phoenix Elder**	Fiery Phoenoc***

*Requires Advanced Classification Level 1 (Complete)	** Requires larger Core Size and Advanced Classification Level 2	*** Requires larger Core Size and Advanced Classification Level 3

There was an interesting multi-element selection of Divine Beasts, which included Griffins, Cockatrices, and even a flying Serpent. If she was looking for something that could fly and could tear up anything else in the air, then those would probably be the way to go. Unfortunately, they would likely suffer even more from the attack by the Undead in comparison to her constructs, as they all seemed like creatures – at least from what she could tell from her limited knowledge of them from myths and legends – that were more about brute force than anything…which was pretty much covered by some of her current Dungeon Monsters.

The Thunderbird option in the Divine Beasts Classification, on the other hand, was something she could only imagine would be able to use elemental energy to toss out lightning bolts to strike its enemies. Again, something that sounded neat, but would it be useful against undead? She wasn't quite sure, so she passed on that unless she couldn't find anything else.

Sandra remembered when Felbar had mentioned using Fire to help defeat the Undead that he had fought against, and some of the choices would definitely contribute to that. The Phoenix-type of Monsters, for example, were flying creatures that could start assaulting the Specters up in the air – they were vulnerable to Fire from what he had said. Having an aerial force that could destroy the ever-growing numbers of Specters floating above the forest would be highly beneficial; at the moment, all she had that could attack them were her Shears, and those would perhaps take a hundred or more to kill a single mist-like Undead – not a good exchange on Sandra's part.

As for the two Classifications that seemed uniquely suited to combating the Undead, there were two: Unicorns and Angels. The Unicorns list also included some Monsters on the list that weren't unicorns – like the Glowing Lemur and Mirrored Lynx – as well as what she would classify as unicorn-adjacent options – like the

Radiant Pegasus. She knew from stories that unicorns were reportedly supposed to have some sort of natural protection against elemental spells because of their horn on the top of their head, though she wasn't exactly sure how it worked. The Pegasus, being basically a flying horse, was something that drew her attention; if it had some sort of natural protection as well, then it would be ideal.

"I can actually help you out there; I helped what I thought was a decent Holy-based Core once...which eventually tried to consume me, but that's a different story entirely," Winxa said abruptly as Sandra was mentally thinking about her choices. "Anyway, the horn on a Unicorn can provide a measure of protection to the Monster that negates nearly any elemental energy directed towards it, even going so far as to eliminate area-of-effect spells and effects. A Pegasus, however, is a bit more limited; they exude a Holy-based aura that does the same for those surrounding it up to a certain range – but it only works against Nether-based spells and effects. Essentially, Unicorns are protected against *all* elemental attacks themselves, while Pegasi protect themselves and others against only Nether-elemental attacks."

Thank you, Winxa – that helps make my decision much easier.

With the valuable information that the Dungeon Fairy had provided, Sandra knew what she would choose from that list: Radiant Pegasus. While having a Dungeon Monster that was basically immune to elemental-based spells and effects would be helpful, having one that could help the other members of her planned Dungeon Core-destroying army stay safe against attacks was more valuable. She might eventually get a Unicorn as well, but for the moment the Pegasus was the more important of the two.

Lastly, there were the Angels, which was a multi-element Classification of Holy and Spirit. Neither Sandra nor Winxa had any information about them, though the Dungeon Core had heard stories of them when she was still Human. They were apparently beings made of pure Light that were the exact opposite of Demons – which she was glad she hadn't met yet, because, apparently, they were quite scary. Of course, the Undead were bad enough, but at least they had a semblance of being something "normal" that had been alive at one time; Demons, on the other hand, were completely unworldly and unlike anything found in nature.

With no information about any of the other selections available, Sandra settled on three choices: Rising Phoenix, Radiant Pegasus, and Celestial Authority. That last was entirely a "shot in the dark" entirely based on the name – it sounded powerful, which was exactly what she needed. She still had more AP if she needed it to acquire more if her selections didn't work out, but she'd rather save some for later if she had the option.

New Dungeon Monsters unlocked through Advancement!

Unicorns (Holy):
Radiant Pegasus now available!

Radiant Pegasus
Mana Cost: 10000 Mana

Angels (Holy/Spirit):
Celestial Authority now available!

Celestial Authority
Mana Cost: 18000 Mana

Phoenix (Holy/Fire)
Rising Phoenix now available!

Rising Phoenix
Mana Cost: 15000 Mana

Sandra now had 15 AP less to her total – still giving her 24 to use if she needed them. She was briefly worried that her new Dungeon Monsters were quite expensive, but it turned out that the Mana Cost listed on the notification didn't account for her Advancements. Still, almost 13,000 Mana for a Celestial Authority was quite a bit to spend on a Dungeon Monster that she wasn't sure would work or not, but there wasn't anything for that but to try them out.

Over the course of the night, she stopped the production of her Rolling Forces and the build-up of her AMANS (which was able to reach nearly its previous total); instead, she used the Mana she was accumulating on Steelclad Ape Warriors, Unstable Shapeshifters, and her new acquisitions. By morning, she had managed to build her small army of constructs and Shifters back up to the point where they could go out and defend her entrance again if necessary, but not quite to the point where they could go out and start destroying the more-powerful Undead roaming around. With the addition of her new Dungeon Monsters, however, that could change fairly quickly.

The Radiant Pegasus was a resplendently white horse that was 8 feet tall when it held its head straight up, with a 12-foot wingspan when it fully opened the feathered wings that could lie flush against its sides. It was also capable of emitting a steady glow that seemed to infuse the air around it, extending up to approximately 15 feet on all sides; after looking at it closely like she could the Goblin Worker and Unstable Shapeshifter she had obtained earlier, she knew this was its special ability.

Radiant Pegasus

Current Elemental Energy:
Holy – 10000 energy

Special Ability:
Nether-negating Protection Aura: 2 Holy energy per second

It was an expensive ability at 2 Holy energy per second, but it could also last over an hour if it was kept on continuously; that could potentially extend if, say, she hung a Holy Energy Orb around its neck. Sandra didn't really have a way to test it without going into battle against something that would use such devastating effects against her Monsters, but if it worked the way it was supposed to then it could be a huge benefit.

The Pegasus wasn't just a winged horse that had an aura, however, because it had some potential for offense as well. She inadvertently found out – after she had it gracefully fly around her Home room a little – that it had trouble landing and stopping right away; this was in part because its hooves seemed to act essentially like small warhammers as they hit the stone of her floor, cracking the hard material as the Pegasus attempted to come to a complete stop just after landing. Apparently, the winged horse needed some sort of runway to slow down after touching down after a flight to avoid breaking the ground; nevertheless, the lesson she learned was that it could certainly defend itself if it were attacked up close.

The Celestial Authority was unlike anything she had seen or heard of before. Once she created it, she found that she couldn't stare at it for more than a minute or so; it was a being of pure light approximately 5 feet tall that appeared very vaguely like a person – as in it had a head, two arms, and walked on two legs. It held what appeared to be a longsword made of the same light in its hand, which seemed to be its *main* method of attacking. Looking closer, she could see that it had other abilities that could be useful – expensive, but useful.

Celestial Authority

Current Elemental Energy:
Holy – 9000 energy
Spirit – 9000 energy

Special Abilities:
Divine Light Explosion: All remaining Holy energy
Arrows of Spiritual Ascension: 1000 Holy and 1000 Spirit

Of course, she had to test them – outside of her dungeon, obviously, with a name that contained the word "Explosion". She first tried the Arrows of Spiritual Ascension, which were interesting and powerful. After telling the Authority to activate it, the being would reach inside of itself and pull out an orb of light in its hand; as soon as it had it in hand, the Angel would toss the orb ahead, which would immediately fracture into 5 equal parts and shoot forward up to 50 feet…sort of like arrows shot from a bow, though they spread out in a narrow arc.

The Divine Light Explosion – the Celestial Authority's other Special Ability – used all the remaining Holy Energy it had left to…well, *explode*. An extremely bright light – even brighter than the Angel itself – built up in the Authority's form over the course of five seconds, before it shot out in all directions at once. She didn't really have anything near it to test how destructive it was, but furrows left in the barren dirt of the wasteland where she was testing it gave enough evidence that it was fairly powerful – and *final*. After consuming all of its Holy energy in the explosion, the Angel was also *consumed*, leaving behind its Monster Seed in the process.

The last Dungeon Monster she acquired access to – the Rising Phoenix – was one that she thought would currently benefit her the most. Unfortunately, it was also the one that caused the most problems for her. The firebird was a lot larger than she had expected; at 12 feet long from wicked-looking beak to the end of its tail feathers and featuring a 25-foot-wide wingspan when fully extended, it was an impressive creature. It was also burning so hot that it melted some of the smaller original constructs she still had wandering around in her Home.

That wasn't too bad, however, compared to the nightmare of trying to get it up and out of her dungeon. When the Phoenix didn't have its wings extended, its body was relatively sleek, so it could fit down the tunnels – if just barely; the problem was getting it through the doorway to the VATS, which she had to redesign the tunnels outside the doors so that it could turn to the side and enter through that way. Then, when it got to the air traps that sent it upwards, the sheer heat from it caused it to rise much faster than normal, where it ended up crashing against the ceiling above the trap. Fortunately it didn't seem hurt by it, but the stone ceiling required a little repair from the impact.

It was a good thing that it hadn't been hurt, because there was no way to heal it with her Repair Drones – they couldn't get close enough. The heat emanating from the Phoenix was so great, in fact, that it almost caused the Gnomes' supply wagon to catch fire as it made its way through the workshop and out to the sky above. Once it soared through the open air, Sandra wasn't sure exactly what it could do other than burn brightly; its special ability gave a hint of what the Phoenix was known for, but without testing it she wasn't sure how effective it could be.

Rising Phoenix ***Current Elemental Energy:*** *Holy – 7500 energy* *Fire – 7500 energy* ***Special Ability:*** *Born from the Ashes: 3700 Holy and 3700 Fire*

She didn't want to risk killing it herself just to test the ability – especially after the effort she went through just to get it out of her dungeon – so she sent it against the Undead that she had a hard time eliminating: the Specters. As the flaming bird screeched through the sky on its way over the forest, she watched it go with some of her other constructs out there; she had to admit that even if it turned out not to be very effective, it was impressive to look at, nonetheless.

Fortunately, it was just the thing she needed to combat the mist-like Undead that were busy accumulating ambient Mana above the trees. The Rising Phoenix didn't attack so much as just pass through the insubstantial forms of the Specters, destroying them utterly in seconds. Sandra thought that they didn't even do any damage to her Monster, but after a few Undead were destroyed, she noticed a significant drop in the intensity of flames that were running all over the Phoenix. After destroying just over 20 Specters, the flames were extinguished completely and the bird fell from the sky, crashing through the trees below and scorching leaves as it passed by.

Some nearby Rolling Forces finally located it after a minute; she normally would've kept watching through the Phoenix's senses, but as soon as it fell she lost all contact with it. When they finally "rolled" up on the crash site, she saw what appeared to be a tiny, baby Phoenix bird waddling around the ashes of its former self. The firebird appeared completely helpless and didn't even have any flames around it, though the ashes that would flare up a little as it hopped around showed that it still generated a bit of heat.

It was only after 10 minutes of watching the bird hop around looking lost that something finally happened. The Phoenix began to grow at a rapid pace, getting larger and larger...before it stopped when it was only about half the size of the original Phoenix. It immediately lifted off the ground and burst through the trees; as soon as it hit the open air, flames burst out over its body and wings, though they were noticeably not as bright as before. *Interesting.*

More experimentation showed that it was able to destroy another 10 of the Specters before falling again. This time, however, she was too late getting to the crash site; her nearby rolling constructs made it to the location just in time to see a zombie bear smash flat the poor baby firebird under its paw, though it appeared to scorch said paw in the process. So, obviously, soon after the "resurrection" the Phoenix was extremely vulnerable, which meant she had to plan better where it crashed after its flames were extinguished, otherwise it wouldn't be able to come back if it was caught by some other Undead.

It wasn't a perfect trade-off, but Sandra still thought that even if the Phoenix was destroyed before it could resurrect even once she came out ahead. Therefore, she decided to create another one to start hunting more Specters. Since she'd seen that the flames of the newly reborn Phoenix were dimmer than before, she tried focusing on her new Monster to see if she could duplicate that intentionally. After getting nowhere issuing orders to the Phoenix, she finally found that if she directly controlled the Monster, she could dampen the flames considerably for a short time – at least while it was on the ground. Learning how to fly and do it at the same time proved to be beyond her at the moment.

Each of the Dungeon Monsters she had acquired proved to be just what she needed, so she kept the rest of her remaining AP for the future. The last thing she did that night was to start to plan out where she was going to place all of the Dwarves that could potentially be there later in the day, as well as where to put all of the new crops she was going to need to plant. She dismissed the idea of just adding on to her current growing room for the simple reason of Mana availability; the current growing room took quite a lot of her Maximum Mana to set the trap up with Natural and Holy elements – for the actual growing portion and "sunlight" – and making it much larger would probably be impossible until she increased her Core Size.

Therefore, she started the slow process of creating another growing room down below near the long line of rooms she had made before; she was thinking that all of the rooms she had excavated to acquire more AP and for their Raw Materials would be ideal for the Dwarves to live in. With easy access to the "farms" she was going to make, they would hopefully feel more in control of things – and it would free Sandra up from having to do the whole process of planting and harvesting and whatnot herself.

Before she could really start that, though, morning arrived, and her Visitors were up and raring to go for the day.

Chapter 24

Gerold rode on the back of a large metal cat, feeling relieved, vulnerable, nervous, and hopeful all at the same time. His position on the back of the monster wasn't the most comfortable, because the large...*Jaguar Queen, I believe the dungeon called it*...was essentially a skeleton made from some unknown metal; he had his short legs wedged between its ribs and he was holding onto its spine with his hands. When it moved – even if the movements were relatively smooth – the spine of the Jaguar rubbed roughly against his lower body, causing a little pain after a while.

Nevertheless, it beat having to walk and got him quickly across the wasteland. He felt extremely vulnerable without his armor and passing through the dangerous land was something he never thought he'd have to do, so having a giant cat to help him flee from danger was a bonus. Gerold had refused some basic leather armor that Sandra had said she could craft for him fairly quickly, mainly because it didn't feel...right...to wear something that wasn't his old armor. He did take a small battle-axe that she apparently had lying around somewhere, though it wasn't nearly the same quality as his old one – and couldn't absorb and use his energy, either. It was a poor substitute – and he *almost* refused even that – but he felt a few degrees safer with at least some sort of weapon at his side.

Relief washed over him as he looked up and saw Nurboldar in the distance. Despite the fact that the Core of the dungeon had saved him from death, given him two powerful objects that helped to restore his elemental energy (at the expense of temporary unimaginable pain, of course), and offered his people a refuge when the threat of the Undead dungeon became too much, Gerold had never felt comfortable being in there. The thought that he had been in a dungeon *at all* was hard to believe, let alone that he had survived after seeing things he'd never dreamed of seeing before. *Honestly,* he thought, *I don't even know how I managed to sleep last night, considering where I was.*

To be fair, he barely remembered collapsing on a bed made from leather material last night; he had been so physically exhausted that he didn't think he could've stood up for much longer. The only thing he remembered was waking up the next morning ravenous, his stomach threatening to eat itself from the inside. He belatedly remembered feeling some of the same hunger the night before but had been too focused on staying alive by doing what the dungeon wanted; he had followed the strange metal ape at first because he wasn't sure what would happen to him if he refused. Well, that, and because of the slim hope that he could find a way to regain his former honor after losing his armor.

He was still a little mad at the dungeon for that, but reflection during both the tour of the miraculous rooms and his current ride on top of a big metal cat made him realize that it really was his own fault. He had interfered with something that wasn't any of his business and paid the price for his stupidity and curiosity; if he could take back the decision to investigate the source of the

Nether energy, he would, but now he had to live as well as he could with the consequences.

Speaking of Nether energy, he could vaguely feel some sources of the element out towards the southeast; the very faint sense of them meant that they were likely fairly distant, so he wasn't too worried about them attacking him on the way back to his village. At least, he *hoped* it was still his village; he was nervous about the response he would get from the villagers and the other Shieldmen...especially Second-shield Bregan.

Will they shun me? Will they cast me out because I lost my armor on what was essentially my first day? Will they even listen to me?

Regardless of his nervousness, he was hopeful that they would listen and believe what he had to tell them. By taking refuge in the dungeon, they'd be able to survive the undead that were sure to make their way to the village as soon as they could; in fact, the closer he got to the forest to the southeast of Nurboldar, the more he could sense faint traces of Nether energy. It reminded him of the amount that one of the skeletal rats had possessed, so he was sure there were more scouting out the border of what Sandra had called an "Area of Influence".

I better convince the others before it's too late.

To help with that, he was bringing along the large cat he was riding that the dungeon had graciously allowed him to borrow. That wasn't all he was bringing, however, as he had a small bag of the same things that were embedded in his palms – "Energy Orbs" he was told they were called; his case was apparently unique, because others could use the orbs to regenerate their elemental energy by just holding them against their skin. It was what he saw with the other people in the dungeon he saw – which still confused and shocked him, with there being two Gnomes and an Elf *living* there. It was that, as well as the fact that they looked like they were well-fed, comfortable, and hopefully *not slaves of some kind* that convinced him that the dungeon's Core might actually be telling the truth about wanting to help.

He supposed he should still distrust that whole unbelievable premise, as well as question her insistence that his people come to the dungeon to take refuge; thinking about it, however, he couldn't find it in himself to disregard what he had seen with his own two eyes. Sure, it could be an elaborate plot to lure the 115 Dwarves – including all of the villagers and Shieldmen presently there – to their horrifically painful deaths inside the dungeon…but what if it was all true? For all he knew, the Creator may have sent Sandra there precisely to help them all out, and it would be foolish to dismiss the possibility that everything was exactly the way she said it was.

The delicious breakfast consisting of all the meat he wanted that morning didn't hurt, either. If it was a bribe of some sort, it was a good one.

The Jaguar Queen and the bag of Energy Orbs weren't the only things he was bringing with him, however. Gerold looked to his right, where Felbar – the older Gnome – was bringing his large machine along, to hopefully give a little credence to his claims. It was still a longshot, but he was aiming to get as much help as possible in convincing his brethren of the importance of what he was going to convey to them. Short of some Undead attacking them, or the willingness of some of the Shieldmen to journey through the wastelands to see the source themselves, he was limited with what he had to work with.

Unsurprisingly, he and the machine the Gnome was piloting – which was nothing short of amazing, he could easily admit – were seen from a distance away. Just as he had feared and was expecting, Second-shield Bregan was right out front with two other Shieldmen that had yet to leave for the day.

** I've told Felbar to wait until you need him, though I'll be translating everything that's said so that he can understand what's going on. **

Sandra's voice in his head surprised him, as he wasn't aware she could speak to him outside of her dungeon. It surprised him so much that he nearly fell off of the metal cat he was riding, though a quick grab of a rib kept him from sliding off and likely sending a horrible confirmation of his incompetence as he fell to the ground.

Before he could say anything, Bregan spoke first in his gruff voice, sounding somehow angry, curious, and cautious all at once. "Gerold? Where have you been? Where is your armor, boy?"

Gerold hated when the Second-shield called him boy, but then again he called everyone that; when you were as old as the old Shieldman was, almost everyone could be classified as a boy or a girl to him. White hair streamed out from the helmet that Gerold thought was never taken off, even to sleep, and his equally white beard was so long that the end of it had to be tucked away inside his armor to keep the Dwarf from tripping over it. The lines on his face were so deep that Gerold thought he could put his pinky in one and it would disappear, which was in complete contrast to his own jet-black hair, short beard, and unwrinkled visage.

Despite his older age, the armor he was wearing was the original one he had received as a brand-new Shieldman a couple hundred years ago – or so the rumors said. Unlike what the older Dwarf's body had undergone over the years, the armor – and the battle-axe attached to his side – appeared unblemished, like it had just been crafted and hadn't seen a day of battle.

"Second-shield Bregan, I have some dire news that you need to hear. Yesterday I discovered that there is an undead-filled dungeon that is threatening to expand into our lands—"

"That didn't answer my questions, boy. Where have you been and where is your armor?" Bregan cut him off, his voice louder this time.

"Sir, that's what I was trying to tell you. I sensed a great surge in Nether energy out in the wastelands and went to investigate—"

"You deliberately deserted your duty here to go chasing some sort of sense you had? And I suppose this is where you left your armor?"

"No, sir...I mean, yes, I left, but that was after I found a skeletal rat in the forest here—"

"So, because you saw a rat, you went off into the wasteland to see if there were more of them? And were there any?"

"Uh...any what, sir?" Gerold asked, confused at the line of questioning but slowly dreading what it was leading to.

"Rats, boy. Skeleton rats, if that is indeed what you saw."

"Well, no, I didn't see any more rats—"

"And if you didn't see any more rats, then what was the point of your travels out there? Everyone knows there's nothing out in the wastelands; it sounds as if you deliberately went into an area that is off-limits without permission, leaving us wondering if you had died fighting Golems – which we're going to have to double our culling today, thanks to you," Second-shield Bregan again cut him off with a curt, admonishing, and accusatory tone, before his voice went soft and somehow...*cold*. "I'm not going to ask again, boy...where...is...your...armor."

Gerold swallowed a lump in his throat. "You see, there was this big undead army, and then there was a metal ball that started to suck up everything – including the ground beneath it – and then I—"

Bregan's face turned so dark with anger that it looked like he was going to explode. "ARE YOU TRYING TO TELL ME YOUR ARMOR WAS DESTROYED?"

"...uh...yes? But it wasn't my fault, it was Sandra's use of the—"

"I don't care who you want to blame for it, *your* armor is *your* responsibility, and your foolishness has caused its destruction. It would've been better if you died along with your armor, boy; you've dishonored the reputation of the Shieldmen with your actions over the last day," the older Dwarf continued in disappointment, his voice calmer but hard as granite. Gerold looked over at the other Shieldmen next to the Second-shield and saw equally disappointed expressions on their faces. Strangely enough, he had been so consumed with his training that he hadn't even learned their names – and now it was looking like he never would. "Now tell, me who is this Sandra you're blaming for all your failures?"

The question was like a cold bucket of water dumped on his head; the fact that he was just thinking about how he had unfairly accused the dungeon of destroying his armor and axe resonated with him. Added to that, Gerold hadn't meant to mention the dungeon by name quite yet, as he didn't have to guess how the whole situation must sound; giving something that had historically been a source of death and destruction against their people a name and personality went against everything he knew of them. Truth be told, *he* was still getting used to it, and here he was trying to convince the others to go there.

"...um...well...Sandra is the name of the dungeon that is fighting against the undead and is here to help us. She is also the one that healed me after I—"

"—became so delusional after the loss of your armor that you're now giving a dungeon a name? There aren't any dungeons in the wastelands, by the way, or we would've heard about it before now; and even if there were, if it's fighting against the undead – which is even more far-fetched than anything else you've said today – then we should just let them do it and stay out of it. We have enough going on here as it is, which has just been made that much harder by your incompetence."

"There is a dungeon out there, and she only wants to help. Where do you think this thing I'm riding came from? And then there's Felbar in the—" Gerold began, using his hand to point to the massive machine that was standing still to the right and a little behind him. He heard a gasp come from someone he was addressing, and a quick look showed that at least one of them had seen the gear and embedded orb in his palm.

"I know what a Gnomish War Machine is, boy – I saw a couple in my youth, though I never thought I'd see one here," Bregan said, not even bothering to look at the towering construct that could undoubtedly chop him in half. *Then again...I've seen the old Dwarf fight before, and I'd probably put my odds on Bregan.* "The more important thing that you need to explain, *boy*," he said while putting particular emphasis on the word, "is what that thing on your hand is."

He tried to explain what it was, but as he had only the barest understanding of it, it all came out a garbled mess.

** Tell him that is a simple bond between yourself and my Core, which allows you to communicate with me and not be killed by my Dungeon Monsters or traps. That's the truth, so you should be able to communicate that. **

The sound of Sandra's voice startled him again, mainly because she had been entirely silent during the entire exchange, though he supposed that it might be because she was translating everything that was said to the Gnome. Apparently, the reaction to her voice betrayed him, because Bregan became even more suspicious.

"Is there something wrong, Gerold? Is this...*thing*...on your hand some sort of brand that marks you as part of the dungeon's property? Are you hearing voices in your head?" the older Dwarf scathingly asked. Then he shook his head slowly. "What have you gotten yourself into, boy?"

"Look, whatever you might think about me and how—" Gerold swallowed again— "*incompetent* I may or may not be, there is still a danger to the village! At least come and visit the dungeon or see for yourself by going through the wastelands—"

"I don't know what was done to addle your mind, but you're sadly mistaken if you think I'm going anywhere. I won't fall into the same trap you did, and I won't put the people of Nurboldar – nay, the entire Kingdom – at risk because of your foolishness. Now, begone and go back to wherever it is you found these things; I won't have your nonsense here."

"But I also brought some of these orbs for you to try; they'll help regenerate—"

"We don't want anything from you, or this supposed 'dungeon' of yours; as far as I'm concerned, you're dead to us. I'll be sure to send word back that you died doing your duty, though, so your family won't be dishonored along with your name; that, and because I have no idea how I'm supposed to explain how imbecilic you are."

And that was it. No matter what he said, even following after for a short distance, none of the others would even acknowledge he was even there. When he came upon the first of the farm's fields, Bregan turned back to him and gave him a stare that made even the Jaguar Queen step back – or at least the thing controlling the monster. He knew from that look that there was nothing he could say or do to convince him or the others, so he gave up. "Fine...Sandra, take me back, if you would. I can see that they are too closed-minded and set in their ways to accept the help offered."

There was no reaction other than the barest twitch in Bregan's eye that said he even heard what Gerold said.

** I'm so sorry he wouldn't listen to you. I wish there was something else I could do, but short of allowing the Undead dungeon to quickly expand to show them the error of their ways, there's not much I can do. Maybe if Echo came to talk to them? **

"No, I doubt that would work. Thank you for trying, though."

** Just curious; do you mind if I take a few...samples...from your farms here? **

I wonder what she means by samples? He knew she didn't mean any harm to the Shieldmen or the villagers, so he said that was fine. "It's not like they're going to need it in a few weeks anyway."

From above, he saw the same shapes that he had thought were going to impale him during the battle he observed between Sandra's forces and the undead horde shoot down to the fields.

"Hey! What are those and what are they doing?" Bregan shouted, running towards where the nearest monster – that looked like a large pair of shears – was snipping off a few parts of a wheat stalk. It was gone from the field and up in the air with something stuck through the loop of its handle before he even got close; Gerold watched as it slowly flew back towards where he knew Sandra's dungeon was located. In a few other places he saw more rising up with their own “samples”, including one that appeared to have impaled a potato and was wobbly flying away.

** Time to go – I don’t think that guy looks very happy. Thanks for the permission, by the way, even if* ***he*** *doesn’t approve; the last time I tried to take an acorn, I was set upon by a group of powerful Elite Elves, so I’ve been more than a little cautious about what I take. Now, however, I guess it doesn’t really matter; they know about me anyway because you told them. Whether they believe you or not is their problem. **

Gerold hung on as the Jaguar turned around and slunk away from the edge of the field, heading back in the direction he had first taken when he was investigating the day before. *Has it only been…what…less than 24 hours?* It seemed like it was much more, considering that he had lost his armor, shield, weapon, and his place in Dwarven society. As far as his parents would know, he died while fighting and culling the Golems near the village, doing his duty to his people and Kingdom. He had no home now, no place where there was someone who wanted him around…and he felt lost.

** They may yet come around, just give them time. The offer still stands for them to take refuge here if they change their minds. Meanwhile…I could use your help if you would like to contribute a little. **

He slowly nodded, knowing that he didn't really have any other options. He could always walk away and hope to find something he could do in another land – perhaps the Gnomes would be willing to take him in – but he was curious what the dungeon needed help with. *I guess home is wherever I make it…even down in the depths of a dungeon…*

* * *

"Shouldn't we have at least checked out his story, Bregan?" Marleth asked him after Gerold on the ridiculous metal cat and the Gnomish War Machine were gone.

Absurd! "Ridiculous! Are you telling me you actually believe him?"

Second-shield Bregan glanced over at Third-shield Marleth, seeing that the other Shieldman was picking his words carefully. "No, not necessarily. However, the fact that he was riding…whatever it was…sends up some warning signs to me. I've never seen anything like that before, so what if he was telling the truth – or something close to the truth?"

Bregan harrumphed, annoyed that he had to explain it to the Third-shield, who should know better. "Whatever it was he was riding was probably constructed by the Gnomes; the presence of that War Machine should've been clue enough. Most likely, Gerold felt like shirking his duties to explore the wastelands, came upon some Gnomes camped out there, and lost his armor to them in some sort of swindle. Can't trust Gnomes, you know – they'll steal the boots right off their mother's feet if it benefited them in some way."

Marleth seemed as though he wanted to protest, but he snapped his mouth shut and said no more about.

"Now, it looks like I'll have to be slotted back into formation with the unfortunate *death* of a Shieldman," Bregan said, doing his best to end the matter by stressing the word. Fortunately, the other two took the hint and nodded, going about their business of culling dungeon monsters. When they were far enough away, his whole frame sagged in his armor and he sighed heavily.

Gerold, you stupid Dwarf, what have you done? I thought this was supposed to be my retirement...

Chapter 25

With the convincing of the Dwarves to come to her dungeon a bust, Sandra turned her attention back to doing what she could to minimize what damage the Undead Core could do; it was practically inevitable that it would upgrade its Core Size before she was ready for her assault. Not that she wanted to delay, but her reserves of Mana via her treasury were quickly drying up. *I think I need to build a bigger vault for next time.* She had previously stopped adding to her treasury because she had thought that what she was saving was more than enough for a "rainy day", but this was turning out to be a violent downpour she hadn't accounted for.

Regardless, she was determined to let that be her last mistake, and to strive forward with her plan. While Felbar and Gerold were heading back to the dungeon, Sandra started working with Violet on enchantments while Echo finally got the go-ahead to bring another shipment of Energy Orbs back to her village. The Dungeon Core only had the opportunity and Mana to create a few over the last day, so they had to take some from the Gnomes' shipment; she figured that they wouldn't be leaving until the Undead dungeon situation was taken care of anyway, and by that time they'd likely be able to make many more to replace what was "borrowed". Plus, she was hoping to add some Cubes to the shipment, which she hadn't had a chance to do yet since most of her Mana had been used for more important matters.

** There are a few things that I want to work on as far as enchantments are concerned. First, I need the warhammers that my Steelclad Ape Warriors will be wielding enchanted so that they provide a little extra "oomph". Second, I'll be working with Echo when she gets back to make a new bow for her, and I'd like both that and some arrows enchanted. Lastly – and I think Felbar will like this – I want to place some more enchantments on the War Machine. **

The Gnome was nodding along with Sandra's words, but her face became confused at the mention of the War Machine. "What are you talking about? We already enchanted that and from what Felbar said it's working perfectly."

** We can talk about that when he gets back with Gerold; right now, I want to look at how we can utilize Energy Orbs for other weapon enchantments. **

Violet still seemed confused, but she was excited enough about doing some new enchantments that it didn't seem to bother her. "What did you have in mind?"

** Well, first I want to forge all-new Titanium warhammers for my Apes, but I want to add two different enchantments to them; one will be Fire-based and the other Holy-based, so I'm going to need to work with you through my Shapeshifters to complete them.*

Especially as I want to incorporate those Orbs to make them stronger and last longer. *

Again, she seemed skeptical, but the Journeyman Enchanter was up for the challenge.

Most normal weapon enchantments that Sandra knew of – that weren't the temporary ones that she knew the Gnomes favored in battle – could be quite useful but had some limitations. Most of those limitations came in the form of energy usage; for instance, it could be a powerful enchantment – like one that would cause lightning to erupt from the end of a sword when it came into contact with an enemy – that could be used maybe a score of times before the energy ran out. Or, on the other end of the spectrum, a simple enchantment that strengthened the metal so that it was less susceptible to breaking or kept the blade as sharp as a newly crafted weapon could last for years depending upon use.

Of course, there were hundreds of enchantments that were in between those two extremes, but the limiting factor was the same: elemental energy. With the new Energy Orbs, however, that would all change; by incorporating them into the enchantment with the **Limiter** rune, she was hoping to make powerful enchantments last a whole lot longer.

Sandra started with the crafting of the Titanium warhammer, but she made some alterations to the end of the haft; normally there was a small round pommel on the end that helped to prevent the hammer from completely slipping out of the wielder's grasp, but the Dungeon Core changed that up a little. Instead of what was essentially just a nub, she expanded it until it could contain two Average Energy Orbs; it made the pommel a bit oversized, but the weight wouldn't change too much – because they were going to be hollow.

Before the Orbs were inserted, Sandra used her Shapeshifter in Felbar's form to enchant the Average Fire Energy Orb with the **Limiter** rune and then placed it as well as a Spirit Orb inside the hollow pommel. When that was done, she used her Steelclad Ape – that was doing all of the metal-crafting – to seal it up, containing the Orbs inside the warhammer. From there, things got a little...difficult.

The **Activate** rune sequence – when incorporated into an enchantment – worked the most reliably when made from Spirit elemental energy, which was why most of the best Enchanters Sandra knew of that made weapon enchantments had access to that particular element; it wasn't as though it couldn't be made from other elements, but they usually consumed more energy than a Spirit-made one for some reason. Sandra thought it had to do with the particular aspect of the element that worked best with "command"-driven runes, but she had never really gone that deep into enchantment theory to know if that was the real reason.

Regardless, Sandra wanted the weapon enchantment to be as efficient as possible, so a Spirit-based **Activate** rune sequence was the way to go. The problem with that was that Sandra had yet to master the precise way to create the Spirit-based activation sequence, despite weaving the relatively simple Fire-focused one – so she needed Violet's help to attach them together. The obvious difficulty with that, of course, was that Violet couldn't actually see the Fire-based enchantment Sandra was planning on adding to attach it properly. After some experimentation that left them both frustrated as Sandra tried to create a simple Minor Heating Fire enchantment on a piece of stone and Violet tried to attach an **Activate** rune to it, they almost gave up when they never seemed to line up and attach. However, the Gnome had an idea that seemed obvious at the time but took the frustration they were feeling to figure it out.

Since Sandra could see the Fire enchantment she was creating and also had access to the Spirit element in Felbar's body, all Sandra had to do was place some un-powered Spirit-based enchantment indicators where the sequence had to be lined up perfectly. A simple solution it was, but it also worked.

"I'm sure that I probably would've learned more about working with Enchanters wielding different elements...if the Academy were still there," Violet said sadly after she had successfully connected everything together. "But I guess there's no substitution for working in the field, is there?" she asked wistfully.

** There is some truth to that. Now that we have this figured out, we can finish this. **

The next part seemed quite easy in comparison to their difficulties earlier. Sandra created the Fire-based enchantment, connecting it directly to the pommel and running it around the rest of the haft, before completing the simple rune sequence for the main enchantment there. Before it was completed, Violet added the **Activate** rune sequence where Sandra indicated it needed it to go, which she did flawlessly – even though Sandra split it so there were two activation areas.

On either side of the warhammer – the flat head and the spike on the other – there was now a spot that would activate the Fireburst enchantment, a relatively simple and basic enchantment that was normally not that powerful. Upon striking something, it would emit a small burst of flames that conveyed a bit of fire damage to a target, but it was more focused than, say, a Flame Edge enchantment – which would coat an entire blade with flames that could be used repeatedly.

Fireburst, on the other hand, typically only conveyed the flames in short spurts in a concentrated area, instead of an entire slice with a sword. It wasn't used as much because it was only activated when *something* came in contact with the activation portion of it, which could make it a bit hazardous to carry it around. Flame Edge and others like it could be activated and deactivated with the simple placement of hands on the hilt in a specific way, and the flames would go away when the wielder wanted it to.

With the Average Fire Energy Orb with the **Limiter** rune attached to the Fireburst enchantment, however, and the flow of energy turned up a bit, Sandra was hoping for some more impressive results. Once the enchantment was done, she took it outside the workshop with her Steelclad Ape Warrior and tested it.

Whoops – too much!

When the Ape swung the enchanted Titanium warhammer down to hit the dirt, there was a discharge of flames that was so powerful it blasted a large hole in the ground, partly destroyed the head of the warhammer, bent the haft of the weapon, and launched the Ape backwards through the air; when it landed, about 80 feet away, the impact deformed both of the construct's legs and one of its arms. Fortunately, it wasn't destroyed completely, but a Repair Drone needed about 15 minutes to get it back to normal.

"Whoa – what was that?" Gerold asked when he came running up on the Jaguar shortly after the unexpected explosion. "Are you under attack?" Felbar was right behind him, looking ready to attack anything that moved.

** No, everything is alright; I was experimenting with an enchantment that didn't quite go the way I was expecting. Sorry for alarming you. **

"That...was an enchantment?" Felbar asked, shock on his face. "I've never heard of anything like that."

** Yes, well, I think I know what I did wrong; with a hopefully simple adjustment, that shouldn't happen again. That was a mistake on my part – I'm just glad I tested it outside the workshop. **

"That was a mistake? I could see some potential uses for something like that," Echo asked, coming back from her visit to her village. Sandra realized she was broadcasting her response to everyone in the vicinity, which she thought included Felbar, Gerold, and Violet down in the workshop; she wasn't expecting the Elf back so soon from her trip, but apparently she didn't want to spend any more time there than was needed.

Sandra had been so focused on crafting and testing the enchantments that she hadn't really been paying attention to the immediate area; if she had started the test a minute or so later, there was a possibility that the others might've been hurt by the explosion. The Dungeon Core quickly looked around her AOI to make sure she hadn't missed anything else while she was so focused elsewhere and was relieved when nothing seemed out of the ordinary. Or, as ordinary as a Phoenix hunting down any remaining Specters in the open air and her Rolling Constructs finishing up the elimination of all of the smaller Undead roaming around was.

** I'm glad you're all back, because I wanted to talk to everyone about what the plan is for taking out the Undead dungeon. However, before we do that, why doesn't everyone except Violet*

wind down a little, get something to eat, and maybe eve
nice relaxing bath before we get started – because we have a lo
*go over followed up by a lot of work. **

They were more than agreeable to that, especially Gerold – who was still obviously dealing with the rejection by his people. Echo perked up at the mention of a bath, though she mentioned something that made Sandra a little worried. "That sounds like a great idea, but there's also something I heard while in the village that may be a cause for concern for the future. It's nothing urgent, so I'll tell you later."

When the War Machine was parked back in the partially destroyed workshop and Sandra sent the Mechanical Jaguar Queen to go roam around the wastelands, Sandra got back to work with Violet. The warhammer had been so damaged that some of the enchantment on it was damaged as well, so they had to basically start over. Fixing it in the state in was in was out of the question, but fortunately Sandra had made two other Titanium Warhammers with her Ape while they were trying to figure out the enchantment in the first place. Instead, she just absorbed the halfway-destroyed weapon, noticing that the Average Fire Energy Orb that was placed in the pommel was now two-thirds smaller from just the single activation of the enchantment.

The second enchantment went much easier and faster, now that she knew that she had to drastically turn down the flow from the **Limiter** rune. When she tested it – aboveground again for safety – it had the desired effect; a brief burst of flames erupted from the head of the hammer, creating a small dent in the dirt and making the hammer rebound from the force of the mini-explosion just a little. It was exactly what she needed to make her Steelclad Apes into the warriors they were meant to be.

That wasn't all, however; because they were going against the Undead, she also wanted to create some Holy-based enchantments that were offensive. That was going to be a little difficult, because most of the enchantments she knew of were primarily defensive – but with the added potential energy behind one, it could prove to be just as deadly as the Fireburst...if not more.

She finally settled on the Holy Light enchantment, which was an extremely basic enchantment that was normally crafted on simple wooden sticks and used as a torch of sorts while delving through Nether-based dungeons. The enchantment gave off a steady light that could last for days of constant use; Nether Dungeon Monsters tried to avoid being close to it (likely because the light made them a little uncomfortable), though it apparently didn't actually hurt them unless they were touched by it directly – and then it was essentially like burning them with a hot brand. Again, not normally that powerful or even deadly except against the smallest of Undead, but when it had a bit of an extra boost behind it...who knows?

When they were done, it was hard to tell exactly how powerful it was; all she could say when her Ape experimented with it outside, was that it created a brief flash of light that was as bright or brighter than anything she'd seen before. It only lasted for a fraction of a second, but it was impressive for all that. Before she created any more of those, she'd have to try it against an Undead to see if it actually did anything.

** That's a good start, don't you think? Now, let's focus on the War Machine. **

"You mentioned that before, but it's already working the way it's supposed to," Violet said, after the warhammer experiments were complete. Sandra was planning on creating more of them once they had figured out all of the other enchantments she had in mind.

** No, that's all fine – perfect, even. You did a really good job on that, you know? No, what I'm talking about is adding some extra **elemental** weaponry to it, to make it even more versatile. **

The Gnome seemed to consider that for a moment. "Ok...but I'm not sure how that is going to work. With the warhammers, we used an **Activate** rune sequence, but if the War Machine is already touching something, it's probably already being destroyed by its weapons."

** That's a good point, but the way I'm thinking it will work will be just a bit different. I have some thoughts about what I'd like to include, but instead of the* ***Activate*** *rune sequence being at the point of contact, I want it to be inside where Felbar is piloting the construct. **

She cocked her head to the side as she thought about it, before smiling wide as she understood. "Ah, I see now. What did you have in mind?" Sandra mentally smiled back.

It required a bit of manipulation of the inside cockpit where Felbar controlled the Machine, but it was relatively minor and done fairly quickly. When Sandra was done, there were now an Average Fire Energy Cube and its accompanying Spirit Energy Orb wedged into the inner wall, as well as **Limiter** and **Activate** runes sequences running down the left arm and to the tip of the warhammer fused to the end. On the right side, there was an Average Holy Energy Cube with the same setup, though instead of just the right arm the sequences roamed lightly over the entire War Machine. That enchantment required Sandra to contribute four of her Shapeshifters in Echo form to complete because of the sheer size of it, though at least the enchantment itself wasn't complicated.

Felbar came back into the workshop just as Sandra and Violet were finishing up the new additions. "What are you doing to my girl?" he asked worriedly, rushing over to put his hand on the War Machine's leg possessively.

Sandra couldn't help but laugh at his reaction and proceeded to tell him that they had made some changes for him to try out. He looked suspiciously at Violet, who looked back at him with an innocent smile on her face, before climbing up with the help of some boxes into the pilot's area. "What are these Cubes doing in here?" he asked, seeing them immediately.

** I'll explain it in a moment. Head out of the workshop and I'll show you. **

The Gnome grumbled under his breath about secrets and about having no respect for his baby, but he did as Sandra asked. As soon as he was out there and safely away from anything that could get hurt, the Dungeon Core pointed out the activation symbol on the nearby wooden wall, just to his right, along with a similar one on his left.

** Now, touch the one on your left and hold your hand there. **

Felbar did as he was instructed, and a semi-transparent shield of light sprung up around the entire War Machine.

** If you sort of turn your fingers to the right, the Holy Protection Shield will stay on until you turn it off, though you won't be able to attack through it. Let me demonstrate. **

Sandra had the Steelclad Ape that had followed him outside pick up and throw a small rock at tremendous speed at the War Machine; as she had predicted, the rock bounced off, ricocheting off and leaving the Gnome construct unharmed – even though it probably wouldn't have done much in the first place. She then asked Felbar to try to attack the Ape, but the Gnome soon found that he couldn't fully extend his arms up, as they were slowed to a stop by the shield from the inside. He could walk and even run but trying to attack anything through the Holy Protection Shield was nearly impossible.

Felbar proved her wrong, however, as he physically barreled into the Ape with his entire body – shield included – and sent it flying backwards. Fortunately, it wasn't hurt that badly, but it did go to show that the Gnome could at least do *something* while shielded.

** The Shield doesn't consume a lot of energy by itself but uses more when it stops an impact or even an enemy spell – which will drain it rapidly. It's meant for extra protection when you're in trouble or see an attack incoming, and not for constant use.*

** The other enchantment, on the other hand, is best used in short bursts and you'll have to keep your hand on the activation rune because you'll not be able to "lock" it. It's also on your right side because it'll leave your left hand free to control your Machine's left* *arm. Now, stick your construct's left arm out and we'll see if Violet and I set up the enchantment correctly.* *

Felbar hesitated as he reached up to the activation rune, and Sandra nearly giggled at the look on his face as he likely remembered the "mistake" she had made earlier. Fortunately for him, Sandra had learned from that and Violet had double-checked everything before she approved of its safety. With a shrug, Felbar closed his eyes and pressed down on the rune sequence.

A cone of fire erupted out of the end of the warhammer, starting from its tip and extending almost 10 feet before dissipating. The noise of crackling flames made him open his eyes and stare at the flames coming from nowhere, and he began to giggle himself as he moved his War Machine's arm around, making the cone of fire go where he wanted.

* *Oh, good – it didn't even explode this time!* *

Felbar froze for a moment and gave a half-hearted grunt at Sandra's poor excuse for a joke.

* *Anyway, we've determined that you can keep that going for about 20 seconds before it starts heating up your Warhammer too much; after 30 seconds, the hammer will probably start to deform a little; at a minute, the Titanium will likely start to melt. Like I said, this is best used in short bursts, otherwise you'll have to wait a while for*

the hammer to cool down again before you even use it to attack with. Not only that, but the Flame Cone enchantment uses a lot of energy, so you have approximately 10 minutes of full use before the Cube runs out. We would've put large Cubes in for these enchantments, but then you'd have a lot less room to move. *

The flames cut off after just over 20 seconds of Felbar playing with them, and the warhammer was noticeably hot, with waves of heat flowing off of it. After having done so much blacksmithing lately, Sandra could tell that another second or two and the entire thing likely would've started to change color from the heat.

"This is...this is like nothing I've ever seen before. Thank you," Felbar said, a hitch in his throat as he appeared to be holding back tears.

* *You're welcome, but you can also thank Violet for helping a massive amount with those enchantments. Anyway, head back inside and get out of that thing – we have a lot to talk about.* *

He looked disappointed, but he turned the War Machine around and jumped back down to the workshop. By the time it was parked, and he was out, the others had arrived.

Chapter 26

** I'm going to keep this as brief as possible, because we have a lot we need to get to. Which brings me to my first question: how many of you are willing to help me do this? While this is my dungeon and I control the different things in here, I don't control* ***you****. If any of you wish to leave, you can do so whenever you like. I appreciate whatever help you're willing to give to eliminate this threat once and for all, though. **

Sandra thought that it was the best idea to give them an out if they wanted it, because she didn't want them to do something they had no desire to do. Now that the War Machine was done as they had agreed, Violet had already helped with quite a few of the enchantments that the Dungeon Core had wanted done; at the same time, Sandra had practiced a lot more and could actually create a lot of the easier enchantments by herself. She was pretty sure she could do most of the others that she still had planned if necessary, so if the Gnomes wanted to leave, they could go with her blessing.

Echo was only there to deliver Energy Orbs to her village and her people, though she had been a great help in teaching Sandra how to manipulate elemental energy well enough to cast some spells. The Elf didn't have to do any of that, though the Dungeon Core certainly appreciated all that she did; that being said, there was no obligation for her to continue helping.

Gerold was newly added to her Visitor's list and had been around her dungeon for less than a day, in fact, so Sandra didn't expect much enthusiasm from the Dwarf. He had just been essentially exiled from his home, and it wasn't likely that he was up to helping, considering the circumstances.

Sandra shouldn't have been surprised by their responses, but, nevertheless, she was.

"We've already talked about it and Violet and I are seeing this through; the undead were our responsibility, so we're staying until the situation is taken care of – which means that dungeon is destroyed, obviously," Felbar stated first without hesitation. "When it's gone, then we'll take the wagon back to Gnomeria and discuss with those in charge about you and what you have to offer with some cooperation. The only thing is...." He trailed off, visibly searching for words.

** What is it? **

"Well...I want to go with you when you destroy this dungeon; I want to see it through to the end."

** That's extremely dangerous, Felbar. When I sent my constructs against that Reptile-based Core, every single one of them perished and I almost didn't succeed. This Undead Core is much stronger, has more Mana available, and therefore I would only assume will be* *much harder to destroy. That, and it probably knows I'm coming for it, so it's had time to prepare.*

** Not only that, but there's no way the War Machine will fit down into the dungeon, so I don't know what you're planning on doing there. **

He didn't seem to be persuaded by her warning. "That's completely understandable and I understand the risks, but it's something I feel I need to do," he said confidently. "As for the War Machine not fitting, I'm well aware of that – which is why Violet thinks with your help, we can make a Deep Delver."

It took Sandra a moment to remember Violet's mention of a special Gnome construct made for destroying dungeons back when they first met. The Apprentice Enchanter at the time had never worked with one and barely even knew what they looked like, so there hadn't really been a point in asking about it before this.

"The War Machine is specially designed to cull dungeon monsters *outside* of the dungeon, where they can take advantage of the space and can match just about anything they come across," Violet explained, taking a cue from the other Gnome to speak. "The Deep Delver is very different from that, as it's approximately 5 feet tall and made entirely of steel; it's also much more agile, allowing whoever's piloting it to move quickly to avoid danger – which is important, because it is also not as...tough...as the War Machine."

"I piloted one in my youth, before all of the troubles we've been experiencing lately," Felbar said, continuing the explanation. "I was one of 120 others that went into a Goblin dungeon that was getting way too powerful to easily cull anymore, and which had expanded its territory to encompass one of our smaller villages – unbeknownst to us. It was only after multiple disappearances that we discovered what had happened, so the Dungeon Destroyer Brigade – of which I was one – was dispatched to destroy it before it could cause any more problems.

"Only 92 of us made it back from that expedition, which was actually one of the best results over the last few decades, if you can believe that," the older Gnome said while looking off in memory. He shook his head after a moment and then continued. "So, yes, they aren't nearly as powerful as the War Machines, but they are a heck of a lot better than just me going in there with a knife expecting to kill some undead. So, we'd like your help and permission to build one, so that I can at least contribute some."

Sandra wasn't exactly sure what to think about that. She didn't want him unnecessarily risking his life, but she also knew that it was his life to do with as he pleased. *Hmm...perhaps this might actually coincide with my overall plan of cooperation between the races; I always knew that it was probably only going to happen with my help, so I guess it has to start somewhere.*

"If you can make me one as well, I'd like to go with you into that dungeon," Gerold suddenly said. Sandra had been automatically translating everything the Gnomes were saying to the others, but his statement was so unexpected that it took her a moment to figure out what he was saying – and to translate it to the other three.

** What? Why? **

"Because it's *my* village that's in danger, and despite their refusal to listen to me, I still want to do whatever I can to stop them from being overrun and killed. That being said, without my armor, I'm pretty useless; hearing about this 'Deep Delver', though, I think that could be just the thing to allow me to do...something."

That actually made a bit of sense to Sandra, because it was true that he didn't really have much to contribute to the whole thing. She was going to ask him to help with any information he had about planting the "samples" she had taken from the Dwarves' fields, because farming had been more of a profession rather than a craft to her in the past. She had some knowledge of it from some of the other crafting information she had pursued, but other than being able to make it grow, the types of food she was going to plant she had no clue about – unlike many of the other plants she had already grown and cultivated, because they had alternative uses.

But if he was willing to fight for his people, to delve through the dungeon with the intent of destroying the Core, then he could definitely be a big help. It would probably take a little to get him up to speed with controlling this Deep Diver if it was anything like the War Machine, but that might actually be a good thing. It would allow her to continue to build up her forces so that there was no way they would be in danger of losing; overkill was something she would rather experience than the risk that they wouldn't succeed.

** Fine, if we're building one already, we might as well build another one and you can come along if you like. Just remember that it's extremely dangerous and you may not make it back alive— **

"I'm going too."

** You too, Echo? Why? It's nowhere even near your lands and there's no reason for you to risk yourself. Gerold and Felbar I can understand – even if I don't agree – because they were either in charge of culling the undead or at risk of falling to them, but that doesn't apply to you. **

"For the simple reason of what they are, Sandra: undead. Our people hate undead dungeons and immediately stamp them out when they are found, even if their dungeon monsters drop the rarest, most valuable loot," she said, before she hesitated. "Well, we'd probably cull them for a couple of weeks to get that loot if it were something really valuable to us, but *then* we would destroy it so completely that you'd never even know it was there."

By that time Sandra had given up trying to convince the others that it was too dangerous, so she didn't argue with the Elf. Besides, she was secretly happy that they were willing to work together – even if it was through an intermediary (namely, Sandra) – to accomplish a task. From the history of the area, as far as she knew it, such a thing hadn't happened in centuries, ever since Wester and his dungeon threatened all four races; it was only through banding together that they were able to defeat him and his elemental dragons. In complete contrast to that, Sandra was there to bring them together...not to destroy her, but to work together to secure their continued survival against the other dungeons.

Echo wasn't done, though. "I'm also hoping that this will prove to Wyrlin and the others he has gathered that you're not what they think, and that you're actually here to help. There's nothing like destroying an undead dungeon to get us Elves on your side."

** Wait...what was that about Wyrlin? **

"Oh, sorry – that was the news I overheard back in Avensglen. Apparently, Wyrlin has managed to spread his message that I'm under your thrall and that you're planning on making slaves of all of us. They're only rumors right now, but even if what those rumors say are even partly true, then it's possible that he's gathered maybe a dozen or so followers that are intent on destroying you," Echo said nonchalantly, like it was no big deal. *It's a big deal to me!* "Like I said earlier, though, I highly doubt they would attack for a while, especially as I heard that he and his followers are heading to the capital looking for additional support."

** Uh...that sounds like it was pretty important to know, Echo. How long do you think I have until I should be worried? **

"Hopefully years, because I also heard that the response from the Energy Orbs I've been delivering have been thoroughly welcomed, and it's not likely that they will gain much support there." She shrugged. "The distance is too great for much better information, so your guess is as good as mine."

Sandra couldn't even devote enough of her mind to think about something that may or may not occur in the future, because there was way too much to do.

** Fine, then; I'm going to ignore that unless I have some more information regarding imminent danger, because if you're all coming along then we have a lot of work to do...and not a lot of time to do it. **

That was absolutely true; by adding the three that were coming along – Sandra was very glad Violet hadn't insisted on going – it would add to the list of things that needed to be done. On the flip side, Echo's accompaniment might solve a problem the Dungeon Core had been worried about earlier...

* * *

Echo watched in fascination as very thin, narrow lengths of yew wood appeared on the table in Sandra's woodworking shop, until they stopped at 40. Right next to them were 10 even thinner sheets of what Sandra said was titanium, so thin that when she first picked one up it was a bit wobbly and flopped around – unlike any type of metal she'd seen before. All of that was joined by a cylindrical-looking titanium tube that she couldn't see the purpose of.

When Sandra said she was going to help make another bow for her, this wasn't exactly what she was thinking of. When she had made her current bow, she had collected yew wood loot over a period of time, before asking one of the other Rangers who had access to the Natural element to "connect them together". It wasn't as perfect as finding a single piece of yew wood to make a bow, but sometimes it allowed the bow to be stronger, with less likelihood of cracking.

Once they were all pieced together to make one large rod, she had painstakingly used her time off to bend and shave off portions of the wood after it was briefly soaked in water, making the wood more flexible. Over a few days of work, she had slowly curved the new bow so that when it was pulled by the string connected to it the wood bent evenly in all the right places, indicating a strong structure to it. After a few times using it, she had made what some might say were imperceptible adjustments to it, but it worked perfectly after that.

That was before it was broken by Wyrlin and she needed to have it mended using some Natural elemental energy again.

There were those who specialized in bow-making using their energy, of course, and their bows were some of the best you could obtain. However, the effort in their production usually meant that they were rather rare, and for someone like Echo – or any of the other Rangers in Avensglen – it was unlikely that she'd ever get her hands on one of their quality. The rest of them had to make do with what they could craft themselves, applying techniques passed down from generation to generation and using locally obtained wood for that purpose.

She had been lucky to have acquired enough yew wood to make her bow, but now that Sandra had demonstrated that she could create it on demand, she was confused as to what, exactly, she was doing. "What is all this for?"

** This bow is going to be a little different from what you're used to, but many of the bows I've seen crafted were what we call "composite" bows, made from altering layers of materials to aid with strength under pressure – as well as allowing for some specific enchantments to be placed on it. **

Looking across at herself was starting to become "normal" – *it's clothed at least* – as Sandra liked her Shapeshifters to use her body to perform more delicate tasks, as well as for enchanting. The thin boards and metal definitely qualified for a delicate task, as she could imagine one of the metal Apes she had would probably crack the yew wood as soon as they were picked up with its large fingers.

She didn't blame the dungeon for wanting to use the right "tool" for the task, but she couldn't deny that it was still a little unnerving.

Rather than explain any further, her copy started to pick up the different pieces on the table, slotting them into a spot that she didn't even notice on the titanium tube; at first she thought Sandra was just randomly placing them inside the small slot, but after a while she seemed to see a pattern. She started with 6 of the yew lengths on one side, before adding 1 of the titanium sheets, then 2 more yew, then another titanium sheet, and so on until there were a total of 5 titanium sheets separated by 2 yew, ending with another 6 at the end.

Then she did the exact same thing on the other side, until Echo could finally begin to see something take shape. It looked very unlike any bow she had seen before; in fact, it really just looked like a really odd stick. Before she could say anything, the other Echo closed her eyes and ran her hand over the bundled pieces she had inserted starting nearest the tube; wherever they passed, the yew and titanium lengths seemed to combine together and fuse to the tube as well, sort of like what she had seen the Ranger that had used his Natural elemental energy to combine her pieces of yew together to make her current bow.

** It's a little bit of a cheat, because they normally use a flexible glue to combine the layers together, but this works too – and it's much faster and easier. Now that these are together, I need to enchant this. **

Her double abruptly vanished, and the clothes seemed to fall to the floor, blocked by the work table; concerned, Echo rushed over to see what had happened, only to see a copy of Violet practically swimming in the previously right-sized clothes. That didn't seem to faze the Shapeshifter Sandra was controlling, however, as a nearby wooden box was at hand to lift the Gnome Enchanter up to the table height. As the small figure managed to get her hands out of the now too-long sleeves, she grabbed the "bow" and started to do...something...to it.

Reaching into the folds of her clothes, the Gnome eventually fished out two pairs of fairly small Energy Orbs – one colored green and three colored grey. Then, in a small slot on the back top of the titanium tube that she hadn't noticed before, the little person stuck two orbs inside it until they were hidden, followed up with two more on the back bottom. When they were inside, the metal seemed to flow over the slots, hiding them completely from view. Then, she continued her fancy hand-waving – which seemed unnecessary to Echo – for a couple of minutes. Fortunately for the Elf, who was looking at the whole process in confusion (she had tried enchanting something after looking at some examples in the Sandra's Repository, but couldn't manage more than a few lines and almost a complete rune – but not quite) it wasn't completely silent as Sandra/Violet did her thing.

** So, what I'm doing here is putting two enchantments on this bow, with a simplified* ***Activate*** *rune compared to some of the ones Violet put on the War Machine and warhammers wielded by my Apes. Normally, you'd have to be able to see Spirit elemental energy to use one of them, but I have a feeling you'll be fine even if it's invisible to you; I'll go over that once I'm done, because otherwise it probably won't make sense.*

** The Natural enchantment, however, should be easy to understand; it works in a similar way to the ones on the War Machine, allowing the wood and metal layers to bend* ***much*** *easier than they would normally, which should allow you to pull on the bow with minimal effort. It's activated as soon as you nock an arrow to the string, and when you let go the enchantment deactivates, straightening the composite materials almost instantly – and I'm sure you can guess how quickly and powerfully that would send your arrows forward. **

"Uh...what string are you talking about? There isn't a string on—"

** ...and that should do it! Okay, this may seem a little strange, but I want you to nock one of your arrows like you normally would. **

Sandra was just talking nonsense now – there was no string to nock it to! The Gnome copy, sensing her confusion, picked up the bow and handed it to her; she held onto the tube – which she assumed was the grip (*and it needs some sort of leather wrapped around it to stop it from slipping from my hands*) – and felt silly standing there with it. Sandra/Violet indicated the quiver at her side and mimicked nocking an arrow with her hands, so as she rolled her eyes – feeling ridiculous – and did what was asked of her.

She noticed that there was a little lip on the tube that she assumed was the arrow rest, so she placed her arrow on it and pretended to "nock" it just to get the silliness over with. As she placed her hands where she would imagine a string was, however, she felt something...something invisible. Holding onto the arrow with the fingers wrapped around the grip, she used her free hand to feel the invisible whatever it was, running up and down it until she was pretty sure it was exactly what she thought it was – a string.

"What? How?"

** The string is made from a thin strand of Spirit elemental energy, so that's why it's invisible to you. You never have to worry about it breaking or getting wet, and it'll be there as long as the enchantment lasts. When I learned about this bow and the enchantment associated with it, the enchantment would last for up to 1,000 pulls before having to be replaced. Holding the pull for longer uses a little more energy, so it could be less. With the Energy Orbs I placed in there, despite them being the Tiny variety, I estimate that it could be anywhere from 20 to 50 thousand pulls* *before they'll need to be replaced, with the Natural one running out first. Not too bad, huh? **

Echo was barely listening, as she nocked the arrow to the invisible string, pulled it back and took aim at the side of a wooden table on the other side of the room. She released and immediately lost her grip on the bow; the recoil from the wood and metal snapping back straight was so intense that it shook out of her hand. As for the arrow, it hit nowhere she had aimed, hitting the far wall so hard that it shattered into a hundred pieces, leaving a small gouge in the stone.

** Sorry about that; I forgot to warn you that you don't necessarily need to perform a full draw to get it to fly – and that the recoil when you do is quite heavy. With practice – and forewarning, of course – you'll get used to it.*

** You may also notice that it didn't quite fly where you were likely aiming; that's because the bow needs to be adjusted – and that's where you come in. I have almost no skill in firing one of those things, but* ***you*** *do; you'll need to pull on it and then use some of the tools in here to start shaving at the thicker outer layers— **

"I know exactly what you're talking about; it's how I created my own bow. It still seems a little odd, but I think I can do it," Echo said, finally beginning to see how the strange new bow worked. It was exciting having something so powerful in her grip – it felt like something out of legend, in fact – except she was part of creating that legendary bow. "When I'm done, what else do you need help with."

** That's actually what I wanted to talk to you about. You know how my Shapeshifters are going to be involved in the assault on the other dungeon? Well, I'm not wholly sure that they can perform spells fast or accurate enough, because my connection to them will be limited while they are inside the Undead dungeon. Reaction times are much slower and the commands I give them cannot be too complicated, but if you're there...well, I think I can have them copy what you do. **

That sounded...weird. "Copy? What do you mean by that?"

** Exactly what I said – copy. They will cast their spells wherever you cast...and shoot their bows wherever you shoot. **

"Shoot their bows—are you saying what I think you're saying?" Sandra didn't reply, but the start of a new pile of yew wood and titanium sheets, followed up by a familiar tube was answer enough.

I guess I'm a bowyer now...

Chapter 27

The next five days were a bit of a blur of activity in Sandra's dungeon; Deep Delvers were constructed with the aid of Felbar and Gerold and then enchanted by Violet; Titanium warhammers were crafted and then enchanted; composite bows were crafted, enchanted, and then fine-tuned for firing by Echo; additional constructs, Rising Phoenixes, Celestial Authorities, and Radiant Pegasi were created; and a very small section of Wheat, Barley, Hops, and even Potatoes were planted with the help of Gerold (who knew a little about it at least, having lived in the village for more than a month).

New Origination Materials found!

Wheat Seed
Barley Seed
Hops Rhizome
Potato Cutting
These materials cannot be directly used as a Monster Seed, nor can they be used in specific applications to create whole new Monster Seeds.

It didn't seem as though she would eventually be able to just create grown Wheat, Barley, Hops, or Potatoes, but she could at least create as many seeds, rhizomes, and cuttings as she needed to make more. She didn't spend a lot of time on them, however, because she had neither the time nor the Mana to devote to something like that at the moment; what she had done with them was more of a proof of concept than anything else.

She didn't have much time to look at the new food she could grow for a couple of reasons; namely, she was directing her ever-growing force of Dungeon Monsters and, of course, she was crafting. Starting on the second day, she had 5 Steelclad Ape Warriors armed with the new enchanted Titanium warhammers as well as 2 Radiant Pegasi and 6 Celestial Authorities with which to start destroying the larger, more powerful Undead roaming around the forest. With a trio of Phoenixes roaming the sky looking for Specters, she was finally gaining some ground with what was already outside the other dungeon.

Her Apes, with their new more-powerful weapons, performed better than expected; half of them had the Fireburst enchantment on their warhammers, while the others had Holy Light – and both worked just as well as she had hoped. The first Undead her small force of Monsters tackled was another Ogre Skeleton; the Apes with the Fireburst enchantment managed to get in close and smash their weapons into its leg, blowing out chunks of bone from both the impact and small explosion of flames. Not only that, but the bones around the impact site – maybe because they were dry or for some other reason – caught fire, burning through the surrounding skeletal figure at a fairly rapid pace.

The Holy Light enchantment was equally impressive. Upon being struck, a brief flash of very bright light enveloped the point of contact, spreading out and causing a large part of the bones around it to crack and virtually fall apart. Both enchantments were about equal as far as the damage they inflicted, but Sandra suspected that the Holy Light enchantment might have an even better result against some of the Undead that were protected by Nether-based effects – like those Liches that Echo had mentioned.

The Celestial Authorities were equally impressive, using a surprising agility to jump into the fray and avoid being smashed by the Ogre's huge bone club. Every slice of its longsword made of pure light cut completely through bone like it wasn't even there; even though it wasn't quite as "destructive" as the warhammers her Apes were wielding, it was possibly even deadlier – especially when they could slice and slash their longswords much more rapidly than the Apes could swing their weapons. The only downside was that their light seemed to dim a little after each strike, but when the battle was done they were back to their original brightness; she took this to mean that interacting directly with a Nether-based Monster – while effective – "hurt" them a little, though it was obviously not directly proportionate to the damage they doled out.

The Pegasi, for their part, dampened the Ogre's special ability that it tried to use to speed itself up; they had to be within about 15 feet for it to work, but that wasn't a problem, because they were flying circles around the Undead. Every other second, one of them would swoop in and stomp their hooves on the head of the Ogre, cracking it apart bit by bit. That didn't really even matter, though, because within 15 seconds the Undead Monster was blown or hacked apart – all without even touching one of her own.

When her force entered the forest, they set about destroying every Undead Monster in their path; there were a few times when there would be gatherings of the Undead in another attempt to trap her forces, but rather than risk them dying she went around them and mopped up all of the stragglers she could find. Sandra figured that she would eventually be able to get into a pitched battle with them – just not quite yet.

By day three, all of the Specters above the trees that Sandra could reach were eliminated, though she could visually see a large number of them in the Undead Core's Area of Influence further to the east that she couldn't reach. That alone let her know that it was quite possible the rest of that area was crawling with Undead, which was likely still funneling quite a bit of Mana to the Core; as far as she could estimate, though, her own intake was at least twice as much at that point from her various constructs roaming around. In fact, she estimated that she was gaining just about 650,000 Mana every day, which was only increasing as she created more Dungeon Monsters and sent them out into the world.

By the end of the fourth day, she had added enough of her Dungeon Monsters to finally take down one of the gatherings of Undead that had plagued her so far. With dozens of Apes, Pegasi, and Authorities comprising her force – along with two Repair Drones, which really hadn't been needed yet – she pitted them against a dangerously large force of over 100 Undead of various types, which also included Liches, the black-colored armored undead, ghouls, large zombie beasts, and even a couple of Ogre Skeletons.

But she also had a secret weapon – Felbar had joined the fight with his War Machine. After he asked her to soften them up with her Celestial Authorities' special long-range Arrows of Spiritual Ascension attack – which literally punched holes in the Undead wherever they hit – he waded into the small horde like a madman. A particularly skilled and deadly madman that laughed as he destroyed the Undead with abandon, at that.

His Flame Cone attack swept across the front line, lighting on fire and burning at least two dozen of the enemy in the first few seconds, before he swept away those close to him with his warhammer and literally sliced an Ogre Skeleton in half with his double-bladed axe. He had gone ahead of the others when he attacked and nearly became overwhelmed, but he was quickly backed up by her Apes and Authorities, who tore into the Undead crawling at his flanks. Her Pegasi, on the other hand, went straight for the Liches who were staying near the back of the group, preparing their powerful Nether-based attacks. As soon as they got close enough, the black-ish energy that the robed Undead were gathering started to dissipate, but not completely. There was still enough gathered by that time for them to launch their attacks, though they were drastically decreased in potency.

The black clouds that shot forward and surrounded her constructs and other Monsters slowed them down considerably and dimmed the light in her Angels, which resulted in a few being killed from the affliction they were experiencing by the other Undead. Fortunately, none were destroyed from the dangerous effect of the Liches' casts, which would've been deadly if they hadn't been diminished by the aura coming from her Pegasi. Felbar and his War Machine were spared any of that, luckily, as he had activated his Shield and the spell was absorbed into it without harm. It also had the effect of making a few of the Undead attacking him rebound backwards, freeing him from being surrounded.

There were no additional spells from the Liches, fortunately, because their relatively fragile bodies were pounded into oblivion by the hooves of the Pegasi. Their aura – now a bit diminished after sucking a lot of the power out from the Undeads' spells – was still enough to dampen the Nether shields protecting the powerful robed Monsters, which left them highly vulnerable to physical attacks.

The entire battle lasted no more than 5 minutes...and it was a massacre that made Sandra inwardly smile at how well it had gone. She felt a little vindicated after her last showing against the foul Undead, and she was actually looking forward to pitting all of her might against the dungeon in a few days' time.

All in all, she lost 4 Apes, 6 Authorities, and a single Pegasi that was jumped on from below by a trio of ghouls as it flew too close to the ground, though there were a few that needed repairs or "healing" from her Repair Drones. Considering that they had destroyed a little more than 10 times their number, the casualties they experienced were worth it.

By the middle of the fifth day, her Monsters and Felbar had wiped out every single Undead they could find, though her Rolling Forces had all split up and were literally combing the forest for more. Some Specters tried to hide in the trees which the Phoenixes above couldn't reach, so Sandra had to improvise by having some of the Celestial Authorities ride on the backs of the Pegasi, where they could slice the mist-like Undead from where they were trying to stay out of sight.

She took a page from the Undead's strategy book and surrounded the dungeon entrance, as well as a second "exit" that was much larger – which was probably where that massive horrific abomination of corpses had come from the other day. Unlike the Undead Core, which had grouped its Undead up into a massive horde, she had her forces spread out just in case there were any surprises coming from the other dungeon. She couldn't plan for everything, but she hoped she was prepared enough for most eventualities.

Felbar came back once everything was secured and took a much-needed rest – but there was no rest for Sandra and the others. Production of everything was still ongoing, including a special project that was inspired by a suggestion from Echo.

"Do you know how your Ape practically blew itself up the other day? I was thinking...is there any way to maybe, I don't know

– put that kind of enchantment on an arrowhead?" she had asked, innocently curious whether such a thing was possible.

With Sandra and the burgeoning talents of her Journeyman Enchanter in residence, such a thing was merely a challenge, not an impossibility.

It was relatively simple in design, but executing the enchantment took some ingenious design. First, instead of using wood for the arrows, Sandra had to create a thin Steel tube – it wasn't necessary to be Titanium – to help with preventing the arrow from destroying itself when it was shot. She could've made it from a lighter material, like Copper or Nickel, but it needed to be a little heavier to support the weight of the tip – which was quite different from a normal arrowhead.

Instead of a sharp point, the tip of their new arrows were bulbous in shape – because they contained two Tiny Energy Orbs, one Fire and one Spirit. It was a thin Nickel oval ball that was stuck on the end, with a small point on the end to help it cut through the air a little better, but would crumple upon impact; as soon as it did, there was a small **Activate** rune sequence that was the barest distance away from touching the front portion of the tip which would activate upon impact, discharging the contents of the Fire Energy Orb into the Fireburst Enchantment placed upon the arrow tip. With the **Limiter** rune turned all the way up, all 50 Mana inside the Tiny Fire Energy Orb was sent into the Fireburst Rune, creating an impressive explosion that had metal fragments shooting in all directions near the impact. It was slightly dangerous if one of her

Dungeon Monsters was too close to the explosion, but it was worth it for the sheer devastation it caused.

The only issue was the fletching on the arrow, which was normally made from some sort of bird feathers. No bird feather was strong enough to make much of a difference for the heavy arrow – more like a *bolt*, actually – so Sandra put Steel fletching on it at a slight angle, which helped to stabilize it during flight...and then the problem was when it would hit the grip on the bow when it was released, sending it tumbling away instead of flying straight. It required moving them slightly on the arrow and creating two additional notches on the bow grip that the fletching could pass through, which Echo said would work fine – as long as it was held and released in a certain way.

Each of those arrows required approximately 100 Mana for the Energy Orbs and materials – which wasn't that much considering what it could do – when she wanted to have a full supply of them for each of her Echo "copies" via her Unstable Shapeshifter Monsters, it added up. She wanted each of them to have at least 50 of them and although that was technically only 5,000 Mana apiece, the time it took to complete all of the crafting and enchanting was what slowed the process down.

By the end of the fifth very productive day, Sandra was pretty sure they'd all be ready to go by mid-morning the next day; she was already planning on working through the night, and Violet volunteered to stay up later to do so as well, which would help immensely to finish on time. Sandra was feeling good about their chances of success, especially as the Deep Delvers that Felbar and Gerold were going to be using were complete.

The Deep Delvers were a whole new class of Gnome construct – and looked quite a bit different as well. Instead of 20-foot-tall behemoths, the one that Felbar was going to pilot was 5 feet tall, while the one the Dwarf was controlling was a foot taller because of their height differences. Also unlike the War Machine, all of the movements of the all-Titanium Delver were controlled by the actual arms and legs of the pilot as they put their own limbs into the construct; essentially, the entire thing was like a large shell around the person inside of it, making them approximately the same size as a Human or an Elf – just thicker and a lot more durable. A warhammer and double-bladed axe was included as weaponry for Felbar – attached to the ends of the arms similar to the War Machine – while just a warhammer and a flat piece of Titanium (acting as a shield of sorts) was attached to Gerold's.

Because of the size difference and less space to place Energy Orbs or Cubes, there were weaker Flame Cone and Light Shield enchantments on the Deep Delvers, but they would still work well enough – just not quite the same length of time. The Delvers were actually completed on day three, but it was taking Gerold that much time to get used to controlling the construct – especially after he fell on his face dozens of times in just the first few hours of getting inside.

It also took him some getting used to being almost fully enclosed with just a small area to look outside the Delver through some slits, as well as the fact that it was *extremely* difficult to get in and out of the hatch that allowed him to enter the construct from the back – by himself. After nearly an hour of hyperventilating and acting a little claustrophobic, either his fear was overshadowed by his need to contribute or he hid it pretty well – because he seemed fine.

I think this is going to work out; I think I'll even see if Echo would be up to riding on a Pegasus to keep her out of harm's way. Then with all my Monsters and the two Deep Delvers coming along, we should be good.

Halfway through the night, she realized she had made a mistake: she had begun to think that things were going well, and that everything was going to be alright. *I should know by now to put my pessimism first, because being optimistic only seems to invite trouble.*

Just after midnight – *very* early in the morning of the day they were going to attack the dungeon – the situation became a little more complicated. Sandra immediately felt the expansion of the Undead Core's Area of Influence...and she quickly sent her awareness of her own AOI to see if she should be concerned. Of course, when she went to go check, she found that the other Core could now reach just barely through the village – which was definitely a concern.

So was the large horde of Undead that streamed out of the inaccessible eastern part of the Undead Core's AOI, heading west and slightly north...directly towards the Dwarven village.

*   *   *

What? What was that?

Something made Gerold sit up straight in his bed, though he couldn't for the life of him figure out what it was that made him do it. He wiped the sleep out of his eyes, feeling like he had just gone to sleep only minutes before.

** Gerold! You're awake! Hurry and head up to the workshop; the Undead Core has expanded and can now reach your people's village! **

Gerold was up and out of his bed before his body could catch up with his mind, and he stumbled badly enough that he slammed up against the nearest stone wall with his face. Picking himself up, he rushed through the tunnels leading to the clever vertical transportation rooms, where he met Felbar on the way. The two didn't even have to say anything, as they had been working side-by-side the last few days without even having to communicate; many of the things they needed to convey could be done non-verbally with hand movements, other visual cues, and a few words that they had learned over the last few days of the other's language.

He had never really had any friends growing up because of his unique Nether sensitivity, and he was starting to think of the old

Gnome as one – even if they didn't speak the same language. Gerold knew that Felbar was committed to destroying the undead as much as he was, and it created a sort of bond between the two.

It only took them a couple of minutes to arrive at the workshop above, and despite the late hour and not a lot of sleep, Gerold felt wide awake. He jumped into the Deep Delver construct with a little help from Felbar, who locked him in when he was all set; in return, the Dwarf lifted the Gnome up with his warhammer so that he could get into the pilot's area in the much larger War Machine, and within moments he was strapped in and ready to go.

** I've sent the majority of my Monsters guarding the entrance of the Undead dungeon to intercept them before they arrive, but I fear they will arrive too late. I also had some of my Shears sent down to the village to knock on doors and walls to wake everyone up, though I can't really communicate the danger to them. If you both rush, you might make it in time – but you better hurry! **

Gerold didn't wait for anything else and he ran for the workshop's exit, his practice over the last couple of days showing in the way he didn't trip himself up. All the hesitation and fear he had initially felt being trapped in what was essentially a large metal suit of armor was gone, and the movements needed to control the Delver were basically natural to him by that point.

Seconds later he hit the dirt and stone of the barren wasteland and took off, the partial moon above lighting a little of the way. A few times he had to turn on his bright shield to see a few particularly dark areas bathed in shadows, but for the most part he could see well enough to navigate through the hills and valleys of the broken land successfully.

Running next to him was Felbar, who – despite having longer legs on the War Machine – was barely keeping up with his rapid pace. It was one of the benefits of the construct he was controlling, he was told; it wasn't nearly as powerful, but it was faster and more agile than the larger behemoth. Gerold ate up ground faster than he thought possible, and within minutes he could see the burning torches of Nurboldar ahead of him.

As he crashed through the fields of wheat near the border of the wasteland – deliberately uncaring about what he trampled – he could see that there was a commotion near the village as more torches were lit and were moving around erratically, as if someone was carrying them around and trying to smash them into something.

** They've outpaced my larger forces, but some of my Rolling Forces near the forest border are seeing them almost there – you better hurry! **

True to her statement, Gerold could start to sense a large concentration of Nether Energy coming from the east. It was hard to tell, but he didn't think it was *quite* as large as the one he had sensed outside of Sandra's dungeon nearly a week ago – though it was large enough to cause him some concern. He could only hope that one of those gigantic, disturbing corpse-piles wasn't accompanying them, otherwise they likely had no chance to survive.

It didn't take long for him to arrive at the village proper, only to see every Dwarf out of their houses wandering around and obviously wondering what was going on.

"What are you doing back here, Gnome? Is this your doing?" Second-shield Bregan asked in Dwarven as they arrived and practically slid to a stop. The old Dwarf obviously didn't know that Gerold was inside the smaller construct – *how could he?* – and the dishonored former Shieldman got a kick out of startling him.

"No, he's here to help – the undead are just about to attack! They'll be streaming through the trees in a matter of minutes, if not less!" Gerold shouted, pointing towards where he sensed the concentration of Nether elemental energy.

"Boy? What are you doing back here – and what in the name of all that is holy are you wearing? That's a poor excuse for your old armor, whatever it is – you look ridiculous," the old Dwarf said, completely ignoring the danger that Gerold was trying to warn him about.

"Danger. Fight." Felbar's accent was horrid and was barely understandable, but the few words that the Gnome had learned of Dwarven were clear enough to those assembled.

"I don't take orders from a Gnome—" the Second-shield began, before Gerold angrily cut him off.

"Look, I don't care what you think of me anymore, or about how I may have dishonored myself and my family with my actions. But the undead are coming NOW, and if you can't get over that, then everyone here could DIE! If you won't fight, then get out my way and I'll do your duty for you," he said, before turning towards the forest, feeling the appearance of the incoming undead at the cusp of exiting the trees.

"Now listen here, *boy*—"

Anything else he was about to say was tuned out when he saw some movement towards the tree line, right at the edge of a barley field. Fortunately, the village was on a small rise in the landscape that allowed for seeing farther than normal, and the others around him seemed to glimpse the movement by the moonlight on the thankfully cloudless night, and they stopped their conversations and protests.

His protests apparently forgotten, Bregan started barking orders to the Shieldmen. "UP FRONT! Protect the villagers at all cost and prepare to engage!"

More and more stalks of barley started to twitch as a veritable wave passed through the field, aiming unerringly for the line of armored Dwarves that assembled next to Gerold and Felbar – leaving him and the Gnome to defend the middle. The villagers fell back and locked themselves in the Hall, the strongest and most defensible building in their small village. Thinking about the night before his disastrous first day, he remembered being in there drinking at a small impromptu party with the other Shieldmen, celebrating his training completion; that memory also brought back how he had good-naturedly thrown one of the others through a wooden wall in a wrestling match – and the "strongest and most defensible building in the village" didn't seem that strong.

My father probably could've built that thing out of stone and then nothing would get through; with it made almost entirely out of wood, however, it won't last long versus one of those more powerful undead.

His roaming thoughts were brought back to the present as the constant stream of undead made its way through the barley field; he tensed up as the twitching stalks arrived at the edge nearest the village…and a small skeleton rat poked its head out and stared at the assembled Dwarves with the empty eye sockets of its skull.

"Boy, if you got us all worked up over a tiny rat—"

The rat was soon joined by the appearance of hundreds more, just barely visible at the edge of the light thrown out by the torches. Gerold couldn't help but think that if they had actual eyes, they'd be looking at hundreds of accompanying reflections – though the appearance of undead rats in their skeletal forms was bad enough.

At some unknown signal, the rats streamed out of the stalks and started to swarm over the assembled Shieldmen, as well as Gerold; they completely ignored Felbar in his War Machine…but he didn't ignore them. The ground shook a little as he slammed his warhammer down, completely demolishing a dozen rats at a time, before sweeping his weapon back and forth, picking up and tossing the rats aside in the process. Gerold followed suit, smashing the rats which were fortunately having a difficult time climbing up the smooth metal of his Deep Delver; he eventually activated his Flame Cone enchantment with a flick of his right pinky finger to the activation spot, sending out a relatively small swath of fire around him, which was very effective against the weak undead.

The others were good at what they did, and despite the hundreds – or potentially thousands – of small rats swarming around them trying to reach the villagers in the back, they kept the line against the waves of undead.

* *That's just the first wave – the larger undead are arriving...now.* *

Gerold's senses had been overwhelmed by so many Nether monsters around him, but when he focused on that sensitivity, he could see that she was right...these were just the appetizer; the main course was coming up.

Chapter 28

Watching from above the village and fields from three dozen Reinforced Animated Shears, Sandra watched as hundreds of Undead streamed out from the trees, trampling the field of Barley in their effort to reach the Dwarves and lone Gnome. She heard Gerold warn the others of the incoming horde, but they were still having trouble against the swarm of rats; well, not *trouble*, but the small skeletons were literally throwing themselves suicidally at the Dwarves. Too late, she saw the plan: they were there entirely as a distraction, as the Dwarves were too busy trying to kill the smaller undead to prepare for the other, more dangerous ones.

** Tell them to ignore the rats – they're coming! **

Both Felbar and Gerold tried to convey the problem, but the rats were just annoying to completely ignore. As the Undead closed in, Sandra brought in her small force of 6 Phoenixes – who were able to arrive faster than the others – and swept them over the field, burning through over a hundred Specters before they burned out and crashed to the ground. That was beneficial enough, but their bright appearance highlighted the rest of the field – and the horde of powerful undead heading their way.

The Dwarves finally understood the danger and did their best to ignore the jumping and biting of the skeletal rats as they prepared to withstand the charge of Undead. "HOLD THE LINE!"

the old Dwarf that Gerold said was named Bregan shouted, getting everyone's attention. They immediately faced towards the incoming enemies, letting all of the other distractions go as they settled themselves to receive the first wave.

Sandra briefly looked at her own main forces to see how far away they were and estimated that they wouldn't get there for at least two minutes; the line of Shieldmen with Gerold and Felbar looked impressive – but she doubted they were going to hold intact for that long. She didn't think they were necessarily going to be overrun, but there would likely be casualties before they could be relieved.

The Undead dungeon had either gotten lucky or had planned exactly when their Core would be upgraded, because the attack turned out to come at probably the worst time possible for the Dwarven Shieldmen; after only 30 seconds of defending the line admirably against Ogre Skeletons, ghouls, the armored Undead, and a variety of zombies (there weren't any smaller skeletons other than the rats), the first of the Dwarves fell, his armor disintegrating around him as he fell unconscious when his energy ran out.

Sandra could only imagine how different this would've gone if they had listened to Gerold and at least taken the Energy Orbs, because after a long day of culling the Dungeon Monsters in either forest hemming them in, most of the Shieldmen were dangerously low on energy already. When their sleep was interrupted – the only way for them to regenerate that energy – they arrived at the battle only semi-full, which led to them fighting at a severe disadvantage.

Felbar took matters in his own hands when he saw the first – and then the second of the Dwarves fall near him – and opened up with his Flame Cone, shooting out a large swath of flames that blanketed dozens of incoming undead…as well as the barley field behind them.

"Those are our crops! What do you think you're doing?" one of the Shieldmen next to the War Machine asked, distracted enough that he got smashed by a massive bone club from his blind side. Needless to say, Felbar didn't answer him – not that he could understand it anyway.

But the Gnome didn't stop there, as he continued to light up everything he saw, including more of the field; the Undead still making their way through the field ended up getting burned, showing the real intent behind the fire attack. Those that made it through – which, granted, was still quite a few – were on fire, the elemental attack doing continuous damage that helped to drop them faster.

The Undead Core wasn't done with its strategy, however; the Specters that survived the attacks by the Phoenixes – approximately a score of them – had held back at that point, and Sandra hadn't even noticed until they started moving. As they shot downwards from behind the line, Sandra reached out to the two that could hear her.

** Gerold, Felbar – the Specters are moving in! **

The warning came too late for a dozen Dwarves, as the Specters went right for a gap in the Shieldmen's armor and disappeared; moments later, the Dwarves' armor started to break apart, as the energy inside of them was literally sucked out by the mostly transparent undead. Only two of them survived the next couple of seconds as they collapsed, and before the others could react they were overrun. Those two that survived just happened to be next to Felbar, who had responded to Sandra's warning by shooting his flames up in the air and burning some of the Specters out of the night sky, before turning to those around him and protecting them as well as he could.

Unfortunately, he had held his flames going for far too long, and the warhammer began to literally melt and drip from the end, sort of like a candle. When the head of the hammer was almost gone, the enchantment lost cohesion as what it was enchanted on disappeared, and the flames shut off abruptly. Luckily for Felbar, there was no backlash from the cessation, but the enchantment had collapsed so thoroughly that it would have to be completely built up from scratch.

The sacrifice of two of the War Machine's weapons was worth it, though, as it had helped to clear out dozens of Undead and left a large space in the middle of the line where the Shieldmen could retreat to after their losses all along the line. At that point, Sandra counted only 22 of them left after what appeared to be over 50 – and the battle had only been going on for just under two minutes.

Then, inevitably, the Liches arrived. There were a dozen of them bringing up the rear, as they always appeared to instinctively stay behind the others. As the survivors were gathering together to put up a last defense against the scores of Undead still looking to kill them, the robed Monsters started to gather their Nether energy for their deadly attack.

A dozen Pegasi shot down from the sky behind the spell-casting Undead, diving straight for them as the rest of her forces arrived and streamed through the trees, running for everything they were worth. Everything seemed to be in slow motion as Sandra continued to observe from up high, and some quick calculations showed that her flying horses wouldn't arrive in time to stop everything.

** Gerold, tell all of the Shieldmen to jump on the War Machine or get as close to it as they can! **

Gerold immediately shouted the order, knowing that Sandra was keeping an eye on things from above. The other Dwarves looked extremely confused, and only just over half of them followed the strange order – including, miraculously, the stubborn form of Bregan. When the older, white-haired Shieldmen leader saw that there were a handful still fighting, he added his own order for them to move towards the War Machine.

As the stubborn ones turned to obey, they were hit from behind by a mass of dark clouds that almost appeared to consume the armor straight off of their body; the energy drained from their bodies so quickly that they didn't even get knocked unconscious – which made the next part hard to watch. The Nether-energy attack, having consumed all of the elemental energy inside of them, next started to consume their bodies...leaving the 7 Shieldmen to scream as their bodies started to age rapidly, before being eaten away from the inside.

Felbar, for his part, took the cue that Sandra had given him and activated his Holy Protection Shield as soon as everyone who could make it was close enough. The shield made of light lit up the village and burning fields nearly as bright as daytime, and the Nether-based attack – that the Liches managed to get off before having their rotting brains bashed in by Pegasus hooves – splashed ineffectively off of the powerful protective bubble and dissipated a few seconds later. The thirteen remaining Shieldmen looked around in shock as they were saved by the powerful enchantment, before the light disappeared and they were once again back to defending themselves.

Gerold had also activated his own personal Shield, though it was only just large enough for him. As he let it fall as well, he joined the other Shieldmen in a wavy defensive line with a one-armed War Machine in the middle.

"We have to evacuate the villagers! Marleth, run back and—" the old Dwarf began.

One of the other Shieldmen wearily interrupted him. "Marleth is dead, sir."

"Fine, fighting retreat! Let's get in between the houses to present them a better line of defense." Putting actions to his words, Bregan started to back up, keeping the Undead at bay ahead of him with great sweeps of his axe. The others followed suit and in less than a minute they were in a relatively narrow space between two buildings, with a much more cohesive line of defense.

Meanwhile, Sandra's forces were attacking the Undead from the rear and were absolutely devastating them. It wasn't just that her Angels, Pegasi, and Apes equipped with Steel Warhammers were Undead-killing machines, it was also that none of the Monsters in the rear of the horde seemed to pay them any attention or defend themselves. They were all so intent on reaching the Dwarves that they apparently had no orders to do anything but that.

Things were looking good before one of the villager Dwarves hiding in the large building in the middle of the village looked out the window at the approaching horde and screamed; it was apparently just loud enough that the Undead heard her...and when one of them heard her, *all* of them heard her. Two wings of Undead broke off from the side of the horde pushing against the Shieldmen, Gerold, and Felbar, and started to circle around the buildings to either side.

"NO! Drecker, you're with me; the rest of you...HOLD THE LINE!" Bregan shouted, tapping another Shieldman next to him and disappearing with him back behind the defensive line, aiming for the large building's entrance. It was likely locked, but when there was a duo of Ogre Skeletons accompanied by two dozen ghouls on the way, a wooden door wouldn't present much of an obstacle.

Their absence didn't seem to make much difference, as the horde was finally starting to ease up a little from the Undead that had moved away and the pressure on them from behind. Gerold and Felbar eventually told the others to fall back for a moment while they took over, knowing that the exhausted and nearly spent Shieldmen likely didn't have much left to give. Luckily, large sweeps of the double-bladed axe the War Machine was wielding was all that was needed to push the incoming Undead back, giving them some room to recover. Shortly thereafter, her constructs and other Dungeon Monsters finally managed to work their way through, destroying the rest of the horde with ease.

For the rest of the Undead that had gone around the building to go after the Dwarven woman who had screamed, it was another case entirely. Bregan and the Shieldman named Drecker arrived moments before the undead, and they immediately went to work slicing through the ghouls who had outpaced the Ogre Skeletons, but there were too many of them to handle easily. Not more than 10 seconds after they started to slice up the Undead with amazing speed and technique – especially considering the age of the older Dwarf – Drecker fell to one knee, the armor already starting to deteriorate as the Shieldman was emptied of energy. The wounded ghoul he was fighting immediately fell upon him and helped the armor finish falling away, ripping out hunks of flesh at the same time.

Bregan, apparently conscious of his co-defender falling, seemed to go berserk, moving faster and at one point actually spinning in a circle as he chopped three ghouls in half with one swing. He appeared to be winning...but then the two Ogre Skeletons arrived with their heavy steps reverberating the ground beneath his feet.

** Gerold, the old Dwarf is in trouble— **

Sandra tried to warn Gerold, hoping that he or one of the others could get there in time; the pressure on them was easing to the point where all of them could help, but it was too late. Ignoring a ghoul trying to claw through his armor, Bregan just stood there and held his axe out, as if he was daring the Ogre to strike him with its bone club. So, naturally, the Ogre obliged.

As soon as the club swung downwards and impacted the axe the Shieldmen leader held aloft – which amazingly stopped the heavy weapon – Bregan emitted a shout that seemed to come from his very soul. As his voice rose in volume and the Ogre continued to try to push downwards, a fire began in the middle of the Shieldman's chest, building larger as the seconds ticked by, until finally it burst out of him, hitting the Ogre with a massive burst of intense fire. The Skeleton cracked apart and practically melted as it fell to the ground, before dissolving and leaving behind an Onyx Monster Seed.

Bregan, unfortunately, suffered nearly the same fate. The fire that had burst from him appeared to consume both him and his armor in a flash, leaving behind a small pile of ash where a Dwarf stood just a moment before. He had given his life in a blaze of glory to save his people...but they were still in danger.

The explosive fire had killed off all of the other ghouls surrounding the Dwarf – whether that was intentional or not, Sandra figured she'd never know – but the remaining Ogre was completely unharmed. As the Dungeon Core watched it turn its attention to the large building, she heard more screaming coming from inside; looking back at her Monsters and the remaining Dwarves, she could see that they were quickly making their way there, but the massive Skeleton would have more than enough time to destroy half of the building – and kill quite a few of the villagers inside – before they could stop it.

The Ogre took a single step forward...and then was knocked flat on its back as an explosion shattered half of its ribcage. Three more explosions followed in quick succession, blowing off a leg, an arm, and finally its skull shattered, sending bone fragments everywhere – before they dissipated as the last Undead that had assaulted the village was finally destroyed.

** It's about time – what took you so long? **

Echo was seated on the back of a Pegasus, her bow still held out in front of her and to the side of the flying horse's neck, trying to avoid being smacked in the head by a flapping wing. "It's not my fault this thing is so slow; you'd think being able to fly would make it quicker somehow, but I swear I could've ran here by myself even faster," she said with a sneer to the open air, looking at the pair of Shears Sandra had brought down to talk to her. "Besides, it was your idea that I ride it, so it's ultimately your fault that I'm late."

Her sneer went away, however, as she patted the side of the Pegasus fondly. "I have to admit, though – this is quite the steed to ride into battle. I think I might even name her."

** Her? I don't think my Monsters are either a him* ***or*** *a her. **

"Doesn't matter, I can just think of her whatever I like since you gave her to me." Echo smiled as she waved down to a couple of Dwarves that were staring at an Elf sitting on the back of a pure-white flying horse that had a faint light aura around it.

I guess that's something you don't see every day.

Chapter 29

By the time the pre-dawn light was brightening up the barren landscape of the wastelands, the villagers and the surviving Shieldmen were already on their way towards Sandra's dungeon. Actually, Gerold told them it was – not inaccurately, even if not the whole truth – a safe haven and refuge for them; apparently, the only ones that had known where Gerold had actually gone had perished in the battle overnight, so his report that there was somewhere safe they could go made it much easier to convince them to evacuate than it probably would've been otherwise. Even the Shieldmen hadn't argued about it, though that was likely because they were practically dead on their feet, their energy levels so low they couldn't think straight.

With a third of their fields burned, 80% of the Shieldmen dead (including their leader) and facing the possibility of another attack by the Undead, it wasn't really that hard to get everyone to pack up everything they could carry and bring it with them. In all, every single one of the 62 villagers had survived, but of the 53 Shieldmen that had been alive at the start of the night...only 11 of them had made it through – if she counted Gerold in that count. It was a dour bunch that shuffled slowly across the wasteland, their exhaustion from the night obvious as they walked into the unknown. She had asked Gerold if any of them wanted to ride on one of her Apes or Pegasi, but none of them trusted her Monsters enough yet despite the fact that they had been saved by them.

Sandra couldn't blame them, really; they had lost a lot over the last couple of hours and it was undoubtedly hard to trust Dungeon Monsters so soon after such a tragedy. Fortunately, the villagers – as well as the surviving Shieldmen, veterans as most of them were – looked towards Gerold as an authority figure that they were happy enough to follow…for the moment, at least. When the shock of the events wore off and everyone got some sleep, that could change, but as the one that supposedly "brought reinforcements" Gerold was ostensibly in charge.

All of which was a good thing, because Sandra expected some further attacks against the Dwarven village. Half of her forces were currently escorting the Dwarves to her village, while the other half had gone back to the Undead dungeon entrance; while they had been absent going about their reinforcement duties, however, the few Shears she had kept back keeping an eye on the entrance had seen scores of Undead streaming out – and there was nothing she could do to stop them. The flow of Undead only increased as over 40 Shieldmen were killed, and now they were scattered over the forest with Sandra unable to keep track of them.

Sandra also got an equal amount of Mana from those deaths, as unintentional and unwanted as it was; since it had occurred in her Area of Influence as well as the Undead Core's, she received half of the resulting Mana – as much she'd rather not benefit from the deaths of sentient people, she wasn't going to waste it. The flow of Mana coming from their deaths "dwarfed" the previous amount she had received from the deaths of the

Gnomes for some reason, though – especially when Bregan, their leader, had perished.

"It's because of their greater capacity to hold and use elemental energy compared to those who haven't trained that part of themselves," Winxa informed her. "The Gnomes weren't Enchanters that had constantly worked on building up their elemental energy, so they weren't…'worth' as much, as callous as that sounds. If those Elite Elves that were in your dungeon not so long ago had died, you'd probably have seen *even more* from them."

Sandra guessed that made sense, though putting a value on someone's life like that was indeed callous. But it also explained how she was able to fill up her entire treasury with Elemental Orbs and Cubes while the battle was ongoing. She didn't have enough focus to funnel the Mana into anything more productive at that time, so it seemed like the best idea; now it was going to come in handy when all the Dwarves arrived, because she had plenty of Large Elemental Orbs to complete the Visitor's Bond with all of them.

That was, if they agreed to it – though she was hoping they would, because she didn't want any unfortunate accidents between her Monsters or Traps and them. She had already had to stop her forces out aboveground from automatically attacking the Shieldmen when they first were encountered, and she didn't want inattention in the dungeon to have unintended consequences. Not only that, but Sandra would be extremely limited on what *she* could do with non-bonded “invaders” in her dungeon, so she was considering making it a requirement.

She also used a relatively small portion of the Mana she received to furnish all of the rooms they were going to stay in and live, though they weren’t very fancy; basic wooden bedframes with a simple Bearling Leather mattress comprised of multiple layers, followed by Cotton sheets and a Cotton pillow filled with raw Cotton bolls. It took some impromptu growing of Cotton in the cleared fields she had for future food production as well as harvesting, but she had plenty of time while the Dwarves were trying to figure out what they were doing in the late night and early morning.

It also took a small army of constructs consisting of Hyper Automatons, Iron-Banded Articulated Clockwork Golems (which, as the name implied, had a much greater range of motion than its previous incarnation), and Large Armored Sentinels that harvested the cotton, assembled all of the bedframes, and worked with Sandra to craft all of the Cotton Cloth pillowcases. By that time, however, she had gotten so adept at controlling and directing her constructs that it was all done before the Dwarves even started on their journey. She knew it was certainly going to be a rough adjustment for them, but hopefully not too bad.

The plan to delve through the Undead Core’s dungeon had been delayed, but it was only a matter of sending her Monsters forces to clean up the surrounding areas again before she sent them down to attack; the last thing she wanted was to have them attacked again by those Undead roaming around right now, like what had happened when she destroyed the Reptile Core. As much as they needed to destroy the Core *now*, she didn't want to jeopardize the expedition right from the start; it had been necessary before, because the Elves had been directly threatened and there was very little choice in the matter.

What made that scenario different from now was that she was pretty sure she had the necessary means to carry out the destruction of the Reptile Core with just her constructs; this time, with the Undead Core being so powerful, she knew she needed to improve what she was going to send against it to ensure victory. She might've waited *too* long, unfortunately, which resulted in what happened that night, but it could've been much worse if she had gone into the dungeon with forces that didn't manage to succeed. It would've put Sandra further behind, while giving the Undead Core the means to upgrade even more, making them even more powerful.

I have to stick by the choices I make, even if they don't turn out to be the correct ones; I know I'm no expert in these types of matters, and I'm doing the best I can with limited information. The fact that the Undead Core seemed to be just the opposite of her limited knowledge of strategy and tactical matters only made it more difficult to make correct decisions...but she was learning. Sandra had tried to be adaptable during the battle between the Dwarves and the Undead and it might've even saved some lives, though she was fairly confident she had been outclassed in that by the other Core again. She was just thankful that the Core seemed so bloodthirsty and out to kill the Dwarves that it didn't really defend properly against her Monsters when they arrived, otherwise it may have turned out differently.

Regardless, it was over and done with and she could only work towards the elimination of the Undead Core now with focus, and despite the timeline being pushed back momentarily, Sandra was confident it could still happen by the start of the next day. She just had to deliver the Dwarves safely and then start destroying all of the Undead outside the dungeon again—

...Oh, no – what now?

Sandra had been constantly monitoring the borders of the wasteland for any threats, because she didn't want to be surprised by something; although most of her focus had been near the forest filled with Undead, she still periodically looked towards the Elves and Orcs to make sure they were fine. One of her Shears near the Orc lands spotted something running into the wastelands, stumbling and floundering from apparent exhaustion; dawn was just starting to touch on the horizon, so it was unusual enough at that time of day for an Orc to be out of the village, so she sent her Shears closer to get a better look at what – or, as it turned out, *who* – it was.

She immediately recognized Kelerim, the half-Dwarf/half-Orc Blacksmith that had left her dungeon no more than two months ago, hoping to help the Orcish people with his new Blacksmithing skills – and to find his father that he just learned about from his unexpected half-brother, Razochek Bloodskull. She brought her flying construct down farther, only to see what appeared to be bloodstains on his torn shirt, accompanied by a look of extreme weariness on his face.

"Sandra! *cough* I don't know...if you can hear me...*cough*...need your help..." he said to no one in particular, before he collapsed to his knees, unable to go on any farther. Sandra immediately dispatched two of her Apes along with a Repair Drone from her dungeon, which was the closest force she had to him – the others were quite the distance away. One of the Apes physically carried the Drone because it didn't move very fast, and as they sped away they were joined by a Jaguar Queen and Dire Wolf that she had on the constant prowl around her dungeon entrance.

* *Kelerim! What are you doing here – and what happened to you?* *

Kneeling down seemed to ease some of the pain and lying on his side seemed to ease it even more – enough that he was able to talk without much coughing. "Sandra! Thank goodness you heard me...I'm so sorry...I didn't mean for any of this happen..." he managed to get out, before his body was wracked by another coughing fit and the Dungeon Core could see spots of blood on his hand that he used to cover his mouth.

** I have help on the way, Kelerim – just stay awake until they arrive, which should hopefully be in a few minutes. Now, explain what happened. **

Sandra was worried about her friend, but despite the wounds on his body – which apparently also included his lungs – he appeared to be hale enough to survive until her constructs arrived. Kelerim coughed once more, which seemed to help calm him a little, and he began talking softly, just slightly louder than a whisper.

"I went to find my father, using the coinage you created for me or trading my skills to create fine blades to work my way to where the Bloodskull Family Compound was located. I had never been there before, and it was a lot larger than I had expected; it appeared as though my father was a much more powerful Warlord than I knew. It was then that I knew that I couldn't just come out and pronounce myself his offspring; mainly it was because I was worried there were more there like my half-brother that would kill me as soon as they learned of my existence, but also because I couldn't easily prove my claim.

"I needed to see him, however, so I came up with a plan. After some time talking with the guards, then showing a few attendants of my father what I could offer with my Blacksmithing skills, I was finally granted an audience with the leader of the Bloodskull Family – my father – on the pretense of offering myself to his services. During the audience, I managed to convince my father of who I was by telling him what I knew about my mother, and he welcomed me with open arms."

He paused as a tear fell from his eye and he coughed again. "It...was everything I had ever dreamed of; having a family and a father who cared about me, feeling...loved, I guess. But that lasted all of fifteen minutes, when I couldn't hold back the reason I needed to see him. I told him how I had met Razochek and learned of who I was, and how my half-brother tried to kill me.

"My father wouldn't believe that of his other son, however, and accused me of lying – and then calling for Razochek to come back and refute the claims. Then...and I'm not proud of this because I fear I'm a coward...I told him that a dungeon near Grongbak killed him instead of it being me. I...just couldn't do it; I could sense at that point that if I told my father the truth, he would kill me. Instead, he put me under watch – not quite a captive, but unable to leave the Compound – while he assembled a small army of his people to go destroy the dungeon that had dared to kill his son."

That really doesn't sound good. Her fears were only a little alleviated when Kelerim continued. "I didn't tell him which dungeon, or even where it was located, so he doesn't know it was you out here, but I don't think that matters. When they learn of Razochek's disappearance out in the wastelands, they're sure to investigate; I can only assume that my father doesn't know what happened before I even arrived because the Warbands still around here don't want to be blamed for his death. That'll probably change with an army that I estimated to be nearly 1,000 Orcs strong."

** Ok...but that doesn't explain why* ***you*** *are here. **

Another coughing fit interrupted his response, but he managed to get over it enough to answer. "I was able to escape from the Compound because I wasn't technically under guard, but I was followed by one of my father's retainers who tracked me down to approximately a dozen miles west of here. He captured me and told me he was bringing me back to my father, but I managed to swipe a knife from his belt and stab him deep in the gut before he could react; it wasn't anything near a killing blow, unfortunately, and he enacted his revenge with his sword as I tried to escape, stabbing me shallowly a couple of times – including my chest.

"The blood loss from the much deeper wound I inflicted on him slowed him down considerably, though, and I was able to flee; I managed to make it this far in desperation before my strength started to give out."

Kelerim's voice started to get weaker and weaker, until the last part was just barely above a whisper. Fortunately, her constructs were already arriving, having run the entire way with the Repair Drone – which immediately went to work healing him.

** Kelerim, you're going to be fine, though likely tired until you get some rest and something to eat. Before my constructs bring you* *back to the safety of my dungeon, however, tell me this: how close is that Orcish army. **

The half-Dwarf/half-Orc's eyes started to drift close, as his wounds were being healed and the absence of pain made him drowsy after everything he had gone through. His exhaustion was plain to see in every part of his body, and the stress of his desperate flight was obviously catching up with him.

"They're...not far behind..." he was able to get out before his body and mind gave into the unconsciousness that it had been threatening to unleash upon him.

Less than a minute later the healing was complete, and one of the Apes picked him up and slung him over its shoulder, while the one that had carried the Drone there did the same for the way back. They were still flanked by the Jaguar Queen and Dire Wolf as they started running back to her dungeon, though it was a little slower because they were carrying someone that probably wouldn't appreciate being bounced around uncomfortably as they ran full-out.

Kelerim, Felbar, and the Dwarves all arrived at approximately the same time at her dungeon, though her oldest friend – non-Fairy, at least – was shuffled down below immediately. Gerold assembled the weary Dwarves in the workshop, who looked around disinterestedly at their surroundings, only caring that it looked relatively safe.

Felbar helped the young Dwarf out of the Deep Delver and Gerold addressed the crowd. "There is something that everyone needs to do before you go in. There is a sort of…tattoo…that needs to be applied before you can pass within, which will grant you safe passage throughout the entire…facility." He was presenting them with half-truths, which didn't really sit well with Sandra, but she had also impressed upon him on their journey across the wasteland the importance of having the Visitor's Bond. She even asked him to offer the same special Bond that he himself had, with his embedded Energy Orbs in his palms, though she doubted any of them would take that deal when warned of the pain from it.

He showed them his own hands and the gears on the palms, as well as the blue and black Orbs there. "This is a special…tattoo that not all of you will have; it's normally just this little part here," he continued, pointing to the bronze-colored gears surrounding the Orbs. "For the Shieldmen, however, I would recommend the…upgrade…like I have – though I will warn you that it is…hmm, how do I say this without scaring you…well, it's the most painful experience you'll ever have the pleasure of enduring, but it fortunately doesn't last that long. The tattoo doesn't normally hurt, but this process is a bit different."

The villagers unsurprisingly didn't seem to want the "upgraded" tattoo, but all of them agreed to receive one in order to pass into the "facility"; Sandra was prepared to tell them all exactly what they were getting themselves into, but she didn't want to start a panic before they were all done. In contrast, the Shieldmen seemed interested in what exactly the upgrade meant – and all of them immediately agreed to undergo the painful experience as soon as they held one or a pair of the Energy Orbs in their hands.

The screams from the first to undergo the procedure was almost enough to dissuade the others, but when he appeared relatively unharmed – if haunted – from the experience, the remaining Shieldmen insisted that they could withstand the pain for the benefits they would receive. In the end, all 10 of the armored Dwarves took the upgraded Visitor's Bond – and immediately followed the villagers on their journey deep into her dungeon, barely flinching at the VATS they had to traverse down hundreds of feet. An hour after they arrived at her dungeon, as the sun was fully above the horizon, all of the Dwarves that had survived the attack on their village were safely tucked away in their beds and fast asleep. Felbar and Sandra's other Visitors also followed suit, as Violet had continued enchanting through the night and the others had been woken up early to fight a difficult battle.

Sandra had sent her Monster escorts back to the Undead forest to join up with those she had already sent there, where they began their systematic extermination of every Undead they came across. They had barely started when Kelerim's warning from earlier reared its Orcish head.

The half-Dwarf/half-Orc had been correct in his estimation; Sandra took as accurate count of the army of Orcs that was entering her Area of Influence as possible and stopped counting at nearly 1,000. Anything more definite was practically impossible, as they were too undisciplined to stay in neat ranks – they were more like a mob than anything. Regardless, she didn't think it was too many more than what she counted, which was alarming enough.

What was even more alarming was how they didn't even head towards the village of Grongbak. Instead, they left the road that would bring them to the village and turned to the northeast, heading in the general direction of the Unicorn-based Dungeon Core located there. She had already seen many of the Dungeon Monsters available under that particular Classification when she was perusing options in her Advancement Menu, and she was fairly certain they wouldn't stand a chance against the Orcs. *Even if they have shoddy weapons,* she couldn't help but note when she went in for a closer look with her Shears.

Sandra followed them as they quickly tore into the forest holding all number of Unicorns, shiny Lynxes, and other Holy-based Monsters – and they all fell without trouble, barely slowing the force down. Within a half hour they had marched far enough to find the dungeon entrance, though they had to backtrack a half-mile when they initially missed it. It seemed as though they knew in general where it was but didn't have any local guides with them.

"What's going on?" Winxa asked suddenly. Sandra hadn't really been paying attention to the Dungeon Fairy lately with everything that had been going on, and she realized that she hadn't even told her about Kelerim yet. As the last of the Orc army went inside the dungeon, she recounted it all to her guide, to which Winxa looked thoughtful, though worried.

"That won't be good if they manage to find out your location, of course...but for some reason I feel like I should be warning you of something else," the Fairy finally said, tapping her finger against her lips as she looked off away from her Core. "Hmm...I'm not sure what it was, though it seemed relevant and rather important. Oh well, I'm sure I will remember given enough time."

** Well, if you remember, let me know – I don't want any more surprises especially with those Orcs sniffing around and the Undead Core still a major threat I need to eliminate. **

Twenty minutes after the Orcs entered the Unicorn dungeon, Sandra suddenly felt the AOI surrounding it completely disappear. She was expecting it, but the shock and quickness of its happening shook her a little. *They did it...am I next on their hit-list?*

Sandra wasn't *really* worried about being destroyed by the Orcs despite their numbers, because she was confident her traps and Dungeon Monsters could hold even that quantity off without too much trouble. Given that they didn't have any special way to negate her traps like the Elite Elves had (at least, she didn't think so), they should be highly effective. No, the problem was that she didn't want to *have to* kill them all, but she couldn't see any way around it at the moment.

She could now see inside the former Unicorn Core's dungeon through her Area of Influence, as its presence was the only thing keeping her from seeing inside before. Looking through the entire space – which was now devoid of any traps or Monsters – she saw the corpses of at least 30 Orcs, a few here and there throughout the rooms. She also saw the broken blades of at least a hundred Iron swords, though she was distracted from seeing more than that as the dungeon started to collapse from the Core's former Core Room and the Orcs scrambled to escape being buried alive.

Minutes later, they all escaped safe and sound, leaving their fallen brethren to their new burial site. The second that the last room collapsed near the entrance – which was essentially just a hole in the ground similar to the Reptile one she had gone into – something appeared in Sandra's awareness.

Winxa?! What is this?!

The Dungeon Fairy snapped her fingers and pointed a finger up, as though she finally remembered something. "*That's* what it was! How could I forget something so important?"

I'd say it was important! This could change everything…

Chapter 30

Temporary Dungeon Core Enhancements	
These temporary enhancements are a safety measure implemented by the Creator as established by your contract. These enhancements are granted upon any Dungeon Cores within a certain distance from recently destroyed Cores; this is to reduce the likelihood that the destruction of additional nearby Dungeon Cores will occur while new Cores are brought in and raised to a minimum Core Size to continue the objectives of the destroyed Cores. ***These enhancements are not granted to any Cores that – in any way – participated in the destruction of any neighboring Cores, whether through overt, clandestine, or inadvertent means. In addition, any previous mentoring benefits are now instantly null and void for any Dungeon Cores taking advantage of these enhancements.*** ***As soon as the number of new replacement Cores all reach the New Core Threshold (which will also employ a rapid growth cycle during Core Size upgrades), these enhancements will be negated over the course of 7 days, and any mentoring benefits will be reestablished.***	
(Your Core is not currently eligible for any enhancements)	
Current Nearby Dungeon Cores Destroyed:	**2**
Current Distance Threshold:	**100.0 Miles**
Current New Core Threshold:	**Core Size 20**
Current Temporary Enhancement for 2 destroyed Cores:	
Area of Influence is increased by a total of 50% over the course of 50 days and stays until the current New Core Threshold is reached.	
Next Temporary Enhancements for 3 destroyed Cores:	
Includes all previous Temporary Enhancements, plus: Ambient Mana Absorption directly by the Core is increased by 10000%, Area of Influence is increased by an additional 10% over the course of 10 days, Distance Threshold is increased by 10%, New Core Threshold is increased by 2 Core Sizes	

So what, would you please tell me, is this? Because from what I'm seeing here, we could be in big trouble.

"Trouble" was an understatement; she narrated the entire notification to Winxa so that she could understand what Sandra was looking at, and the second time reading it only made her more worried. In essence, it was saying that if any more Cores were destroyed, the remaining ones around the area would start to become more powerful – and quickly. As it was, the remaining dungeon near the Orcs, the two near the Elves, the two near the Dwarves' former village, and of course the Undead dungeon would have their AOI increased by 50% over the next 50 days.

"Yes, well, something like this hasn't happened in a long time so it didn't even occur to me to tell you about it – because I can't even remember the last time this actually came into effect."

Yes, fine, you forgot, we'll deal with that later – but why does this exist in the first place?

"Well…the best way it was described to me…well…let's just say it was long ago, was that the Creator designed the dungeons for a specific purpose – as I'm sure you remember: to keep the races from warring on each other by making them concentrate on maintaining the safety of their own lands and people. This purpose would fall apart if the Humans – let's just say – got together and formed a larger-than-normal force to start destroying dungeons one after another.

"If they manage to destroy one or two, those areas are then freed up from having to cull the nearby dungeons and are thereby safer; the Heroes or whatever that were previously involved in defending the nearby land could join this force and move on to the next dungeon and destroy it, freeing up those Heroes, and so on and so forth. In a matter of a year or two, your former homeland could be completely freed up from every single dungeon around them; of course, there would start to be some growing dungeons just making it out of their underground areas and into the wider world that replaced the ones that were destroyed – but they would be so weak that they wouldn't prevent the Humans from going off into other lands to conquer. Are you following me so far?"

In general, I am. What I can't understand is why they ***didn't*** *do that; I'm almost positive that they certainly could've done it easily.*

The Dungeon Fairy nodded. "That's what I'm getting at, in fact. If the Monster Seeds that were left behind as your 'Dungeon Loot' aren't enough to dissuade a race from doing that to the dungeons, these Temporary Dungeon Core Enhancements were created to make such a premise nearly impossible. Or at least so difficult that it would result in many deaths of those Heroes in order to destroy the final few dungeons, which would be extremely powerful. In addition, while they're trying to finish them off, brand-new Cores would replace the ones that were destroyed and would rapidly grow until they were again a threat within a few months or sooner.

"Fun fact: this was actually attempted by the Humans when the dungeons first came into existence, but they stopped after four dungeons were destroyed, for some reason that was never revealed to us. It's my own personal opinion that the Creator somehow visited the leaders of all the races at that point to warn them of the consequences of continuing down that path, and that was then passed down from generation to generation as some sort of rule that should never be broken."

Sandra didn't really consider that a "fun fact", though it did certainly explain some things. She remembered back when she was a merchant learning that the Heroes were *very* particular about what dungeons they destroyed, and that if they were forced to destroy two that were close to each other, they would destroy one and then actively "contain" the other until a new dungeon appeared nearby – then they were free to destroy it. While she always thought it was because they didn't want to miss out on the powerful Loot that was dropped by destroying too many at once, but now it made sense with what Winxa was saying.

Then how does that explain what the Orcs are doing?

"Well, in their defense, they probably didn't know that the Reptile dungeon was just destroyed not too far away, triggering these enhancements," she replied with an apologetic tilt to her head. "That, or the warning has been lost to the ages, and they don't know any better."

That's just great – what am I supposed to do now?

"I...don't know. This could have some drastic consequences for this entire region if more Cores are destroyed; because you're at a crossroads between the races, *all* of them would be impacted by this, and further destruction would only spread further into their lands. You could potentially speed up the demise of each of the races, though it would at least temporarily help those people living around here."

It was quite the dilemma.

Logically, the greater good was now to leave the Undead Core alone and just cull the Monsters outside, preventing most of the potential expansion of its Area of Influence in the process. After asking Winxa about the "mentoring benefits" included in the notification, she found that the possibility of another dungeon accessing her AOI was now impossible due to the Enhancements in play, so this option was a real possibility – because she could now upgrade her Core Size without fear. At least until the Enhancements ended, at which time she was hopeful she could handle any threats with her greater Size.

In her Core's fictitious heart and in the deepest parts of her mind, however, Sandra wanted to destroy the Undead Core and call it a day. Thoughts of revenge on the Dwarves' part motivated some of it, but deep down she could feel that it was the right thing to do, despite the danger it could impose on the towns and villages nearby, as well as those farther into their lands. By the "right thing", she meant that it was a mistake that she had made that needed to be corrected, and not necessarily because she thought that she was specifically put there to eliminate all of the dungeons.

Sandra was still undecided as to what she wanted to do as she spent the morning and afternoon creating even more Dungeon Monsters to add to those she already had out and about, including an additional half-dozen Phoenixes to replace those that had perished in the attack the night before. She also expanded her Hyper Automatons force that she used to bring back dropped Monster Seeds, because she was planning on looting the Dwarven village. She already noticed a few skeletal rats sneaking in and snatching some of the Seeds dropped from the battle, and she was sure that the Dwarves had a lot of Loot stashed away from their constant culling of the nearby Monsters.

It wasn't through any desire for it herself – though she wouldn't deny it would be beneficial – but because she knew that if she didn't, more and more Undead could potentially slip through and grab it for their Core. She couldn't allow any such advantageous looting from helping the other Core, not if she had any hope to contain it in the future.

Sandra figured that she would at least continue the cleanup of all the Undead roaming around before making a final decision on that, as well as potentially talking it over with her Visitors later when they woke up.

Meanwhile, she now had constant observation over the Orcs, which was revealing some interesting happenings of their own. The first thing Sandra thought they would do once they destroyed the Unicorn-based Core was go to the nearby village, but that appeared to be the last thing on their mind. Instead, they immediately camped in the middle of the forest that once contained the now-destroyed Core's Monsters – and probably still did have a few roaming around somewhere. When they finally stopped moving and lay down to sleep, not even bothering to have someone keep watch for potential Monsters, she was finally able to get an accurate count: 973 Orcs. Most of them still had swords, but 72 of them appeared to have nothing but smaller daggers now, as their shoddily crafted Iron swords were now gone.

What was even stranger was that not a single Orc said a word the entire time. Sandra briefly thought that something might be wrong with them – as she had heard of elemental energy being used in the past to subtly influence someone's mind – but as she initially observed them setting camp, that notion went away. It appeared as though the force was just tired and had worked together so much that no words needed to be spoken. They were efficient in their movements and did everything with a minimum of fuss, so there was apparently no reason to communicate.

That all took place just past mid-morning, and they were up again approximately 8 hours later as the setting sun was very nearly touching the horizon. The darkness didn't seem to deter the Orcs, however, as they exited the forest and made for the road to the village.

Except…they kept going instead of heading for the settlement.

Winxa, the Orcs aren't stopping. I can see them going straight for the other dungeon to the southwest of them.

Throughout the day, something had been bothering her about the whole situation, and it took the entire day to figure out what it was: the Warband that had taken over for Razochek and continued the culling process of the nearby forests was nowhere to be seen. It was only when she looked closer at a few of the Orcs in the army that she thought she recognized one or two of them integrated with them.

Why would they accompany the new army when they could just tell what happened to Razochek?

Then she remembered that the others of Razochek's warband that hadn't perished with him didn't actually *know* what happened to Kelerim's half-brother, only that he disappeared in the wastelands.

Winxa backed that thought up for her a moment later. "They could be pleading ignorance and be blaming his disappearance on something else. It's quite possible that they don't know what happened to the Orcs that died in your dungeon and would rather seem incompetent rather than complicit."

That was true, but the Orcs that had come from the Bloodskull Compound had to have been informed that a *dungeon* had killed Razochek – otherwise what they were doing didn't make sense. Sandra figured it was only a matter of time before they put things together and determined that something in the wasteland killed Razochek and went hunting for it – even if it didn't turn out to be a dungeon, for all they knew.

As the Orcs entered the trees heading towards the Avian dungeon, Sandra had her flying Shears follow along for as far as it could before something unexpectedly dive-bombed her construct and destroyed it nearly instantly. She didn't bother sending any more into the forest after that, because she already knew where they were going.

The Avian-Classification Core and accompanying dungeon were apparently a little tougher, because it took some time for anything to happen. While Sandra was waiting, most of her guests were starting to wake up and look for food, which she easily supplied from a small kitchen she had replicated down below near the Dwarven bedrooms – though she didn't really have a dining area set up quite yet. The villagers and Shieldmen were happy enough to be eating meat and especially fruit, as it was apparently quite the luxury for them, sitting on the floor wherever they could find space to eat.

She took that opportunity for Gerold to come forward and finally fess up and tell them precisely where they were and who Sandra was – and she promptly freaked out half of the villagers with her voice in their heads. The Shieldmen were a bit more stoic about the whole thing, but that could also be because they were all still reveling in the Energy Orbs embedded in their palms to care that much one way or another. Luckily none of them started screaming and demanded to be let out immediately, though she certainly let them know that they weren't prisoners and could leave at any point.

They calmed down even further when she showed them the growing room she had created to plant their crops, and that they could produce as much as they wanted – and do it much, much quicker in the process. She also found out that a few of the villagers had extensive experience back in their strongholds brewing and distilling, so the potential for making the drinks that they so desired was now a real possibility for the future.

She also talked to Violet, Felbar, Echo, Gerold, and the Shieldmen about the new development concerning the destroyed Dungeon Cores. She would've included Kelerim, but he was still sleeping, and he seemed like he needed it more than he needed to be awkwardly introduced to the others to take part in the conversation. Besides, he probably didn't want to hear about what a mess he had caused with his actions immediately after waking up.

** ...and that's pretty much all the information I have at this point. We've got two choices: leave the Undead dungeon and its Core alone and attempt to contain it so it doesn't expand even further, including the extra Enhancement it'll receive over the next 50 days, or destroy it and make every other dungeon within 100 miles or more that much more powerful. Though, if the Orcs do succeed in destroying the Avian dungeon that they just entered, it could make the whole situation even worse. **

"If that does happen, I think we'll have no choice. If what you said is true—" Violet said – and Sandra translated for everyone else— "then it will become more powerful no matter what you try to do to contain it. So will every other dungeon, though it will happen a little more gradually; regardless, the issue isn't really what will happen immediately, but what will happen in the future if these 'enhancements' continue to grow more powerful."

"I know for a fact – because I was one of the ones doing it—" Echo chimed in— "that we were maintaining a comfortable balance in the nearby dungeons, and this change will already upset that precipitously. What you said about not destroying dungeons too close to each other and in rapid succession is true, as that has been passed down to us for as long as even our elders can remember. I thought it was true everywhere, though I also thought that since Sandra was doing it that the rule didn't apply…I was obviously wrong."

The Shieldmen and Felbar acknowledged that they had also heard that rule, so it was apparent that the limitations had been in place for quite a while everywhere. Sandra was sure it was the same with her former race as well, even if she hadn't heard of it before; Violet and most of the villagers seemed not to know about it, so that kind of information might've only been necessary to pass on to those that actually had to abide by the rules.

"As much as I want to destroy that dungeon for what it did," Gerold finally added, which garnered nods from the other Shieldmen, "I say wait and see what happens with the Orcs; the situation is probably barely manageable right now, and I fear what will happen if you start something that could have serious implications not only to my people, but every race nearby."

The others reluctantly nodded, even Echo – who was naturally predetermined to want all Undead dungeons to be wiped off the face of the land.

** I guess that settles it, then. I'm already starting to mop up many of the scattered Undead that emerged during and after the battle in Nurboldar, though I can't reach nearly all of them. It will require an upgrade to my Core Size to accomplish that, which I can't afford to be down for right now; once we find out what happened to the Orcs— **

They didn't have to wait long, as Sandra could feel the collapse of another Area of Influence. Sending her attention there immediately, she roamed the now-destroyed Avian dungeon rooms, seeing hundreds of Orc corpses, some lying on top of each other and ripped to shreds. In the final room, the Avian's Core Room, there were only about 50 Orcs left alive, though even they were wobbling around on their feet unsteadily from multiple wounds. Not a single one had an intact sword, though most of them had some sort of dagger or destroyed sword in their hands.

They ran as fast as they could through the rooms, the dungeon collapsing behind them, striving to make it out before the entire thing buried them. A few minutes later 45 of them emerged, leaving 5 of them that had fallen behind to suffer the fate of being crushed by tons of falling dirt and rock.

** It looks like our choice has been made for us. **

Temporary Dungeon Core Enhancements	
(Your Core is not currently eligible for any enhancements)	
Current Nearby Dungeon Cores Destroyed:	**3**
Current Distance Threshold:	**110.0 Miles**
Current New Core Threshold:	**Core Size 22**
Previous Temporary Enhancement for 2 destroyed Cores:	
Area of Influence is increased by a total of 50% over the course of 50 days and stays until the current New Core Threshold is reached.	
Current Temporary Enhancements for 3 destroyed Cores:	
Includes all previous Temporary Enhancements, plus: Ambient Mana Absorption directly by the Core is increased by 10000%, Area of Influence is increased by an additional 10% over the course of 10 days, Distance Threshold is increased by 10%, New Core Threshold is increased by 2 Core Sizes	
Next Temporary Enhancements for 4 destroyed Cores:	
Includes all previous Temporary Enhancements, plus: Mana Cost to upgrade Core Size is decreased by 25%, Mana Cost of all Dungeon Monsters decreased by 25%, Ambient Mana Absorption within the Core's dungeon is increased by 2500%, Area of Influence is increased by an additional 25% over the course of 25 days, Distance Threshold is increased by 25%, New Core Threshold is increased by 3 Core Sizes	

Chapter 31

By the next morning, the undead that Sandra's Dungeon Monsters could locate, and reach of course, had been wiped out – though she suspected that there were again hundreds hiding out in the Undead Core's AOI that she couldn't see. There hadn't been any large gatherings of Undead like they had done before, but she was starting to learn how the other Core went about their strategies; making her have to hunt down the Monsters was a delaying tactic and only temporarily kept her from doing what she needed to do. Whether it was because there was some other sort of attack planned or perhaps because the Core already had enough Mana to upgrade again, Sandra didn't know.

It didn't matter though, because she currently couldn't move any faster; there were people coming along that needed sleep to function properly unlike her Dungeon Monsters, so the earliest it *could* happen was late the next morning as everyone got up from another nap they took overnight. Kelerim eventually woke up in the middle of the night and Sandra let him know what had transpired, as well as the unfortunate results of the Orc army's action – both to their numbers and the Temporary Enhancements the nearby dungeons were now experiencing.

He didn't take it well.

** There's nothing we can do about it now, but I fear there are going to be some hardships in the future before we can fully get a handle* *on the situation. There have already been sacrifices made to protect everyone here in this dungeon, and we'll all be doing our part to keep further casualties to a minimum. So cheer up, my friend, because we've got a lot of work to do. **

"That's easy for you to say; you're not the one that caused all of this."

** That may be, but I think I was already heading in this direction from the get-go, so it was inevitable. So stop moping around and be useful; make some blades for your Orcish heritage – because those things they are using are utter garbage. **

Having something to do was the best thing for him, and while he grumbled a little, he didn't protest. While she could certainly make better swords and other weapons for the Orcs – and probably would, with what was likely going to be coming their way – she didn't have the time nor inclination to do it right then.

Knowing his way around, he went right to work in the forge where Sandra had taught him the basics and a few advanced techniques of Blacksmithing; luckily for the others, she had moved their rooms further down below, otherwise the banging would've certainly woken them up. In fact, he was still going when Felbar, Violet, Gerold, and Echo woke up and got some food from the nearby dining area.

"Who are **you**?" Echo asked Kelerim after hearing his incessant banging from down the tunnel. The others had come along, just as curious as to who this new person was.

Sandra translated, but didn't bother introducing him – he did that all by himself.

"I'm…Kelerim. Sandra said I could work in here – did I disturb you?" he said, wiping the sweat off his forehead with the back of his arm. He had taken his torn and ragged shirt off from the heat at least an hour earlier, so he was essentially just there with threadbare pants and a leather Blacksmith's apron.

"Uh…no. I'd just never seen anyone actually use that thing other than Sandra's constructs. Are you coming with us to destroy the undead dungeon?" Echo asked with a strange tone in her voice.

"Me?" Kelerim laughed depreciatingly at the question. "No, I'm not a fighter – I'm a Blacksmith by trade."

"You're a Blacksmith? You don't look like any Blacksmith I've ever seen before, but for some reason you look oddly familiar," Gerold interjected himself into the conversation.

"Um…well, my mother was a Dwarf and my father was an Orc, but I left the mountains of my birth a long time ago—"

"Now I remember! You were just a little lad when they forced you out; I remember that vividly because I didn't agree with it just because you were different. I was a little odd myself, and I always worried they would put me out like you were." He paused for a moment. "I'm glad to see you survived, at least."

"If you call being beaten daily, half-starved, and forced into a trade without my say-so surviving, then I guess it qualifies," Kelerim said dejectedly.

"Well, that's enough catching up – we've got to get going. Nice to meet you, Kelerim," Felbar said abruptly, likely sensing the dour mood that had fallen over the group. The others also said their goodbyes as they realized what he was talking about.

"Yes...it was nice to meet you...*Kelerim*," Echo said last with particularly slow emphasis on his name, following the rest out of the room – though her eyes lingered on the half-Dwarf/half-Orc longer than necessary.

Hmm...

Kelerim went back to work on the sword he was making, completely oblivious.

For her part, Sandra made sure everything was assembled for the trip to the dungeon. Most of her Dungeon Monsters were already there, surrounding the entrances/exits again, but a few that had just been created were going to join Felbar and Gerold in their Deep Delvers, as well as Echo on her Pegasus that she named...Starlight. *Not a particularly inventive name, but I guess it fits.*

Five of the Shieldmen also insisted on going because they wanted to be a part of eliminating the threat; Sandra was sure that revenge was also playing a factor in their decision, but at least they had the presence of mind to only send half of their number away, electing to keep the rest to protect the villagers. Not that they really needed protecting at the bottom of Sandra's dungeon, but she could appreciate where they were coming from.

Violet was of course staying, but she had plenty to work on – including trying to figure out how to fix the War Machine's left arm that had melted. Sandra had already repaired much of the actual physical damage, but now many of the movement enchantments were all messed up and might need to be replaced completely.

One spot of good news – at least she hoped so – was that the Orcs that had survived the destruction of the Avian dungeon had left the area first thing in the morning; they headed back northeast up the same road they came down, though with only about 5% of the number they arrived with. She told Kelerim the news and his reaction was one of surprise and then suspicion.

"Either they think they completed the mission they were given, or they know they don't have enough of them to search for your dungeon – or whatever it is they think killed Razochek. Let's just hope that it's the first, and that they're not heading back to get more help."

** That's something I don't even have time to consider right now, so I think I'll shelve that for another time. No need to borrow trouble at this point in time. **

The group left just after mid-morning, off to join the rest of her forces outside of the Undead dungeon entrance. Just so that she hopefully wouldn't be surprised by any last-minute strategies by the other Core, she took 500 of the Shears in her AMANS and spread them throughout the border of her AOI to inform her if the Undead started to stream in from the areas she couldn't reach. It wouldn't necessarily prevent them from attacking, but she heard Felbar say the other day: Forewarned is forearmed...or something like that.

It took a little over an hour and a half for them to walk all the way to the dungeon entrance, mainly because the Shieldmen Dwarves – though they tried to walk quickly – couldn't move nearly as fast as Echo and the Deep Delvers. Regardless, the sun was high in the sky above the trees as they approached the large assortment of constructs and other Dungeon Monsters.

When they were all together, it was an impressive display: 50 Steelclad Ape Warriors armed with Titanium warhammers enchanted with either a Fireburst or Holy Light enchantment; 50 Celestial Authorities holding their longswords made of light and wearing Leather necklaces around their necks containing Large Holy and Spirit Energy Orbs to regenerate their elemental energy; 40 Unstable Shapeshifters that had accompanying enchanted bows made from Yew and Titanium, each with a leather quiver that held 50 of the special arrows that would explode upon impact; 20 Radiant Pegasi that would help dampen the severity of Nether-based traps and effects, which the Shapeshifters (in Echo form) could ride, also with supplies for the Echo copies strapped to their backs; 8 Multi-access Repair Drones to heal anyone who was hurt (she made sure to have one for each living person going); 5 Shieldmen with full sets of plated armor, shields, and battle-axes that became stronger through the use of elemental energy – which was also helped by the Energy Orbs embedded in their palms, along with more hanging around their necks underneath their chest plates; Felbar and Gerold in their Deep Delvers (with Gerold's Energy Orbs connected to his attack enchantments replaced from the battle in the Dwarven village); and finally Echo, riding on the back of her Pegasus Starlight, who would have a commanding view of the fights to come to direct the Shapeshifters in battle.

Sandra and Echo had already practiced with that portion of the plan earlier, and it worked well enough; all she had to do was order the Shapeshifters to target whatever the Elf targeted, and they immediately shot their bows – which only worked if Sandra wasn't directly controlling them, otherwise they would fumble about like the novice archer the Dungeon Core was – or sent out a spell using their elemental energy. Along with the bows, quivers, and arrows they were bringing, each of them had a pair of Holy and Air Energy Orbs that they could wear to keep them from running out of that energy too quickly.

"So...what? Do we just go in?" Gerold asked when they were all assembled and ready to go in front of the Undead dungeon entrance.

** Not quite yet. I'm sending in some...sacrifices...first to hopefully trigger some of the traps and get a better look at what's inside.*

Hold on. I need someone living to go with them, though, to keep the Core from changing anything afterwards. Just stepping inside the entrance should do the trick. *

"Is that the reason you needed these…tattoos?" Felbar asked, rubbing the chest on his Deep Delver with the side of the warhammer attached to his left arm.

* *Precisely. Without those Visitor's Bonds, I can't create much other than Monster Seeds – you know them as Dungeon Loot – and the Monsters themselves; it's a hindrance to me, but it also ensures that anyone entering a dungeon with the intent to destroy it won't have to worry about new traps springing up or walls collapsing on them.* *

If Sandra had learned anything from her previous experience dealing with the Reptile-based dungeon, it was that she probably would've been better served to send in some of her smaller constructs first to draw out some of the attacks, instead of letting the bulk of her forces suffer from it. With that in mind, she pulled up the 500 Rolling Forces she had gathered over the last hour, as well as over 1,000 Reinforced Animated Shears from her AMANS. She was already in the process of replacing them back in her dungeon, so they wouldn't be missed for long.

The only drawback from having her "sacrifices" scouting the way without someone following along was that the Monster Seeds they dropped would be absorbed and used by the Dungeon Core right away; normally, Sandra – and she assumed from what Winxa had told her, the Undead Core as well – had to wait until the invaders left the room to absorb them, but if there was only someone stationed at the entrance, then it wouldn't matter. It was a price she was willing to pay, however, to save the lives of her Dungeon Monsters and the people coming with them.

Felbar volunteered to stand inside the entrance while Sandra sent in the first wave of scout "sacrifices": 100 Shears and 50 Rolling Forces. Rather than have them all go in at the same time, she figured it would be better to space them out – it would defeat the entire purpose of this plan if they all went in and were destroyed in the first room.

As soon as they passed over the threshold of the dungeon, Sandra felt her connection to them become muted, similar to what happened before in the Reptile dungeon. Commands to them immediately became difficult to get through and were delayed, and she again felt that she couldn't give them more than basic commands. Fortunately, she had been expecting that, and she had already given them specific orders before they went in – which they had no trouble following.

Sandra immediately saw through her constructs that the first room was dark; she could tell that the ambient light inside it had been turned all the way down to its lowest allowed setting by the Core, which was even darker than what she herself had done in the bathing room she had designed. Luckily, her constructs didn't rely on physical light to see by – mainly because they didn't have eyes – so everything in the room was visible, if not well-defined.

There were a dozen humanoid-looking zombies inside the relatively small 30-foot-wide ovoid-shaped room, who reacted immediately to the invasion by her constructs by shuffling quickly towards them. For their part, her Dungeon Monsters completely ignored the Undead – which was one of the specific orders they were given – and instead rolled or flew around the room, looking for traps. She knew that her constructs *might* have been able to do some serious damage to the zombies, if not kill them all, but that wasn't their purpose; their purpose was to trigger traps and unveil surprises waiting for her other forces.

They found the trap near the exit tunnel to the next, right where someone who had confidently destroyed the zombies would trigger it on their way onward. Hundreds of shadowy tendrils shot out of the floor and nearby wall, latching onto everything in range – which happened to be more than half of her constructs in the room. The shadow tendrils seemed to pulse with a deeper darkness as the Nether-based trap ate away at the captured constructs, destroying them in a matter of seconds.

Her other Shears and Forces tried to bypass the trap and move on to the next room, but as soon as they got close to the trap, more tendrils shot out and grasped onto them. Within moments, all of her constructs had been caught and destroyed, leaving her blind to what was happening inside the dungeon.

** Ok, so…new plan. There's a trap in there that we may need to neutralize first, otherwise I'll just be throwing my sacrificial constructs away. Eventually the energy in the defense will run out, but I'm not sure how long that will take; I'm sending in some of my Monsters to see if I can speed up the process. **

She sent in 6 of her Apes and 6 of her Angels, and then asked Felbar to follow them – but to stay just inside the room near the entrance. Her constructs led the charge with their warhammers and made short work of the zombies, blasting them apart with a few swings of their weapons. She knew from her own experiences and from what Winxa had told her that most Cores put their weakest Dungeon Monsters first and had stronger ones as the invaders made their way down, so she wasn't going to start getting overconfident in how easy they had been destroyed. The Undead in the dungeon were the least of her concern – it was the traps from the last dungeon that had destroyed so many of her constructs, and it was likely that the ones inside the current one would be similar.

Once they were down, she had her Celestial Authorities use their special Arrows and send them forth over the space where she knew the Nether-based trap was. As she hoped, the shadowy tendrils shot out faster than she could even see them and snatched the arrows of Holy and Spirit energy out of the air; unlike the constructs, what the trap grabbed wasn't quite the same. Within a second, the Arrows' lights started to dim, but the Mana inside the

Nether trap was strained in order to do it; with Nether and Holy being opposites, it made sense to Sandra that they would react that way.

Out of the 30 Arrows shot and caught by the trap, 2 of them were released to finish their previous journey down the exit tunnel as the Mana in the trap ran out. As soon as she saw that happen, Sandra brought in another group of 100 Shears and 50 Rolling Forces and sent them through the space where the trap was...and nothing happened. She was going to have to act fast, though, because she knew that the trap would eventually regenerate from the ambient Mana around it, though she didn't know how long that would take; to have a little forewarning, she had one of her Shears and one of her Rolling Forces stop where she felt it trigger before, acting as a way to know when it was active again.

As her constructs rolled and flew down the tunnel leading to the next room, something struck her as odd.

Winxa, why would the Monster Seeds still be inside the first room from my destroyed constructs? I'm quite sure that the Core could've absorbed them, even though Felbar was in the entrance tunnel.

She thought about that for a moment. "You're right, it should've been able to. Either it deliberately didn't do so for some unknown purpose...or it isn't paying attention."

It's not paying attention? It's being invaded, and it doesn't care? That doesn't make sense—or are you saying what I think you're saying?

"I don't know for sure, but yes – the Dungeon Core could already be upgrading its Size again."

If that were true, it was both a good thing and a bad thing; on the one hand, it meant that spur-of-the-moment reactions from the Core would be almost non-existent, so hopefully there wouldn't be any major surprises. On the other, it could finish upgrading at any time; with the Temporary Enhancements as well as its already fairly large AOI, it was possible that it could reach some other settlements. Maybe not the Elves quite yet, but the chance that it could potentially reach the Orc village was worrying. She was hoping to destroy the Core before it could get the chance to upgrade, but now it appeared as though she had waited too long. With who knew how many Undead were in the "dead zone" she couldn't reach, the potential for disaster was right on the forefront of her mind.

** We might need to move a little faster than I had planned; I'm halfway convinced that the Core is already undergoing its expansion process and it'd be better if it was stopped before that's completed. **

Although she was confident they would eventually destroy the Core, she couldn't quite tell how long the dungeon was from looking at it underground from her Area of Influence. All that she could tell was that it was at least twice the size of what the Reptile-based dungeon had been, but even that could be deceiving as it seemed to branch off into different directions multiple times. If the Core had enough time to send its Undead aboveground to the Orcs and destroy them all there, the influx of Mana would allow it to create more hordes of Undead…or potentially something more powerful that she had yet to see.

Fortunately, everyone seemed to understand the danger that would arise if that were to come about and pushed for speed. Therefore, sending caution to the wind, she ordered everyone to slowly start filing inside, while the Shears and Forces already inside were approaching the next room. The second room contained skeletons – a lot of them. Sandra counted 60 of them inside the 50-foot by 50-foot room with a relatively low 7-foot-tall ceiling; the tight quarters meant that a few of her Shears were snatched out of the air as they flew by, though her Forces were unharmed even as they were kicked around like children's play balls. Again, as per their orders, her constructs flew and rolled around until they found a trap – which just so happened to be a small trigger in the precise middle of the room.

The room went from dimly lit to complete darkness; it was somehow so dark that even her constructs had trouble "seeing" despite their lack of physical eyes. Their sense of things around them dropped to only about a foot, which caused many of them to crash into the skeletons or the walls, doing some damage to the Undead but doing even more to themselves. It took all of 5 minutes for her constructs to be destroyed, though they took a few of the enemy with them in the process.

Sandra immediately sent in her Apes that had been sent to destroy the zombies in the previous room, and she finally saw the delay in their responses as it took almost 5 seconds for them to respond. Thinking back to the Reptile dungeon, she was convinced that it actually took longer now than it did back then. *It must be because of its higher Core Size or something along those lines; that also means that any future dungeons that I may need to destroy that are even more powerful could be a major pain.*

Her Apes crashed into the room and started swinging their warhammers around, smashing through the skeletons there in the same complete darkness that was still activated. The Undead didn't stand a chance and most of them were quickly destroyed; then, because her constructs couldn't "see" that well, some accidents started happening where they inadvertently started to hit each other with the powerful weapons. One of her Apes was hit so hard with an impact by a Titanium warhammer and a Fireburst enchantment that its Steel chest caved in and the glowing "power source" inside of it was extinguished. A few others were damaged as well – with one now even missing a leg – before they finally stopped fighting at her delayed command.

She brought in the 6 Celestial Authorities next to help mop up the remaining skeletons, who were ineffectually beating on her Apes that were frozen in place by Sandra, which she belatedly realized she should've done in the first place. She was so used to her Apes being such powerhouses of destruction that she didn't even think about it, and that was something that was going to have to stop if she hoped to succeed; unthinking actions like that could result in the deaths of more than her constructs and Dungeon Monsters if she wasn't careful.

Her Angel-type Monsters walked into the room and the darkness was pushed back – but not completely banished. Her Authorities dimmed a little themselves, but it wasn't progressing more than a slight amount; they immediately ran forward and mopped up the rest of the skeletons, making the room "safe" once again. Sandra wasn't sure how long the trap would last, however, because from her experience something like what was being done to make the room darker didn't expend as much Mana as the shadowy tendrils from the previous room.

Therefore, she had her Angels park themselves around the room, which helped to brighten up the place just enough to see everything without tripping over the Monster Seeds that were still on the floor.

I guess that proves it; the Core definitely had the opportunity to absorb all of these – because Felbar was in the previous room. It has to be upgrading right now.

Sandra brought in another group of sacrificial scouts from outside, determined to keep going quickly but still trying to be as safe as possible. Meanwhile, the last of her Dungeon Monsters were coming in behind the Dwarves and Echo astride her Pegasus – though she had to duck to fit inside the tunnel. They couldn't all fit inside the first room, so Sandra kept them going until they were inside the second room, which was just large enough to hold them.

Her Repair Drones she brought along immediately started to patch up the Apes that had accidentally hurt themselves, while the Shears and the Forces she had recently brought in were already heading for the next room.

Now that everyone was inside, she was hoping that would speed things up. Sending in small forces at a time would certainly be safer, but it was also very time-consuming. Eventually she'd have to make do with what she had when she ran out of her "sacrificial" constructs, but hopefully by that time they'd have a good rhythm going.

Speaking of them, the third group of Shears and Rolling forces were entering a room that had a half-dozen larger beast zombies—

Something was happening towards the entrance of the dungeon. Sandra looked through the viewpoint of her Shears and Rolling Forces waiting outside to the hole leading into the ground, only to see the roof collapsing. *What? How?* She didn't have time to investigate further, because she could feel her connection to everything inside the dungeon start to fade as the tunnel leading down started to fill up with dirt, stone, and a nearby falling tree that was caused by the ground crumbling underneath it.

With a split-second thought, she – hopefully – sent some orders to her Dungeon Monsters before she lost all connection to them, as well as a quick message to the others.

** The entrance is collapsing and I'm losing connection to my Monsters – they're under your command now, Felbar! I'll try to— **

She wasn't able to finish her message, as she felt any connection she had to anything inside the Undead dungeon cut off completely.

Winxa? What happened? I lost all connection to anyone or anything inside the dungeon. How was the dungeon able to collapse the ground, sealing off the entrance? I thought that was impossible!

The Dungeon Fairy looked shocked. "It *shouldn't* be possible to close up your initial entrance to the world above; any action that would do that is unable to be taken. Just like you couldn't block up your entrance here, even when there weren't any invaders inside, the Undead Core shouldn't be able to either." Winxa paused for a moment, before thinking out loud. "Unless...that entrance...wasn't the initial entrance. If it were a secondary entrance, sort of like your workshop that was connected to the now-destroyed Bearling lair, then physically rigging something up to collapse – and that didn't require the use of your Dungeon Core abilities – would perhaps work. Which means—"

— that the initial entrance is probably the larger exit I was guarding earlier but had been basically ignoring up until now. I figured it was the same as the Reptile dungeon and it was blocked off, so I didn't check it – I'm so stupid!

Sandra was mad at herself; she had thought she had everything covered, but the Undead Core had managed to pull one over on her again. Something still didn't add up, however...

Ok, so if the real entrance is through the other large "exit" tunnel, then why can't I reach my Dungeon Monsters or the others with them?

"Well, the reason being inside the dungeon diminishes your connection with them already is because of the Core itself; in this instance, it's acting as a sort of stopper that you can't get past right now." Winxa started to demonstrate an example using her hands, forming what looked like a bowl or something similar. "Think of it like a bucket of thick jelly with a plug at the bottom; you drop your Monsters inside the jelly and your connection to them is a little muted and diminished, but you can still reach them – like what you've already experienced."

The Fairy then used one of her hands to poke the side of the "bucket." "You can't go in from the sides to touch your Monsters because the bucket is in the way, obviously; now, if you were to put a lid on the bucket—" she continued, placing her hand on top of the invisible prop— "then the only way to get to them would be from the only other option – the stopper. So, unless you can dig all of that up within the next few hours, the only way you'll be able contact them again is if the 'stopper', or Core, is removed."

Great, just great. Sandra looked at the collapsed entrance again, trying to calculate if she could create and send a large group of her new Automated Sharp-bladed Diggers there to start excavating the area fast enough to make a difference. After a couple of seconds of also peering at it from underneath via her Area of Influence, she determined that it was possible – though it could take 5 hours or more. For one, her Diggers didn't move very fast, so half that time would probably be spent traveling there; for the other, there was only so quickly they could dig without getting into each other's way, so it would end up taking a bit of time to complete.

She went ahead and started to create them despite not knowing if everyone was still alive inside. While 15 of them were being created through the use of some of her treasury resources, she sent her remaining Shears and Rolling Forces over to the other entrance to see if there were any way through there.

Undead were streaming out in waves and spreading out to apparently cover as much area as possible – but they were also quite aware of where her constructs were and the direction they were coming from. A swarm of Specters enveloped her 700 Shears and basically ate them up, though there were quite a few casualties on their part; that again didn't deter them, as they immediately fell upon her Rolling Forces before they could escape.

Then, seemingly out of nowhere, more Specters flew out of the "dead zone" that she couldn't reach and destroyed all 500 of her Shears that were keeping watch for anything moving within. Within a minute, she had basically lost a view from most of the forest, though she still did have an aerial view from her flock of Phoenixes roaming around. They were wholly ineffective at seeing through the trees, and she didn't want to risk lighting the entire forest on fire by having them go down in a full blaze; that might solve some immediate problems, but as there was no way to stop it, the fire might spread for hundreds of miles.

That Core has been one step ahead of me this entire time; there's no way it could coordinate all that before it started its upgrade, which means that whole thing with not absorbing the Monster Seeds was just a ruse. It's been aware of everything this entire time, just waiting to strike.

She canceled her plans to send the diggers, instead keeping them safe back in her dungeon; she could always send them later, but she doubted they would live long enough to make it to the collapsed entrance in the first place, let alone being allowed to dig for hours in their excavation.

As she tried to develop some alternative plans, she hoped that everyone trapped down there was alright – because it was all up to them now...

Chapter 32

Echo watched as the others stumbled below her as the ground shook and the sound of rocks and dirt crashing together filled the tunnel behind them.

** The entrance is collapsing and I'm losing connection to my Monsters – they're under your command now, Felbar! I'll try to— **

The rest of whatever Sandra was trying to tell them was lost as Echo felt some unknown connection sever itself within her mind. The destruction behind them finally settled, and Echo turned her Pegasus Starlight around to see what happened – only to find the way behind was blocked.

"Is everyone alright?" she yelled out, as dust seemed to fill the tunnel and she coughed as she made her way to the second room again.

No one answered her and she got a little worried, until she realized that no one could understand her; the automatic translation that Sandra normally did for them was no longer there. She looked around and saw Felbar and the other Gnomes – including Gerold in his all-metal construct – and sighed in relief...before a little part of her mind started to panic.

We're trapped! There's no way out!

Elves weren't very comfortable underground, and it had taken a while to get used to being inside Sandra's dungeon – and she still wasn't completely at ease. The only thing that had made it more bearable was the knowledge that she could leave at any time, and the exit was only a relatively short distance away; now, trapped underground in a dangerous undead-filled dungeon, Echo was starting to lose her nerve.

I should've never insisted in coming!

Her panic was only increased when she saw the way all of Sandra's monsters were frozen in place – though they were staring at Felbar for some reason. The only one that wasn't doing that was Starlight, which Sandra had specifically told her would follow her commands. Looking around some more, she also realized that they were missing some of the monsters that had come with them; looking back down the tunnel, she realized that at least a dozen of the metal monkeys, a handful of Pegasi, and nearly 20 of the strange beings made of light were still behind her in the tunnel – and were now buried under tons of dirt and stone.

"What are we going to do?! We're all going to die!" she cried out, the panic now ramping up as she began to realize their situation. She hadn't realized she had been relying on Sandra to coordinate everything, and without the Dungeon Core there she was feeling lost.

Luckily, no one could understand her, and they ignored her hysterical panicking; *it's all good for those Dwarves*, she thought, *because they're used to living underground and probably don't care, but I swear the low ceiling in this room is getting lower.*

Felbar barked out something – which was completely foreign to her – and every monster in the room…except Starlight and the creepy Shapeshifter things for some reason…turned to the right. Another barked command and they all jumped, followed by another that made them all attack some invisible enemy ahead of them with their weapons – or hooves.

Well that's good at least; if Felbar can control them, then maybe we have a chance. Though, without the Shifters following his commands—wait a minute! Sandra put ***me*** *in charge of them!*

The knowledge of her responsibility towards the others in commanding the Shapeshifters dampened her panic further, though it was still simmering under the surface of her thoughts. With her own barked command, "Begin!", 10 of the multi-colored monsters morphed into a naked version of herself. She was beyond caring at that point, but the 10 that had shifted went to the backs of the nearest Pegasi and opened up the packs that were strapped there and pulled out some basic beige-colored cotton clothing. When they put on the outfit – more for her and the others' sake of modesty than for any real protection – they unstrapped the bows and quivers as well, before climbing on top of the Pegasi.

A different command came from Felbar and it was obviously directed towards just the white flying horses, because they immediately turned towards Echo. She smiled in the Gnome's direction, assuming that he had just given her control of them – or at least told them to listen to her commands. While Echo had originally been in charge of the Shapeshifters, apparently Sandra hadn't made the Pegasi as part of that deal.

There were still 30 Shapeshifters and 6 Pegasi not being used – they were going to have to adapt without the extra mounts and supplies – because they were all going to be on a rotating "shifting" schedule. Since they could be in the form they were in for an hour, followed by an hour off, the plan was to start with 10 for 30 minutes, add another 10 for 30 minutes, and then when the original 10 shifted back, a different 10 would shift into Echo's form. That way, except for the first 30 minutes, there would always be 20 shifted Echos riding Pegasi and following the Elf's instructions. Of course, with 4 Pegasi crushed behind them, some of the Echos would have to be land-bound and only use their energy to cast spells – but it was better than nothing.

Sensing that they were as ready as they were going to be, Felbar somehow directed his commands to just a select few Apes and the beings made of light that Sandra called Celestial Authorities – but Echo had a feeling were actually Angels, which she had heard of but never seen before – to make their way through the tunnel ahead of them. After a few moments, everyone else followed behind them, starting with the rest of the Angels and Apes, then the Dwarves and, finally, Felbar. As he passed by her, his construct held its weapon up to its head in some sort of awkward salute...and she strangely felt a little better.

Echo took a deep breath to settle her nerves, before she too called out to the 10 Echos creepily facing her and waiting for orders. "Follow me and attack what I attack." The other unshifted monsters stayed near the back of the pack, along with the 8 white cylindrical constructs that were acting as their healers. *At least we didn't lose any of those.*

When she entered the third room, the battle against some large zombie bears was just concluding, with the last one being sliced apart by three separate Authorities at the same time with their longswords made of pure light. She felt a slight kinship with them because of their obvious Holy-element affiliation, and she was happy they were on their team against the vile undead that were infesting the dungeon.

There was a trap inside the room as well, though fortunately none of their constructs were...*stuck*...in it. Near the end of the room just off from the exit, there was a rectangle of a black so deep it seemed to suck in every bit of light around it – including the light being shed by the Angels in the room. An exact copy of the rectangle was on the ceiling right above the other one, and there were a dozen of Sandra's strange metal ball constructs falling from it. As soon as they would hit the black rectangle on the ground, it would reappear a split-second later from above, before falling into the one below again.

She barely recognized the balls, though, because they were falling *fast*. Faster than Echo could run, and she thought that was pretty fast; those metal constructs, though, were moving so quickly that they were essentially a blur. The others stood around in fascination for a moment, before Felbar said something and everyone started to move towards the exit. As they were making their way around the strange trap, the rectangles suddenly disappeared, and the balls hit the ground with such speed that they hit the ground and exploded, sending shrapnel everywhere.

One even hit her across the room in her shoulder and she hissed in pain and surprise; placing her hand on the wound, she saw that it was relatively shallow and not too serious, so she looked around at everyone else to see how they fared. Luckily, the only one to get seriously hurt by the shrapnel was one of the extra Pegasi, which practically had its right wing sheared off by a large metal fragment moving at high speed.

The healing "Drones" moved around to those wounded and automatically healed them with their strange, thin, padded arms and they were ready to move on. *Note to self: stay away from traps still in operation, even if they seem relatively harmless.*

The fourth room held a trio of large Ogre Skeletons, which were again dispatched by the monsters they had with them, though an Ape had its lower half smashed flat by the downswing smash of a massive bone club. The healing construct was able to repair it, but now they faced a problem. The previous rooms had been scouted out by Sandra's smaller constructs, but this room hadn't had that done yet; they had managed to kill the Ogres without triggering anything by staying near the entrance, but now it was difficult to determine how to go about either bypassing a trap that they didn't know the location of, or sacrificing one of their more powerful monster allies to definitively find it.

No one moved as Felbar looked at the Dwarves and even Echo as if he was asking for her opinion. She shrugged and briefly considered offering to shoot some arrows to see if she could trigger it, but she didn't want to waste what they had – especially since the other Echos would follow suit.

Gerold stepped forward unexpectedly, saying something to the other Dwarves and a single word to Felbar. Echo had no idea where he was going, but he seemed to be trying to find something as he looked at the floor, holding his arm out like some sort of dowsing rod. Finally, he stopped about two-thirds of the way through the room and knelt down awkwardly in his construct. A deep black essence flowed from where his hand would be underneath the metal arm of his "Deep Delver", pooling along the ground until it seemed to concentrate and outline a large rectangular shape.

Echo knew he had access to Nether energy, which at first made her a little wary of him because of that fact alone, but she eventually ignored it. Now, though, seeing him do something she'd never heard of before surprised her – mainly because it almost appeared as if he was casting some sort of spell like she and others of her kind were able to. *That's very strange...but also very useful, if that is indeed where the trap trigger is.*

The Dwarf stood up and waved everyone forward in a hurried gesture. Already she could see the smoky essence starting to dissipate, so it was obvious that it wouldn't last long; now that they knew where it was, though, everyone avoided it on their way through to the next room. She gave him a thumbs up when she passed him, letting him know that she was appreciative of his help, despite it coming from a source of Nether.

His ability to locate the trap triggers wouldn't have mattered in the fifth room unless he went first, because it was set off shortly after 5 each of the Apes and Angels entered the room. From what she could see from behind the crowd down the tunnel, dozens of large black orbs appeared from across the room and shot towards the entrance of the room where the trigger apparently was. They slammed into the unfortunate monsters who set the trap off at high speed, extinguishing the light coming from the Angels after 4 or 5 hit them one after another; the Apes were hit so hard that they were launched backwards against the near wall and were basically flattened, while one was sent down the tunnel again and collided with some other Apes, causing major damage to a half-dozen of them.

After everyone pulled back a little and they were able to fix the damaged Apes – including the one that was hit into the tunnel – Gerold walked forward cautiously and inspected the ground ahead of him. After a quick look, he boldly walked towards where the trap was likely triggered...and nothing happened.

Good to know it has been deactivated, but he better not get too cocky.

With the trap now used up for the moment, they were able to enter the room, which was large enough to hold them all easily and then some; there didn't appear to be any undead in the room at all, which was strange, but it also gave the next round of Shapeshifters to shift into more Echos, though 4 of them were forced to stay naked and weaponless. Just as the 6 that actually did have clothes started to put them on as the Dwarves nervously hefted their axes, talking softly amongst themselves – probably at the lack of undead monsters in the room – when Gerold suddenly bent his Deep Delver's head back enough to look up.

Echo didn't have time to think, she just reacted instinctively as she pulled up her bow and nocked an arrow all in one motion and fired above her head without aiming. Her arrow released and she barely held on the bow as it snapped back straight, but her focus was all on where she had aimed. Barely visible in the dim light, dozens or maybe hundreds of Specters were starting to descend from the ceiling; it was hard to tell how many of them were there because they all seemed to blend into each other.

Her explosive arrow went straight through them because there wasn't anything substantial to them, but the undead had barely started moving when it smashed against the hard stone ceiling. A large explosive fireball erupted from where it hit, enveloping the nearby Specters and burning them completely away. Less than a second later, another 10 arrows shot upwards from the Echo copies who did exactly what she did, though they fortunately didn't aim exactly where she shot; instead they too shot straight upwards which meant that there was a painfully loud explosion that blanketed most of the ceiling in temporary flames.

Small shrapnel from the arrows fell back down at high speed, though fortunately no one was hurt – though she could hear some *pings* as some hit a few Apes and bounced off. When her vision cleared from the sudden brightness of the explosions, she saw that very few of the Specters were actually still alive, and they continued to descend. She didn't bother to fire another arrow because it wouldn't do much good, but before she could start to gather the Holy energy to launch a Lightstrike spell, Felbar and Gerold had already raised their left arms and blasted some quick flames in their direction, burning them out of the air.

When the rest of the Specters were dead, they all stood around in the deafening silence as they all tried to wrap their heads around the pure destructive power of the arrows Echo and her doubles had shot. It was one thing experimenting with them outside in the wastelands, but it was something else entirely to use them in a confined space – and so many at the same time.

She reached up to her ears as she felt something warm trickling down it; she briefly wondered if she was wrong about no one getting hurt from the shrapnel...when she realized it was coming from both of her ears. *Those explosions certainly were loud, I guess.*

The healing Drone stopped by her and the Dwarves to fix their blown-out eardrums, though it seemed as though the Deep Delver had protected Gerold and Felbar enough that they didn't require help. When she could hear again, she looked around and smiled at all of the others, who hadn't been expecting the destructive power of all of them shooting together. *I don't think I was either.*

She shrugged as if to say, "What are you going to do," before settling herself with a small smile. The panic that had set in earlier was all but gone as she realized she was doing what she had always wanted to do: be a part of an "elite" team of individuals that had the express duty to cull Monsters and destroy dungeons. It also helped that it was an undead dungeon that they were bent on destroying, as that would make success that much sweeter. In fact, if it weren't for the fact that they were trapped underground with no chance of escaping, she would say that she was having a good time.

Without further ado, the others turned toward the exit and Felbar ordered the monsters he controlled forward. Echo and her cadre of copies followed after, and for the first time since she stepped foot into this dungeon, she was actually looking forward to testing herself against whatever was upcoming.

* * *

Echo wasn't having a good time anymore, nor was she looking forward to destroying any more undead. She couldn't be quite sure because she had lost track of how many times her Shapeshifters had switched forms, but she was pretty sure they had been making their way through the dungeon for at least 6 or 7 hours; it could be longer, but she was starting to get really hungry even after having a huge breakfast earlier – and no one had thought to bring food along in what was supposed to only take a couple of hours. Then again, her extreme hunger could be because she had to be healed a few more times and had used her entire reserve of Holy elemental energy reserve at least once, though fortunately it had been regenerated by the Energy Orb around her neck.

The others looked ragged as well from the constant stress of killing undead and worrying that the next room would have a trap that could kill them all. Luckily, through some sort of miracle, no one had died; well, that wasn't quite true – no *living* person had died. Their force of monsters was now whittled down to a fraction of what it had been at the start. From a small army of powerful dungeon-created constructs and monsters, they barely numbered more than herself, Felbar, and the Dwarves.

She had the most left on her team, in fact; 10 Shapeshifters – whittled down from 40 – was all she had left, which meant that only 3 or 4 of them were in Echo form every 45 minutes, with a 15-minute overlap where there was more. The smaller number of them was probably good, because they only had 5 Pegasi left – including Starlight...actually Starlight *"2"* because the original Pegasus she had been riding had been killed by a trap a few rooms before. *She was a good flying horse...*

She didn't have the opportunity to mourn, however, because their supply of Apes and Angels was also dangerously low. They only had 8 of the Apes wielding their special warhammers and 4 of the Celestial Authorities left, as they had paid the price for traps that were unable to be identified in time, or because of attrition due to fighting undead. In fact, the only one of Sandra's monsters that had survived intact were the healing Drones, mainly because they always stayed at the back of the group and no one wanted to risk them not being there when they needed them.

The reason they were still inside the dungeon when they doubtless should've been done by that point was a point of contention between them all and had led to some heated arguments; they were made all the more stressful because precise communication was still an issue because of the language barrier between them all, so it had devolved into a lot of finger pointing and gesturing to get their points across.

The issue was that the dungeon didn't seem to have a straightforward path to where the Dungeon Heart/Core was located. The first indication of this had been in the seventh room, where similar-looking tunnels led out from it to the left, right, and straight ahead. After a few minutes in which they had all pointed off to different tunnels, they had finally settled on straight ahead, which made the most sense to Echo and obviously Felbar at the time; she figured that the others were just distractions and if they wanted to get to the end as quickly as possible, then straight would get them there.

She was horribly wrong.

They took the straight route, which slowly began to angle off to the right as they went, though it wasn't completely noticeable at once. Still, Echo was marginally sure they all thought that was the way it was supposed to be and didn't turn back. After fighting through more zombies, skeletons, a large contingent of ghouls that emerged from a cleverly hidden pocket beneath the floor in a room, more Specters that filled a pit on either side of a narrow walkway, and scores of the black-armored undead that were lined up in ranks, they finally emerged into a large room after 3 or 4 hours – to find it was the exact same one they had needed to choose their pathway from earlier. The straight path had led around in a circle, ending up in the right-hand tunnel...with nothing but the loss of some of their monsters to show for it – not to mention their mounting exhaustion.

Echo remembered Sandra saying that she could "see" the outside of the dungeon from underground, so the Dungeon Core probably could've told them that going down the left tunnel was the correct way to go without wasting time – but how were they supposed to know? After a few minutes of silence followed by accusatory finger-pointing and arguing in different languages that the others couldn't understand, they eventually went down the left tunnel, hoping that their destination was close at hand.

More skeletons, zombies, and other undead met them along the way – including some of the hated Liches. She knew that rationally they weren't *actually* undead Elves that had chosen to embrace their Nether element and practice Necromancy, but from the glimpses she had of their hands and the barest hints of their faces she couldn't picture them as anything else. She had sent countless Lightstrikes in their direction (which were then copied by her Shapeshifter forces), interspersed by an arrow or two, which kept them so off-balance that they were unable to respond and were destroyed before they did any damage. Of course, she ended up almost completely draining herself of Holy energy at the time, but it was worth it even though it regenerated slowly over the next hour or two.

As for traps, which were still the deadliest foes they faced in the dungeon, there were some variations of what they had seen before, but many of them were brand new. There was a trap that had walls of Nether set up to act like a maze, where if you touched the walls it would essentially burn with an intense cold; that one was actually a little frightening, because undead could emerge from the walls and attack out of nowhere, which was difficult to defend against. Another trap had super-thin diamond-shaped slices of pure darkness randomly descending from the ceiling like raindrops, and whatever they touched would get sliced up; after they had attempted to traverse the room while avoiding the "raindrops" and Starlight had her head severed from her body, they found that the dark slices couldn't penetrate through metal – only flesh – so the Apes acted like shields for her and her Shapeshifters as they crossed through the room.

The deadliest trap so far had been one that was activated as soon as one of the Apes stepped into the room, but it didn't manifest for nearly 15 seconds, when dozens of their monsters were already inside the room, fighting some puny skeletons. "Whoa, stop – call them back, Felbar!" Gerold had said (or she assumed that's what he said, since she didn't have a translator handy), just as he was about to enter the room ahead of the other Dwarves. It was too late for most of them, however, as little black motes were scattered all around the room, and where they touched the Angels and Apes already inside the room it somehow *ate* away at them. Luckily, Felbar was able to save some of them, which immediately got fixed up by the healing Drones, but the damage was already done.

The one thing that had prevented all of them from dying, strangely enough, was Gerold's strange Nether-sensing ability, which highlighted many of the trap triggers – but certainly not all. Over half of the traps that could've taken an even larger toll on them – and possibly kill some of the *living* elements of their group – were never even activated, as they were bypassed after they were found. The use of that ability, though, took a higher toll on him than normal; he was looking the worst out of all of them; a few times his Deep Delver had even stumbled and fallen, and it took a few moments for his exhausted body to respond and pick himself up.

The dungeon seemed never-ending, and Echo was starting to despair that they wouldn't ever escape from there with their lives, let alone actually destroy the vile undead Core. Just as she was starting to think that, they entered a room that was at least 5 times bigger than anything they had seen so far; her first glimpse around the room had her questioning her sanity.

If this nightmare isn't the final room, I don't even want to know what's next.

Chapter 33

There were only three visible undead in the room, but they were monstrous. Two of them were massive piles of various corpses all smashed together in a horrific abomination that brought the bile in her relatively empty belly up to her throat, threatening to make her gag and throw up whatever was actually still in there. She had heard mention of one of them outside of Sandra's dungeon when they were basically under siege but hadn't seen it in person – and wished that she hadn't even now. *If nothing else was proof enough of why we destroy undead dungeons immediately when we find them, those things should convince even the most hesitant.*

The one that was outside of Sandra's dungeon had been destroyed along with everything else when she used that disturbingly destructive construct, so she wasn't even sure how powerful it was. She was told that it had some sort of "healing" aura – if fixing undead that were damaged could be called healing – that had manifested itself before it was destroyed, but that was all she knew about whatever they were. *It's a good thing there isn't a horde of smaller undead in here, otherwise this could be even more difficult.*

Those were the least of her concerns, however, because it was the third undead in the room that worried her the most. The ceiling of the room was almost impossible to see over her head because of the same dim interior that the rest of the dungeon had, but she suspected it had to be over 200 feet tall; of course, she was basing that on the horrifically tall giant zombie she was looking at, which towered in between the two abominations. It appeared to be an actual *Giant* that had been turned into an undead, with open wounds all over its body, rotting flesh falling off of it in chunks that didn't seem to make a difference in its size, and open eye sockets that looked like the eyes had been forcibly removed from.

It was wearing a loincloth that was hard to tell what color it started as – because it was drenched in dried blood – and nothing else, though it held a wooden club in its hand that looked suspiciously like a tree that had been ripped out of the ground.

None of the undead so much as twitched as they entered the room, though once everyone was inside there was finally some movement – though not from the monstrosities. Behind the towering giant was a very large tunnel that she presumed was that big to let that particular monster through; emerging from that tunnel was a horde of undead that made the rest of the dungeon seem tame. There were more skeletons, zombies, ghouls, armored undead, Specters, Liches, and even a few smaller ones that she had never seen before anywhere.

As soon as they passed within range of the two abominations, the "healing" aura that she had heard about surrounded them, indicating that they were now even harder to destroy. Hundreds of undead streamed into the room and took places in front of the three monstrous undead, lined up and ready to attack. When the flow finally stopped, she looked over at Felbar and Gerold, seeing the same hopelessness in their gazes that she was sure was in her own.

In preparation, Echo wearily looked over at their supplies and saw that she and each of her copies had exactly 5 more exploding arrows to shoot – and that was even combining everything they had left from the other Shapeshifters. They all had a small amount of Holy energy with which to cast spells, but it wouldn't be much; she briefly tried to get the unshifted ones to change into her form, but she belatedly realized they were all still on a cooldown – with the next batch nearly 30 minutes away from shifting.

Nothing in the room moved as both groups just looked at each other, waiting for some sort of signal to start the attack. With a big sigh, Echo raised her bow and figured she might as well get it started, watching as the 4 other shifted Echos did the same. *I think the explosions* ***should be*** *powerful enough to negate any healing they might receive, so I might as well try to destroy as many as possible right away.*

Just before she was about to release, she saw Felbar waving his arms back and forth in a gesture she had learned to translate as "stop". Echo lowered her bow, confused, and shot him a questioning look. He didn't say anything, but he looked at the others and then at the monsters they had left; she had noticed that whatever commands he would give them he could practically whisper and they would hear it, and he was obviously doing so now as she barely saw his lips moving in the construct he was controlling. No sound reached her even though she was only about 10 feet away, though it was obvious that Sandra's monsters could as they quickly started to move.

Their movement must've alerted the undead that something was up, or the Core had somehow heard him, because they immediately ran, shambled, or flew forward. Echo froze at the scene in front of her, with hundreds of undead rushing towards her with killing intent. The floor rumbled under the first step of the massive zombie Giant, which amazingly had the effect of snapping her out of her fear-driven paralysis.

Out of the corner of her eye, she watched the three Angels rushing forward as fast as they could; without a thought, she used her Air elemental energy to cast a spell that reduced the air friction in front of them and pushed them forward like she could do to herself. She started to get an inkling of what was planned, so even though it rapidly drained that particular element, she was essentially full of it since she hadn't used it all during their experience so far. Right after she did that, she shouted, "Spread!", which was an order she had designed that would spread out the attacks of her Echo copies – or in this case, spread their Air spells in between the three Celestial Authorities.

They shot forward and closed the distance between them and the approaching undead horde within seconds, spreading out so that there was one in the middle, one on the right, and one on the left – exactly where the massive giants were behind the ranks of the smaller undead. Instead of attacking, though, they used the extra boost to their speed to leap high into the air and over the heads of the undead horde – which didn't stop and kept rushing forward.

Meanwhile, 8 white cylindrical objects flew through the air towards the approaching horde, as the Apes dropped their warhammers, grabbed one of the healing Drones, and then threw them with their enormous strength over the heads of the leading wave of undead as well. "Echo!" Felbar shouted, and she instantly knew what he wanted.

Letting go of the Air-based speed spell on the Angels while they were in mid-leap, she nocked one of her arrows and released with just a modicum of aiming, before doing so again just under a second later. Her copies followed suit, launching their own barrage, and 10 arrows flew through the air towards the 8 thrown Repair Drones.

The Angels seemed to explode in a bright light a fraction of a second before the arrows hit the Drones. She had been briefed on the abilities of the Authorities by Sandra just as much as the others were, though Echo thought Felbar had apparently forgotten about any of them, as the Angels were primarily used in melee instead of tossing out their Arrows. That meant that they were still almost completely full of Holy elemental energy; the resulting Divine Light Explosions were so bright that the Elf had to look away, but she could sense that they were large enough to encompass the majority of the abominations behind the horde and the lower half of the zombie Giant.

The explosions from the Drones being hit from her and her copies' exploding arrows were smaller, though no less destructive. Massive swathes of the undead were destroyed in seconds leaving behind their Loot sometimes in piles as the monsters were packed so closely together. Hundreds were killed as a result of the attack...but there were still dozens of undead outside of the blast radius heading their way.

Looking behind them when the light disappeared from the detonations, she saw that the two abominations were starting to dissolve into the ground after being destroyed by the intensely bright destructive light of the Angels exploding, though the Giant was still alive – and falling forward, its bottom half essentially obliterated. On a person or even another *living* beast, that kind of damage probably would've been enough to kill or incapacitate them; since it was a *zombie* the rules were a little different. It didn't feel pain and wouldn't bleed to death – losing its legs was more of an inconvenience than anything.

It slammed down, luckily squishing the middle portion of the undead still racing towards her group. The others all fell down as a result of the massive impact, and Starlight 2 danced around for a second before flapping her wings to bring her off the ground. Echo made ready to launch her remaining arrows towards the 50 or so random undead heading their way (with no Liches she could see, fortunately), but was stopped again as Felbar picked himself up and saw the situation.

"Echo, *berchke*!"

Obviously, she had no idea what *"berchke"* meant, but as he pointed off to the tunnel with his weapon she figured it out fairly quickly.

"No, I'm not going to leave you—"

"*Berchke*!" he repeated, so loudly that it was almost as painful as listening to an arrow exploding in a confined space.

Rather than argue anymore, and since Sandra had obviously put him in charge for a reason, she directed Starlight 2 to head towards the tunnel; before she got a few more feet upwards, though, she noticed that the other Echos were trying to follow her. "Follow Felbar's orders now!" she shouted at them, before urging her Pegasus onward with speed. She looked back to see them returning back down to just over the Dwarves' heads, and they shot their arrows into the undead that were just on the edge of being too close to do so safely.

Whipping her head around at something out of the corner of her eye, she barely ordered her flying mount to dive as a wooden club wider than the wingspan of her Pegasus whipped over their heads. The disturbance in the air was so great that she felt them both spiraling out of control, so she used the little Air elemental energy she had left to stabilize them. Finally looking around after the recovery, she saw that the zombie Giant had lifted itself up and was balancing itself on its left arm as it started swinging its tree club with its right.

Luckily, the Giant moved relatively slowly and it was easy to see where the club was going to swing, so she was able to avoid one, and then another before she was able to fly past its range; she figured that it would have to find some way to turn itself around before it could hit her again, and that she was in the clear.

Of course, looking back, she saw at least a dozen Specters that had survived the explosion earlier closing in on her. As she directed Starlight 2 to keep flying, she turned and launched Lightstrike spells in their direction, which rapidly expended her Holy elemental energy. They didn't even try to avoid her casts, so she ended up destroying 8 of them – but she counted 5 of them still there...and they were closing in fast.

Urging her flying mount to move faster, she contemplated her options. She was out of essentially all of her energy, though it was regenerating – but it wouldn't be in time to save her. Her arrows, if she shot them, would just pass right through the insubstantial undead, so that was also out. The only thing she had left was her Pegasus and its Nether-negating Protection Aura special ability, which she had used sparingly and even when she did, it wasn't as effective as she would've liked. The original Starlight had the aura on while negotiating its way through the trapped area that had ultimately killed her, though she was sure it had *some* effect on the trap. With no other choices she had Starlight 2 activate it and prayed that would be enough.

The first Specter hit the aura and made it approximately two feet before it dissipated, dropping a small black stone as Loot. The second and third hit the same spot moments later, carving out a large portion of the 15-foot aura radius before disappearing. The fourth was there less than a second later and it managed to progress through the quickly fading Aura until it reached to within inches of Starlight 2's tail.

The fifth one was right behind the fourth, however, and as the previous Specter was destroyed, it pressed through the Aura to hit the Pegasus in the rear end. Starlight 2 neighed loudly – the first time she had ever heard it make a noise and it shuddered underneath her; in a matter of seconds they were falling out of the air, rushing towards the ground at dangerous speeds. Just as they entered the dark tunnel, a last-second wing-flap prevented them from both being smashed flat, though she could feel that Starlight 2 was almost out of the energy that was being sucked out of her. The Aura disappeared as they crashed, and Echo tumbled over her mount's head; she heard and felt a pop in her left wrist as she fell, and by the time she stopped rolling an enormous pain bloomed from the spot.

Holding her scream in while she took stock of the situation, she could see the Pegasus starting to fade away, dissolving into the ground. Fortunately, the Specter seemed to be consumed at the same time, because there was no sign of it. Echo picked herself up and found her bow – which had rolled away from the crash site roughly 20 feet – and it appeared to be undamaged. The same couldn't be said for her arrows, as two of them had been bent out of shape with the crash, but she was just glad that one was still fine – and that they hadn't exploded with such an impact.

Holding the one arrow and bow in her left hand, she stumbled as the ground shook underneath her feet, the sound of a cracking wood resounding from behind her. She held in her screams from the pain in her left wrist as she landed on it, but she again picked herself up and ran down the relatively short tunnel, hoping that the zombie Giant hadn't just flattened the rest of her group just a moment ago.

She quickly found herself in a similar-looking room with nearly the same dimensions as the one before, though there were luckily no massive undead there to greet her. Instead, Echo saw a glowing black crystal-like gem floating in the middle of the room at least a hundred feet above her which reminded her a little of what Sandra appeared like, though the feeling of Nether energy wafting off of the Dungeon Core she was looking at made it much more sinister. In comparison, Sandra's Core was bright and almost cheerful, which matched the personality of the voice she had heard inside her head on many occasions.

How am I supposed to destroy it from here? Normally, hitting something from that distance wouldn't be a problem, even with compensating for the powerful draw of the bow and the heavier exploding arrow. With her obviously broken wrist, though, she didn't think she'd be able to hold the bow up, let alone steady it enough to aim.

Echo looked below the Core and saw that she better decide what to do quickly, because there were more skeletons and zombies forming on the ground. There were already a half-dozen undead and more were appearing every few seconds, and they started to shuffle in her direction. Looking around the rest of the room for some sort of other solution, she saw that it was empty of anything...except another massive tunnel leading to who knew where.

I might as well try something, otherwise I'm dead...though I'll probably not survive this either way. Trading my life for the destruction of this Core would be a worthy endeavor any Elf would appreciate. She gathered the remnants of her Holy energy that had regenerated and formed another Lightstrike spell, adding what Air she had to help speed it on its way. When it was as large as she could get it, she released it towards the floating Core.

It flew straight and true, but the farther it got from her, the more it shrunk; she knew that was going to happen, which was why she tried to make it as big as possible to begin with. Time seemed to slow down as she watched the now-small streak of light hit the undead Nether-Core, and she held her breath as it seemed to splash against the glowing black crystal. Echo heard a sharp *crack* and she rejoiced for all of a second...before she saw that it was still intact, other than a long crack running up the side of it.

With no other choice, she decided to see if she could hit the Core with her bow by switching hands; however, her left hand couldn't even pinch the arrow to set it on the invisible string, let along pull it back. With great pain, she shifted it again and held the bow loosely in her left hand, and then held it up; she let out the scream she had been holding as she pulled back the arrow she had nocked and aimed...then she released.

Her left wrist snapped, and she lost control of the bow almost immediately, which was probably why she could tell right away that her arrow was going to go wide – though just barely. She sighed and waited for it to miss—

A flash of metal zoomed into her field of vision, aiming straight for the Core in the center of the room – or at least she thought it was aiming for it. Instead, what she quickly realized was a pair of Sandra's flying Shears hit her arrow mid-flight, causing it to change the angle of its flight enough that it slammed into the Core.

A familiar explosion engulfed the undead Dungeon Core and it shattered into hundreds of pieces, falling to the ground in a rain of crystal fragments. Echo stood there in shock at the sight, unable to understand what had just happened. Looking down, however, made her realize that although she had succeeded, she wouldn't survive long; the skeletons and zombies were still heading for her and she had nothing with which to defend herself.

"Echo! You did it!" she heard from far behind her and she whipped around in surprise. Felbar and Gerold were running towards her down the tunnel without their Deep Delver constructs, but even if they were armed they wouldn't be able to reach her in time. The undead were very nearly upon her, and she was too tired and injured to run from them.

** Echo! Felbar! Gerold! Bring the Shieldmen and run up the other tunnel – the dungeon is about to collapse! **

Sandra's voice precipitated hundreds more Shears flying in and slamming into the skeletons and zombies coming for her; they didn't do a lot of damage by themselves, but the sheer quantity of them caused bones to crack and shatter, as well as tearing away zombie flesh. She doubted they would do much good against something more powerful, but it was enough to save them – though they were destroyed in the process.

"I'm so glad to hear your voice, Sandra, I thought we were going to die down—"

** Less talking, more running! You don't have much time! **

Echo heard another *crack* coming from above, but instead of a Core cracking it was the ceiling of the room; another few seconds went by and a huge chunk of it broke away and fell, crashing with an ear-shattering explosion of stone chips as it hit the floor. In addition, the dim light of the room was starting to become even dimmer, so Echo quickly joined the Gnome and Dwarf as they passed by her and ran for the other tunnel.

As soon as they got there, she could see Angels and Apes attacking another force of undead there, and they were ridiculously outnumbered. Luckily, there were also eight Pegasi waiting for them there that flew over to the three.

** Are the Shieldmen behind you? **

Gerold said something that Echo couldn't understand with a hitch in his voice. Sandra didn't translate, however, probably because there was entirely too much going on.

** Their sacrifice will not be in vain – but we have to get you out of here. **

The Pegasi folded their legs down so that even the Gnome and Dwarf could climb up on their own winged horses. As soon as they were settled and were holding onto the mane of their flying mounts with a death grip, they took off towards the entrance.

Down below, the last of the Apes and Celestial Authorities were quickly overwhelmed by a horde of Undead, which then started rushing up the tunnel after the fleeing Pegasi. Before they could get far, the Core Room and then the tunnel started to collapse, crushing the back ranks. In a cascade of destruction, the rest of the tunnel fell apart just behind Echo and the others, coming so close to killing them all that one of the lagging Pegasi was smashed by a falling boulder from the ceiling and crashed to the ground.

Less than 5 minutes after the Core was destroyed, 7 Pegasi and three riders shot forth from the tunnel just ahead of its complete collapse and Echo looked around to see that they had emerged into a dark forest. *We must've been in there longer than I thought.*

As the Pegasi burst through a small space in between the foliage above, she looked over at the others who appeared to have the same shocked expressions she was sure was on her own face. *We…did it? We're…alive?*

It seemed impossible that they had both succeeded and were still alive – but it was completely and unequivocally true. *Unless I died and this is all a dream?*

Almost as if on cue, the pain in her wrist decided to come back at that moment as if to prove it wasn't all just her imagination.

Chapter 34

When the Undead around the forest and open areas started to make their way back towards the dungeon her friends were trapped within, Sandra had a feeling that Echo and the others were making some progress and making the Core nervous. When they all disappeared at about 5 hours after the entrance's collapse, she began to hope that they would succeed.

She had already been building up some more forces for an assault that she wasn't sure would even be successful, so she cautiously began to send them towards the other entrance at that point. Sandra wasn't convinced that the whole pulling-back of the undead into the dungeon wasn't another trick, so she sent them in separately, and from different directions, just in case there was something waiting for them. If one or a few were attacked, then she could pull them all back at the same time, but if she had sent them as a full group it might be difficult to escape with all of them.

Her hopes rose as they arrived at the entrance without any trouble, though she was still cautious. She was right to be cautious, too, because the few Shears she sent in to look around found a massive tunnel filled with undead. She couldn't make out the end of the tunnel from the entrance, but from underground and outside of it she could tell that it was all one long passageway that led directly towards what she assumed was the Core Room; it seemed a little crazy to Sandra to have it so open and vulnerable, but then again it might've been for some strategic purpose that she didn't know about.

She briefly thought about just sending in thousands of her Shears to see if they could fly down and destroy the Core, but the sight of dozens or possibly hundreds of Specters in the tunnel floating around dissuaded her of that notion. She still thought that if she sent enough they could probably get through, but then she considered what would happen to the others if she succeeded. If they were still an hour or so away from the Core Room, then if she destroyed the Core they would be crushed with no way out when it collapsed afterwards.

It was another hard choice, because she wasn't sure if she would have another chance like the one she was looking at, and while she had more Dungeon Monsters on the way, they would be hard-pressed to defeat what was already in the tunnel. Eventually she decided to just bring in approximately 3,000 of her Shears in preparation of an attack if it seemed like the others had failed.

When 75% of the undead she could see from the entrance left the tunnel – she supposed they went further into the dungeon – she knew that her friends were likely close to the end, and that the Undead Core was panicking. Still, with it at least marginally aware of her presence outside the second entrance, it kept some in reserve to prevent her from coming in. With the reduced number of Specters in the tunnel, though, she figured it was about time to go for it – she couldn't wait any longer.

So she sent her ground forces inside and they pushed back at the undead inside. They were making fairly good progress, but additional ones started to reinforce them from further inside; the Undead Core was probably working to replenish those that Sandra killed, and it made their progress stall. That's when she sent in half of her Shears to see if she could get through.

As if reading her mind, the remaining Specters assembled across the tunnel in an unbroken wall of mist. Her Shears hit them at full speed and punched through but dissolved soon after from the powerful essence of the undead; her constructs just weren't powerful enough to survive even the briefest contact. However, it wasn't as if her Shears had no effect; the wall of Specters appeared to have shrunk from the touch of her own constructs, but it was still full enough to prevent anything from getting through.

She sent some of her Pegasi in next, using their Nether-negating Auras to try and thin it out. It worked, but as soon as they got close enough to use the Aura, the Specters would rush forward and overwhelm the individual Pegasi; she lost four of them before she decided to just go for it and send the remaining 16 she had in – because she was running out of both time and her other Dungeon Monsters fighting the Undead down below.

With her own "wall" of Pegasi using their Auras, she managed to thin the Specters enough to send her Shears back in; 500 of them went first and punched through the mist, but only one survived to keep going. She wasn't sure if that was enough to succeed in destroying the crystalline Undead Core, so she pressed her Pegasi to close the distance with the Specters.

Their Auras ended up destroying most of the Specters, but it ended up killing half of her Pegasi in the process. The other 1,000 Shears then were free to go towards the Core, while her forces in the tunnel were slowly being taken apart.

The single pair of Shears that made it through from the 500 that had tried rushed ahead, seeing the Core in the distance. As soon as it entered the room, however, she saw Echo releasing an exploding arrow at the Core from the ground, but her scream let Sandra know she was in quite a lot of pain. The world seemed to slow as she saw the arrow knocked out of alignment as Echo's wrist snapped and the bow went flying; there was nothing she could do, however, as the delay between her orders and the Shears actually doing anything was too great.

Luckily, the Shears had been coming in the room at a lower elevation as it passed through the tunnel, and it had to angle itself upwards to hit the Core. Through some miracle or sheer accident, the construct hit the exploding arrow and knocked it back on course; when the Core shattered along with the arrow's explosion, it took her Shears with it.

From there, Sandra managed to get in contact with those left alive – she felt horrible that the Shieldmen didn't make it – and was able to facilitate their escape before everything collapsed. The rest of her forces perished along with all of the undead, though she supposed that it was quite possible there were more scattered around the forest that hadn't been called back. She doubted it would be many, however.

As for the Shieldmen, Gerold and Felbar told her when they got back to her dungeon that they were smashed by a tree wielded as a club by a giant zombie. Glancing blows from that same club were also what damaged their Deep Delvers enough that the Dwarf and Gnome couldn't move inside of them, so they escaped from the constructs and made a run for it. The Giant was apparently still alive at that point, and it had killed the rest of the Undead in the final room with the incessant flailing of its club, but the surviving Gnome and Dwarf were small enough that they were able to sneak past as it kept stupidly smashing ineffectually at the deceased bodies of the Shieldmen. The Undead Core had obviously been occupied in other matters – namely Echo's and Sandra's efforts to reach the Core – to direct the zombie Giant and stop it from doing that.

"So...what do we do now?" Echo asked later, when everyone was safe and healed up back in the dining area of her dungeon. Kelerim and Violet had joined the three that had survived the destruction of the other Core and its dungeon.

Speaking of that, the notification had come up from the destruction of the Undead Core as soon as the dungeon had collapsed completely, and Sandra wasn't looking forward to what would happen soon. The Area of Influence for all of the remaining dungeons in the area – and possibly even farther, as the Distance Threshold had increased – would start to expand, the Cores would begin to accumulate Mana at a faster rate than they did previously, and they would start to upgrade their Core Sizes even faster than normal.

Temporary Dungeon Core Enhancements	
(Your Core is not currently eligible for any enhancements)	
Current Nearby Dungeon Cores Destroyed:	**4**
Current Distance Threshold:	**138.0 Miles**
Current New Core Threshold:	**Core Size 25**
Previous Temporary Enhancements for 3 destroyed Cores:	
Includes all previous Temporary Enhancements, plus: Ambient Mana Absorption directly by the Core is increased by 10000%, Area of Influence is increased by an additional 10% over the course of 10 days, Distance Threshold is increased by 10%, New Core Threshold is increased by 2 Core Sizes	
Current Temporary Enhancements for 4 destroyed Cores:	
Includes all previous Temporary Enhancements, plus: Mana Cost to upgrade Core Size is decreased by 25%, Mana Cost of all Dungeon Monsters decreased by 25%, Ambient Mana Absorption within the Core's dungeon is increased by 2500%, Area of Influence is increased by an additional 25% over the course of 25 days, Distance Threshold is increased by 25%, New Core Threshold is increased by 3 Core Sizes	
Next Temporary Enhancements for 5 destroyed Cores:	
Includes all previous Temporary Enhancements, plus: Mana and Raw Material Cost of all Monster Seeds is decreased by 30%, Ambient Mana Absorption from outside the Core's dungeon is increased by 30%, Area of Influence is increased by an additional 30% over the course of 30 days, Distance Threshold is increased by 30%, New Core Threshold is increased by 3 Core Sizes	

She looked at their tired faces, wishing that they had a lot of time to rest and relax after the exhausting last couple of days.

** I'm not quite sure, but I do know that this whole situation has now become bigger than just this little area around my dungeon. I think it's about time we have a chat with some of your leadership, because we can't do this all by ourselves. **

They looked at each other and sighed, all of them putting their heads in their hands as they shook them in defeat. "Good luck with that," Gerold said, which was echoed by everyone else in the room.

Apparently, that might be more difficult than even destroying the Undead Core...

End of Book 3

Author's Note

Thank you for reading The Crafter's Dilemma!

A lot happened in this book, including plenty of crafting through enchanting, discoveries of the larger Energy Cubes, contacting the Dwarves, and even the creation of a powerful War Machine and Deep Delvers. The most important part of everything that Sandra was able to accomplish, however, was the way people from three races – despite not being able to speak the same language – were able to work together to defeat a common foe. That, and the fact that someone other than Sandra can control her constructs and Dungeon Monsters will have a major impact in the future...

Again, thank you for reading and I implore you to consider leaving a review – I love 4 and 5-star ones! Reviews make it more likely that others will pick up a good book and read it!

If you enjoy dungeon core, dungeon corps, dungeon master, dungeon lord, dungeonlit or any other type of dungeon-themed stories and content, check out the Dungeon Corps Facebook group where you can find all sorts of dungeon content.

If you would like to learn more about the GameLit genre, please join the GameLit Society Facebook group.

LitRPG is a growing subgenre of GameLit – if you are fond of LitRPG, Fantasy, Space Opera, and the Cyberpunk styles of books, please join the LitRPG Books Facebook group.

For another great Facebook group, visit LitRPG Rebels or LitRPG Forum.

If you would like to contact me with any questions, comments, or suggestions for future books you would like to see, you can reach me at jonathanbrooksauthor@gmail.com.

Visit my Patreon page at https://www.patreon.com/jonathanbrooksauthor and become a patron for as little as $2 a month! As a patron, you have access to my current works of progress, which I update with (unedited) chapters every Friday. So, if you can't wait to find out what happens next in one of my series, this is the place for you!

I will try to keep my blog updated on any new developments, which you can find on my Author Page on Amazon.

To sign up for my mailing list, please visit: http://eepurl.com/dl0bK5

To learn more about LitRPG, talk to authors including myself, and just have an awesome time, please join the LitRPG Group.

Books by Jonathan Brooks

Glendaria Awakens Trilogy
Dungeon Player (Audiobook available)
Dungeon Crisis (Audiobook available soon)
Dungeon Guild
Glendaria Awakens Trilogy Compilation w/bonus material

Uniworld Online Trilogy
The Song Maiden (Audiobook available)
The Song Mistress
The Song Matron
Uniworld Online Trilogy Compilation

Station Cores Series
The Station Core (Audiobook available)
The Quizard Mountains (Audiobook available)
The Guardian Guild (Audiobook available)
The Kingdom Rises (Audiobook available)
The Other Core (Audiobook available soon)
Station Cores Compilation Complete: Books 1-5

Spirit Cores Series
Core of Fear (Audiobook available)
Children of Fear

Dungeon World Series
Dungeon World (Audiobook available)
Dungeon World 2 (Audiobook available)
Dungeon World 3 (Audiobook available)
Dungeon World 4 (Audiobook available)

Dungeon Crafting
The Crafter's Dungeon (Audiobook available)
The Crafter's Defense (Audiobook available)
The Crafter's Dilemma

Made in the USA
Monee, IL
30 October 2020